DOMINION

JOHN CONNOLLY
DOMINION
JENNIFER RIDYARD

THE CHRONICLES
OF THE INVADERS SERIES

headline

First published in 2016 by
HEADLINE PUBLISHING GROUP

1

Cataloguing in Publication Data is available from the British Library

Hardback ISBN 978 1 4722 0976 4
Trade paperback ISBN 978 1 4722 0977 1

Typeset in Bembo by Avon DataSet Ltd, Bidford-on-Avon, Warwickshire

Printed and bound in Great Britain by Clays Ltd, St Ives plc

For Cameron and Alistair . . .

. . . but isn't everything?

And let them have dominion over the fish of the sea and over the birds of the heavens and over the livestock and over all the earth and over every creeping thing that creeps on the earth.

Genesis 1:26

EXTRACT FROM THE CHRONICLES, BOOK 7, SECTION 13

OF THE ASSASSINATIONS ON EREBOS AND THE INTERVENTION OF SYL HELLAIS

It is recorded that the Second Illyri **Civil War** started with the destruction by the **Diplomatic Corps** of the vast Military base known as **Melos** Station, but in truth the killings began earlier that day, on the nearby moon of Erebos. It was there that the **Archmage Syrene**, public face of the Nairene Sisterhood, was due to wed the Military hero **Lord Andrus**. Under the guise of the celebrations, Syrene dispatched a group of **Novices** with psychic powers to murder all those who might have opposed the Corps' seizure of power. This effort succeeded only in part, for the assassins were themselves destroyed at the last by the intervention of another

$\alpha = 3.58113$

$A = bc^2$

Novice, the only child of Lord Andrus, the child known as Syl Hellais – Syl the Earthborn. **Syl the Destroyer.**

But she was not alone in disrupting Syrene's plans, for another force, led by the human Resistance fighter **Paul Kerr**, infiltrated Erebos in the hope of rescuing Syl from the Sisterhood. Using a captured Illyri vessel renamed the *Nomad,* and aided by the Illyri officer, **Peris,** as well as the biomechanical organisms known as Meia and Alis, Kerr's human crew succeeded in freeing Syl, and fleeing Erebos.

The Nomad was pursued relentlessly, as those on board knew of the Corps' dark secret: the Diplomats had allied themselves with the parasitic alien species known as the **Others,** and had agreed to deliver entire worlds to them. The greatest of these sacrifices was to be **Earth,** the most advanced civilization yet encountered in the Illyri Conquest. Even Syl herself was not unaffected by the Others, for her own father had been an unwilling victim of the contagion.

The Corps, bound to the Others, had set about transporting infectious spores from the harvesting facility at Archaeon to the planet Earth.

They had become complicit in **genocide,** but at the time only the *Nomad* and its crew had the knowledge to stop what was to come. Under threat of capture or destruction, the *Nomad* vanished into the **Derith** wormhole, from which no ship had ever returned.

War raged. Friends no longer recognised one other. Families were ripped asunder: brother against brother; wife against husband; father against daughter.

And the **Illyri Empire** began to tear itself apart.

I
THE PRISONERS

CHAPTER 1

Together the two old soldiers strolled the hallways of Edinburgh Castle. On a fine morning such as this, the building appeared more beautiful than ever, vast and imposing, a vision of its former glory. Jasmine bloomed heady and sweet in the courtyards, its scent wafting through open doorways on a summer breeze. Grey doves cooed at the windows, and shafts of light spilled onto freshly swept floors. Even the sandstone walls had been buffed, and now the buttresses and buildings of the castle gleamed atop their rock in the pale Edinburgh sun.

All of this had been done at the command of the last Illyri governor of the islands of Britain and Ireland, Lord Danis.

It was blissfully quiet, also at Lord Danis's instruction, quieter than the old castle had been in all its long history. No soldiers bustled past, no patrol vehicles rumbled by, no airships zipped overhead, no gunfire sounded from beyond the walls, and so the lifelong comrades could continue their daily walk without interruption. It was as if the Illyri race had never been here, nor the tourists that once thronged the cobbled courtyards, nor the medieval kings, Jacobite rebels and Celtic fighters who had preceded them. Perhaps even the long-ago footfalls of the English conquerors had never worn slow pathways into the flagstone floors. Here, in the company of his long-standing companion, Captain Peris, Lord Danis hoped to find a little peace.

The pair moved gradually towards the main castle entrance, tracing the routes they'd known for so long yet meeting nobody they knew – in fact, seeing nobody at all. They were alone in the castle. At the gateway they stood beneath the Latin script carved above the archway.

'*Nemo me impune lacessit*,' Danis read, and there was mockery in his voice.

He always stopped and considered the words at this point on their regular walks. Sometimes he made no comment; sometimes he shrugged; sometimes he shook his head; sometimes he swore. On more than one occasion he had broken down and wept, though that had not happened for some time now. Perhaps his heart was finally mending, thought Peris. Or hardening.

'No one who harms me will go unpunished,' translated Peris, as he always did.

'It would be better if it read "no good deed will go unpunished",' said Danis, and after a moment he sighed. 'I should never have let them go, Peris.'

Peris managed a weak smile. 'You must miss her terribly,' he said.

'Miss who?' said Danis, and he jabbed angrily at a button on the wall. Immediately the hologram of the castle disappeared and they were once again standing beside a window overlooking a nighttime garden, where milky moths supped from heavy, stinking blossoms. Dual moons shone brightly in the sky above, illuminating the high wall that enclosed the grounds of their gracious residence.

Their gracious prison.

'Why, the Lady Fian, of course,' said Peris. 'Your wife. You miss your wife.'

'Yes, of course,' came the governor's reply. He had been forced to abandon Fian on Earth during the last panicked exodus from the planet, and it was assumed that she was dead. He lived with his guilt, but only barely.

Danis laughed, but it was a hard, clattering sound. 'For a moment I thought you meant my darling daughter,' he said.

'Well, you miss Ani too, naturally,' agreed Peris.

'No!' Danis spat the denial out like a piece of bad meat. 'Not my daughter. Never her. Ani is no longer blood to me.'

Peris opened his mouth to protest, but Danis had turned to leave, and his back was as solid and impenetrable as the walls surrounding the lush garden. The stooped Illyri muttered to himself as he went, declaring that he had had quite enough with today, that he was fantasising about his bed, and as the governor shuffled away, the security bracelet on his ankle flashed once, transmitting details of his movements to those who watched them, night and day.

Alone but not tired – for how could one be tired after a virtual stroll around a non-existent castle, around buildings that had long since been reduced to rubble and ash – Peris stared out into the silver-lined darkness. In truth, he wasn't sure what to think about Ani, or what to believe.

As far as Danis was concerned, his daughter had betrayed them all. She was a true Nairene, turning her back on family and friends in favour of the red witches. She had stood by while her own father was locked up, leaving her mother forsaken in an alien world, and Danis refused to believe her claims that his imprisonment was necessary for his own protection. His only child, whom he had once loved so much – and still did, deep in his soldier's heart – was dead to him.

Ani was nearly twenty-one now, and in terms of the planet where she had been born, according to the traditions of Earth, she would soon come of age. Yet Peris suspected that Ani had grown up much earlier than that, four years earlier in fact, on the day of the teenage killings on Erebos.

The day that started the Civil War.

He remembered it as if it were yesterday, but sometimes he wondered if he truly remembered it at all. Could he really trust his own recollection when, at the time, the flesh on his arm was being eaten away as if by virulent, ravenous bacteria, apparently at the instigation of a teenage girl, a mere novice to the Nairene Sisterhood? He wouldn't have believed it himself if those around him hadn't been dying too, by fire, or in fountains of blood, or with their bones inexplicably broken by invisible, violent hands, the audible snapping a soundtrack to their agonies.

And then Syl Hellais – the first Illyri born on Earth, the only daughter of Peris's old master, Lord Andrus – had intervened, a tornado of fury turning all the destructive forces in the room back on their makers, and there had been more suffering, more death, and the bodies had piled up around him, so many young, broken bodies. Ani had arrived too, and words were exchanged between the two friends, harsh words that could not be unsaid, and a lifelong friendship had crumpled as if it were nothing.

When Syl had left, Ani had stayed. Like a silver-haired angel, she'd remained by Peris's side, holding his hand until the Archmage Syrene had appeared.

What happened since that time now seemed inevitable – that much Peris had come to understand. Yet still he clung to the words Ani had uttered before Syl had fled, for they seemed to be the only hope left for his fractured, war-torn people.

'You seem determined to forget that the Sisterhood was founded with a noble purpose,' Ani had told Syl, 'but I shall make it my mission to reclaim that purpose, however long it takes . . .'

Peris had tried to explain all this to Lord Danis, but he would hear none of it.

As for Paul, Syl and those who had fought alongside them, they were surely dead, because nothing that entered the Derith wormhole had emerged from it again. Peris just hoped their deaths had been clean, and quick. Sometimes a quick death was all that one could hope for. But perhaps they were all beyond hope itself now, even those still left alive.

What they really needed was a miracle.

II

BEYOND THE
DERITH WORMHOLE

CHAPTER 2

The ship before them was less mechanical than organic. It was clearly made of some kind of alloy, but its form resembled that of a great manta ray freed from the hold of the sea and now swimming through the immensity of space: smooth, flowing, elegant – a creature of great beauty and potential lethality.

The surface of the vessel showed no lights, no windows, and no sign of weapons. It reflected the space around it, so that it seemed a thing composed of darkness and stars. It dwarfed the *Nomad*, and was significantly larger than even the greatest of the Illyri destroyers and carriers that moved back and forth through the wormholes.

About the length of ten or eleven football stadiums laid end to end, Paul Kerr calculated, and half as wide. Even in this desperate situation – tired, hunted, and having committed the *Nomad* to a wormhole from which no ship had ever returned, only to be confronted by an alien craft of unknown origin and intention – he was almost amused to find himself thinking in terms of football fields, although as a source of amusement it was only one step away from hysteria.

For he was terrified; they all were.

And as the majesty and dread of the unknown craft impacted upon them, the crew of the comparatively tiny *Nomad* – as inconsequential as a beetle before a buffalo, a minnow before a whale – found themselves truly lost for words. Perhaps, then, it was fitting that the first of them to speak was neither Illyri nor human, but biomechanical.

'It's wonderful,' said Alis, and Paul wondered if the Mech had somehow busted a circuit coming through the wormhole. Perhaps it was a case of the mechanical responding to the mechanical, because

Alis was an artificial lifeform; when faced with an engineering marvel like the one that currently dominated their field of view, she might have been more inclined to appreciate its construction than the four humans and one Illyri who stood alongside her, and were instead worried about the distinct possibility of dying. To Paul's left, Meia, the other Mech, remained silent, but her face betrayed graver concern than Alis's.

'Please don't let "It's wonderful" be the last words that I hear,' said Thula.

The big Zulu was Paul's sergeant, and it was clear that their thoughts were running along similar lines.

'Maybe they're friendly?' suggested Steven hopefully. He was Paul's younger brother, and was currently occupying the co-pilot's chair beside Alis. He glanced at Alis as he asked the question, but his girlfriend – if that was the appropriate term for a biomechanical organism at least twice his age, thought Paul – was too in awe of the ship even to hear the question.

'Activity,' said Meia. 'Starboard wing of the vessel. It's firing something.'

Paul saw it seconds after Meia. A hatch had opened in the alien ship, and now an object was approaching at speed.

'Ah hell,' said Thula.

'What is it?' asked Paul. 'A torpedo?'

'Our systems can't identify it,' said Alis.

'Come on, Alis! I don't want to find out its purpose only when it blows us to pieces.'

'I'm trying!' said Alis.

'I can target it and take it out,' said Rizzo, the fourth human on board the *Nomad*. 'But our weapons are almost exhausted. If we end up in a fight, we may be reduced to throwing our shoes at them.'

'Lock on to it,' said Paul. 'On my command—'

'No.'

They all looked to the owner of the voice, even Alis.

Syl Hellais stepped forward, and Paul felt his skin prickle as she brushed against him. She was no longer the Syl with whom he had fallen in love on Earth, the Illyri girl struggling through the Highlands, hunted by her own people and surrounded by the hostile faces of the human Resistance who fought the Illyri occupation. Back then she had been dependent on Paul to keep her safe, or so he had believed. But in the time that they had been apart – Paul conscripted to the Brigades with his brother, Syl a virtual prisoner of the Nairene Sisterhood on the Marque with her friend Ani – she had become a being transformed, a creature who was both Syl and Not-Syl. She had powers beyond Paul's comprehension. She could bend others to her will, cloud their minds, even kill them, all without the slightest physical contact. Paul had watched her do it, and he realised to his horror that he was now slightly afraid of this female for whom he also felt so much love. He had no idea how long she had kept this secret hidden, and he wondered how much else she might be hiding from him. He had to be able to trust her, for the sake of his crew as much as for himself.

For if he could not trust her, neither could he love her.

'Syl!' he snapped, frustrated.

'Don't do anything,' she said, then, as an afterthought, she added, 'please.'

'We can't just sit here and let it come.'

'We must,' she said.

She wasn't even looking at him. Her eyes were fixed on the ship.

'Why?'

But Syl had blocked him out. All of her attention and energy were directed at the vessel before them. She allowed her mind to drift, passing through the hull of the *Nomad* and out into the depths of space. She shivered for a moment. Paul saw it and reached out for her in concern, but then thought better of touching her when a blue crackle of static electricity snaked out from her body like a tiny bolt of lightning and struck his hand, causing him to snatch it back in pain.

Syl's consciousness passed through the approaching alien object – *stone metal circuit unknown unknown scan weapon scan* – and drew closer to the ship, seeing it, feeling it, exploring its surface, probing for weaknesses, a point of entry, a—

Her thoughts exploded in a babble of voices, as though she had inadvertently tapped into a million – no, a billion – different conversations. The force of it flung her consciousness back into her body, the recoil sending her stumbling against the *Nomad*'s hull.

'Don't fire,' she said, as she recovered herself. 'Please. Don't even move. Do nothing. Do you hear me? Do *nothing*!'

The tone of her voice changed on the final word. It echoed and resonated. Paul felt his body grow still, as though held in place by unseen bonds. He did not struggle against them, though. He did not want to. He found he was no longer quite as afraid. Only his head was capable of movement. He looked at Syl, and her eyes flicked to his. Her lips did not move, yet he heard her voice speak to him.

'*Trust me*,' it said.

And he knew that it was Syl who was doing this, Syl who was holding them in place, Syl who was keeping them from acting against the incoming threat. They had no choice but to do as she said. She had taken all other options from them. Even Meia had lifted her hands from the controls.

Syl's influence might have reduced Paul's fear of the alien threat, but as he stood fixed in place, watching the unknown object grow from a gleaming dot to a revolving orb the size of a small car, his fear of Syl increased. *Trust*: she had picked the very word that had passed through his mind only moments before. Was it a coincidence, or had she somehow been listening to his thoughts? Could she do that? Were her powers that great?

And then the extent of Syl's abilities, and the alien ship, and the orb were no longer his only sources of concern. The Derith wormhole behind them bloomed for an instant, like a flower opening then collapsing upon itself, and from it emerged another threat: the sleek silver form of their Illyri hunter, a ship of the Diplomatic Corps that had been pursuing them for days, seeking their destruction. From the corner of his eye, he followed its approach on the screens embedded in the intelligent glass of the cockpit windows, so that it was superimposed over the reality of the alien vessel, like a small pale ghost.

Syl's hold over him diminished as she was distracted by the new arrival. Immediately he barked instructions to his crew.

'Steven, hard to port, then come around. Rizzo, prepare to engage. The Diplomat ship is closer, so that's your first target. All weapons.'

And then Paul turned to Syl.

'Don't ever do that again,' he said softly. 'Not for any reason. Do you understand? I am in command of this ship and its crew, not you.'

Syl seemed about to argue with him, then saw the fury on his face. She nodded, and looked away, but her eyes were like red-hot coals.

Yet even as the *Nomad* began to move, its engines gave a deep sigh, and died.

CHAPTER 3

They didn't panic. Later, that would be what Paul remembered most clearly about those first seconds after the engines failed, and he was hugely proud of his crew for the way they responded. Rizzo, Thula, Meia, Steven, and Alis – each contributed to the diagnostics check, trying to determine the source of the failure. They worked fast, constantly communicating with one another, each telling the others what had been done and what was about to be done.

And all the time Paul watched as the Corps pursuit ship came around in a fast arc to bring them into its sights.

It was Meia who came to the correct conclusion before the others.

'Our systems have been targeted,' she said. 'We've lost propulsion, weapons and navigation, but life support and ancillary power are untouched. We've been carefully disabled.'

Paul looked past the cockpit screens to the sphere, which had slowed its approach and commenced a lazy orbit of the *Nomad*. Beyond it waited the alien vessel.

'That won't be much consolation when we're dead,' said Thula, who was tracking the Corps ship.

'We're in their sights,' said Steven. On the cockpit screen, the Corps vessel turned from green to red.

'They're firing!' said Rizzo.

And they were. From the underside of the pursuit ship appeared two balls of light: torpedoes. The *Nomad*'s computer instantly calculated their trajectory, and offered a series of avoidance measures for the pilots to take, none of them applicable for a ship that had no engines upon which to call.

The torpedoes exploded, but long before they had gotten anywhere near the *Nomad*. Paul and the others watched the blasts ripple in a convex shape and disperse, as though the missiles had been fired from inside a great bubble, and their power had failed to breach it. Immediately after the explosions, the pursuit ship gave a lurch and lost all momentum. It, too, had been crippled by an outside agency, apparently completely immobilised, and nobody had to look very far to figure out just what that agency might be.

A series of thuds came from the body of the *Nomad*.

'What is that?' asked Paul.

'The thing circling us has fired a number of devices,' said Steven. 'They've attached themselves to our hull.'

Meia turned to look at Paul.

'We're being scanned,' she said. 'My CPU has detected it.'

'She's right,' said Alis. 'They're moving through all non-organic systems.'

'But this ship is immune to scans,' said Paul.

'Not any longer,' said Meia.

'It's not only non-organics,' cut in Syl. 'I can sense them examining me too.'

It was an odd feeling, and she could only compare it to a kind of caress. It was intrusive, but not entirely unpleasant. She closed her mind to the probing, just in case, but she believed the scan to be physical, and not in any way attuned to psychic activity.

'I don't feel anything,' said Thula.

Suddenly there appeared before him an image of his own body, skinless but identifiable by the shape of his nose, which had been broken so often when he was a boy as to be highly distinctive. Thula could see his lungs pumping, his heart beating, even the twitch of individual muscles. Then the image was magnified rapidly, until within seconds he was staring into the deepest workings of his brain, watching as synapses flared.

He risked a quick glance away, and saw that all of the others were also staring at maps of their bodies in varying stages of magnification. Only three were different from the rest. The brief glimpse that Thula got of Meia's insides was much like Alis's, showing pale tubes and hints of circuitry, alongside unidentifiable organs that were part mechanical and part laboratory-grown flesh. When the scan reached Meia's brain, the patterns revealed were more regimented than his, and the paths taken by the electrical pulses more ordered. He wasn't entirely surprised. He'd never considered himself particularly logical.

Then there was Syl. Her brain scan showed nothing – nothing at all. It was like looking at a ball of dough. A scan of a dead person's brain would probably have revealed something similar.

The projections vanished and the *Nomad*'s lights began to flicker on and off. The food processors and heaters powered up, then just as quickly ceased to function. The chemical toilet flushed. Doors opened and closed of their own volition.

'They're deep in our circuitry,' said Meia.

'Why?' asked Paul.

He saw Meia discreetly plug herself into the *Nomad*'s systems.

'Careful, Meia,' he said.

Meia jolted as she connected with the ship's computer, but she quickly recovered herself. Her eyes danced in their sockets, flicking back and forth, up and down, following code unseen by the rest of them.

'They're searching,' said Meia.

'For what?'

'Contamination. It's extraordinary. This is scanning on a subatomic level. We have nothing like it. It's—'

Meia spasmed, and her head began to shake uncontrollably. Her hands opened and closed repeatedly, and then the shaking spread to her entire body.

'What the hell?' said Rizzo.

It was Paul who acted first, yanking the connector from Meia's arm and breaking the link with the ship. Meia flopped in her seat. A trickle of white fluid mixed with red leaked from her mouth where she had bitten deep into her artificial flesh. Alis moved from the co-pilot's seat to examine her.

'Meia?'

Meia's lips moved. She reached up with her left hand to wipe the mixture of ProGen blood and Mech plasma from her mouth. She looked embarrassed at the sight of it.

'I'm okay,' she said.

'What happened?' asked Paul.

'They didn't like me looking over their shoulder while they went about their business,' said Meia.

'Did you pick up any hint of who or what they are?'

'No.'

'They are many,' said Syl.

They all looked to her. She was fiddling absently with the scruffy brown locket she wore around her neck on a strip of leather.

'That's all I know,' said Syl, pulling the amulet backwards and forwards on its string. 'I've heard them. There are billions on that ship.'

'How is that possible?' asked Rizzo. 'It's big, but it's not that big.'

'I don't know,' said Syl. 'But it's the truth.'

Nobody argued with her. Already they knew better than to do that.

Around them, the *Nomad* began to hum as its engines powered up again. Seconds later, they felt it begin to move. Paul turned to his brother questioningly.

'It's not us,' said Steven. 'I didn't touch anything.'

'We're not in control,' said Meia. 'They're bringing us in.'

'What about the Corps ship?'

Steven examined the screens.

'No sign of movement there. It looks like it's staying where it is, for now.'

Paul walked to one of the starboard windows. He could see the other vessel as a shard of silver hanging in space. And then, as he stared at it, a mesh began to appear, so fine that, for a moment, he thought that it was an imperfection on the glass. It slowly extended until it surrounded their pursuers in a honeycombed oval.

Thula joined him at the window.

'It doesn't look like we have the same thing around us,' he said.

'No, it doesn't.'

'Do you think that's good or bad news?'

'Relatively speaking,' said Paul, 'it's probably good. In reality, though, this is all bad news.'

'When do you think we might start getting some good news?' asked Thula.

'Not anytime soon.'

Thula considered this.

'I hate space,' he said at last. 'And I reckon space hates me right back.'

CHAPTER 4

It would not be true to say that Paul was feeling optimistic, exactly, but a situation that had seemed desperate only minutes earlier was now starting to feel just slightly less terminal. Admittedly, they were being dragged towards a massive alien ship that had taken control of their little craft, but the recent alternative outcomes had included being destroyed by their unknown captors or being blown to pieces by the pursuing Corps vessel. The fact that they were still alive was something.

He watched the Corps ship growing smaller and smaller behind them. He realised that he had never seen the faces of those who had followed them into the Derith wormhole, intent upon the *Nomad*'s annihilation until they all found themselves at the mercy of a greater power. So far his crew had destroyed four of their pursuers' vessels, including the massive cruiser that had followed them to the Archaeon system, but the only direct contact with their enemies had occurred right at the start, in orbit around the planet Torma. There he and the others had engaged in bloody combat with Illyri who had been stripped of all identifying marks, even down to the neural Chips in their skulls. Paul believed them to be allied to the Corps – probably Securitats, the security police who did most of the Corps' dirty work.

But back then these killers had been hiding themselves, disguising their advanced craft as rustbuckets held together with scavenged parts, just as they had discarded any uniforms or insignia before commencing their assault. Now they had emerged from concealment: their ships were no longer flying under false colours, and they had attacked and destroyed Melos, the most important Military base in the Illyr system.

If this was the work of the Corps, then civil war had surely broken out in the Illyri Empire. Paul just wanted to know for sure.

Alis had already tried contacting the alien ship, but to no avail. Now Paul asked her to open a channel to the Illyri vessel trapped in the alien net.

'This is the *Nomad*,' said Alis. 'Calling unknown vessel off our stern. Identify yourself.'

There was no reply. Paul took over from her.

'This is Lieutenant Paul Kerr of the Military Brigade vessel *Nomad*,' he said. 'Requesting formal identification of unknown Illyri craft, and confirmation of mission.'

Now came contact, but it was not verbal. Two Illyri words, transmitted by the other ship, appeared on the cockpit screen. Paul's Illyri was good enough to be able to understand the message, helped by the fact that it wasn't very long, but he wasn't sure if the other humans on board were fluent enough to translate it. Alis looked at Paul enquiringly, and he nodded.

'Sir, the message reads *Mission: Destroy*. That is all.'

'Well, that was helpful,' said Thula. 'I'm glad we could clear it up.'

'They're not very talkative, are they?' said Rizzo.

'I think they still believe there might be a way out of this for them,' said Paul. 'If I was their captain, right now I'd be trying to reroute the ship's systems away from the central computer, and put as much of them under manual control as possible. Then as soon as that net, or whatever it is, comes down, I'd make a break for the wormhole.'

'So why aren't we doing the same thing?' asked Thula.

'Because it has no hope of succeeding,' said Paul. 'And also, I want to meet whatever is in that big alien ship.'

'I'm guessing aliens,' said Thula. 'Maybe big ones.'

'See?' said Paul. 'You're already becoming quite the expert.'

'You think they might be friendly?' Rizzo asked Paul.

'They haven't killed us yet.'

'But nothing that entered this wormhole has ever come out again. Now I think we know why.'

'You see all the things you're finding out?' said Thula to Rizzo. 'Bet you're glad you came now.'

Rizzo threw a clipboard at him, but Paul didn't notice. He realised that Syl had been quiet for a long time. He saw that she was standing close to the starboard hull, her right hand braced against it.

'Alis,' said Paul. 'Give me a view of our hull.'

Alis brought up the outline of the *Nomad* on the screen. It showed four raised bumps where the alien scanners had locked on to the exterior. Syl's right palm was directly beneath one of them.

'Syl?' he asked.

Syl lifted her free hand, signalling him to be quiet. Paul found the gesture more bemusing than irritating. He wondered if he should simply surrender his authority to her and go back to being a grunt. It would certainly make life a lot easier, and he'd have someone to blame when everything went wrong. He moved to her side, standing close but, as before, not touching her.

Syl risked another mental exploration, reaching out to the alien ship ahead of them as the *Nomad* drew closer and closer to it. She did so cautiously, for the intense babble of voices she'd encountered the first time had been immensely painful to hear, like suddenly finding oneself plugged without warning into the speakers at a particularly loud rock concert. Now those voices were silent, but Syl was aware of a great presence in the ship beyond, as though untold numbers of beings were holding their breath in the vessel's depths.

'They're listening,' she whispered.

'Can they understand us?' asked Paul.

Syl detected a flutter, a slight change in the nature of the silence, an involuntary mass response to Paul's question.

'Yes.'

'What do you feel from them, Syl? Hostility? Anger?'

Carefully, Syl probed. She had never attempted anything like this before, or certainly not on this kind of scale. Yes, she had manipulated the consciousness of individuals, even their actions. In turn, others in the Nairene Sisterhood had tried to enter her mind, mostly unsuccess-fully. This was different, yet even as she roamed, a part of her stood to one side, marvelling at her own powers. They were growing so fast, yet she was beginning to understand that they had always been there, and were as much a part of her as the colour of her eyes and the texture of her skin. Only now was she really exploring her own capacities, her own limits.

If there were any limits.

She pushed those thoughts away, and concentrated instead on what she was sensing. It was like being blind, and exploring only by touch, yet the touch brought to her shapes, and the shapes were sounds and feelings.

'Curiosity,' she said.

'About?'

Syl turned to him, but barely saw him. He was a shadow Paul.

'You,' she said to him.

'Me?'

'They've seen you before.'

'That's not possible.'

'Yet it's true.' She looked away from him. 'There is also fear.'

'Of what?'

With a small squeal of alarm, Syl yanked her hand away from the hull, as though it had suddenly become hot to the touch. She smiled weakly at Meia, who had been watching quietly from the other side of their craft.

'I think they just did to me what they did to Meia earlier,' she said.

'They'll only tolerate a certain amount of interest,' said Meia.

'Yes.'

With a twitch of her head, Meia indicated to Paul and Syl that they should follow her to the rear of the *Nomad*, where they could not be overheard by the others – or monitored by whatever else might be listening through the hull. Meia found a pen and paper, and began to write.

You're becoming stronger, Syl.

Syl shrugged, but did not disagree.

What you just did back there – did you learn it on the Marque?

Syl found a pen of her own, and wrote beneath Meia's question.

No. I don't think so. It's new. I have a sense that it's linked to the wormhole, but I can't say why.

You probably shouldn't have used that power here.

Why?

Because now they know what you can do.

Syl's pen remained poised above the paper for a second or two before she wrote:

Nobody knows what I can do.

With that, she put down the pen and walked away.

CHAPTER 5

Syl retreated to the rearmost seat in the main cabin, far away from the cockpit. She ignored Thula's raised eyebrow – it was unusual for Paul to exclude him from any discussions, and he was clearly interested to know what might have been discussed – and Rizzo's indifferent gaze. Steven and Alis were running a diagnostic check on the *Nomad*'s systems in an effort to find out if the alien incursion had left any nasty bugs in the ship's computer, so they were otherwise distracted.

The unknown ship hung before them. Syl was tempted to try and explore it again. It was as if a greater consciousness was willing her on, and she understood that something on the other vessel was as curious about her as she and the others were about it. But there was a risk involved, because to explore she had to open herself up, and that left her vulnerable. She could not examine without being examined in turn. About that much, at least, Meia and Paul had been correct.

Nevertheless, Syl was furious at them for interfering, and for treating her like some kind of child. They didn't understand what was happening to her, or how she was growing and changing; they didn't realise that she was only beginning to tap her new potential. But, then again, how could they, when Syl herself didn't entirely understand what was happening either, and a small but very real part of her was absolutely terrified by the increase in her powers. She found herself again holding on to the amulet that hung around her neck, the little item of jewellery that had once belonged to Elda – sad Elda, brave Elda, dead Elda - and from which she now drew a kind of consolation. Back on the Marque, the home of the Sisterhood, Elda had been seen as little more than a drudge, but ultimately she had been so much more – a spy, a freedom fighter – and her discovery had led to her inevitable death at the hands of the Gifted, Syrene's most vicious Novices, which made her a martyr too.

With a weary sigh, Syl activated the nictitating membranes over her eyes. It was the closest thing she had to eyelids. She didn't envy human beings much, but one aspect of their physicality that she would gladly have spliced into the Illyri DNA was the gift of eyelids. If nothing else, they enabled humans to shut out most visual stimuli, bright light apart, and send a signal to others that any disturbance would be unwelcome. In the absence of them, the semi-transparent membranes would have to suffice.

Syl had felt different ever since the events at the palace at Erebos, when she had been forced to unleash herself on the Gifted. At the time, she had experienced a kind of surge of exultation and energy as she had brushed aside each of the young Nairene novices. Initially she had put it down to anger and adrenalin, and – perhaps – the secret joy of at last being able to test herself against worthy opponents. On Erebos, Syl had killed, and she was troubled by how little guilt or regret she had felt at taking the lives of others.

They made me do it, she reminded herself over and over. The Gifted had murdered unarmed Illyri, and had been about to kill Paul when she intervened. Had Syl faltered, even for a second, they would have murdered her too. They had given her no choice.

But – and here was the terrible truth, the secret dark stain that could not, must not be revealed to anyone, not even Paul – Syl was *glad* that they had forced her to act. She hated them – Sarea, Xaron, Mila, Nemeine and, most of all, Tanit – and their viciousness had given her an excuse to act on that hatred. They had been dangerous, but Syl was far more lethal than they could ever have imagined.

Now, in the tense quiet of the *Nomad*'s cabin, Syl recreated those moments, and felt again those bursts of elation, like lightning flashing through her system, and realised that they had been strongest when she caused the death of one of the Gifted. It was as though in dying they had released their essence, the thing that gave them their psychic abilities, and it had immediately transferred itself to Syl, seeking to earth itself in her. Each time one of the Gifted breathed her last, Syl's powers had grown. But even that could not explain the leap in her abilities since she had passed through the Derith wormhole. These were powers on an entirely new scale: to be able to escape the physical, to escape the confines of the *Nomad*, to roam across the void and touch an entirely alien consciousness, sensing its mood, its intentions, however primitively at first. And she would get better at it, oh yes, of this she was certain. And while it scared her, the possibilities made her almost breathless with excitement.

Right now, sleep was the furthest thing from her mind.

The membranes slid sideways, shapes and light becoming clearer as they did so. She took in the cockpit: Steven and Alis, still at work; Rizzo behind them, concerned only that whatever was left of her weaponry would still function if required; Thula stretched out across three chairs, seemingly asleep, the presence of the alien threat off their bow less worthy of his concern than the possibility of snatching some much-needed rest after the events of the previous days. Meia and Paul were still absent.

Go on, thought Syl. Do it. Explore them. You know you can. You've already done it a little, and none of them even noticed.

No, that wasn't true. She hadn't tried it on Alis or Meia – especially not Meia. They were different. Their intelligence was artificial but, conversely, they were also more sensitive in their way than any of the others. Like Syl, Meia and Alis were also altering, mutating. They were capable of emotional responses, and that was most certainly not part of their original programming. For Syl, the only surprising aspect of the Mechs' evolution was that their creators had not anticipated it. Their framework might have been plastic and metal, but they were essentially biomechanical: advanced models fitted with ProGen skin, flesh and internal organs. ProGen was grown in laboratories, but it was the same material that was used in surgery on Illyri, replacing damaged tissue with its artificial equivalent. The point about ProGen was that it formed neural connections. On a nanotechnological level, it repaired damaged pathways. You could feel someone's touch on your ProGen skin, and taste a kiss with your ProGen lips and tongue. And each new version of ProGen incorporated lessons learned from the previous one. Its nanobots adapted.

Syl forced her body to relax, in imitation of sleep. Her remarkable eyes became like vivid golden marbles, both absorbing and reflecting the light. Her thoughts were racing. Thinking about the concepts that had apparently come lately to the Mechs — sensation, emotion — brought her back to Paul and the other manifestation of her gifts that she had so far thought best to keep from him. She allowed her mind to move through the *Nomad*, searching for him. She encountered Meia along the way, but slipped around her. It was Paul she wanted. She found him in the captain's cabin. She should not be doing this, she knew. It was wrong, an invasion of his privacy that should have been beneath her, and yet what girl had not wished she could know a boy's deepest, secret musings?

Syl entered Paul's head, and read his thoughts. Just as with the alien intelligence, she experienced them not as coherent pieces of logic or emotion but as disparate clouds of colour and banks of sound, within which could be found scattered images, voices, words. She saw his mother — *green yellow warmth love fear miss you die not die sorry father sorry* — and Steven — *orange green anger envy loyalty love Alis danger home mother sorry sacrifice live* — before she came to herself. She felt and saw blue and red, hints of green and black, a mass of confused emotions, but two that overwhelmed most of the rest, swirling together like smoke: *fear love fear love love Syl love fear love fear anger love fear anger Syl.*

She left him, and returned to herself. She was aware of a figure standing before her. Meia was staring down at her.

'What?' asked Syl.

'You're not sleeping,' said Meia. 'Which raises the question of what you *are* doing.'

She watched Syl for a moment longer before going to assist Alis and Steven with their checks.

CHAPTER 6

The *Nomad*'s progress halted when they were about a mile from the alien vessel.

'What's happening?' said Paul.

'I don't know,' said Alis.

'Try asking them.'

'It hasn't worked before.'

'You never know.'

Alis opened all channels.

'This is the *Nomad* requesting communication with commander of unknown vessel,' she said. 'Please respond.'

Nothing.

'Try again,' said Paul.

'Unknown vessel, this—'

All displays vanished from the cockpit screens, to be replaced by a single word rendered in the Illyri alphabet:

WAIT

So they waited, for what else could they do?

In a strange way, the break was almost welcome. Many hours passed without any further communication from the alien ship, and the *Nomad*'s crew became somewhat inured to its presence. Alis even darkened the cockpit windows, which made the massive bulk of the strange craft much less intimidating and helped the crew to take turns sleeping. They had spent so much of the previous weeks fighting and fleeing that they were exhausted. With their fate taken out of their hands, all they could do was eat and rest. The *Nomad* had been resupplied at Melos Station, so it had a full larder. Okay, so most of it was Illyri food, but some of it wasn't bad. In addition, their Illyri Brigade officer, Peris, had managed to requisition some human rations from the station's huge stores, so there were chicken and noodle dishes that required only rehydration, along with coffee, tea, and even some chocolate. They ate well, and took turns to wash.

Alis and Meia did not sleep or eat, but they availed themselves of the opportunity to get clean, and afterwards Steven and Alis slipped away together into the rear cabin. Paul didn't object: after all, there was a limit to what they could get up to back there. At least, he hoped so. He sipped his coffee standing in the ship's tiny galley, and tried not to listen to the sounds of lips squelching together coming from somewhere over his right shoulder.

'Young love.'

Syl laid a hand on his arm as she spoke.

'I worry about him,' said Paul. 'Actually, I worry about both of them.'

'I don't think it can end happily.'

'How could you say such a thing?' Paul replied. 'A teenage boy filled with raging hormones, and an artificial being coming to terms with unanticipated emotional responses?' He smiled, but just a little sadly. 'How can it possibly go wrong?'

'What about an older teenage boy, also filled with raging hormones, and an Illyri girl who likes to think she's slightly more in control of her hormones, but not by much?'

Paul turned and opened his arms to her. She melted into his embrace with something like relief. She was as tall as him now and doubtless would grow taller yet, but her hair was still soft against his cheek and her warmth as enticing as ever it was, and he pressed himself against her.

'I remain optimistic,' he murmured.

'So do I,' she said. 'Can we talk?'

'Isn't that what we're doing?'

'Actually, I think what you're doing is trying to kiss my neck.'

'Maybe.'

'Not that it isn't lovely, but I do need your full attention for a moment.'

Paul sighed and disengaged. Good grief, he thought, I'm even thinking in ship's terminology about physical interaction with my girlfriend.

'I'm listening.'

'What I did earlier, when the alien ship sent out that scanning device—'

'You mean, taking away our ability to act against a possible threat?'

'Yes, that.'

'You know, given that I'm supposed to be in charge, I could have had you court-martialled.'

She made a dismissive noise at him. 'Oh yeah? You and what army, exactly?'

'It was dangerous, Syl. And wrong.'

'Could you just listen to me without adding a sermon?'

'Go on.'

Syl took a deep breath and looked away from him. She started fiddling with her necklace again, as if it were worry beads. As she began to speak, her voice was so low that Paul could barely hear her. He leaned closer.

'I don't think I could have blocked you all in that way even a few days ago; one person, maybe, but not an entire crew.' She glanced at him quickly to make sure she had his attention, then immediately looked away. 'Also, this ability to . . . *probe*, this deep psychic contact, for want of a better description, that's new too. It's like my consciousness can now float free. I didn't even have to think about what I was doing, Paul, it was just a natural reaction, in the same way that you might raise your hand to catch a ball when it's thrown at you. But all this has happened only since we came through the wormhole. It could be that it's somehow amplifying my abilities.'

The words that had spilled from her abruptly stopped. Paul waited a moment while considering what she was telling him, and was about to reply when she started speaking again, though still not making eye contact.

'And I couldn't admit this to anyone else, only you, but it frightens me, Paul. It's like – I don't know, but the only comparison I can find is that I thought I was walking on solid ground, but then I looked down and saw it was thin ice, and under it were these incredible depths, but also the risk of drowning. I'm sure whatever I've already done is just the beginning. It feels like there's more to come. Much more.'

Now she looked at him and he held her eyes. There were so many questions that he just couldn't seem to formulate, and he wanted to say so much, to console her, to confront her, but all of his words seemed small and trite. What finally came out of his mouth surprised even him.

'If you can control minds,' he asked, 'can you also read them?'

Syl almost laughed. For a moment she thought about lying, but decided not to. Paul looked both ashamed and worried – ashamed to be concerned over something so personal at a time such as this, and worried that she had glimpsed his private self – and she knew that this was important to him. She cared so deeply about the young man before her. She hoped that he truly loved her, and if he did then surely he should understand what he loved, she reasoned, and would forgive her a moment of weakness. Anyway, she needed to know she could rely on him to be there for her. How could he ever be there for her when he didn't truly know who she was, and what she might yet become? More than anything, she wanted to be honest, even at the cost of alienating him.

'Yes,' she replied, 'I can.'

'Have you read mine?'

'Yes. I shouldn't have, but –'

Again, she was tempted to be evasive, to find some excuse for her intrusion upon him, but she settled for the truth.

'I wanted to,' she finished. 'You mean so much to me, Paul, and I wanted to know that you felt the same way.'

'So what did you see?'

'I saw that you . . . care . . .' she said, trailing off, leaving the rest unsaid. 'I won't look again.'

He seemed to consider this, then stepped away from her, and for a moment she was certain that she'd made a mistake in confessing all to him. He looked around, agitated, as if searching for something.

'Syl, they're listening to us,' he said. 'You told me so. This conversation – they'll hear. They'll know what you can do.'

Syl shook her head.

'No. We're in a box,' she said, 'just you and I. No sound can penetrate it. They can't hear or see us through it. I know, because I created it.'

Paul frowned, and looked away from her again. Syl saw that his cup was sitting on the galley counter.

'Your coffee has gone cold,' she said, for want of something else to say.

'Right.'

'Are you angry with me?'

'About the coffee?'

She pushed his arm a little crossly.

'No, about everything else.'

'You mean like digging around inside my head without even saying "please"?'

'Yes, that.'

'Just a bit, but I'll get over it. Anyway, if I could, I reckon I'd probably have done the same.'

'You want to look into my mind?'

He hesitated, but only slightly. She watched him expectantly, and he saw himself reflected in the warmth of her eyes.

'Yes.'

'Then do: look.'

Syl took his hands in hers, placed his fingers against her temples, and opened herself to him.

Their minds coiled in the greatest of intimacies, and they walked through each other's hopes and fears, amid all that was good and all that was bad. She showed herself to him, and he to her, and when they were done there was nothing left of which to be ashamed, for everything had been revealed. In that moment, no two beings had ever been closer, and the universe shifted and was reborn.

The contact ended, but they reached out and held onto each other, his face lost in the thick fall of her bronze hair.

'Did you see?' she whispered.

'Yes,' he said. 'I saw it all. I saw love.'

And then the *Nomad* started to move.

CHAPTER 7

The alien ship dominated the view from the cockpit windows. Space was gone, and there was only the vessel. Now that Paul could examine it more closely, he was astonished at the smoothness of the hull and the absence of any obvious windows or observation ports. Then again, it was entirely possible that this was some kind of automatic sentinel, dispatched to monitor the Derith wormhole and capture or destroy anything that came through it. It would be a dull posting, and an entirely automated system would probably make a better job of it than a crew, as the former was unlikely to become bored or distracted by the absence of very much to do. But how did that fit in with what Syl had told them about hearing many voices from the ship, or her belief that their conversations were being monitored by a reactive consciousness?

But he also had a strange feeling about the vessel, one that he chose not to share with the others because it seemed so ridiculous. There was something deeply organic about the alien craft, and he returned once again to his own earlier comparison with a manta ray. It seemed to Paul that, had he reached out and touched the ship, it might have responded to the contact much as a living thing would: moving slightly beneath the weight of his hand, or perhaps darting away in alarm. He was still considering this when a bay opened in the centre of the hull, ready to admit them. He saw no doors: rather, the skin of the ship simply folded back. It called to mind a mouth widening, and Paul thought: *We are about to be eaten.*

They entered the body of the ship, but could see nothing before them. The lights of the *Nomad* seemed unable to penetrate the murk, and the scanners were no longer under their control. For the most part, they were entirely reliant on their own eyes and ears, and whatever extra powers Syl might be able to offer, although she did not speak as the ship engulfed them, for she was as overwhelmed as the rest of them.

Now all was silence and darkness. They had not even heard the bay doors close behind them.

And then the shadows began to retreat, like black smoke being sucked through unseen vents, and slowly the interior was revealed to them. It was huge and spherical, and the *Nomad* hung unsupported at its heart, like the tiny nucleus of some great atom. The surfaces around them were reddish-purple, dotted with pits. Red cables dangled, and a series of raised mounds rose at either side of them. Lights shimmered at irregular points, buried beneath thin membranes so that they shone pink instead of white.

And the whole mass pulsed. Paul knew that his first impression had been correct all along.

'It's alive,' he said. 'This ship is a living organism.'

Syl and the humans had all seen and endured so much in their short lives, but they had never encountered anything like this. Even Meia, older than the rest of them, appeared awed. Only Rizzo resorted to practicalities.

'And we're in its belly,' she said. 'Great.'

It struck Paul that Rizzo might be entirely incapable of wonder. It had seemingly been removed from her at birth.

'Look!' said Syl.

She was pointing out of the window next to her. The others moved to the port side of the *Nomad*. A length of tubular organic matter, like a massive vein, was extruding from the bay, growing from the flesh of the ship and extending itself towards their vessel.

'That's just gross,' said Rizzo.

The *Nomad* rocked slightly as the tube connected with the door on the port side. Seconds later, the door unlocked and hissed open. Paul walked to the doorway. Before him stretched a tunnel of bluish tissue. Like the bay, it was lit by what Paul could now see was bioluminescent matter. Carefully he reached out and tested the wall. It was rigid, slightly warm, and smelled faintly of meat, like a very hygienic butcher's shop. It also curved about halfway down its length, so he could not see the end.

'Syl?'

She joined him. Behind her, Meia tilted her head and frowned a warning at Paul.

'They already know about her,' said Paul. 'That ship has sailed.'

He turned back to Syl.

'Are we in danger?' he asked.

Syl extended her right hand and touched the tunnel. She could almost feel the colour that instantly flooded into her mind, so vivid was it: greenish-yellow, shading at its edges to red. The voices were present again, a low hum in her consciousness.

'Not yet,' she replied.

'What does that mean?'

'For now they're still just interested, but if we act strangely, or give them any cause for concern, they'll kill us.'

That wasn't reassuring, as Paul wasn't precisely sure what counted as acting strangely when moving through an organic spacecraft populated by unseen aliens.

'Any clue yet as to who "they" are?'

'No,' said Syl. 'I can hear them, and sense their feelings, but only as much as they'll allow.' She lowered her voice so that only he could hear. 'Paul, I'm the one of whom they're most distrustful. I'm the one putting us at risk.'

'Because of your powers?'

She shook her head.

'No. Because I'm Illyri.'

Paul took her left hand in his right.

'We're together,' he told her. 'You let them know that.'

Syl smiled at him.

'I don't need to tell them. Just as I can sense their feelings, so they can sense mine. I think you may be the only reason that I'm still alive.'

'Wow, it's almost like you need me.'

Her grip tightened.

'Isn't it?' she said.

Thula tapped Paul on the shoulder.

'Perhaps you could concentrate on the problem at hand,' he said. 'You can discuss your wedding plans later.'

Paul reddened, but he did not release his hold on Syl.

'Steven, Rizzo, Alis: you stay with the *Nomad*,' he ordered. 'Meia, Thula: you're with us.'

'Weapons?' asked Thula.

Paul looked to Syl for advice. She shook her head and turned to Meia.

'Meia, they know you're armed.' Among Meia's adaptations was a piece of internal weaponry buried in the workings of her right arm. 'If you attempt to use it, they'll destroy you.'

'I understand.'

After only the slightest hesitation, Paul and Syl stepped onto the docking bridge and began walking. It was slightly springy underfoot, as if inflated.

Thula grinned at Meia.

'After you,' he said. 'You won't take it the wrong way if I don't stand too close, you being targeted first for destruction and all?'

'Nothing would make me happier than to keep you at a distance,' Meia replied.

She moved past Thula and left the *Nomad*.

'You're developing a sense of humour,' said Thula.

'I had to,' Meia replied over her shoulder. 'With you around, I needed one.'

Thula glanced over at Steven. 'And to think one just like her is all yours,' he said. Then he followed the others into the heart of the alien ship.

CHAPTER 8

They only discovered that the far end of the connector was blocked when they were over halfway across, because the curvature had hidden their ultimate destination from them.

'That's not good,' said Paul.

The connector began to shake.

'I've got worse news,' said Thula, looking back in the direction from which they'd come. 'The other end has detached itself from the *Nomad*. This thing is closing on us.'

Paul took a few steps back and saw that the *Nomad* was indeed no longer visible, for the tube had sealed itself and was now retracting, curling quickly towards them as if it were a heavy stocking being turned inside out.

'We go on,' he said. 'We don't have much choice.'

They kept moving forward, the shrinking of the connector apparently keeping pace with them, so that for every metre they travelled, they lost one behind them. Then, when they were almost within touching distance of the barrier ahead, it opened with a disturbing sucking sound, like a muscle relaxing. Thula eyed the resulting gap warily.

'It looks like a mouth,' he said. 'That, or someone's arse.'

'It's fantastic,' said Meia.

'I knew you'd say that.'

'So do you agree that the ship really is alive?' Paul asked Meia.

'I don't know if you could call it alive, exactly,' she replied. 'The vessel's exterior is clearly some kind of alloy, which functions as a kind of exoskeleton, but so far the interior is organic. It appears to be biomechanical.'

'Like you?'

'Perhaps, but on a much vaster scale. The interesting question is one of consciousness.'

Like you, Paul was tempted to add, again, but held his tongue. Instead he asked: 'You mean, is it capable of independent thought and action, or is it under someone else's control?'

'Or even if it's an actual creature, or simply organic matter adapted for purpose,' said Meia.

'Syl spoke of multiple presences,' said Paul. 'Whatever this thing is, it's not out here alone.'

He looked to Syl for confirmation.

'It's all quiet now,' she said. 'I don't sense anything.'

Paul peered through the opening. It was darker beyond than in the connector, which had now shrunk so far that the closed end was almost at Thula's back. With little alternative, Paul stepped through and found himself in a small, enclosed oval space, no bigger than the *Nomad*'s main cabin and with only the faintest of pink luminosity to it. Again, the surface beneath his feet was relatively firm, but with a little give. It was like standing on thick rubber matting. The others joined him. As soon as Thula was inside, the doorway sucked shut behind him.

The light grew brighter. Veins and arteries appeared in the walls, the floor, the ceiling as, slowly, the entire oval became almost entirely transparent.

'Oh my God,' said Syl.

They were in another massive chamber, but this one dwarfed the dock to which the *Nomad* had been brought. Now the fleshiness of its walls was clear to them, and they could pick out muscles and tendons. Strangest of all, it was filled with some kind of fluid, faintly yellow in colour, through which bubbles moved, propelled from one side of the chamber to the other by muscular spasms coming from suckered openings similar to the one through which they had just passed. Syl thought of a great womb, to which their tiny bubble was attached like an egg, surrounded entirely by amniotic fluid.

And they all heard as well as felt a rhythmic vibration, like a great drumming, and they knew that it was the beating of the ship's heart.

The floor of their bubble shifted, causing clear vertical projections to rise behind each one of them, which then expanded to gently enclose them around the legs and upper body, holding them in place. With only the slightest of jerks, the bubble was released from its mooring, and shot through the fluid. Particles of tissue floated before them, or bumped against the outer skin, but not so hard as to cause even a ripple in its surface. They also glimpsed what looked like bacteria, but so great in size as to be visible to the naked eye: small systems of spirilla, clusters of cocci, and rod-like bacilli with flicking flagella.

Then, less than a minute after their trip had commenced, it came to an end as the bubble reached the far side of the chamber, and a new sucker reached out to catch them and pull them to the wall. Their restraints fell away, and another doorway opened before them. They passed through it and found themselves in an observation gallery, its window many storeys high and hundreds of metres wide. The window gave a clear view of space, and the distortion caused by the Derith wormhole, as though the stars were being manipulated and obscured by an imperfect lens. Over to the left they could see the imprisoned Corps craft, the net around it barely visible from this distance.

The image before them began to recede, and it took them a moment or two to realise that the ship they were in was moving, reversing so that more and more of the galaxies beyond became visible. The stars shimmered, and whole systems appeared to detach themselves from the fabric of space. Darkness and light slowly turned to silver before them as other ships were revealed, their alloy exoskeletons seemingly growing before the eyes of Paul and the rest as each one deactivated its camouflage. One, two, three, ship after ship, until an entire fleet was displayed, each vessel different from the next: some angular and geometric, others flowing and wavelike; some perfectly symmetrical, others with disproportionate bulges or unevenly balanced, yet still strangely graceful and harmonious, as though their apparent instability was a reflection of purpose; less a flaw than a conscious design.

And the Corps ship hung at the heart of the fleet, like a small fish surrounded by the predators that would inevitably consume it.

Paul stepped closer to the windows. A thin mesh of transparent scales covered it on the outside, which probably explained why the exterior of the alien ship had appeared entirely solid when they looked upon it from the *Nomad*.

'Paul!'

He turned at the sound of Syl's voice, and saw fear naked on her face.

'They're coming!'

CHAPTER 9

The hull of the observation deck began to bulge close to where Thula was standing. He stepped back in alarm as the shape of a man appeared in the red flesh of the ship, like a figure emerging from a vat of blood. He was naked but unfinished, a showroom mannequin come to life, created not from plastic but meat, and entirely without skin. He was an anatomical model made flesh, a flayed man, every muscle laid bare to them.

When he opened his heavily lidded eyes, they displayed the pupils and irises of an Illyri.

He stood before them, space at his back, the vessels of the fleet visible behind him, and gazed intently at each of the visitors in turn. He spent the longest time staring at Syl and Paul, as though trying to come to some understanding of the connection between them.

Then he spoke, slowly but clearly, in English, his voice soft and only a little hesitant. There were pauses between certain words, even between some syllables. And as he spoke, a translation appeared in the air before his face, rendered in the letters of the Illyri alphabet.

'Welcome,' he said. 'It is a' – pause – 'pleasure to have you. Here.'

'Who are you?' asked Paul.

He had almost asked 'What are you?' but that seemed impolite.

'We are Cayth.'

Meia was circling the being, examining him. He appeared untroubled by her attention.

'Syl?' Meia said.

'Yes.'

'I can hear no heartbeat.'

Meia's faculties were far more acute than those of humans or Illyri.

Syl reached out with her mind to the one who called himself Cayth with her mind, trying to get some sense of him, but found nothing. He was like a skinned, walking corpse.

'It's just something for us to focus on,' she said. 'It has no life.'

'It's a composite,' said Meia. 'I see aspects of Illyri musculature and bone structure, but human too. And then there are the eyes. They've created a fusion of both species, probably from the scans they made of our bodies.'

'You told us they were coming, Syl,' said Paul. 'Is this what you meant?'

She shook her head.

'No, they're here. They're all around us. I can feel their presence.'

'They're invisible?' asked Thula. He looked unhappy. Skinless bodies were bad enough; unseen beings peering over his shoulder were another matter entirely.

'It's more than that,' she said. 'I don't think they have any physical form at all.'

'We are Cayth,' repeated the being before them, but his movements and gestures had changed. They were less mechanical and mannered than before. Syl saw an expression on his face that reminded her of Paul, a little flick of the left eyebrow that he used when he was amused, or sceptical.

'It's learning from us,' she said. 'It's imitating our gestures, our expressions.'

'We want you to be. Comfortable,' said Cayth. 'We want to communicate.'

Then it tried switching to Illyri, but no equivalent translation into English appeared in the air.

'What's the deal?' asked Thula.

'It's simply repeating what it already said,' Meia informed him. 'I think it learned English from listening to us talk on the *Nomad*, and some Illyri the same way. Perhaps it picked up the Illyri alphabet from the ship's systems, but it has no idea how the English alphabet might look.'

Seeing Thula's puzzled expression, Cayth returned to English.

'We wish to communicate,' he said, again. 'We want you to be. Unconcerned.'

'Skin might help,' said Thula. 'And maybe a pair of pants.'

Cayth's body jerked, his back arching to such a degree that his face turned to the ceiling. He stretched out his arms and legs, and his feet left the floor, so that he became a crucified figure hanging before them.

And then he was gone. He fell apart before their eyes, muscle, flesh and bone reduced to a thick red soup that fell to the floor and was reabsorbed into the body of the ship.

'Was it something I said?' said Thula, looking appalled.

'Clearly that wasn't working for anyone,' said Paul.

'Is this preferable?'

The voice came from behind them, deeper and more organic than the unfortunate Cayth's. They turned.

Before them stood a dense hologram, easily seven or eight feet in height. The creature it depicted was black and exoskeletal, like a shadow version of the ship itself. It resembled a hybrid of a predatory insect and an armoured knight on horseback, with six long limbs arrayed in pairs. Those on its upper body ended in sharp, striking talons that, as they watched, flared into a delicate star pattern, each phalange capable of independent movement, so that the alien could just as easily pick up an egg without cracking it as strike a lethal blow. Its head was a great elongated bone mask, dotted with multiple black eyes at its thickest part before narrowing to a point barely wider than a man's hand. They could see no sign of a mouth or jaws.

'Again,' said the voice, 'is this preferable?'

'Man, bring back the other guy,' whispered Thula to Paul. 'Even without pants.'

The head of the hologram tilted in his direction.

'No offence meant,' Thula added.

Syl stepped forward.

'You are Cayth, aren't you?' she said. 'All of you.'

'There is not one. There is only all. I am Cayth. We are Cayth.'

The hologram flickered and vanished, to be replaced by a series of rapidly changing images, in which each of them saw some of those whom they knew and loved: parents, brothers, sisters, friends, comrades.

'Where are they getting these from?' asked Paul.

'Some of it is from the databases on board the *Nomad*, I imagine,' said Syl. 'But most of it is from us.'

'How?'

'When they scanned us, they saw the things we care about, the things we hold dear: memories and images, families and friends – all that we treasure. They also probably saw what we had in the ship: those mementoes we all keep.'

Paul glimpsed his mother, smiling at him, uncannily like the old passport photo of her that he kept in his pocket. Thula watched one of his brothers grinning at him, just as he did from the picture of them together that was one of his most prized possessions.

Syl saw her father, and she stumbled backwards, the shock of him there, apparently in the living flesh, clear on her face.

'But when they scanned you, you were blank, Syl,' said Thula softly. 'I saw it.'

She swallowed hard, and when she spoke her voice was high and sharp.

'Well, obviously they saw more than you did,' she said.

Paul caught Thula's eye, giving him a warning look; he kept little from his long-time comrade, and Thula was aware that Syl possessed some very strange abilities. He'd even seen some of them for himself. She was an odd one, he thought, watching her surreptitiously as her honeyed features smoothly recast themselves and her face became a mask once more. She was the sort of complicated girl his mother had warned him to avoid. Clearly Paul's mother had not done the same. Perhaps she should have.

And still the images continued to change, like a reel of tiny films.

Meia saw Danis, to whom she had spoken just before she left Earth, and whom she trusted; and she saw the human called Trask, too, leader of the Resistance movement in Edinburgh, as much friend as enemy. Curious, she thought.

And from all of these images, the Cayth created a single figure, containing a little of each of those whom the others found reassuring, trustworthy. It was vaguely masculine and middle-aged and, like the original composite, it combined human and Illyri features – skin as dark as Thula's, its face set with entirely lidless Illyri eyes – but it had a kind of gentleness to it, as though the Cayth had somehow managed to pinpoint the finest qualities of each of those remembered. It wore the uniform of a Brigade officer. The campaign badges on the left breast were familiar to Paul. It was a replica of the uniform worn by Peris, their old guardian, now left behind on Erebos.

'Is *this* preferable?' the composite asked, and there was humour in the voice.

Nobody objected. It seemed that this was, indeed, preferable.

CHAPTER 10

The observation deck, previously empty of furniture, produced chairs from the floor, and an oval table, precisely like those on board the *Nomad*. A shape began to form in the wall, and what might almost have been a female version of the Cayth figure appeared, sliding effortlessly out of it with a soft plop. Paul heard Syl gasp beside him, but he was too distracted even to look at her. The new arrival bore traces of Paul's mother – vague, and impossible to identify precisely, but present nonetheless. He felt a huge rush of need and emotion unlike any that he had experienced since he was a young boy. All of his feelings for his mother – love, guilt for being forced to abandon her on Earth, sorrow for all of the times he had hurt her, gratitude for all that she had done for him and his brother, and other sensations too complex to name – threatened to overwhelm him.

He became aware of sobbing from his left. He looked at Syl, and saw that she had broken down. The sounds she was making seemed to come from the very depths of her being, and there was something so primitive and painful to them, and something so desolate yet awed about the expression on her face, that all he could do was try to pull her to him in order to console her. Yet she brushed him away, her eyes fixed on the alien, captivated by her, and Paul was reminded of the illustrations in the books of religious instruction at his old Catholic school, of Bernadette kneeling before the Virgin Mary, bathed in radiance.

Somehow, Syl managed to force the words out.

'My mother,' she said. 'It's become my mother.'

Paul, who had never seen any pictures of the Lady Orianne, looked from Syl to the alien. He had thought that the alien perhaps bore some slight resemblance to Syl as well as his own mother, but he had put it down to the possibility that the presence of Syl had partly influenced its creation. Now he knew differently. He wondered just how much the alien resembled Orianne. He suspected, from Syl's reaction, that it was not merely a passing similarity, or simply a hint or suggestion as with his own mother. No, whatever the Cayth were, they had somehow tapped into Syl's wellspring of love and loss, and so powerful was it that it had influenced the appearance of this latest manifestation.

The alien tilted its head, watching Syl in turn, fascinated by this emotional response to her presence. As it did so, its appearance altered, shifting like sand, and now the resemblance to Syl was unmistakable.

Careful, Paul wanted to say. *Careful, Syl.*

And a little of his concern got through to her. He saw her force herself to look away, although it clearly pained her to do so.

A hatch in the table opened. Ornate glass bottles appeared, filled with water, and bowls of Illyri and human food, squares of chocolate among them. There was also a steaming pot and cups. Paul smelled fresh coffee.

'Please,' said the female Cayth, gesturing at the table and chairs. 'Sit.'

They sat, the male Cayth at the head of the table, the female to his left. She had not taken her eyes from Syl.

Meia picked up a piece of chocolate and examined it. She sniffed it carefully before returning it to its bowl.

'It appears to be real,' she told Paul. 'Either they raided our larder, or they scanned our stores and replicated everything in them, just as they scanned us in order to create these hybrid forms.'

Thula took a square of chocolate and paused for a moment to say what might have been a small prayer before popping it in his mouth. He nodded as he ate, and poured himself some coffee, then picked up two more pieces of chocolate and sent them the way of the first.

'They might have been poisoned,' said Paul.

'Still might be,' said Thula. 'But what a way to go.'

Paul returned his attention to the Cayth.

'You haven't introduced us to your friend,' he said to the first figure.

'We are Cayth,' the female replied.

'We can't call you all Cayth,' said Thula, through a mouthful of chocolate and coffee. 'It'll become confusing.'

The female frowned. They watched as she struggled with something – memories, perhaps.

'Fara,' she said at last.

The masculine form looked puzzled at this latest development.

'Fara?' he asked her. 'Why?'

'It was a name that we once knew.'

The male regarded her curiously. 'Yes,' he said. 'It was.'

He turned back to Paul.

'Kal,' he said, indicating himself. 'That, too, is a name we once knew.'

'Kal,' Paul repeated. 'I am Paul Kerr.'

'You are the leader.' It was a statement, not a question.

'Yes.'

'We saw you.'

'Where?'

'On a planet of sand and stone.'

A system map appeared in the air before them. Paul saw a wormhole, and a series of moons and planets. He recognised Torma, where all this had begun: the attack on their ship, the deaths of their comrades, and the fleeing and fighting that had led them at last to the Derith wormhole. The image changed, and Paul saw a Brigade shuttle hovering against the Tormal landscape. The image was magnified, over and over, until Paul could make out the silhouette of his brother at the controls, and glimpsed a perfect ghost of himself standing beside a window, staring out. If the image was a photograph, he was staring directly at the camera.

'That rock,' he said. 'It was covered in symbols.'

'Yes.'

'I sensed something there.'

'You sensed us.'

'But it was just a rock.'

'No, it was much more than that. It was a sentinel.'

'You left it there?'

'Long ago. We left many like it.'

'Why?'

'To watch. To warn.'

'Of what?'

Kal did not answer. Instead, he pointed to the observation window, and the Corps ship that hung trapped beyond it.

'The Illyri?' said Paul.

'The contamination.'

'The Others,' said Syl. 'That's what he means.'

'Others?' said Fara.

Syl could still not quite bring herself to look at the female form, as though she did not have faith in her abilities to keep her feelings under control.

'That's what we call them,' Syl mumbled. 'Those—'

But Fara interrupted her.

'Does this appearance disturb you?' she asked.

'A little,' said Syl.

'Why?'

'You look like someone who' – Syl tried to find the right words, but couldn't – 'was – *is* – important to me.'

'Your mother.'

'Yes.'

'We – no, that should be I – *I* thought you would be pleased,' said Fara. 'I thought you would be reassured. I felt your love for her.'

'She died when I was very young,' said Syl. 'I have no memory of how she looked, except for pictures. When you appeared, you were so much like her, or so much like how I imagined she might have been.'

Syl seemed to be talking more to herself than to Fara, or perhaps even to the ghost of a dead mother.

'I can change,' said Fara. 'I do not wish you to be distressed.'

Syl raised her eyes from the table and held Fara's gaze, although perhaps it wasn't a gaze, for the alien was an organic composite. It had no need of the five senses, for it was a sense all its own.

'No,' said Syl. 'I don't want you to change.'

Thula caught Paul's eye. *Not good*, his expression said. *Not good at all.*

Back on the *Nomad*, Steven, Rizzo and Alis were growing increasingly concerned. They had lost communication with Paul and the others from the moment that the docking bridge disengaged from their ship, and since then they had been watching what appeared to be signs of activity in the bay around them. The lights embedded in the fleshy walls had begun to form particular recurring patterns. At first, Steven thought that it might have been a trick of his imagination, caused by staring out of the cockpit window for too long, but Alis had picked up on them too, and had begun analysing them, trying to determine what they might mean.

'I think it's a form of communication,' she said. 'They're signals being sent from one part of the ship to the other.'

'By the crew?' asked Steven.

'I assume so, except . . .'

'Except?'

'There doesn't seem to *be* a crew. On a vessel this size, we'd surely have seen some sign of them by now. It's like a ghost ship.'

'But Syl felt them.'

'Syl felt something,' said Alis. 'I don't doubt that. I'm just not sure it was the crew.'

'Maybe they're dead,' said Rizzo matter-of-factly.

'Then what was she hearing?' asked Steven. 'Spirits?'

'When we were in basic training, Peris told me about an Illyri warship called the *Margus*. Did you ever hear of it?'

Steven shook his head, but Alis retrieved the details from her memory.

'I know of it, Rizzo. It was long before the Illyri encountered humanity – or any other advanced species, for that matter – and they had to do their own dirty work on far-flung planets. An infection was brought on board the *Margus* following an exploration mission to a new moon: a virus of some kind that the ship's medical systems failed to detect. It killed the entire crew, almost six hundred Illyri, all wiped out in a matter of hours, and the virus left no trace of its presence, beyond the bodies. When the remains were examined, they were found to be entirely clear of any lethal contaminant. It's one of the great mysteries of Illyri exploration: a ship floating through space, steered by corpses.'

'Yes. It was the early days of neural Chips,' said Rizzo. 'They were always malfunctioning, according to Peris, and surgeons were forever having to perform tweaks on them. When the crew started to die, the Chips responded with some kind of spontaneous upload of data: fragments of speech, last messages to loved ones, all sent directly to the ship's systems. So when the first rescue crews entered the *Margus*, all they heard were the voices of the dead.'

'Ghosts in the machine,' said Steven.

'Even after they powered down the computers and rebooted, the voices were still there,' continued Rizzo. 'No one could ever figure out where in the system they'd embedded themselves. Eventually the *Margus* had to be entirely refitted, but even then a lot of Illyri preferred not to serve on it, apparently. It was said that the voices could still be heard, whispering in the background of open channels.'

'I thought the Illyri weren't superstitious,' said Steven. 'They don't believe in an afterlife.'

'Oh, they didn't think that the ship was haunted,' said Alis. 'It was just bad for morale. Eventually, the *Margus* was scrapped.'

'Bad for morale?' repeated Rizzo. 'Right.' She blew air through her nose disdainfully.

'You think this might be another *Margus*?' said Steven to Alis.

'No, this is something stranger, and more advanced. Whatever is controlling this ship, it's not spirits.'

Steven was staring at her curiously.

'What?' she said.

'I don't want to offend you.'

'You won't.'

'That phrase, "ghosts in the machine", I think I once heard it used about the Mechs' belief in a god. Your conviction that you had a soul was—'

'A system defect,' Alis finished for him. 'A glitch. But what is a soul? Perhaps it's nothing more than a manifestation of our consciousness that survives the final destruction of our bodies. It is what continues. It is what endures. It is the ghost in the machine of the universe.'

The *Nomad* shook, and its cabin door opened. Once again, a bridge had connected it to the alien ship. As they turned to look, pinkish gel oozed into the cockpit and began to form a figure before them: first legs and a torso, then arms and a head. Rizzo leapt for the shotgun that was never far from her reach, but Steven shouted at her to stand down, his voice snapping out the command, and the highly trained fighter within Rizzo's nonchalant, tough-girl exterior had the sense to listen. Finally, a layer of pale skin formed itself over the figure, and it stood naked before them. It was female, and human, or apparently so.

'Follow me,' it said.

'I don't think so,' said Rizzo instinctively. She had never seen any reason to follow a naked stranger anywhere before, and wasn't about to start now.

Suddenly an image of Paul appeared between them and the woman, something like a hologram.

'It's okay,' Paul told them. 'Just do as she asks. I think you need to see what we're seeing.'

CHAPTER 11

The crew of the *Nomad* stood together at the centre of a vast chamber filled with millions of sparkling lights that seemed both part of, and separate from, the alien vessel. As one light appeared, another was extinguished: a constant flickering that dazzled the eye. At first there was only silence, but gradually a low hum could be heard, and as it rose in volume they discerned the babble of an untold number of voices, all speaking in unison. This was the sound that Syl had heard.

This was the Cayth.

They were a race without physical form, a species that had long ago abandoned bodies. Bodies wasted away. They contracted diseases. Bones shattered, and organs failed.

But the mind . . .

How frustrating, how unjust, that a lively, active consciousness should cease to exist simply because the delicate frame that housed it went into decay. If the mind could be freed from the limitations of the body, then it might become virtually eternal.

And so the Cayth evolved, but they did not entirely abandon flesh, blood and bone. They created organic computers, and biomechanical ships, and these they inhabited with their consciousness. They were both individual and collective: billions of distinct minds working together, so interwoven and interdependent that their identities had become, for all intents and purposes, one. Yet, as Fara and Kal had demonstrated, some element of their former individuality still remained, a dream of what once had been.

★ ★ ★

They returned to the observation deck, their eyes and ears still filled with the sight and sound of the Cayth. The hum continued though, like a soothing white noise. Now they all looked at Kal and Fara differently, knowing that within their temporary physical forms, assumed for the benefit of their guests, they contained multitudes.

'It is interesting that you call them "Others",' said Fara, 'while we refer to them as a contaminant.'

'How so?' asked Paul.

'Because to them, we are the others. We are the contamination.'

'I don't understand.'

'They are ancient,' said Kal. 'They may well be the oldest living beings in the universe. To them, all other life is inferior.'

'To them,' Fara corrected him, 'all other life is *prey*. They may appear simple – in their most basic form just a spore, a tiny thing – but they are impossibly complex. Within each spore is the potential for any number of evolutionary paths, depending upon the requirement of the species: food, knowledge, reproduction, infection. Destruction.'

'And they are in constant communication with one another,' added Kal. 'They are not quite a collective, but individual manifestations of the life-form are capable of remaining in contact with others, even when light years apart.'

'How?' asked Meia.

'Through what we believe is a form of quantum entanglement,' said Fara.

'Quantum entanglement remains a theory,' said Meia. 'It has not been proved.'

'Nevertheless, we can find no other explanation for how the contamination' – she paused and then corrected herself, deferring to the visitors – 'no, for how the *Others* behave.'

'Excuse me a moment,' said Thula, ' but could someone explain what you're talking about? What the hell is this quantum entanglement business?'

'How long do you have?' asked Meia.

'Explain it to me like I'm five,' said Thula, folding his arms across his chest in a challenge.

'And me too,' chipped in Rizzo, 'but preferably in Italian.'

'It is a theory concerning very small particles – electrons, for example – that have interacted in the past, and then moved apart. Anything that affects one of those particles, such as an adjustment to its position or velocity, should instantaneously affect the other particle, no matter how distant they are.'

Now they all stared at Meia in bafflement.

'And that's the bambino version? Is it even worth telling you that nobody understood a word of what you just said?' said Rizzo.

'Don't feel bad – it's not you,' Thula told Meia. 'Someone could be explaining to Rizzo how to open a door, and she wouldn't get it. Unless she can blow it up or shoot at it, it's all just Greek to her. Or Zulu. *Ngicela ukhulume kancane*, hey, Rizzo?'

'Screw you, Thula,' said Rizzo. 'And what the hell does that mean, anyway?'

'It means, "Speak more slowly",' said Thula, and he winked at her.

Rizzo said something presumably obscene in Italian, though no one felt the need to ask for a translation, before returning her attention to Meia.

'What he just said,' Rizzo told her.

'That probably goes for all of us,' Paul added.

Meia sighed, and even rolled her eyes. Sometimes Paul had to remind himself that she was an artificial being. She grew more human – or more Illyri – with every passing day.

'Imagine you had a twin sister,' Meia explained, focusing on Rizzo, 'and she was on Earth, and you were here. Well, quantum entanglement is the equivalent of someone tickling you here, and your twin sister back on Earth laughing.'

Rizzo considered what she had been told.

'That,' she said, after a few moments, 'is the stupidest thing I've ever heard.'

'Albert Einstein agreed,' said Syl, dredging up a memory from her lessons on Earth. 'He called it "spooky actions at a distance", so he wasn't a big fan of quantum theory either.'

'Anyway,' said Fara, who had watched and listened with a

combination of bemusement and irritation to these exchanges, 'we believe that only some form of entanglement can account for the exchange of information between the Others.'

'What else can you tell us about them?' asked Paul.

Both Kal and Fara looked almost embarrassed.

'Very little,' said Fara. 'They are hostile, without mercy, and concerned only with the propagation of their own species. They resist examination. If necessary, an individual spore will destroy itself rather than submit to testing of any kind, but that's purely a last resort. They prefer to attack. Infection is their best defence: a single spore lodges in a host organism, then uses the energy of the host to breed fragmentarily through asexual reproduction, with each new fragment capable of growing into a mature individual. Basically, one spore can turn its host into a kind of spore bomb.'

'We've watched it happen,' said Syl.

'My crew saw an entire planet being used as a breeding facility,' added Paul.

'And what did you do?' asked Fara.

Paul hesitated.

'We destroyed it,' he said.

'An entire world?'

'Yes. We irradiated it. On my orders.' Paul spoke defiantly, but he was annoyed to feel a blush of shame coming to his cheeks.

Fara smiled at him, but it was not triumphant or gloating, merely sad.

'It's okay,' she said. 'Nothing on it could have been saved from them.'

'You seem very certain of that,' said Meia.

Meia had not been present when Paul was forced to act so ruthlessly to halt the breeding programme. She had heard something of it from Alis, but had kept her opinions to herself. Privately, though, she was appalled at the probable eradication of all life on the planet, and alarmed at the capacities of the young human lieutenant. But she also recognised a kind of muted admiration for him. No one so young should have been forced to make that decision – nobody of any age, if it came to that – yet he had acted as he thought best, and was now living with the consequences. Still, Meia did not want him to get a taste for such actions.

'I am,' said Fara, 'because we were forced to do the same.'

'We tried to halt their spread,' said Kal. 'We failed.'

'And then you fled here,' said Meia.

'We were vulnerable to them in ways that conventional species were not,' said Fara.

'Because you're a collective consciousness,' said Syl.

'If one was infected, all would fall,' said Kal. 'Like the Others, we knew of the existence of wormholes, although their knowledge far exceeded our own. This wormhole – the one the Illyri call Derith – is unusual. It is the most remote of those mapped, and the systems beyond it are bordered, at their farthest reaches, by a ring of neutron stars and decaying magnetars.'

'Again?' said Rizzo.

'Natural defences,' said Meia. 'Neutron stars have magnetic fields more than a trillion times stronger than the earth's, and incredibly powerful gravitational forces. A magnetar is a rapidly spinning neutron star, again with a colossal magnetic field. They're not perfect fortifications, and magnetars don't live long – maybe ten thousand years – but they're a start.'

'Beyond them we have capture fields, like the one that trapped you and the pursuing vessel,' said Cayth. 'Nothing gets through. Here, we are safe.'

'Or prisoners,' said Syl.

'It is necessary,' said Fara. 'From here, we can watch. We created the ancient transmitters that are our sentinels aeons ago, when we still had form, when your kind were just a whisper. Through them, as your conquests grew, we learned more of the Illyri.'

'And what about humanity?' asked Paul.

'Not until we glimpsed you on Torma. You are the reason that your crew are here, and not out there.'

He gestured to the Corps ship.

'What are you going to do with it?' asked Syl.

'It's contaminated.'

'What does that mean?'

New images appeared before them: the crew of the Illyri pursuit vessel moving about their cabin, or resting in their bunks, but presented like the pictures from an MRI scan, with their internal organs visible: lungs, spinal cord, heart.

Brain.

'My God,' said Paul.

The creatures were clearly visible, wrapped around the brain stems of some of the crew, minute tendrils snaking into their hosts' brains. Paul counted twelve figures on the ship, and more than half of them were carrying one of the Others.

'You asked them their mission,' said Fara. 'They told you that it was your destruction. Now we must ask you your purpose.'

'The Illyri are planning to give Earth to the Others,' said Paul. 'We have to stop them. Already, ships bearing spores are no doubt on their way to my home planet.'

'You can't stop them,' said Fara.

'I have to.'

'You don't understand,' said Fara, and her voice was softened by sympathy. 'It has already happened.'

'That's not possible,' said Syl. 'We would have heard about it. Syrene wouldn't have been able to resist taunting me with it.'

'And an evacuation of all Illyri personnel would have been required,' said Meia. 'That was still only in its early stages when I left Earth with Syrene, and it will be a mammoth operation. It'll take months, perhaps even a year. And I was monitoring all communications. Even if the infection of Earth had been imminent, I would have known. But the fact remains: none of that could have been achieved so quickly.'

'Time,' said Fara. 'It is not the same here.'

'Stop speaking in riddles!' snapped Paul. 'Tell us what you mean! We have family on Earth, and friends. It's our world, our species.'

'And they are gone,' said Kal. 'All gone.'

'A higher gravitational field,' said Meia. 'No, oh no . . .'

'What?' said Paul. He looked at his brother. Steven had gone very pale. His chin was trembling, and Paul thought that he might cry.

'Time passes more slowly in higher gravitational fields,' said Meia, 'and the gravitational field surrounding the Derith wormhole is immense. But there is also the wormhole itself.'

She looked to Fara for confirmation. Fara nodded.

'One mouth of this wormhole accelerates to near light speed, then reverses, but the other remains stationary,' Meia continued. 'The moving mouth ages faster. We're at the stationary one.'

'So time passes more slowly here,' said Syl.

'How much more slowly?' asked Paul.

'We don't understand these things in the same way—' Kal began.

'*How. Slowly?*' repeated Paul, and his tone brooked no argument.

'A day on this side for a year on the other,' said Fara. 'Approximately.'

'We've been here almost two days now,' said Steven. 'So two years have gone by back on Earth?'

'Yes. Or thereabouts.'

Steven leapt from his chair, his hands twitching frantically as if he was already at the controls of the *Nomad*. 'We must leave,' he shouted. 'We have to get back.'

Rizzo stood too, her hand automatically reaching for the holster where she normally kept a gun. Alis rose and joined them.

'We have to return!' said Rizzo, slapping in frustration at the empty holder on her hip.

'Return . . . and do what?' asked Kal.

'Help them!' said Steven. 'What do you think?'

'You knew this?' said Paul to Kal and Fara. 'You knew about the passing of time, yet you kept us here?'

'We saved you,' said Fara. 'Without our intervention, your pursuers would have killed you. And we did not know about the Others' plans for Earth until you told us.'

'Two days!' said Paul. He was shouting too now. 'You marooned us for one day, and brought us here for the next, and for what?'

'To give us time,' said Fara. She did not seem even remotely troubled by Paul's rage.

'Time for what?'

'To decide whether or not to destroy you,' said Kal.

It was Steven who cracked first. He lunged across the table at the Cayth, but he had barely stretched himself before cords of tissue snaked upwards from the floor, holding him where he was. Rizzo tried to help him, but she too was gripped and held in place.

'Stop!' shouted Syl. 'Everyone, please stop!'

She reached out and took Paul's hand, willing him to be calm so that he might in turn calm the others, then turned to Fara.

'We're alive,' she said. 'You let us live.'

'Yes.'

'Now will you let us leave?'

A pause.

'Yes.'

'And will you help us, against the Others?'

Another pause.

'No.'

'Cowards!' cried Steven. He was struggling against his bonds, and weeping as he did so. 'You're just cowards!'

As before, Fara and Kal remained unfazed.

'If you leave here now, and go back to Earth, you will die,' said Fara.

'We can't abandon it,' said Paul. He was keeping himself under control, but whether solely through his own efforts, or helped by Syl, he wasn't sure.

'They have taken your world, just as they have taken many worlds before, just as they will again. The Illyri will keep feeding the Others new planets as the price to be paid for the continuation of the Conquest: life forms, species, whole civilisations, in return for knowledge. And if by any chance the Illyri were to refuse, and decide that enough was enough – and what conquering race has ever made that decision? – then the Others would destroy them too, and seek new hosts elsewhere.'

'But you won't help us to stop them – to stop it all?'

'We can't,' said Fara. 'We would doom our entire race.'

'Then if you won't, who can?'

And Fara raised a finger, and pointed it at Syl.

'She can. She tries to hide herself, but there are always shadows, and her shadows are great, and terrifying. There is more within her . . .'

But Paul barely heard Fara's words. He could think only of Earth, of his mother, and of everyone else he had known and cared about so much. His friends. His uncles, aunts, cousins. The Resistance: Trask and his crazy daughters, the Illyri deserter Fremd, Maeve, Heather and her little girl, Alice. Maybe even Peris.

Gone. All gone.

III

THE DYING OF
THE EARTH

CHAPTER 12

After the attack on the Military base of Melos, and the killings on Erebos, Captain Peris became a trophy of war. Many in the Diplomatic Corps might have preferred that he were dead, but others had successfully argued that he would be more useful alive.

The situation was further complicated by the fact that Archmage Syrene, the leader of the Nairene Sisterhood, and also a crucial supporter of the Diplomats and their Securitats, had just married Lord Andrus, the great Military leader, and Peris was one of Andrus's oldest comrades. The hurried wedding ceremony took place on Erebos, even while Syrene bled from the shoulder where she'd been hit by pulser fire during the escape of Syl and the others. But the wound was minor, and the marriage crucial: it forged new ties between the Military and the Nairenes, even while the ruins of Melos Station drifted nearby, pretty as falling stars.

Lamentable as the union might have been, this tangled alliance of Nairene and Military was the reason why Syrene had been among those who argued against killing Peris. Under her influence, her husband, Lord Andrus, was trying to bring wavering factions within the Military over to the side of the Diplomatic Corps, arguing that a long civil conflict would only tear the Illyri Empire apart, and it was in their best interests to ally themselves with the new order and force the remaining renegade Military elements to the negotiating table. He had encouraged Peris to lend his voice to this effort, but Peris had resisted. Nevertheless, the fact that Peris was still alive allowed Andrus to declare that the Corps and its allies clearly had no desire for further bloodshed.

And then there was Ani . . .

Peris could not understand it, but Syrene seemed to have taken to Ani, keeping the youngster near her at all times, whispering to her, pulling her ever closer into her web, ever closer. Ani ceased to visit Peris as his recovery continued, and when finally she did return, she had Syrene's handmaiden, Cocile, in tow, and a tendril of budding leaves had been tattooed onto the young Illyri's cheek, as if this was a time for artifice.

'I am glad to see you looking so well,' said Ani.

'I wish I could say the same,' Peris replied.

'I'm not sure that I understand you.'

'That scrawl on your cheek,' said Peris. 'I understand enough about the Nairenes to recognise it as a mark of esteem. If I didn't know better, I'd say you were moving up their damned ladder!'

Which was when Ani informed him that she was now Syrene's scribe. She ignored the way Peris's jaw dropped, tapping absently at her writing device as if she was too important to make time even for eye contact. This was a complete turnaround, in direct contrast to the initial fraught and acrimonious meetings between the Archmage and the Earth-born teenager back in Edinburgh, and Peris struggled to make sense of it. Cocile made her lips tight, as if suppressing amusement at his befuddlement.

'But what about your parents? What about all that the Sisterhood has done, and their allies in the Corps?' he said. He recalled what he'd witnessed on Archaeon, the mental snapshots of living creatures torn apart by aliens, and the resulting spores that were bound for Earth. He'd told Ani about all of it: had she really cast it aside, as if it were nothing? He thought of the Gifted, and the torments they had inflicted, not least of all on himself. Finally, he recalled those he had known on Melos Station, and all the nameless dead who had joined them in the void as the base was destroyed. How could Ani ally herself with those who had done such things? He stared hard at the young Illyri, willing her to look at him, wishing he could reach into her stubborn skull with the force of his mind, but it was a power that he did not possess.

'What about my parents?' said Ani evenly, and as she spoke, the leaves on her cheek appeared to flutter and fall into shadow. 'I have spoken to the Archmage. Everything is in hand. As for the rest, we are at war, but we must strive for peace.'

'But . . . Ani, may I speak with you in private?'

Now Cocile let out her long-suppressed laugh.

'Don't be ridiculous,' she scoffed. 'The Archmage's personal scribe cannot be left alone with a prisoner.'

'Peris,' said Ani, her voice soothing, as if she was addressing a toddler having a tantrum. 'I appreciate that we have a long history – or rather *had* – but I am a Nairene now, of late ordained as a full Sister. In addition, the Archmage Syrene has seen fit to allow me to join her personal staff. I have been singled out for great honour. From now on, I must unshackle myself from my past. I'm afraid that I can't see you again. I wish you well. Goodbye.'

Peris reached for her, but she was already rising. She did not look back at him as the door closed behind her.

'Ani!' he shouted. 'Ani!'

Yet she was gone, and he was alone.

But while Ani might have absented herself from Peris's life, Syrene had not. She began to visit him regularly, assuring him that his 'crimes' against the Sisterhood and the Illyri Empire had been forgiven. She understood from Ani that Peris had travelled to Erebos with the best of intentions, seeking only to ensure the safety of senior Illyri who were under threat from renegade forces. The fact that he had remained behind on Erebos rather than flee with Syl Hellais and her followers was confirmation of his loyalty, Syrene said. She spoke of all the Military leaders who had already come over to the side of the Diplomats. She explained to Peris that, while he was lowly in rank, he was held in high esteem by his fellow soldiers. If he came onside, he could do much to prevent further conflict and loss of life.

The days turned to weeks and Peris continued to spurn Syrene's silken offers. Among them was a promise to have his arm reconstructed, but the operation would be painful, and the recuperation period lengthy. The one thing he didn't have was time. He had to warn Danis, who was now Governor of Britain, of what was coming. He had to warn everyone. Somehow, he needed to find a way to get to Earth, but so far none of Syrene's offers to him had included that possibility.

'Please, Peris,' said Syrene, perching on the old soldier's bed. 'The reconstruction is a simple procedure now. I'd like to know that you're whole. Do it for me.'

'Your Eminence,' he replied, 'that is precisely why I will not do it.'

She laughed gaily at the insult. 'Well then, do it for Ani. You know, she wants me to send you to Earth.'

Peris was surprised. It was as though she had read his mind.

'Ani asked you to send me?'

'She thinks you might be able to convince her mother and father to return to Illyr, for she misses them. No doubt you might find the business of travelling easier with two functioning arms.'

Peris tried to judge the Red Witch as she spoke, for she was being unnaturally talkative, which made him immediately wary, but she remained as unreadable as ever. She had a certain dramatic way of speaking, he noticed. Every line was a performance, every declaration a soliloquy. She was an actress playing a role, but the real being remained unknowable.

'I tried to impress upon Sister Ani the great honour that I had bestowed on her father by making him governor,' Syrene continued, 'but the child is fretting. She is a dear little creature though, and has become almost like a daughter to me and to my beloved husband, especially since' – here her face contorted and her voice rose as her emotions tipped over into blackness – 'that traitorous *spawn* of Andrus's turned on us at our own wedding. The destruction she caused, the death . . .'

She shuddered to a halt and placed her head in her hands, then shrugged her shoulders heavily, as if the weight of Syl's treachery was too much for her to bear. When she finally looked up, her features were once more rearranged into bland tranquillity and, as she continued, her voice was smooth as oil.

'Do you know I was prepared to love Syl Hellais as my own, Peris? Yes, on the surface it would appear that it was I who took her away from her father, and it was I who removed Syl and Ani to the Marque. But consider the facts: was I not offering them refuge from the storm they themselves had created? They were traitors to their own kind, to the entire Illyri nation. They took up arms with those who would destroy us, and yet still I gave them my hand of friendship and transported them on my private craft to the sanctuary of the Sisterhood, saving them from certain death in the Punishment Battalions.'

She waited for his reaction, and when there was none forthcoming she continued, growing ever more self-righteous.

'And I fear you have forgotten that Syl Hellais was also responsible for the death of my esteemed first husband, Consul Gradus. Yet, traumatised as I was, I found it in my heart to provide her with a path back from the abyss, giving her another chance that even she – audacious and wilful child that she is – could not have believed possible. I was gracious, despite my own terrible suffering, despite being so cruelly widowed in my prime.'

Peris watched Syrene closely as she talked, finding himself mesmerised by the ink creatures that spilled down her face, writhing and creeping along with her words.

'And then, once again, how did that vicious hellcat see fit to repay me? With evil, Peris. With pure evil. First, she visited destruction upon my Marque, killing one of our most revered teachers, the Grandmage Oriel – a dear friend of mine, and a gentlewoman whose only wish was to live out her days in peace, surrounded by the eager Novices who hungered for the wisdom that decades of study and quiet contemplation had bestowed on her. Do you know what Syl did to Oriel?'

Syrene didn't wait for an answer, so tied up was she in the lies she had told herself.

'She unleashed a swarm of garniads on her, stinging her to death. It must have been agonising. But that was not enough for Syl Hellais, for she then flew to Erebos, where she murdered numerous important guests at my wedding – including esteemed members of the Military, *your* Military, I might add – and then, when my most gifted Novices tried to stop her, she killed them too. In cold blood.'

Peris thought he might laugh, but he feared if he started he would not stop, so he chewed back the sound and it came out as a grunt.

'But of course, you were there!' Syrene said. 'You witnessed her madness firsthand. You too were a victim. It would be helpful if you could make a formal statement to that effect. My gratitude would be considerable. There are so many rumours, so many lies, about what took place before my wedding . . .'

So this was the game, thought Peris. Sign up to the fiction about Syl Hellais, the tale that it was she, not the Gifted, who was responsible for the killings on Erebos. And while he was about it, he could support Andrus's claim that the attack on Melos had been necessary to prevent the Illyr system being turned into a series of battlefields. We killed thousands to save millions: that was the great argument, the great lie.

Syrene regarded him quietly for a long while and it was as if her thoughts were tapping at his mind. He was powerless to stop her intrusion, so instead he said precisely what he was thinking.

'You know full well that Syl did not injure me. She saved me. And you know too that she did not kill the officers who died that day. It's no good reading my thoughts, Syrene, for I am not the one with secrets to hide.'

She watched him for a few moments longer, unmoving, and the creatures adorning her face went still, poised as if waiting to pounce. Finally, she stood up to leave.

'I am done wasting my time with you, Peris,' she said. 'Your disdain grieves me. Expect no more favours from me. Since you are no longer in pain, please make yourself ready to go to Earth. I shall provide you with a small craft for this purpose. You are to report to Governor Danis, greet his wife the Lady Fian on my behalf, and then transmit a report on their health for the sake of Ani. Unfortunately, they will be unable to return to Illyr as their daughter might wish: we need Illyri of their quality and loyalty to remain on Earth. Incidentally, Ani was also concerned about the welfare of that dreadful governess, Althea, and hoped that she might be able to return with her parents, so please send word of Althea, too. She may return if she wishes. She's of no consequence to me. After that, you are to remain on Earth, for I have grown weary of you. You will end your days there.'

For once, Peris managed to keep his mouth shut. The Red Witch had given him just what he wanted: the opportunity to return to Earth. Once he was there, he'd have to find a way to escape after he'd warned his friends of the threat from the Others, but he'd deal with that problem when the time came.

'Do you have nothing to say?' asked Syrene.

Peris sighed, and shook his head.

'I'll go,' he said. 'I don't have much choice.'

'I'm glad to see that you've stopped fighting me, Peris. You just didn't realise that you had already lost a long time ago.'

'Yes,' he agreed as she turned to go, 'we've all lost.'

But they had not. Now, he thought, at least there is hope.

CHAPTER 13

Peris's journey to Earth was dull, and without company. He was the only passenger on a series of ships that took him, by way of relays, to his old stomping ground. That was unusual: in the past, ships to Earth would have been filled with Diplomats, Military, even the occasional Civilian businessman. Now there was still traffic, but most of it seemed to be heading away from the planet, and Peris thought that he knew why.

The evacuation had begun.

The final shuttle that took Peris from the mothership to Earth dropped him off on the planet in a rush, as if the pilot was a nervous cab driver in a particularly seedy part of town. She had been uneasy from the moment they uncoupled from the ship.

'You all right, officer?' asked Peris, not for the first time. She was making him nervous, but the planet that now drew closer below them appeared as beautiful and blue as it had always been, quiet and untouchable from this distance, marbled with white clouds and golden deserts.

'I told you, sir, I'm fine,' she snapped, yet again, and then they were enveloped in the heavyweight duvet of cloud that lay over Edinburgh. They broke through close to the ground and the city looked as he remembered it, grand and wet.

His feet had barely touched the tarmac when the pilot took off again, speaking in a rush as the door opened, saying that no, she had no reason for stopping on the planet and, no, she did not wish to rest or eat a proper meal, or even freshen up before she flew away.

'Hurry, sir,' she called to him anxiously as the exit slid shut, 'and be careful.' The doors had barely sealed before she was off again, but she waved at him from the cockpit, her lips forming the words silently: 'Hurry! Hurry!'

Peris watched the small silver dot of her craft as it was absorbed by the ominous sky, then turned his face to the rain and the wind, feeling the water and the chill beating against his flesh, pummelling like tiny, angry hands. It had been a long time since he'd known rain on his skin. It felt good. He felt alive.

A voice bellowed across the courtyard into which Peris had been deposited, a familiar voice, the voice of a friend: 'Ahoy! Is that really you, Peris? I didn't dare believe the manifest! I had to see for myself!'

And now something happened to Peris that hadn't happened in so long he'd almost forgotten that he had this ability, this odd power in him. His cheeks tingled and his mouth opened as if it wasn't under his control any longer, and he found an enormous smile was spreading unbidden across his face.

'Danis! You old trout!' he shouted back, delighted.

As the grey raindrops fell heavier, the two veterans moved to embrace each other in the storm, and they held on like drowning men to life rafts; they held on because sometimes that's all there is to do.

Peris sat down to a late dinner with Danis and Fian, Ani's mother, in their private quarters. Althea joined them, and so too did Balen, private secretary to the governor. They had to be careful: the Military and the Diplomats were at war, but the situation on Earth was even more complex than it was back on Illyr. The Military on the planet was already subject to control by the Corps, just like everything else on the conquered world, and the Corps had learned of the outbreak of civil conflict before Danis and those like him. The Military presence on Earth had already been much reduced in favour of Corps troops and Securitats, but now the remaining Military forces were largely restricted to barracks, and Military administrators like Danis were virtually powerless, with all of their decisions requiring approval from the Corps. It was, Danis supposed, better than an eruption of bloody conflict between the two Illyri powers on Earth, but not by much.

'What is happening, Peris? Tell me of my daughter. We get so little news,' said Fian as she topped up his wine glass generously with a robust Spanish Rioja.

'And what of Syl, and the Kerr boys?' added Althea, which brought a slight frown of disapproval from Fian. 'We get so little news about *anything*. The Corps is barely willing to tell us the time of day.'

Peris took a large swig of his wine, almost emptying the glass, and Althea raised an eyebrow. Once a governess, always a governess, thought Peris, and he smiled at her affectionately. Peris noticed that she looked different, thinner, her skin drawn tightly across her cheeks, but oddest of all, she was no longer wearing the typical Illyri robes that had constituted her entire wardrobe in times past. Instead, she wore what appeared to be − what was the word? − *jeans*? Yes, jeans, the uniform of half this world, paired with a plaid shirt, a man's shirt, worn and comfortable. Strangely, it suited her, but when she smiled back, it was strained. She seemed tired.

'Fian, Ani is safe − for now,' said Peris. 'Are these rooms secure?'

'Of course,' said Balen stiffly. 'I swept them for bugs myself.'

Thus assured, Peris told them of everything that had gone before: of Ani, and her apparent surrender to the blandishments of Syrene; of the destruction and killings on Erebos spearheaded by the Sisterhood; of the intervention of Syl, followed by her escape with the Kerr brothers, Meia, and others; and of their disappearance into the Derith wormhole, from which they, like all before them, had not emerged again. At this Althea let out a wail of anguish, and then was silent for a time, her head bowed in mourning for her lost near-daughter.

Finally he told them of the forbidden planet of Archaeon, and of what they had seen there: an alien infestation, the creatures bursting from the bellies of animals, and their spores being sucked up to be shipped off-world.

'To Earth,' said Danis flatly.

'We believe so,' Peris replied, but he was surprised that Danis already appeared to be aware of the threat.

There was a stunned silence. The only one who didn't look like they'd just been slapped was Danis. Instead, the governor put his head in his hands.

'Meia warned me,' he said. 'She told me that she believed this was what the Corps was planning, but I didn't want to believe her.'

'You knew?' said Fian. 'You knew, and you didn't tell us? You didn't tell *me*?'

'I didn't *know* anything,' replied Danis hotly. 'Meia merely suspected. She counselled me to keep what she told me to myself and remain on guard. She feared that if we revealed even the little she did know it would spread panic and might cause the Corps to bring forward its plans. I had to trust her. I had no choice.'

'Well, it looks like you've doomed us all,' said Fian, 'you and that damned Mech.'

Peris felt sorry for the old soldier, his long-time friend.

'Please,' he said, 'you must understand: Danis could not possibly have acted on a whisper. Had he tried to reveal what little he knew, he – and all of you – would have been killed by the Corps.'

There was a pause while they digested this. Peris thought that even Fian appeared to relent a little, although her arms remained folded across her chest, and she refused to look at her husband.

'Meia said she'd be back, with help,' said Danis.

'And she may well be yet,' said Peris. 'She, more than anyone, knows the gravity of our situation. She will do what she can.'

'*If* she can,' said Althea. Her lips were tight. 'After all, she went through Derith too.'

Peris looked around at these four dear, shocked faces, wishing he hadn't been the deliverer of such appalling news, and he felt tears come to his eyes. Embarrassed, he looked away.

'I'm just glad you're all still here,' he said softly. 'I was worried I'd be too late.'

'When, Peris? Just tell us when,' said Althea, and her jawline grew even tauter, her expression grim. She pushed her wine glass away. 'This is no time for sentiment, Captain.'

'I don't know to the day, but I have no doubt that very soon large ships will come and unleash their cargo, and the spores will be swept across Earth. That will be it. You ask me when, Althea? All I can say is that it could be any time now. It might be weeks, it might be days.'

Fian was staring out the window.

'When we learned of the outbreak of war, we thought that was why the Diplomats had already begun to leave,' she said. 'We assumed that they had been forewarned of the conflict. But then I kept thinking that if we were at war, surely they'd have shipped out many of the Galateans too, as cannon fodder.'

The Galateans were one of the first species conquered by the Illyri, and were much like large, muscular amphibians in appearance. The Illyri drafted them in to perform the drudge work of war. To their masters they were interchangeable, disposable even, but the Galateans did not resent their overlords. They even welcomed conscription into the Illyri forces, for anything was preferable to the hunger and despair of their home planet. And, in turn, the Galateans got to lord it over other alien species, whether the slave-race known as the Agrons, or the violent, rebellious humans.

'But no,' continued Fian, 'for while we have fewer Diplomats, the place is still awash with those toads, and no one seems to be in charge of them anymore.'

'Some of them have even gone feral,' added Althea. 'They're roving uncontrolled in the countryside. And the Agrons are dying: their immunity medication has stopped arriving, and they're all getting sick. I thought it was simply cruelty on the part of the Corps, but it's more than that: they've all been left to die with us.'

Balen had called up a screen and was checking information, including activity around the wormhole nearest Earth. The rest ignored him. Balen, in their experience, was always checking something.

'So what can we do to stop them?' said Danis.

Peris moved his glass away too. The wine had lost its appeal. He shook his head slowly, aware of three faces turned towards him — three, because Balen was fiddling about with his data. It reflected in his wide, lidless eyes.

'We can do nothing,' said Peris. 'That's why I've come here. To take you away. To rescue you.'

'What?' said Althea, and he swore that she sneered. She really had changed. 'Are you going to rescue the whole planet?'

'Well, obviously I can't do that. But we can try to get as many Illyri off-world as possible.'

'What about the humans?' said Althea.

Peris watched as Fian reached for Althea's hand, and Althea took it automatically. Their fingers squeezed together tightly and Althea's knuckles went white. Danis looked on with a kind of sadness: Fian had given to Althea the comfort that she would not give to him.

'There are billions of them, Althea, billions,' said Peris. 'We barely have enough ships for the Illyri who are still here, let alone the entire human race.'

'Then we must warn them,' said Fian. 'They can start to protect themselves, to make plans. There must be shelters they can use.'

Althea nodded in agreement and together the two females stood up.

'Right now?' said Danis. 'We haven't even eaten yet!'

'You heard Peris. When else?'

'If you go now, you'll cause chaos. There will be riots. People will kill each other to get to shelters. We need to think about this, Fian.'

However, Fian and Althea were already starting towards the door. The situation was moving out of Danis's control. But then, he realised, he had never entirely been in control. He had always been a puppet of the Corps, and now they were cutting his strings and leaving him to fall.

Before Danis could say anything else, Balen rose slowly from his chair. His golden skin had taken on a sickly, malarial hue.

'Look,' he said. He poked a finger through the images in front of him, deftly swiping them together. His movements were so quick that the points of light swirled together like paint thrown in the air, before rearranging themselves into orderly documents once more.

And they all saw what Balen saw: wormhole activity, barely hours behind Peris. A massive unidentified ship, moving towards Earth.

'I've hacked the system to check for incomings flights to all major stations,' said Balen. 'Tomorrow, at thirteen hundred GMT, a number of large craft are scheduled to dock simultaneously. New York . . . Rio . . . Santiago . . . Cape Town . . . Beijing . . . Abuja . . .'

He slid screens around again, nodding to himself as they watched and waited.

'All documentation and permissions for the incoming craft are direct from top brass, and signed off by the Illyri President himself, General Krake. Chatter between Military bases appears to have reached consensus that additional staff are being drafted in at long last, especially given that the Diplomats have been shipping out many of those they had down here and not replacing them. They think extra help is coming.'

'Help, my sorry arse,' said Althea, surprising Peris even further, although nobody else seemed taken aback by the governess's language. She really had changed. There even seemed to be a distinct Scottish lilt to her cussing.

'And those?' asked Peris, pointing to a series of flight numbers on Balen's screen.

'Corps vessels departing Earth over the next twelve hours,' said Balen resignedly. 'It's an exodus. They're leaving us to die.'

Peris thought of Syrene, and her desire to see him head to Earth. Even then she must have known: he had been sent to the planet to perish alongside Danis, Fian, Althea, and everyone else who had ever crossed her, including the entire human race.

'What about Edinburgh?' said Danis. 'Are we due a special landing too?'

'No,' Balen replied. 'But there's a large ship scheduled to land at somewhere called Dunsop Bridge. Why there?'

'Dunsop Bridge in Lancashire?' It was Althea who spoke. 'I remember it from Syl's geographical studies. It's often said to be the dead centre of the United Kingdom. If those ships contain spores, then the ideal thing would be to start offloading them right in the middle, and let the wind do the rest.'

'Will that work?' asked Peris.

'In due course, although the prevailing winds come from the southwest, so the South and Wales should be spared for a while. Ireland too. They clearly didn't do their homework properly.'

'No,' said Peris. 'They'll have prepared well. This has to be just the first stage. They'll keep returning with more spores until they're done.'

'And Edinburgh?' asked Danis.

'If the first drop is at Dunsop Bridge, then it'll buy Edinburgh a few days, at best, maybe a little longer for the Highlands,' said Althea. 'It depends on the speed of the wind.' She turned to Fian. 'Now we have to get the word out.'

'And how are you going to do that, exactly?' asked Danis, who felt that this was his last stand in an effort to make his wife and Althea behave – as he saw it – sensibly. 'It's not as if the Corps will give you access to the television and radio transmitters.'

'We'll use the Resistance's network,' said Althea.

Danis had long known that Althea had contacts – and perhaps more than that – in the Resistance. He had even used her to open channels of communication on occasion, mostly by discreetly mentioning some detail in the knowledge that she would pass it on, but he had always been careful not to openly acknowledge her divided loyalties. He thought for a moment.

'Do what you must,' he said, resigned now to the inevitable. 'Balen and I will try to get word to the Military commanders we have left. Perhaps they can break out their forces from the barracks and try to stop the landings, or stall them. At the very least, it'll give them time to seize ships and start evacuating.'

But even as he spoke, he knew that there was little hope. Any unscheduled craft trying to leave the planet over the coming hours and days would be blown from the skies by the Corps, either by remote weaponry on Earth or their fighters above. By the time the ships carrying the spores began to descend, he would be surprised if there was a single Corps official or Securitat left on Earth.

A hand touched Danis's arm. His wife was beside him. She leaned forward and kissed him gently, then laid her head upon his shoulder.

It was as close to intimacy as they had come in many months.

'Let's give a chance to as many as we can, Illyri or human,' she said. 'I will see you back here when we're done. I promise you, Danis.'

And then she and Althea were gone.

CHAPTER 14

O vernight, Danis, Peris, and Balen contacted everyone they could think of to warn them of what they believed to be coming, but for the most part their concerns were met with polite bafflement. More often than not, they received raucous laughter in response.

'Have you been drinking again, Danis?' asked more than one base commander. The governor cringed at the *again*. How little weight his supposed authority wielded; how fractured the Military chain of command had become here on Earth, how insubordinate. The sense that they'd been left to rot was pervasive among those who remained on the blue planet, and they were more concerned about their vulnerability to superior Corps forces than about crazy talk from a washed-up figurehead who was known to be too well-acquainted with the bottle.

'You say there are spores being sent from space to destroy us?' repeated Rupe, a former member of the castle guard who now headed up the Military detail in Santiago. 'Alien spores, Lord Danis?'

He sounded worried, and for a moment Danis thought he'd finally found someone outside of Scotland who was taking him seriously, until Rupe added: 'Perhaps you should see a doctor, Governor. You've been under a lot of pressure.'

There was no more that he could do. He could only hope that Fian and Althea were having better luck. Danis did manage to call in one favour, though. He succeeded in contacting Junior Consul Steyr, the Diplomat who had overall command of the European continent. To Danis's surprise, he had always found Steyr reasonable, even honourable, and they had worked well together during Danis's time as governor. Steyr was on his way to a departing shuttle, fleeing like the rest, when Danis got him on-screen.

'You're leaving us, Consul?' said Danis.

Steyr smiled at the older Illyri. There was a hint of sadness to it.

'All Diplomatic personnel have been ordered to leave the planet,' he replied. 'Our time here is coming to a close.'

'And Military personnel?'

Steyr's smile faded.

'For the most part, they are to remain on Earth.'

Danis trod carefully. This was not a secure channel.

'I have a feeling that those left behind may have cause to regret their posting,' he said. 'I would consider it a great personal favour if the restrictions on Military travel could be relaxed to permit some of my staff and family to join the exodus.'

'Those are not the orders we have received.'

'We are all Illyri,' said Danis. 'And my people have done nothing wrong, or nothing that merits their abandonment on this world.'

He held Steyr's gaze. Danis knew what was coming, and Steyr realised that he knew.

'Certain individuals were named as "essential" to the new Illyri presence on Earth and were not to be permitted to leave,' said Steyr. 'The list included your name, and those of a number of your immediate associates and family members.'

'At whose command?'

'The Archmage Syrene,' said Steyr. 'But . . .' He paused. 'I don't take orders from the Sisterhood. Anyway, in the midst of such a chaotic situation as we have here, errors can be made.'

Steyr consulted briefly with one of his aides while Danis waited, his life and the lives of those for whom he cared most hanging in the balance.

'One ship,' said Steyr. 'Those on board will join me on the *Oxion*, but they will officially be prisoners. Do you understand? There's no other way.'

'Thank you,' said Danis.

Steyr nodded, and killed the link.

★ ★ ★

In the morning, the reduced castle staff – or the Illyri staff, at least – were informed of the impending evacuation, and told that a ship would be ready to take them off-world. They would be permitted to bring with them only what they could carry. By noon, Althea and Fian had not returned. At one o'clock precisely, as a precaution, the castle entrance was sealed, for there was limited space available on board the waiting craft. Only those inside could be saved.

Still Danis did not give up hope, muttering to himself as he circled the courtyard near the gate, repeatedly urging the remaining guards – who were themselves itching to leave – to keep a lookout for the missing Illyri females, and particularly Fian.

'Still no sign of them,' said one guard. 'But a mob has formed outside. Humans are demanding to get in. They've seen the Corps ships leaving and want to know what's happening.'

'Keep them at bay,' ordered Danis, 'but don't fire unless absolutely necessary.'

By twenty past the hour, news reports started to trickle in, quickly becoming a deluge, faster and faster from all over the world. Large, unmanned craft had entered the earth's atmosphere, massive silver cargo transporters the likes of which had not been seen before. They were unmarked and apparently automatically piloted, for all attempts at communication were ignored, and refusal of landing permission under threat of Military defensive strikes proved no deterrent to their progress. As soon as they reached their optimum altitude, the silver ships' plump underbellies opened and clouds of red-tinged dust – the harvested alien spores – were released onto the world below. Those beneath the craft, Illyri and human alike, rushed to escape the strange mist, and many were killed in the ensuing stampedes, although none would be alive to count the victims, for what panicked feet had started, the spores would go on to complete. Those who inhaled the spores instantly began to choke and convulse, falling atop the crushed remains of the trampled, their bodies swelling as the spores did their work, turning their victims into gestation chambers for the Others.

This was the first wave.

As word spread, the living fled; cars jammed highways, and boats took to the water with scant supplies, their human cargo looking back appalled at their infected lands, and at those leaping desperately into the sea, swimming after the retreating boats, until sinking exhausted beneath the water, and still the clouds spread. Galateans tore into their Illyri masters and the Illyri responded by mowing them down in their thousands. Those Agrons that hadn't yet died of disease took off into the side streets to escape, frenzied with fear, but as they fled and their panic abated, the hot, iron aroma of spilled blood called to them, and they paused and lapped at it, and became distracted by feasts of fresh flesh, eating their fill until they too succumbed to the threat from the red sky.

Some of the remaining Military craft that tried to leave were swamped by panicked crowds, while others were shot down on the instructions of the Corps. Order collapsed in those cities that had been spared the immediate arrival of the transporters as news reached them of what was happening elsewhere, and the realisation grew that they would be next. There were street battles and looting. Chaos spread.

In Edinburgh, as in other major cities, the last of the Corps craft departed from their pads and bays, heading through the heavy clouds and into space, making for the larger carriers that would begin transporting them to the wormhole and out of the earth's solar system. The citizens looked up, and they raged as their oppressors abandoned them.

Only the small carrier in the courtyard of Edinburgh Castle did not leave, but by mid-afternoon the crowd outside the castle gates had swelled to such proportions that there was no hope of Fian or Althea making it through. The carrier was packed with anxious Illyri, whatever valuables they could carry crushed into lockers, or held between their feet. There were children and adolescents among them, all frightened, all looking to Governor Danis for guidance, for hope.

'Cowards!' the people outside screamed, and they were joined by furious Galateans, the two races briefly allied in abandonment and rage.

'Cowards!' the people cried again. Aided by the might of the

Galateans they tried to storm the gates, but the bullets of the remaining guards mowed the first waves down. The mob faltered and regrouped.

Danis heard the shooting, and watched the heaving throng from a screen in the carrier's cockpit. Time was running out.

'Minimal force,' he said to Balen, who sat beside him, a sheaf of papers on his lap. 'Please – they must use absolute minimal force.'

Helpless to act for his master, Balen simply fiddled with the paper clip holding his documents together and they slid to the floor. He let them go.

'We must leave soon,' said Peris. 'We have a narrow window of departure.'

Danis stared at him. 'We can't. What about Fian? And Althea?'

'Can't we locate them with their trackers?' said Peris, but Danis just shook his head.

'Gone. They removed them.' He stared vacantly through the glass of the cockpit window, his thoughts far from the castle. 'Did you know that Althea has a boyfriend, a human?'

Peris didn't but, having seen her last night, he wasn't surprised. She was an altered creature.

'A member of the Resistance,' Danis continued. 'Someone quite high up in the chain of command, or so I'm told.'

'I guess that's why she had her tracker removed then.'

'*Had* it removed?' Danis laughed bitterly. 'She removed it herself, Peris – dug it out with a blade long ago. Fian followed her example, although a little more recently. You know, things weren't good between us, Peris, between Fian and me, after Ani left. Sometimes I wondered if my wife had somebody else too; a human, perhaps, just like Althea. She denied it, of course, said she just wanted to be free of Illyri surveillance, and free of me too, I suppose.'

Peris was at a loss for words. 'I'm sorry, Danis,' he said uselessly.

There was quiet in the cockpit for a few moments, until fresh volleys of gunfire sounded from the gates, followed by a series of blasts. A guard's voice sounded over the internal speakers.

'They've broken through the perimeter!'

'Danis!' said Peris. 'We must leave. Give the order!'

More blasts, more shooting. Through the glass of the cockpit window, they watched as the last guards commenced a fighting retreat to the carrier, and the first of the horde appeared.

'Danis!'

'Start the engines,' Danis ordered the pilot, and there was desolation in his voice. 'As soon as the last soldier is on board, take us up.'

The gunner on the carrier began to lay down covering fire, forcing the humans and Galateans to run for protection and giving the guards enough time to make the ship. The final one had barely gotten his feet in the door when the carrier began to rise. Danis was weeping, but his tears fell silently as the pilot turned the craft away, pointing it into the sky, upwards towards the safety of the twinkling stars.

CHAPTER 15

When Althea, Trask's Illyri lover, came banging at his door in the middle of the rain-sodden night, calling his name, he hurried to let her in. He noticed immediately that she was wearing one of his plaid shirts and realised, with a rush of affection, that she must have purloined it from his wardrobe when she'd left him in the dark hours of that morning.

He moved to embrace her, but dropped his arms when he noticed another, taller figure behind her, and then Fian, the governor's wife, stepped out of the shadows and into the puddle of light on his front step.

'What the . . . ?' Trask started to protest, angry that Althea had risked his security by bringing her here, but then he saw that Althea's normally placid, smooth face was grave and furrowed with worry, and Fian was trembling with nervous energy, and at once he knew. He stepped back to let them in. The time had come.

'They're coming, right?' he said.

Althea nodded. 'I'm sorry,' she said.

'How much time have we got?'

'We think they're due to start arriving tomorrow. Ships filled with spores.'

As soon as they had revealed what they knew, Trask contacted the Illyri deserter and Resistance leader named Fremd, known to many as the Green Man, and with heavy hearts they set their plans in motion. Those humans already chosen were given one hour to get their families and belongings together. No contact beyond immediate kin – husbands, wives, and children – was permitted. Pets were abandoned to the kindness of neighbours, although those leaving them were as yet unaware they'd never see them again. Grandparents, parents, siblings, cousins, friends – so many would be left behind. Notes of love were slipped beneath doors and through letterboxes, declaring that they'd return soon. Perhaps they believed it, at the time.

In the large garage beside Trask's house, final preparations began. He and his group had the longest trek ahead of them because they were heading for the bunker in Ireland. Althea nodded grimly when she heard this: prevailing winds meant this was probably one of the safest places on the planet, she told him, for the spores would be carried like pollen or seeds, a genocidal pollution borne around the world by currents of air. On that basis, the rugged, windswept coastline of the west of Ireland would be less vulnerable than most places, at least for a while.

Fian – the Lady Fian, Trask reminded himself – stood to one side while other groups arrived, bustling past her, packing, re-packing, arguing and talking over one another. She leaned against a wall, watching them, looking lost. She appeared reluctant to leave, yet remained unmoored and alone as Althea dug in with the work that was needed, alternately murmuring information and issuing instructions in the vague direction of Trask's daughters, Jean and Nessa, seemingly oblivious to her friend's continued lonely presence. Well, either she was oblivious or she chose not to notice, thought Trask. Althea was that kind of a woman – if he could call a female Illyri a woman, for he was never entirely sure if the word referred exclusively to human females, although she certainly felt deliciously all-woman when he held her close and warm in his arms late at night. Whatever, Althea was very focused on the task at hand, almost schoolmarm-like, but that probably came from her years as a governess. Trask shook his head in awe as she corralled his reluctant offspring, and went over to speak to Fian himself. She had no business being here, he felt. While the Resistance members had grown used to Althea, the wife of the governor was another matter entirely. Fian would be lynched as soon as the nature of the catastrophe that was about to befall the entire planet became known. Even Althea might not be entirely safe.

'You may leave now if you wish, madam,' said Trask. 'As you can see, your message has been received loud and clear, and we appreciate your help, but there's nothing more you can do here.' That was good, he thought: polite, but firm.

She turned to face him slowly, but made no reply, and her great unblinking eyes seemed to look deeper than his face, far deeper. Up close, he could see the likeness to her daughter Ani in those swirling irises of turquoise, vivid as a whirlpool in a glacial lake. After a few seconds she merely nodded, and he found he wasn't sure what that even meant.

'I met Ani once, you know,' he found himself saying. 'She was an "interesting" girl.'

'She was,' Fian said. 'Is,' she corrected herself, before adding: 'I fear she's running with a bad crowd.'

Althea had shared with Trask the latest news about Ani and the Sisterhood. As far as Trask was concerned, the term *bad crowd* barely began to cover the Nairenes.

'I know what you mean,' he said. 'I have daughters too, but then my ex-wife reckoned *I* was the bad crowd.'

Fian ignored his weak attempt at humour.

'Is she going with you?' she said. 'Your ex-wife; are you taking her with you?'

Trask looked perplexed.

'Well, um, I hadn't really considered it,' he admitted. Quite frankly, the last person with whom he wanted to be trapped in a bunker was his ex-wife.

'But she's the other parent to your children – she gave birth to them,' said Fian, and her eyes were cooler now. 'Will they not want their mother with them?'

'We've limited space,' Trask blustered. 'Very limited. And given that others are leaving behind brothers and sisters, and parents too, I can hardly insist on taking along the ex, now can I?'

He found himself wondering why he was explaining himself to her, and so he ground to a halt. They stared at each other. He tried not to blink, then realised it was ridiculous to attempt to outstare an Illyri.

'And your girls will still go with you, even knowing that you're leaving their mother behind to die?' asked Fian after a few tense moments. Though she spoke quietly, her chin was tilted in defiance. She was significantly taller than Trask and he felt very much like she was looking down on him, in more ways than one.

'Ah, come on now, that's not fair,' he protested, even as he thought that, actually, yes, it probably was. 'Anyway, I haven't told them what's about to happen. I haven't broken the news of what your people are about to unleash on us to anyone beyond the commanders, or there'd be utter panic – and it would cost you your head, I imagine, because my people would look to take their anger out on the nearest Illyri. My girls will find out soon enough, though, and I'm pretty sure they'll understand. They're fighters too, you know.'

Fian looked scornful.

'But she's their mother,' she persisted.

Trask glared at her.

'Dammit, woman, don't you see? If I take the ex-wife – who I don't much like, frankly – I won't be able to take Althea, who I like one hell of a lot!'

'Althea's going with you?' said Fian, and as she spoke, her voice faltered.

'Of course!'

Fian looked over his shoulder – or rather, over the top of his head – and he turned and saw what she saw: the figure of Althea on the far side of the garage hefting boxes into a trailer, her expression determined. She had stripped to a modest vest, Trask's shirt tied around her waist, and her hair was falling from its pins. From this distance she appeared younger than she was, and with her arms exposed – something that rarely happened – she seemed unusually vulnerable.

Frustrated, Trask looked again into Fian's face, prepared to argue his corner, but then he saw that tears were filling her eyes. They balanced on the rims precariously, and at once he felt a strange, deep sorrow for her. He knew she'd lost her only daughter to the stars, and her estranged husband was a laughing stock: an ineffectual drunk, they said, although Althea's view of him was very different.

As the governor's wife, Fian was isolated by her position, and her disintegrating marriage was her burden to bear alone. Althea had become her sole confidante, her friend. Fian must have assumed that Althea would leave the earth with her once the warning had been delivered to the Resistance, but she was mistaken.

'You can come with us too, if you want,' he said, but even as he spoke the words he knew how rash they were, how ridiculous, even. There would be mutiny if he announced that he was adding the governor's wife herself to the manifest. Anyway, she was an Illyri, and they could presumably still leave the planet when they liked. The rest of them didn't have that option. Only later did Trask learn how wrong he was.

Fian smiled weakly, and finally a tear escaped and ran unchecked down her golden cheek.

'Thank you for the offer, Trask, although obviously that will not be happening,' she said. 'But do take special care of my dear Althea. Please. In return, I know she'll do her utmost to take care of you.'

'Of course,' he started to say, but whether she heard him or not he would never know, for she turned heel and left quickly, disappearing through the entrance, briefly forming a silhouette against the brightening dawn sky before the door closed gently behind her. It was only later that he noticed she'd left her overcoat behind on the back of a chair. He held the coat for a second, considering, and then shrugged and tossed it into a corner along with all the other rubbish.

'It's nearly morning,' he yelled. 'We're moving out – now!'

It had been the most difficult decision Trask had ever been forced to make, but in a strange way also the easiest.

Meia had warned him before she'd left Earth – although precisely of what she'd been unclear, as she'd only surmised a scenario from things seen and heard, and from her own suspicions – and he knew that the end must be coming when the pace of the Illyri evacuation accelerated. It was no longer just the senior figures who were leaving – the junior consuls, the lords and their retinues – but the rank and file. They abandoned the most difficult postings first: Afghanistan,

Iraq, Somalia, Congo, the southern United States, Alaska. Triumphant communications were passed along the Resistance's shortwave radio channels, and the sense of an apparent victory spurred an increase in violence against the Illyri forces that remained. Images of the departing ships found their way onto ResNet, the corner of the Darknet that had become an informal message board for the various factions fighting the invaders, where videos of Islamic fundamentalists in Iraq beheading captured Illyri sat alongside recordings of sermons by Christian preachers in the Blue Ridge Mountains proclaiming the coming of the Antichrist and the end of the world.

Political responses to the Illyri withdrawal varied, and it soon became clear that the world's leaders were as surprised as anyone else by what was occurring. Since the Illyri had kept most democratic institutions – councils, parliaments – in place, even if only as puppet administrations, it wasn't difficult for western societies to begin planning the transition back to human rule, although elsewhere tribal and religious conflicts erupted once again, now that the common enemy was leaving.

But Trask didn't pay attention to any of it. He had been preparing for months, assisted by a handful of the most trusted members of the Resistance, many of them from his own extended family. Ironically, given it was the Illyri who were about to attempt the annihilation of humanity, it was to the Illyri deserter Fremd that Trask first turned. Fremd, the leader of the Highland Resistance, but also the figure in the Resistance movement with the most detailed knowledge of the Illyri and the alien parasites they had brought with them to Earth. Fremd had seen the red dust pouring from the dying Grand Consul Gradus, and had witnessed the violent death of Lorac – another Illyri deserter, and a trusted comrade – when the cloud of spores had hit him square in the face, before everything had been destroyed by fire. Fremd knew what might lie ahead . . .

Before she left Earth, Meia had told Trask to work more closely with Fremd, and in order to ensure that they both cooperated, she had given each of them one half of a set of GPS coordinates. When they came together and travelled to the spot – an abandoned crofter's cottage near Aberdeen – they found, sealed in plastic and placed in an airtight box, a book: a first edition of Isaac Asimov's *I, Robot*.

'She always was a funny one,' Trask had said as he unwrapped the novel. The interior had been hollowed out to enable two flash drives to be stored in the space. When they were accessed, the drives were found to contain the location of a number of underground shelters: three in Scotland and England, and one on the west coast of Ireland. They were not human constructions, but had instead been built by the Illyri in the early stages of the Conquest as safe havens in the event of some unanticipated disaster. All had advanced solar-powered generators, state-of-the-art decontamination facilities, water recycling and purification systems, and vast 'farms' in which herbs, greens and microgreens could be grown in tiered beds using hydroponics and LED lights. Each could accommodate hundreds of Illyri, but now they would be used as arks for humans. Over the weeks and months that followed, Trask and Fremd set about adding further supplies to them, even adapting parts of the shelters for chicken runs, and assigning trusted operatives in the vicinity to start raising chickens for eggs. The Illyri food systems allowed the vegetables grown to be adapted to all kinds of uses, and Fremd had quickly figured out how to alter them to provide a grain-free food source that would be ideal for chicken feed.

The question for Trask and Fremd was who to save – the decision that was both easy (immediate family first) and hard (but who else?). Neither made any apologies for picking their loved ones, but after that it was a question of practicality. They chose on the basis of skill sets – farmers, mechanics, electricians, botanists, scientists – recognising that some of those approached would also want to bring their immediate families. Where possible, they selected single men and women, who were warned to be ready . . .

And now the hour had come.

By the time the church bells were ringing for the Sunday morning services, Trask and his people were already bouncing across the countryside in trucks, heading for the western coast. Other vehicles joined their little convoy as they drew closer to the shore, until finally they reached the long-defunct ferry terminal north of Cairnryan. The buildings were deserted, what windows remained were broken, and hardy creepers dangled over the doorways, their leaves thin and crumpled. The only sign of life was a lone gull, riding the wind. A small fleet of fishing boats was tethered beside the silent dock, unused on the Sabbath, but they were dwarfed by the rusted hulk of an old Stena Line ferry, its gangplank down as if waiting for them. A figure in a captain's cap appeared on deck, and other crew members bustled around him: this was Aitken, who had plied this route across the Irish Sea long before the coming of the Illyri. Aitken had been preparing for this day on Trask's orders, he and his crew secretly readying the old ferry for one last journey.

Several of the vehicles paused. Men and women clambered out and heated words were exchanged with the Resistance leaders, for the weather was far from fine for sailing, although the heavy winds appeared to be lessening in ferocity. Those protesting most vehemently reached for their loved ones and gathered them near as if to protect them, saying they should leave when the waters grew calmer for it would be much wilder at sea, out of the shelter of the bay formed by Loch Ryan. Stony-faced, their leaders pressed them to board, demanding their trust and insisting on their obedience to the chain of command, even when they were holding their tiny children by the hands.

Still, despite the best efforts of Trask and others, a truck and a car turned back towards Stranraer, for those inside saw no reason to risk the lives of their dearest ones on the sea, and they did not yet know of what was about to befall the entire planet. Trask had almost been tempted to share his knowledge with all of them at that point, but he needed to hold his tongue for just a little while longer. If they found out the truth now, some of them would try to go back for relatives and friends, or start to panic. It was better that he and his confidantes maintain the illusion of flight from a more understandable, if fictitious threat: a second Illyri front, designed to wipe out all Resistance, requiring them to hide themselves away in preparation for a great human counterattack.

And so, their numbers somewhat depleted, the Scots finally set sail across the Irish Sea.

They landed at Larne Harbour, surprising the locals with the sudden appearance of a ferry, like a ghost ship after years of no sailings. A small crowd cheered as they docked, but Trask could barely look at them, these walking dead, as they drove past them and inland, across the country and to the West, where the Atlantic winds sent waves crashing endlessly into the cliffs, the islands and the rocks. Here they met select members of the Irish Resistance, who had been summoned to join them under the same pretext: an impending massive Illyri assault. The Irish contingent had been supplied with the coordinates, but told nothing else.

'We may have to hide away for weeks, even months,' they were informed. 'For safety, bring your husbands, your wives, your children – but tell no others.'

And they listened and obeyed because they were soldiers of the Resistance, and that's what soldiers did.

Only when everyone was finally underground in this most secret of bunkers, and the doors secured, was the truth revealed. At first there was shock, then anger. A handful of people made an effort to break out, hopeful of still rescuing parents or friends, but the codes were known to only three of the Resistance leaders, and they weren't going to share them with anyone, even under pain of death, for if those doors were opened again then death was inevitable anyway. The escapees tried calling those they'd left behind on their phones, but down here there was no signal. They sobbed wretchedly as they heard the first news reports coming in, then gradually their wails turned to stunned silence as the broadcasts slowly stuttered out, to be replaced by static. Eventually, a kind of resignation came over those in the bunker, allied with a mixed sense of guilt and relief: guilt at abandoning so many others to their fate, and relief that they were not among them.

And they remained below ground for the first six months, while life on Earth was wiped out by the Others.

IV
SYL

CHAPTER 16

Syl was bewildered. Fara's words echoed senselessly in her head, as though spoken in a language that Syl only half-understood.

'I can't destroy the Others,' she protested. 'I'm not even sure that they *can* be destroyed. Who knows how many of them are floating through space on rocks, or sitting in Illyri storage facilities? We could spend thousands of years scouring the universe and still find only a fraction of them.'

'You don't have to find all of them,' said Kal. 'Only one.'

Fara raised a hand to silence him. Clearly she felt that the discussion was moving a little too quickly.

'You have gifts, Syl Hellais,' explained Fara. '*Powers*. We sensed you as soon as your ship passed through the wormhole, and you felt our presence too. You reached out and you were among us: a being with a physical form, using psychic abilities to move through a mass consciousness. We were, for a moment, vulnerable again.'

'Are you suggesting that I would have harmed you?' asked Syl.

'You could have tried,' said Fara. 'We would have destroyed your ship, and all on it, before you could do too much damage, but the potential was there.'

'You're saying that I could attack the Others in the same way?'

'It's possible. They are an interconnected species.'

Paul intervened, putting aside thoughts of Earth, if only temporarily. Now, more than ever, he wanted revenge on the Others, and to be rid of them forever. If Syl could make this happen, then the subject was worthy of discussion. But even as he spoke, he was already planning their trip back through the Derith wormhole before too many more days passed in the blink of an eye.

'Kal said that Syl would only need to find one of the Others,' he said. 'But we've destroyed some of them in the past, and the species has continued.'

'Not just any one,' said Kal. 'We believe that the Others have a hierarchy. Some of them function like queens in ants' nests. They're larger and more powerful than the rest. They transmit and receive information, using it to guide the actions of the species. The infestation of the Illyri was not a random occurrence. The initial contamination might have come about that way, but not what came after. A bargain of some kind must have been struck between the Illyri and the Others, because without a pact, the Others would have turned the Illyri into gestation chambers for spores.'

'It was a meteor,' said Syl. 'That's how the Illyri came to be infected by them. The meteor was brought to the Sisterhood, and whatever was inside – a spore, or a larva – found its way into the Archmage Ezil. She was the one who struck the bargain with them: spare the Illyri, and she would find host races for the Others to use.'

She had already explained most of this to Paul and Meia, but this was the first that the rest of the *Nomad*'s crew had heard of it.

'That's cold,' said Thula.

'Ezil underestimated them,' said Syl. 'She just wanted to hold them off until she could find a way to destroy them, but they were too clever for her. She was trying to do the right thing, or believed that she was.'

'That right thing may have cost us the earth,' said Steven.

'We don't know that yet.'

'We don't because we're still stuck here trading stories!'

He pushed against the fleshy bonds that held him, but they simply tightened a little more. He gave a cry of pain.

'Let him go,' said Syl to Fara. 'Rizzo too. Please. Surely you must understand why they reacted as they did.'

She looked to Steven and Rizzo.

'We all want to be gone from here,' she told them, 'but we can't leave until we've learned as much as we can about the Others, and decided how to move against them.'

'Every minute that we spend here is days on Earth,' said Steven.

'I know that.'

'I left my mum back there.'

'I know that too.'

'*I know, I know,*' Steven mocked. 'You don't know anything! It's not your planet.'

'Yes, it is,' said Syl. 'It's the only planet I've known, and the only home. I care about it as much as you do. But shouting and leaping across tables isn't going to help anyone.'

'Listen to her, Steven,' said Paul. 'If Kal is right – and we've no reason to think that he'd lie – then the worst has already happened on Earth. We'll find out for ourselves soon enough, but if it turns out that we're among the last of our kind, then we'll want revenge, and that means knowing as much as we can about our enemy. Just give us a little more time.'

After a long pause, Steven nodded, although he still didn't look happy. Reluctantly, Rizzo also consented to remaining calm. The veins holding them retreated back into the floor and Steven and Rizzo resumed their seats, but Paul was under no illusions that this retreat was anything other than temporary. He felt real trouble brewing, with his brother in particular. Had they been alone, he'd have grabbed Steven and tried to shake some sense into him. God, didn't he know that Paul was sickened about the fate of their mother as well? And not just her: he thought of his comrades in the Resistance, his friends from Edinburgh, even girls that he'd gone out with, and each time he did, his mind flashed back to those animals on Archaeon, their bodies twisting in agony just before they burst apart in a cloud of spores.

But Steven wouldn't meet Paul's eye. He was slumped in a chair, his arms folded in front of him like a sulking child. Rizzo reached out to him and rubbed his shoulder, and Paul saw Alis look at this fond action in vague confusion, before tentatively reaching out her own hand and patting Steven's other shoulder. He reached up and squeezed her fingers.

Syl continued speaking with Kal and Fara.

'I think I saw one of the bigger creatures that you're talking about,' she said. 'It had made a web for itself deep in the Marque, and beneath it were the First Five. It had attached itself to them and they were in so much pain . . .'

'Our sentinels have also glimpsed Others such as this,' said Fara, 'but not many. They're rare and they stay hidden. Already, the one that you saw may have concealed itself elsewhere.'

Meia leaned forward.

'Do the Others know of your existence?' she asked.

'They know that we once were, and may still be,' said Kal. 'But not where we have gone.'

'Then some of the Illyri probably know of you, too,' said Meia.

'Peris wasn't too surprised when we found that sentinel on Torma,' said Paul, 'but I didn't get the impression that he knew who had left it there. He seemed happy enough to give a long-dead race credit for its creation and leave things at that.'

'Our machinery has been discovered by the Illyri and other species from time to time,' said Kal. 'Their assumption, we hope, is that those who created it have faded from the universe.'

'How many Illyri exploration ships and drones have you captured or destroyed since you concealed yourself here?' Meia asked him.

'Thirty,' said Kal. 'Mostly drones.'

'So they keep sending them into the wormhole?'

'Drones? Yes. But that ship out there is the first inhabited vessel we've seen in many years, yours aside.'

'How often do they come?'

'Irregularly.'

'Has the frequency of their appearances increased or decreased?'

Kal frowned, waiting for the information to be relayed from the consciousness of which he formed a part.

'Increased,' he said after a heartbeat.

'And the technology?'

'More sophisticated. The drones are faster. The last one almost made it back into the wormhole before it could be destroyed.'

Meia sat back.

'Then they know you're here,' she said. 'Or suspect it. You don't have much time. None of us has.'

Fara and Kal considered this. In her head, Syl heard the background babble of the Cayth increase in volume as the possibility of their discovery was discussed.

'We can't leave,' said Fara.

'We're not asking you to,' said Paul. He desperately wanted the Cayth to take their side, but he knew that he didn't have time for the lengthy, and quite probably ultimately fruitless, negotiations that this might require. 'But we need everything that you can tell us about the Others, and whatever intelligence you've gathered on the Illyri from your sentinels, and we need it quickly. About that much, at least, Steven is right: we cannot remain here any longer.'

'Give us a little more time,' said Fara. 'We will upload the data to your ship, and instruct Syl as best we can.'

'I'm not waiting here another day,' said Steven. 'Tying me up again won't stop me. You'll have to kill me.'

'Steven, we only have one ship,' said Paul.

Syl rose and walked to the window of the observation deck. Deep in the blackness, a silver fish flickered in its net.

'No,' she said. 'We have two.'

CHAPTER 17

A hologram of the pursuit ship's cockpit materialised before them.
It was so real that Syl felt she might almost step into it and touch
the crew of the vessel. The interior was similar to that of the *Nomad*,
with six Illyri clearly visible to them: one was slumped in the co-
pilot's seat, a second stood behind her drinking from a container, and
four were gathered around an open panel by the weapons system,
tinkering with the circuits and wiring. Three of those in the cockpit
were female, and three male.

Paul gestured to the Cayth before speaking, tapping a forefinger to
his right ear.

'No,' said Fara. 'They can't see or hear us.'

Paul noticed that they were wearing Securitat flight suits. The
Illyri killers who had attacked the Military mission to Torma, and
from whom he and the others had captured the *Nomad*, had not been
wearing uniforms. They'd stripped themselves of all insignia and
identifying marks, right down to their Chips. But these ones had no
concerns about showing their true colours. Now that war had been
declared, they had no need of camouflage.

'Can you bring us in closer to the group by the panel?' he asked.

The image was magnified so that they were now peering over the
shoulders of the Illyri. Audio clicked in, and they heard voices
discussing wiring and reboots.

'Any idea what they're doing?' said Paul. 'Rizzo?'

Rizzo was still scowling in her seat beside Steven. She glanced at
the younger Kerr brother instead of answering, which stretched Paul's
temper to breaking point.

'He's not in charge here, *Private*,' Paul barked. 'I am. If you're not able to fulfil your responsibilities as a member of this crew, then I have no use for you. In that case, you can stay here with the Cayth, if they'll have you, or you can float home. So answer me: what are they doing?'

Rizzo had never been chastised by her lieutenant in this way before. None of them had. The shock showed on her face. Even Steven looked a little stunned. He unfolded his arms and sat up straighter in his chair. Rizzo, meanwhile, was just short of standing to attention.

'I'm sorry, sir,' she said. She peered at the Illyri. 'The weapons system on some Illyri craft is equipped with a backup power source. It holds a residual charge from the ship's engines. If the ship's power is disabled, the backup means that the weapons can still be used to defend it. They're probably trying to divert some of that power to the ship's engines.'

'To what end?'

She considered it, scratching her head.

'Well,' she finally said, 'I imagine their intention is to get the weapons online and target them all on a single point in the barrier surrounding them in the hope of creating a breach. Then they could use the remaining residual power to kick-start the engines for long enough to get them back into the wormhole.'

'Thank you,' said Paul. 'Kal, Fara: could that work?'

'No,' said Fara. 'The shield is far too strong. And now that we know what they're planning . . .'

She smiled. They heard a low whine from somewhere deep in the interior of the weapons system. It rose in pitch for a moment before fading to nothing. One of the Illyri swore loudly.

'No more backup power?' asked Paul.

'None,' said Fara.

'Can you open an audio link so I can talk to them?'

'What are you planning to say?'

'I'd like to find out who they are, and what they know about whatever is going on between the Corps and the Military. I might even be able to convince them to surrender, so we can take their ship without bloodshed.'

'Why?' asked Fara. 'It will make no difference.'

'I'm not sure that I understand,' said Paul.

'They are contaminated. Whether they choose to surrender or not, we cannot let them live.'

'That's murder,' said Syl.

'That's necessity,' said Fara.

Syl was about to say something more, but Paul shot her a look that silenced her.

'Just let me talk to them,' he said.

Fara nodded. 'The channel is open,' she said.

Paul took a deep breath.

'This is Brigade Lieutenant Paul Kerr calling the commander of the unknown Illyri vessel. We have you on visual and audio. Respond, please.'

A discussion broke out among the Illyri. Some of them looked around the interior of their ship, as though hoping to spot a hidden camera or microphone. The first group was joined by six more Illyri from the back of the ship, some of them clearly groggy from sleep. Eventually, the female in the captain's chair stood and stepped forward. She wore her hair shaved close to her skull, revealing a jagged scar that ran from the crown of her head to just above her left ear.

'This is Fenuless, commander of the *Varcis*,' she replied.

'Commander Fenuless,' said Paul. 'How is your mission to destroy us progressing?'

Fenuless smiled grimly.

'We still remain hopeful of a successful conclusion.'

'I admire your optimism.'

'We saw you being drawn into the alien vessel,' said Fenuless. 'We assumed that you were dead.'

'We find ourselves among friends,' said Paul.

This clearly wasn't what Fenuless was expecting to hear.

'Can you provide more information?'

'I'll let them introduce themselves, when they're ready. In the meantime, we may be able to help you.'

'Why would you want to help us?'

'I'm not like you: I don't kill without a reason. Also, I can't learn anything from you if you're dead.'

'True soldiers don't require reasons,' said Fenuless. 'Only orders.'

'Come on, Fenuless,' said Paul. 'You and your crew aren't cannon fodder. You're wearing nice Securitat flight suits, and Securitat orders always come with a thick intelligence file attached.'

'We have nothing to share with you,' said Fenuless.

'That's a shame,' said Paul. 'If you'll excuse me for a moment . . .'

He made a cutting gesture with a forefinger.

'Audio is off,' Fara confirmed.

'You have control of all ship's systems?' Paul asked.

'Yes.'

'Turn off their oxygen, please.'

'Paul?' said Syl. 'Are you sure?'

'They're Securitats,' said Paul. 'I could try to bargain with them until I'm blue in the face, and I'd still get nowhere. Instead, let's see what happens when *they* get blue in the face.'

He watched as the net around the *Varcis* briefly surged with orange light as it responded to the Cayth command to shut off the oxygen.

Good, he thought. *Let's see how you like that.*

'Now, if you'll excuse me,' he said, 'I need a moment alone with my brother.'

Paul moved to a corner of the room and Steven reluctantly followed. Paul figured that the Cayth would probably be listening in, but he didn't care. As for Syl – well, he couldn't be sure, but he hoped that she'd keep herself in check. He was trying not to think too much about the ramifications of the massive increase in her powers, and what it portended for their relationship as well as Syl's place in the universe. That way lay madness, and he had enough problems as things stood.

He waited for Steven to join him, before shifting position so that he was shielding his brother with his back. He placed his left hand on Steven's right shoulder and spoke to him softly.

'Listen to me,' he said. 'Thula has family back on Earth, and Rizzo too. I love Mum as much as you do, and the possibility that she may be dead – or, God, worse than dead, after what we've seen the Others do – makes me want to kill everyone responsible.'

'Then why the hell don't you?' said Steven. 'Why don't you convince the Cayth to let us go and we'll head back to Earth and try to rescue Mum, and Thula's people, and Rizzo's? Let's just leave, instead of sitting here talking to Securitats.'

'And whose people would we rescue first?' asked Paul. 'Ours? Our mother?'

'Yes!'

'Don't you think Thula might have an opinion on that, or Rizzo? Why is our family more valuable than theirs?'

'It's not like that. You're twisting my words.'

'Maybe we could draw lots.'

'You're just—'

'And that assumes we can even get past whatever is waiting for us at the other side of the wormhole.'

That shut Steven up.

'Have you even been listening to what's being said back there,' Paul continued, 'to what Meia and the Cayth were discussing? The Others know about the Cayth, and that means that the Corps knows too. By now, I'd say they suspect that the reason why nothing returns from the Derith wormhole may be because of the presence of the Cayth, and the fact that we fled into it has probably only confirmed those suspicions. At the very least, the Corps will have left one ship on the other side of the wormhole, in case we do come back out, but my guess is there's worse to come.'

'What do you mean?'

'Think about it: a whole alien species, just waiting to be infested by the Others.'

Even in his anger, Steven understood. He looked past Paul to where Fara and Kal were sitting.

'But how can they infect the Cayth if the Cayth have no physical form?' asked Steven. It was a reasonable question, asked in a reasonable tone, thankfully. His brother seemed to be calming down.

'In a way, all of this is the Cayth,' Paul replied, gesturing at the ship and their surroundings. 'They don't just drift through their world as spirits. They have to interface with their ships, their technology. You've seen how nervous they are. If even one spore were to get into a Cayth ship, it would be the end of them.'

'And you believe that the Others are coming for them?'

'Yes, with the help of the Corps.'

Steven kicked at the floor of the ship in frustration, and Paul half-expected to see some irate manifestation of the Cayth emerge, rubbing its head. Despite all that was happening, the image made him smile

'What?' said Steven.

'All of this,' said Paul. 'You know, neither of us can remember an existence before the Illyri. I can't recall a time when we weren't scared, or fighting, or just trying to survive. Now we're stuck here in the arse-end of the universe, and all I've ever wanted to do is go home, but I'm not even sure if there's a home to go back to anymore.'

He dug his fingers firmly into his brother's shoulder and stared hard at him.

'Of all the crew, of everyone left who matters to me – even Syl – it's you I have to be able to rely on the most. It's you I trust. You're my brother. We're blood. But I can't have you arguing with me, not like you did. Whatever you may think of my decisions, I have to look at the bigger picture. I'm responsible for everyone on the *Nomad*, and not just them: right now we probably know more about the Others than anyone outside the Corps, and the Cayth can add to that knowledge. One ship won't defeat them, and won't win back Earth for us, but what we learn here might.'

Steven nodded.

'I'm sorry,' he said. 'But when I thought about poor Mum . . .'

'I know. And I think I have a plan. I can't go back there, much as I want to. I need to stay with Syl.'

'Because you love her?'

'Well, perhaps' – Paul's cheeks went a little pink – 'but mainly because of what she can do. What if the Cayth are right, Steven? What if Syl is our weapon?'

Again, Steven nodded. 'All right. I get it.'

'But obviously someone needs to go back to Earth,' said Paul. 'I think it'll have to be you.'

'Me? Alone?'

'You can take Rizzo and Alis. I doubt that she'll want to stay with us anyway if you leave, but that aside, she has some very useful skills that no human has, and no Illyri either, come to think of it. You may well need her more than you know.'

Steven frowned. 'If I take Alis, then who'll fly your ship?'

'Well, Meia, obviously, and Thula can help. Remember he was on the flight commander programme, and doing pretty damned well too if I recall, before he lost his temper.'

'Oh yes.' A glimmer of humour played on Steven's face. Thula had been on his way to becoming a pilot before he'd punched out a tutor who was annoying him and found himself busted back to the ranks, so he knew his way around a cockpit, even if he was nowhere near as accomplished a pilot as Steven.

'Okay,' said Steven. 'I'll do it. It may not be an army, but it's a start.'

Paul smiled at him.

'Oh, I think I may be able to guide you to an army too.'

CHAPTER 18

Paul and Steven returned to the table. While they had been talking, the Cayth had done more than simply cut the *Varcis*'s oxygen supply: they had begun to void it from the ship, so that most of the crew were already in obvious distress, trying to breathe shallowly even as their lungs cried out for more air.

Paul resumed his seat next to Kal.

'I presume you were listening to us,' said Paul.

If Kal felt at all embarrassed, then he didn't show it.

'We hear everything on the ship.'

'And do you agree with my assessment of your situation?'

'I hope that it is inaccurate, but I fear it's true.'

'How long can the Cayth hold out?'

'I have already summoned the rest of the fleet. We'll strengthen the defences and boost the nets. A full-scale invasion might break us, but we can deal with smaller incursions.'

'The Illyri are at war with one another,' said Paul. 'That's good news for you.'

'They *were* at war,' Kal corrected him, 'when you came through the wormhole. Who knows what the situation is now?'

'I've never heard of a short civil war,' said Paul. 'They have a habit of dragging on. Syl, how long did the last Illyri civil war go on for?'

'Almost a hundred years.'

'See?' said Paul to Kal. 'A hundred years. I think it's safe to say that they're probably just getting started. Now, can you patch me into Fenuless? Let's see if she's in more of a mood to talk.'

Kal indicated with his hand that the channels were open.

'Commander Fenuless? This is Lieutenant Kerr. You and your crew seem to be in some difficulty.'

'Our . . . oxygen,' Fenuless gasped. 'The systems . . . are . . .'

'Under our control, like everything else on your vessel. You see, I don't really have time for your posturing. I have questions that I need answered and so do our friends here with me. So here's what I'm proposing: I'll restore your oxygen and you'll answer our questions. The moment you cease to cooperate, I'll let you and your crew die.'

'You're a . . . savage,' said Fenuless.

'I'm Scottish,' said Paul, 'so I've heard that one before. Are we in agreement?'

Fenuless spluttered her assent.

'Restore their oxygen supply,' said Paul.

He was so focused on the image of the *Varcis* and her personnel that he didn't notice how intently the members of his own crew were watching him. Somehow, they had gone from a situation where they were at the mercy of an unknown alien race to having their lieutenant giving orders to that same race.

While Fenuless and her crew recovered themselves, Meia asked Kal to cut the audio again. Paul leaned towards her, curious.

'Can you give me the previous scan, the internal one, as well?' she said.

Kal did, superimposing one image of the *Varcis* on the other so that Fenuless and the others appeared semi-transparent. The parasites they were carrying were clearly visible in seven of them, although Fenuless's was bigger than the rest, and its tendrils spread more deeply through her system.

'Interesting,' said Meia.

'What is?'

'Can you see the development of the Other in Fenuless? Look there, deep in the lateral tissue of her brain.'

Meia pointed at Fenuless's image, and the Cayth responded by lighting up the section of Fenuless's brain beside Meia's finger, a section separating the frontal and parietal lobes from the temporal lobe. A particularly thick tendril from the Other had embedded itself there, with smaller tendrils running from it.

'That is the anterior insular cortex,' said Meia.

'What does it do?' asked Syl.

'In both humans and Illyri, it's linked to high-level cognitive functions: error detection, language processing, self-awareness – consciousness, I suppose – but it also processes empathy. It's the part of the brain that makes you, and those like you, compassionate.'

'Meaning?' asked Paul.

'The Other is clearly tied deeply to Fenuless's consciousness,' said Meia. 'They're close, almost functioning as one. I would theorise that the distinction between them is minimal. Fenuless is the Other, and the Other is Fenuless. On a practical level, it has also probably cut off her empathic responses. Lieutenant, Fenuless is a killer, and almost certainly by choice.'

'How can you be sure?'

'The Other is an infection, and the brain tissue would be expected to exhibit signs of inflammation or irritation in response to its incursions. I see no such signs. The Other may well have suppressed her immune reactions, but the complexity of the connections between them indicates a mutual dependence. The Other also appears to have almost entirely enclosed Fenuless's amygdala, the section of the brain linked to violence and psychopathy. If we assume that Fenuless's transformation is not unique, then it would suggest a heightened capacity for ruthlessness among those members of the Corps and Securitats who have been implanted with Others.'

'It wasn't like the Securitats were lacking in ruthlessness to begin with,' said Steven.

'But it's helpful if you're starting a war against your own people,' said Thula.

The layout of Fenuless's ship was slightly different from the *Nomad* in that the *Varcis* had an elevated captain's seat behind the two pilot chairs. Fenuless was now sitting in that raised seat, the rest of her crew ranged around her.

'Okay, let's see what she has to say for herself,' said Paul.

'Commander, I trust you're enjoying the taste of fresh oxygen again. It does come at a price, though.'

'Ask your questions,' said Fenuless.

'What is your mission? And "to destroy" is not an acceptable answer.'

A game was being played, and they both knew it. Fenuless would do her best to keep as much from Paul as she could, regardless of any threat to her oxygen supply. Paul would have to infer as much from what he was not told as from what she chose to reveal.

'We were initially ordered to be part of the assault on Melos Station,' said Fenuless. 'We were redirected to follow and intercept you.'

'On whose orders?'

'Dyer himself, supported by the Archmage Syrene.'

'Who's Dyer?' Paul asked Syl.

'I think he's a Consul – big in the Securitats,' Syl replied. 'I seem to remember hearing his name before.'

'Consul Dyer is now Vice President,' Fenuless confirmed. 'He assumed the post when civil war broke out, because President Krake was deemed to be out of his depth.'

'Why? Because Krake's with the Military?' said Syl, in Illyri, addressing her question to Fenuless. President Krake had been a member of the Military, but had married a Nairene Sister named Merida. Those in the Military who distrusted the Sisterhood had warned him against it, but had been ignored, for Merida was beautiful, and Krake was as vain as he was arrogant.

'Perhaps,' said Fenuless. 'Even for a politician like Krake, it must have been hard to stand back and let his former comrades die.'

'Why not just get rid of him altogether?' asked Paul.

'I know only that President Krake's retention is considered necessary,' said Fenuless.

'That sounds logical,' said Meia. 'Krake's continued presence as a figurehead, as the nominal President of Illyr, would appease the masses on the planet, particularly those Civilians who would have been more in favour of Military rule.'

Syl sighed heavily, for her father was a Military man, or had been, but now . . . well, who knew what he was, or what he had become.

She looked again at the image of the Other in Fenuless's head and wanted to vomit knowing such a thing dwelt within her own father. Andrus would hate such an invasion of the self, or rather the Illyri soldier that he once was would have hated it. She saw Paul look her way, but she pretended not to notice, refusing to acknowledge the concern on his face. Instead, she swallowed hard, choking back the growing despair, for she knew she had to hope. They all had to hope, or they might as well just lie down right here and die.

'And what was to happen once we were intercepted?' Paul asked the commander.

'Is Syl Hellais with you?' responded Fenuless.

Paul glanced at Syl again. She gave a small nod of her head.

'Yes. It was she who spoke to you in Illyri a few seconds ago.'

Seconds? he thought. That's probably hours on Earth.

'All those on board your ship were to be killed,' said Fenuless, 'with one exception: the order for Syl Hellais's destruction was conditional. We were instructed to bring her back to the Marque alive if the opportunity presented itself. If it did not, she could be terminated with the rest of you. Oh, and by the way, Lady Syl' – some of Fenuless's natural arrogance had returned with the oxygen – 'that decision met with the approval of Lord Andrus. In fact, as I understand it, he expressed no desire to see his daughter returned to him alive at all. Instead, the hand of mercy was extended by the Archmage Syrene.'

'You're lying,' said Syl, but her voice caught in her throat. She fell silent and simply stared intently at the image before them.

The Other in Fenuless's head spasmed, and the tendrils in her brain shifted minutely. Fenuless winced in pain and clutched her temples. Syl made an unintelligible sound – it might have been a cry of effort, or even triumph – and when the *Nomad* crew turned to her, they saw that her face was fixed in concentration. Immediately Paul knew what she was doing: despite what Syl had said, she wanted to know the truth, so she had gone looking for it. But poking around in Fenuless's brain was a risky move because Fenuless's consciousness wasn't alone in there.

'Syl!' he said sharply, but she made no reply. 'Stop it!'

He gripped her shoulder, and she spun towards him in a rage, glaring as he shook his head.

'Syl—' he started to say, but then he saw the desolation on her face, and a tear fell from her left eye, and he understood. Fenuless had not been lying: Syl's father had been perfectly happy to condemn her to death.

'What was that?' squawked Fenuless. '*Who* was that?'

Paul was livid. If only Syl could have held back for a while longer. He wanted to find out what Fenuless could tell them of the plans for Earth, of the timeline for its infection. She might well have told him, too. She would have enjoyed tormenting him, if she could.

'I haven't finished with *my* questions yet,' he said.

'I don't care about your questions!' said Fenuless. 'Someone was in my head. Some—'

She stood up in a rage. Before she could say anything else, Paul spoke.

'But you already have something in your head, don't you, Commander?'

Fenuless stopped moving.

'We can see it,' Paul continued. 'The one inside your skull is big. It's like a tumour at the top of your spine, and some of your crew are carrying its little brothers and sisters. Does it have a name, Fenuless? Is it like a pet? Or maybe you're the pet. I bet it's smarter than you, although that wouldn't be hard.'

They could see the Others' reaction to Paul's words. The infected Illyri on the *Varcis* jerked their heads in unison, as though all had been affected by the same jolt of electricity. Immediately, the Others began extending their tendrils not only deeper into their brains but throughout their entire bodies, with the exception only of Fenuless. Syl had seen this before: it was a defence mechanism. The Others were preparing to turn on their hosts. Now that their presence was known, they would destroy themselves and the Illyri rather than risk being captured and examined.

Then Fenuless spoke her final words, but two voices came from her mouth. One was her own, and the other was like a whisper, an echo.

'Tell the Cayth that we are coming,' she said. 'The Cayth are lost. Humanity is lost.'

Fenuless smiled.

'All is lost.'

In that instant, Paul knew that he had gone too far. He could see it in Fenuless's eyes. But he still had so many questions . . .

'Commander,' he said. 'Wait! We can make a deal.'

But it was too late. Fenuless's mouth remained open and tendrils emerged from between her lips, flicking at the air, spitting the first of their spores from holes at their tips. In that instant, Fenuless's head exploded, and for a brief moment the Other was visible, an embryonic organism clinging to what was left of her brain at the top of the spinal cord, before it became lost in twists and coils. Fenuless's remains fell to the floor as, behind it, the rest of the infected crew cried out in agony, their bodies turning to flailing masses of filament, and then to blood and clouds of spores. Within seconds the rest of those on board were on the floor too, the infection spreading rapidly through them as they ingested the spores and their bodies swelled and erupted.

Kal opened his mouth to give an order.

'Wait! Don't destroy that ship,' Paul pleaded with him. 'Please. We need it. We can't help you without it.'

Kal paused, then said one word: 'Decontaminate.'

A curtain of yellow-green light appeared in the centre of the *Varcis*'s cabin. It separated, one field of light moving towards the bow, the other towards the stern, and as it did so it cleansed the ship of spores and Illyri remains, like a wall of heat burning them to nothing.

'Damn,' said Thula. 'Now *that* was a show.'

CHAPTER 19

Paul could barely contain his fury. He had pushed Fenuless, goading her, and then Syl had intervened – no, interfered! – and the Other had reacted. As a consequence, they had learned almost nothing of use from the Illyri commander before she died. He left the table and stalked to the observation window. His reflected face hung among the stars. Distant suns burned in his eyes.

Stupid girl, he thought. *Stupid, stupid, stupid.*

It was Meia who talked him down, her face joining his in the glass.

'Fenuless would not have told us anything helpful anyway,' she said. 'She knew that she was not going to live, and so did the entity she carried. And at least we now have one more ship, although we will require more than that before we're done.'

Paul nodded, still not trusting himself to speak. How many ships, though? With Meia at his side he stared silently through the glass. He felt his heart rate begin to slow and gradually his anger cooled as his thoughts began turning to practical matters. They would need entire fleets if they were to wage war on the Illyri and their strange, parasitic allies.

But that was not his plan.

He pointed to the Derith wormhole.

'We have to go back through it. We have no choice.'

'They'll be waiting.'

'Talk to Kal and Fara. I don't believe for one moment that they're sitting out here armed only with defensive weaponry that can't be shared.'

'I will consult with them.'

'My brother wants to return to Earth,' he said.

'And you will let him go.'

It was not a question, but he answered it anyway.

'Yes. Someone must.'

'But not you?'

'I'm staying with Syl.'

'I may have to leave you for a time.'

Paul's stomach lurched. He needed Meia.

'You have somewhere better to be?' he asked.

'I know where to find help,' she said.

Paul thought for a moment.

'The Mechs?'

'If they can be convinced to fight. Their increasing pacifism was one of the reasons why the Corps sought to destroy them.'

'I would have thought that having tens of thousands of their brothers and sisters blown to smithereens might have caused them to reconsider their position since then.'

'The Mechs are not like you or the Illyri.'

Paul cocked an eyebrow at her, for he knew she had implanted the equivalent of a small automatic weapon in her own arm; he had seen her use it on Erebos to lethal effect.

'Frankly, Meia, you're not like the rest of the Mechs either. You speak of them almost as a different species, and that weapon you implanted in your own body suggests that your feelings about pacifism may be mixed, to say the least.'

'Which makes me ideally suited to convince them to act.'

'It means that we'll need a third ship before long.'

'Well, we probably know where we can find one.'

Now it was Meia's turn to point to the wormhole.

'Through there.'

'Go and have that talk with Kal and Fara,' said Paul.

'And you should talk to Syl.'

Paul looked around and noticed that Syl was no longer in the room with them.

'Where did she go?'

'Fara showed her to an antechamber. She wanted to be alone, but I think she might make an exception for you.'

Paul found Syl in a small room to the right of the observation deck. It was entirely transparent, like a glass bubble extruding from the hull of the ship, with a small, clear bench at its heart on which Syl was sitting. Entering the room made Paul feel slightly queasy. The glass was so pure, and the lighting so subdued, that it was like walking through space itself.

Syl did not turn around to see who had entered. Maybe she already knew, thought Paul, either because of her abilities or because no one else would have dared to intrude upon her solitude. He reached out to touch her, but saw her tense. It was not what she wanted and he withdrew his hand.

'He gave them permission to kill me,' she said.

'Oh, Syl. He is no longer himself, and you know that.'

'But Fenuless was both herself and the Other. I felt it. They were two linked beings in one body, yet Fenuless was capable of independent action.'

'Only for as long as the Other permitted it though,' said Paul. 'I think if she'd had a choice, Fenuless would not have elected to have her head torn apart, but the decision was taken out of her hands.'

Syl winced, and Paul realised perhaps he was being too brutal. After all, if the Others could burst Fenuless's head like a balloon pricked from within, then clearly the same could happen to Syl's father.

He tried again.

'The Corps allowed themselves to be infected by these things, and now they're at the mercy of them,' he said. 'I'm so sorry, Syl – this may not be what you want to hear, but I think the one that invaded your father probably removed all trace of what he was, all that was good and noble about him, as quickly as it could. Whoever consented to the order to have you killed, it was not Andrus. It might have looked like him, and sounded like him, but it was the Other speaking.'

Now she raised her hand, searching for him, and he took it.

'I hoped that there might be something of him left,' she said. 'I still hope so, despite everything.'

'We'll find him,' said Paul.

'Yes, we will. And Paul?'

She stared up at him, and her hand tightened its grip on his.

'If I sense that my father is beyond rescue, I will put him out of his misery.'

Fara and Kal were waiting for them when they returned to the main chamber. Paul was conscious of the moments slipping by. How much time had passed beyond the Derith wormhole just during his minutes with Syl? Hours? If so, how many? He tried not to think about it, just as he tried not to be afraid of what was waiting for them at the other side of the wormhole, or to worry about the prospect of Thula behind the controls of an Illyri ship, like a teenager without a licence. Sometimes you just had to make do with what you had.

In a way, he could understand the reasoning of the Cayth. Even if what they were saying about their fear of contagion were not true, it would still have been tempting for them to stay quietly in their corner of the universe rather than risk confronting the Others and the Illyri. Maybe if they stayed silent enough for long enough, they wouldn't be noticed. It was cowardice of a kind, but not unreasonable.

Meia was standing beside Fara, directing her questions quietly at Kal. Paul saw how the Cayth female repeatedly glanced towards Syl, seemingly distracted by her presence. There was pity in her face, and what might almost have been love. Paul wondered if, in building an image based on Syl's emotional attachment to her mother, Fara might not also have picked up some of those actual emotions herself. He hadn't been given a chance to ask Syl about it, to find out how she felt about this alien reconstruction so like a mother she had never known. He figured that she had enough troubles at the moment dealing with her feelings about her father. It didn't seem like a good idea to scratch afresh at the wound of her mother as well.

Yet he saw something else in Fara too, something less noble, less pleasant. Something . . . alien. That was the only word he could think of. Alien. Unknowable. He didn't entirely trust the Cayth – he didn't know much about them, so he would have been a fool to take them at their word – but he needed them, and he had to keep them sweet. Without the Cayth's goodwill, he and the others would not be permitted to leave through the wormhole, and without the Cayth's technology they probably wouldn't last long once they emerged at the other end.

But Fara continued to trouble him.

He had no more time to consider the problem. Meia turned from her conversation with Kal and approached Paul once more.

'The Cayth have weapons,' she said, 'versions of what they used to trap both us and the Illyri. They're essentially torpedoes. With a little adaptation, they can be launched from the weapons systems on the *Nomad* and the *Varcis*, but it means that we'll have to come out of the wormhole fighting. We emerge, we fire the torpedoes, and we keep manoeuvring fast in the hope that we can avoid being hit while the Cayth weaponry does its work.'

Two ships, thought Paul, which meant that they could fire only four torpedoes. If more than four vessels were waiting for them at the other side of the wormhole, or one of the torpedoes malfunctioned, missed its target, or was destroyed, it would leave a ten-second delay while the tubes automatically reloaded. In a close fight, ten seconds was an eternity. They'd have to rely on the guns alone, and guns would be of minimal use against a cruiser or a destroyer.

And what if the Cayth engaged in an act of sabotage, deliberately supplying them with weapons that didn't work, or self-destructed? After all, those on the *Nomad* were the only beings in the universe who could now say with certainty that the Cayth were hiding behind the Derith wormhole. It might be better for the Cayth if Paul and his little band of fighters died rather than risk their being captured and sharing the truth with the Illyri and the Others.

But Paul brushed that fear away as paranoia. If the Cayth wanted them dead, they could have killed them long before now. The *Nomad*'s crew already had enough enemies. He didn't need to add to their number by conjuring up spectres from the Cayth.

'How long to make the adaptations?' he asked.

'I'm sorry, Paul, but it will take a number of hours,' said Meia. 'It depends on what we're actually given. Alis can work on the *Nomad* while I take care of the *Varcis*.'

'All right, let's do it. Get started please, Meia. And let me know the moment you're done. And also, let's make sure Steven has some of our stash of unlocked pulsers, in case they need them for what they have to do.'

But please, please, don't let it come to that, he thought to himself, glancing at his little brother, who still looked so young despite the shadow of a moustache on his lip. Soon he'd need to shave every day, and the idea of it made Paul feel curiously depressed. Steven had never had a childhood, and he was fast becoming a man.

'Steven, Rizzo, Thula, Syl: come with me, please,' he said crisply. 'I need to talk with you back on the *Nomad*.'

'With your permission, I'd like to stay with Fara for a little while,' said Syl.

Paul wished that he could read her thoughts.

'You're sure?'

'Yes.'

Fara appeared pleased. Paul didn't like that at all. He could, of course, order Syl to come with him. She had given him that option by asking for his permission. He didn't want to do that, though. He had to assume that Syl knew what she was doing. And if she did get into trouble, she'd let him know – he could be sure of that. The only problem was that he wasn't certain how much he could do to help her if that situation arose. Then again, he'd watched Syl force a Sisterhood assassin to burn herself alive simply through force of will, and that was before her powers began to increase. God alone knew what she was capable of now. When it came down to it, Syl was probably more than able to take care of herself.

'Okay,' he said. 'Be as quick as you can, then I'd like you back on the *Nomad*.'

'Yes, *sir*.' Syl smirked at him, and clicked her heels smartly together. She even gave him a salute. He'd have a word with her about that when they were alone, the minx, although he already knew it would make no difference.

The *Varcis* was growing larger in the window of the observation bay. The Cayth were drawing it to their ship so that Meia could begin work on it.

Please don't let there be more than four ships beyond Derith, he prayed. *Please let this work.*

He saw Fara approach Syl and place a hand upon her shoulder.

Please make sure that Syl knows what she's doing, he added to his prayer.

Then, for good measure: *And please make sure that I know what I'm doing too.*

CHAPTER 20

Kal was gone, melting like hot wax into the floor of the ship. Only Syl and Fara remained. The dimensions of the observation deck altered. The ceiling grew lower, the walls moved in. The lighting became more subdued. The effect was not threatening, merely intimate. Fara and Syl sat across from each other in chairs that moulded themselves around their forms, cradling them snugly. It would be easy to fall asleep in them, Syl thought. All the more reason not to.

Perhaps it was the dimness, but to Syl, Fara seemed more like the Lady Orianne than before. No, it was not the light: Fara had subtly changed once again. Her eyes were different, her jaw slightly less pronounced. She was now Syl's mother come to life.

Syl understood that this was, at least in part, her own doing. She was feeding strands of her memory to Fara, snapshots of her mother taken from the video images of the late Orianne that she had watched throughout her life, her only connection to this lost figure, both so familiar and yet so distant from herself. And Fara was acting on them, using them in an effort to bring Syl closer to her. All this Syl knew, just as she knew that the changes to Fara were not merely superficial. There was now a distinction between Fara and the Cayth. The collective was still part of Fara, but Fara was no longer entirely a part of the collective. That was the trouble with memories, Syl thought: they gave life to the dead, and allowed them to make demands upon the living.

'Would you like something to eat or drink, my dear?' asked Fara.

'No, thank you.'

'I am sorry about your father.'

'As am I.'

'You loved him.'

'Of course. I still do.'

'Despite what he has done?'

'The being that sanctioned my death is not my father.'

Syl's fingers were clasped on her lap. Fara reached across the space between them and laid her own hand gently upon them.

'And yet it is.'

Syl looked at Fara's hand. It felt a little too warm. She was still adjusting to the unfamiliarity of physicality.

'Ask me,' said Syl.

Fara withdrew her hand in surprise.

'Ask what?' she replied, but there was falsity to her tone.

'You want me to stay.'

Fara's mouth moved silently as she tried to find a response that would satisfy.

'*We* want you to stay,' she said at last.

Syl permitted a part of her consciousness to probe her surroundings. She was getting better at it with every hour that went by. Before, it had been one thing or the other: she could either be present or absent. Now she could allow just a fragment of herself to float free. It was like being able to hold two melodies in her head simultaneously.

She could feel the Cayth around her, and could hear their constant quiet buzz. They were listening, curious but not involved. Syl's powers interested them, but only to the degree that they might be used against the Others, just as Kal had intimated. They wished to know more about her and her capabilities, but Syl also detected puzzlement, and it was directed not at her but at Fara.

'Why?' asked Syl. 'Why do you want me to stay?'

'We wish to learn more about you. There are similarities between you and us. Your sensitivities are not unfamiliar.'

'No,' said Syl, 'why do *you* want me to stay?'

There it was again, that faint jolt: her question had provoked a reaction in the collective of the Cayth, because they were all one, and they knew the answer. They waited to see if Fara would reveal

more of her former self, the individual that had long been sub-
merged in the sea of the collective. The buzzing increased and Syl
listened, separating the parts from the whole, as images began to
form in her own mind. The Cayth opened themselves to her, and she
felt herself opening up too, like a forgotten flower placed beneath
a warm sun. She leaned backwards, turning her face upwards, drinking it all in. With a delicious shiver, she allowed her thoughts to
continue expanding outwards until her mind became as clear and
free-flowing as water, trickling freely into secret places, her consciousness and the Cayth's becoming one. It was here, tangled in her own
truth, that she discovered the Cayth female's ancient hurt, and she
understood.

Oh Fara, she thought, and her whole being filled with sadness.

'We – ' Fara began. 'I—'

'What was her name?' Syl asked gently.

'Her name?'

'The name of your dead child.'

Fara turned to the glass and the stars beyond it, as though the word
that she sought might be written among them, or the child she had
lost might be found there.

'Elea,' she said. 'Her name was Elea.'

And Fara opened herself to Syl, engulfing her in a wave of love
and loss. Syl saw a little huddled thing, a blur, barely a mound,
breathing its last, and heard a cry of grief that was beyond consolation,
the echo of which had lingered even until now, hidden only by the
babble of the collective. The clear water still lapped in her mind, like
all the tears ever shed in the universe, and she found her cheeks were
wet with them.

'You were one of the first to give up your physical being,' said Syl.
Through Fara, she watched a body fall away as form was shed by
consciousness. The creation of the collective had begun.

'Yes.'

'Because you could not endure the pain any longer, and you
thought that by abandoning your body, and surrendering your
individuality, you might rid yourself of it.'

Fara's face in the glass was a mask of desolation.

'I thought that if there was no "I" there would be no "her",' she murmured. 'I chose to forget because the memory of losing her was too much to bear. I could not be a mother because I had no child, and I decided instead to become one voice among many, so that my single drop of pain might be consumed by an ocean of consciousness.'

The features on her face softened and went hazy, as though seen through narrowed eyes.

'And I did forget, or perhaps I simply chose to do so, until you came. I felt your loss from the moment we became aware of you, and it called to my own, and woke my memories. We sent Kal, and I followed with him.'

Now it was Syl's turn to reach out to Fara. She rose from her chair and put her arms around her. She closed her eyes and Fara closed hers, and for a time they gave themselves up to a beautiful illusion in which one was the mother of a living child, and the other a daughter in her mother's arms. And when, by unspoken consent, they broke the embrace, each was stronger for what they had shared.

The universe is cold, and life is harsh.

We take comfort where we can.

'Paul?'

Meia's voice came over his coms link. Paul stepped away from the weapons console of the *Nomad* where Rizzo was supervising the reset, while Alis was fitting the first of the torpedoes into place.

'I hear you, Meia.'

'We have a problem . . .'

Paul and Meia stared into the exposed interior of the *Varcis*'s main command console. A smell of burning plastic emerged from the tangle of wires and circuitry.

'So essentially, they booby-trapped it,' said Paul.

'Fenuless knew that even if she and her crew were permitted to live, it was unlikely that they would be allowed to leave,' said

Meia. 'She didn't want anyone taking her ship, so her last act was to fry the wiring.'

Meia held up a small wireless signalling device.

'She must have had it in her hand when she was talking to you. As soon as the Other in her head began to react, she activated the mechanism. It didn't destroy the console completely, but it's done enough damage to delay any departure in this ship.'

'How much of a delay?'

'Many hours.'

'But you can repair it?'

'I'll have to scavenge from non-essential systems but, yes, I can repair it.'

Paul sighed.

'Keep me posted on progress,' he said. 'I need to go and speak to my brother.'

Steven reacted just as Paul had anticipated.

'No! No way!' he shouted. 'We've waited long enough.'

They were in the captain's cabin on the *Nomad*. Paul thought that it might give them some privacy, but it had hardly been worth the effort now that Steven was barking at the top of his voice.

'Steve, if you'd just let me finish,' said Paul firmly, but Steven was having none of it.

'Why should I bother?' he shouted. 'You're just going to *order* to me to stay here while the repairs are done.'

Steven made inverted commas with his fingers when he said 'order', and Paul resisted the urge to bend those fingers back to hurt him, just as he would have done in their shared bedroom in Edinburgh. Instead, he perched on the edge of the cabin's small desk, sat on his hands, and tried to remain patient.

'Stevie,' he said again, 'bruv . . .' But his brother cut across him.

'Don't you dare baby me, Paul! Not here, not after everything. I'm not a bleedin' kid! But that's how this is going to end, isn't it: with you pulling rank? That's how it always ends these days. Right, *Lieutenant*?'

'Actually, that's not what I'm going to do at all,' Paul replied.

Steven appeared confused. 'What?'

'I'm going to give you the choice – you, Rizzo and Alis. You can choose to stay and wait until the *Varcis* is ready to boost through the wormhole alongside the *Nomad*, or you can go through it alone.'

'Seriously?'

'It's not what I want, not in an ideal world, but we haven't lived in an ideal world in a very long time,' Paul explained. 'It's a calculated risk. I don't think the Corps will have left a fleet sitting on the doorstep of the Derith wormhole, not while it's engaged in a war with the Military. Nothing that the Illyri have sent through the wormhole has ever returned, and even if they have suspicions, they've no actual proof. Already years have gone by for them, and the *Nomad* has shown no sign of returning. Neither has the *Varcis*. So I'm guessing that there's one vessel out there, or two at most, with bored crews who won't be prepared for a fight. With the Cayth's weaponry at Rizzo's command, and you and Alis at the controls, no sleepy Illyri are going to stand a chance.'

He sounded more confident than he felt.

'But like I said, I'm not ordering you to stay or go. You'll be in command of the *Nomad* whatever happens, because the rest of us will be in the *Varcis*. Rizzo and Alis will be your crew, but I think you should make sure that they're prepared to go with you willingly. Talk to them and come back to me once you've all reached a decision. I'll wait for you here.'

Steven stared dumbly at his brother, but did not move. Paul was pleased to see that he still had the capacity to surprise his younger sibling.

'I didn't say that I'd wait forever,' said Paul.

Steven snapped out of his daze.

'Okay,' he said, 'and thank you.'

'For sending you through a wormhole to face an unknown force alone, then leaving you to somehow make your way to what may be a home planet overrun by the Others?'

'Yes,' said Steven. He grinned.

'Then you're welcome,' said Paul. 'Go. Talk to your crew.'

Steven left. Paul remained where he was. He knew that he was putting his brother, along with Rizzo and Alis, in mortal peril. It didn't matter if that was what they wanted: the risk remained. Most of all, for the first time that he could remember, he would be sending Steven off without the protection of his big brother. Yes, it would have happened eventually. Even if they'd gone through the worm- hole together, their paths would have diverged not long after. The moment had just come sooner than anticipated, but then it would always have come sooner than expected. It would never be the right time to send Steven off alone, to release him from his brother's guardianship. Paul's guts tightened and he felt sick about what was soon going to happen. He thought of their mother. If she was alive, Steven would find her, or die in the effort, and that was what worried Paul most of all.

Steven bounded back in, eager as a puppy. Rizzo and Alis were behind him, smiling, and the Mech was wiping her hands with a rag.

'The torpedoes are in place,' said Alis.

'And the systems check showed no glitches,' Rizzo added. 'They'll fire when I press the button.'

'We're ready to go,' said Steven. 'All of us.'

Paul went through the plan with them three times. It would mean another delay before Steven could start the trek back to Earth, but he understood the reasoning behind it and made no argument. Thula had been assigned to assist Meia on the *Varcis*, but Paul summoned them both back to the *Nomad* for the final briefing. When they returned, Syl was with them. She looked like she'd been crying, but Paul had only a second to check that she was okay. She kissed him quickly on the cheek.

'I'm fine,' she said. 'And you don't have to worry about me, or the Cayth. They mean us no harm.'

It was the reassurance that Paul needed. If Syl said it, then it was true. For the fourth and last time, he detailed the mission that the *Nomad* was about to undertake.

'How will we rendezvous?' asked Thula. 'The universe is a big place, in case no one else has noticed.'

It was a good point, Paul knew, but right now he was also concerned with how they would find out if the *Nomad* had even made it past any sentinel ships on the other side of the wormhole. He didn't want the *Varcis* to emerge into the wreckage of the *Nomad* and only then discover the fate of his brother and his crew.

'A message in a bottle,' said Rizzo.

'What?'

'We know what this Cayth weaponry does,' she said, grinning. 'It immobilises a ship, then kills its crew. If everything goes according to plan, we'll have at least one more empty vessel. We board it, set the autopilot, and send it through the wormhole emitting a simple signal. That way you'll know we're alive.'

'Excellent, Rizzo! And we'll have access to the ship's records,' said Meia, and she was smiling too. Paul couldn't remember if he'd ever seen her smile properly before, but it made her appear terribly childlike and sweet, even though she was neither of those things.

'We may be able to find out how the war has been going while we've been away,' Meia added.

'Nice thinking, Rizzo,' said Paul. 'Let's do it.'

'It still doesn't answer the question of a rendezvous point,' said Thula.

'One moment,' said Meia.

A series of maps began to flash before them, images of star systems both familiar and unfamiliar. It was the Mech who had called them up: they could see her controlling the images with the movements of her eyes. They waited until she found the one that she was seeking.

'Here,' she said.

Paul saw the name of the remote galaxy: Tessel. He called up the wormhole map and overlaid it on Meia's. There was a wormhole in the adjoining system.

'Why there?' he asked.

'Because that's where I must go,' said Meia.

'The Mechs,' said Paul. Now he understood.

'The refuge lies in the Tessel system,' Meia confirmed, although Paul noticed that she was careful not to say where exactly in the system it might be. Tessel was huge. Lifetimes could be spent scouring it and still only a tiny fraction of its worlds might be explored.

Meia pointed at a small planet in the corner of the system. It lit up like a Christmas-tree light, and its coordinates appeared alongside it.

'This world is uninhabited, and uninhabitable,' she said. 'Its atmosphere is toxic, and its surface is obscured by gas clouds.'

'Sounds great,' said Thula. 'Let's buy it and move there.'

Meia ignored him.

'A whole fleet could be waiting in those clouds and no one would know,' she continued. 'Let the *Nomad*, and whoever else it may bring with it, rendezvous with me there.'

'When should I get there?' asked Steven. 'Months from now?'

Meia shook her head. 'Longer, much longer. We need to get that ship going. It'll take me hours. At max, another day here – that'll be a year on your side.'

'So a whole year?' Steven swallowed.

'Yes, and then I need to get where I'm going. Give me fourteen months. At least.'

'Jesus wept,' said Steven, looking a bit ill.

'And the rest of us?' asked Paul. Syl and Thula – his tiny crew – were gathered closely behind him.

Meia's face could be so expressive, he thought; she didn't even try to hide her sadness.

'I think you three will follow your own path,' she said. 'And it will lead you back to the Marque.'

V
SURVIVORS

CHAPTER 21

Trask – one-time reptile-keeper at Edinburgh Zoo, occasional burglar, and former leader of the Edinburgh Resistance – moved through the dead town, his body shifting with the machine pistol he held, letting its muzzle lead. It was a community that he'd never known when people still lived in it. He only stalked its nighttime shadows now that it was deserted, now that all who'd once strolled this very street laden with shopping bags, or walking dogs, or heading off to post letters, were long gone.

Behind him, to his right and left, crept two similar shapes, encased, like Trask, in protective clothing, oxygen tanks strapped to their backs. A fourth figure brought up the rear, its attention focused behind them.

Keeping to their diamond formation, they scanned the abandoned cottages and stores for signs of movement in the bright moonlight. They wore heavy boots that extended to their knees, and black pads of hard plastic on their shoulders and elbows. They had learned from bitter experience that these were vulnerable spots, prone to snagging on nails or bits of masonry as they scavenged. All it took was one tear. Just one.

The suits limited visibility, and the sound of their own breathing made it hard to hear anything else, even with the addition of external microphones that fed into their earpieces. Nobody liked the suits, but dying seemed like a less preferable option.

This was as far east as they had yet ranged, and they had encountered no other survivors for a long time. The dawn chorus commenced, the sweet song of a blackbird, the earliest riser of them all, soon followed by the robin. The birds hadn't been taken. Neither had any insects or bugs, or the littlest mammals and rodents. It had been suggested that their brains were too small, but that made no sense. The Others were able to wrap themselves around the brain stems of anything that walked, swam, flew or crawled on the surface of the earth, so the size of a creature's brain made no difference. No, the Others only needed warm flesh in which to implant themselves, and after that the host was guaranteed an unpleasant death, the spores multiplying in its body until it eventually burst open, giving birth to more spores in an explosion of blood and bone. They'd seen it happen. They'd all left loved ones to die in that way.

And yet still the birds, bugs and smaller animals thrived. Trask and his people had seen rabbits and mice, even stoats and the occasional feral cat. Once, in the weeks immediately after the infestation, during the early sorties, Trask had glimpsed a horse running across the Burren, silhouetted against the evening sky like a piece of animation. He had gone after it, followed by Davy, one of his fellow survivors, but when they reached the hill on which he had seen it, the horse was gone, and Davy was convinced that Trask had imagined it. But he hadn't. He knew that he hadn't. He also knew that it was probably dead now. Most of the larger mammals were. But it was impossible to know whether the other animals had simply been lucky, and avoided or resisted infection, or if they contained dormant spores within them, waiting for the right moment to multiply. For now, Trask was just glad that anything at all had survived, whatever the reason.

Gradually, as the sky turned a deep cool blue, more birds began to sing, wrens, thrushes and finches adding their voices to the chorus. Winter had culled them, so there were fewer than in the past, but soon they'd begin breeding again. They seemed to be adapting well to the new ecosystem, just like the insects. It was a pity that the same couldn't be said for what remained of the planet's most evolved life-form – his own.

It was the bigger birds – the crows, the ravens, the seagulls – that you had to watch out for. They were scavengers, just like Trask and his kind, and smart with it.

And as for the rats . . .

'Trask.' It was Dolan's voice in his earpiece.

'Yes?'

'I thought I saw something move in that house to your left, the one with the green walls.'

Trask paused at the glassless window of a cottage. Dolan was right. There were signs of movement inside. He slipped his finger under the trigger guard, hit the flashlight that hung beneath the barrel of the machine pistol, and directed the beam into the cottage for a moment before recoiling in disgust. The floors and walls were alive with lazy black flies, still sluggish in the cool air, but their buzzing was like static in his ears. In the centre of the room, between an old couch and a television, lay a body. It was in an advanced state of decay and crawling with maggots, but Trask could still see the great hole that had been ripped in it from belly to neck by the emergence of the spores. It looked like a man. Trask felt a terrible sadness. Someone had survived out here for a while, even without protective clothing, but his luck had run out in the end. The chances were better out on the coast, and that was where they'd found the most survivors.

But that was in the early days. It had been many months since they'd come across anyone left alive.

'Flies,' reported Trask, 'and a body.'

'Recent?' asked Dolan.

'Recent enough for maggots.'

'Poor sod.'

'Hey, look up,' said a female voice, and Trask recognised the tones of his older daughter, Nessa. She was bringing up the rear of the formation. 'There, over to the southwest.'

It didn't take Trask long to find it. They were all used to them by now. The sky was clear, marred only by wisps of stratus, and against it moved a small silver speck. They'd come to realise that three different Illyri ships still orbited the earth: a cruiser, a destroyer, and one of the big transporters that had brought the Others to this world. Earlier, when the infection commenced, there had been more, many more, but they were all gone now. After all, there was no need to police a dying world, and the Others would eventually account for the last of humanity.

The silver dot spotted by Nessa was lost briefly behind a strand of cloud. Trask didn't know why these ships still bothered to hang around. It wasn't as if what was left of mankind could go anywhere, or even take potshots at the orbiting craft. Briefly, there had been a sliver of hope, for a secret advanced missile base had remained intact and undiscovered in North Korea, and another in China, but the North Koreans had botched a test launch and drawn the Illyri destroyer down on themselves, and it was said over the short-wave radio that the Chinese had been sold out by the Russians, whose premier was living in a bunker somewhere in Siberia and still trying to negotiate his way off the planet. Trask found that grimly amusing: the Russian leader had sided with the Illyri from the start, hoping that the aliens wouldn't turn on friends, but he'd been screwed over just like everybody else.

In the first year the Illyri had regularly scattered more spores, using remote-controlled airships that flew over land at low level. When possible, the Resistance shot them down, destroying the spores in fiery explosions, but it was a risky business since an attack inevitably caused the Illyri to come looking for those responsible. The airships appeared more rarely now, and the Illyri no longer sent down hunting parties to try to winkle out survivors. Trask suspected that they had done it mostly to stave off boredom, like a kind of sport, but had eventually grown weary of it.

Meanwhile drones, many of them equipped with snares and claws, searched for signs of movement, and when they caught stray humans they pinned them to the ground and forcibly injected them with spores. But mostly the Illyri were content to leave the work of eradicating the remnants of humanity to the Others alone.

Well, not quite alone. That was why Trask and his team were all armed. It wasn't just to fight off rats and seagulls. Spores weren't the only alien entities breeding here, and the Others weren't the only horrors hunting humanity.

For the Cutters had come.

CHAPTER 22

They moved further into the village, but found no remains as recent as the body in the cottage, and no one left alive. Once he was sure that the area was clear, and the streets had not been mined by the Illyri – another little gift from the drones, which dropped miniature explosive devices that drilled themselves into the ground, and were activated by the vibrations of motorised vehicles – Trask contacted the drivers of the jeep and truck waiting on the outskirts, giving them the all-clear to advance.

The truck had broken down on the road and took three hours to repair. It was a credit to Burgess, the mechanic, that he'd managed to get it up and running again, but the delay meant that they would be forced to work in early morning light. They could have waited until dark came again, but Trask was prepared to take the chance on using daylight to complete their tasks. They'd work, then hole up. Once night fell, they'd be ready to move again.

Now the scavenging could begin. Apart from tinned food and medical supplies, petrol and diesel were the main requirements. They were almost down to the last of their reserves and without fuel they couldn't range, or transport anything too heavy to be moved in a handcart. The risks of using the roads were outweighed by the benefits, and Trask was also determined to continue searching for more survivors. In the early days, they'd picked up communications from Dublin, Cork and Limerick, where people had made it to Civil Defence bunkers before the spores could get to them, but the Illyri had information on the location of many such refuges, and patrols had been sent down to target them. The Illyri didn't bother trying to break into the bunkers. It was simpler just to drill holes in the doors and pump spores into the chambers.

It still amazed Trask that the Illyri hadn't come knocking on the doors of their own bunker, as they had on most of the ones in England and Scotland. Fremd thought that Meia had probably erased the records of the Irish bunker, along with a handful of others, before leaving Earth. Then again, it might simply not have struck the Illyri that humans could have discovered this old refuge, or found a way through their security systems if they had. Not for the first time, Trask gave thanks for Meia's existence. He wondered where she was now, if she still existed at all. He thought of her often as he looked up at the stars.

The village had one small petrol station. Trask's younger daughter Jean, who was driving the truck, parked alongside it, and she, Nessa and Dolan set about accessing its tanks and unloading barrels from the truck bed. Burgess checked the garage at the back of the station for oil and spare parts, while Mackay, who was just nineteen and the son of one of the botanists, kept watch for drones.

Leaving them to their work, Trask got in the jeep with Lindsay, a tiny, round-faced redhead, who drove like a lunatic, albeit a gifted one, and they began gathering tins from store cupboards across the village: beans, soup, fruit – even creamed rice, which Trask had hated as a child and still hated now. They did pretty well, and only had to shoot one rat along the way. It was a small one, by their standards: about a foot in length. The really big ones were in the cities, which was another reason to stay away from urban centres.

They then headed back to a little shop just off the main street. Trask had found its address in a telephone directory, and it was one of the reasons why he'd nominated this village for one of their increasingly rare expeditions beyond the immediate environs of the bunker. The sign on the store read 'Graham's Hunting & Fishing Ltd'. The door was open and the floor strewn with leaves and litter that had blown inside. A corpse, more bones than anything else, lay behind the counter.

The front of the store was mainly devoted to fishing rods and lures, along with waterproof clothing and nets, but a smaller room at the back proved more interesting. To the right was a glass case filled with knives, and knives never went to waste, while the shelves were lined with boxes of ammunition. At the rear of the room, in a curtained alcove, stood a locked gun safe.

Trask turned back to the corpse, but Lindsay was already searching it. She wasn't squeamish. Few of them were, really, not after all they'd seen.

'Found them,' she said, waving a bunch of keys that she'd taken from the dead man's belt.

The key to the safe was the third they tried. Inside were five shotguns, three rifles, and a pair of target-shooting pistols.

'Not bad,' said Trask.

They had found Illyri pulse weapons in the bunker, but they were coded to prevent humans from operating them, so only Fremd had any use for them, although he spent his spare moments trying to break the DNA locks. They wanted every man, woman and child to have a gun, but so far there were only two weapons for every three people. The contents of the safe would help to redress the imbalance.

He helped Lindsay to load the weapons into the jeep, and then the two of them worked in relays to empty the shelves of ammunition. Lindsay also took all of the hunting bows and every arrow she could find. She was one of a number of survivors who had grown adept with a bow, and they were now teaching archery to the children and younger teenagers.

They returned to the garage and helped to load the cans of fuel onto the truck. They'd filled two with diesel and one with petrol – a decent yield, given that the Illyri had controlled fuel reserves while they were on Earth, and had done their best to destroy the supplies in as many petrol stations as they could before they left. The village didn't look likely to provide them with much else, so they parked the truck and jeep in the garage and waited.

This was always the hard part. They all had a bottle of water mixed with protein powder strapped inside their suits, and a tube through which to drink it, but that was the only sustenance they'd enjoy until they returned to the bunker. They replenished their oxygen from the tanks in the jeep and tried to find somewhere comfortable to lie down. At least the protective clothing left by the Illyri wasn't too cumbersome to wear, which helped a bit. The material adapted to fit the body, so it was rather like wearing a slightly loose-fitting wetsuit. A tube took care of toilet needs, and the suit converted urine to vapor, but anything bigger had to be held until the wearer was back in the safety of the bunker. It was one of the reasons why they never ranged for longer than a day, although even that could be a strain.

Trask and Lindsay took the first watch. A couple of books were always kept in the vehicles for situations like this, but Trask had brought his own. He'd come across it by accident on one of their searches. It had been sitting in the window of a charity shop in Galway, and he'd taken it from the display. *The Complete Robot*, it was called, by Isaac Asimov.

Lindsay had found a dog-eared copy of *Middlemarch* by George Eliot beside the oxygen tanks. She looked slightly enviously at Trask's book.

'Want to swap?' she asked.

'I'm nearly finished,' he replied. 'You can have it after me.'

He glanced at her book.

'God, *Middlemarch*,' he said. 'Nobody will admit to leaving that in the jeep. I think about twenty people have started it, and no one has ever finished it.'

'If I'd known, I'd have brought something else.'

'You'll know better in future,' he said.

'Are you planning to build one?'

'Build what?'

'A robot.'

'It's not a "how-to" book. It's a novel.'

'Oh. Why'd you pick that, then?'

Trask marked the page he was on with a finger, and turned to the cover, as though the answer might lie there.

'A friend sort of recommended it to me,' he said.

★ ★ ★

They stayed quiet after that because everyone else had fallen asleep. The comms links had to be kept open in case of an emergency, and the rest of their group could hardly doze with Trask and Lindsay babbling in their ears. Trask was absorbed in his book. The hours drifted by. After four had passed, he woke Dolan and Nessa, and they took over the watch. Lindsay fell asleep instantly, but Trask stayed awake for a while. He was thinking about robots, and how rational they were supposed to be, and Meia. Being rational and principled weren't the same thing. If Meia were truly rational, she'd abandon Trask and the rest of humanity and leave them to survive as best they could, or let them die in the process. But if she were principled, she'd come back to help them.

Trask hoped that she was principled. No, he believed that she was. He prayed that God would prove him right.

He laughed. He couldn't help it. He saw Dolan and Nessa staring at him. Look at me, he thought: I'm praying now. That was what hope did for you.

And Meia was his hope.

CHAPTER 23

Trask was roused from his sleep by Nessa. Years of fighting the Illyri, and of sleeping in strange places while on raids, had trained him to wake silently. Now he looked up at Nessa and saw her right forefinger placed against her mask. He nodded. She pointed straight up, and he heard it: the low hum of a drone.

He wasn't worried about the drone picking up their heat signatures. The biohazard clothing also functioned as darksuits, masking body heat. Neither was he concerned about the drone noticing the truck and the jeep. They were in a garage and it would hardly be surprising to find vehicles under its roof. Had they left them out in the open, by the pumps, it might have been another matter. Still, this was a small village and a drone had no business being there. Trask wasn't a great believer in coincidences. Like lottery wins, they were something that happened to other people.

The rest were awake too, but remained motionless. Nobody wanted to move in case they made a sound in the unfamiliar surroundings of the garage and brought the drone down upon them.

The drone, or worse.

Trask's mouth was dry, but he was too wary even to take a sip of fluid through his straw.

The growling ceased and the ground beneath them shook as something heavy landed outside. Burgess was closest to the front of the garage and risked a quick glance through the window.

'Cutter!' he cried, and then the thing was upon them. The garage door buckled under the first impact and gave way entirely to the second. For a moment Trask saw the Cutter silhouetted against the fading afternoon sunlight. It looked like a great squid, with long flailing tentacles ending in flat, bladelike protrusions that could slice through metal as easily as flesh, hence the name the humans had given to the creatures. But those blades could also come apart to form gripping claws, or narrow to sharp points like spears. The tentacles surrounded a beaked mouth in the heart of its yellowish body, ringed with black, spiderlike eyes. It moved on four jointed legs that could be retracted into its torso, allowing it to roll easily, and regardless of how it landed, those legs immediately appeared again, so it was always upright.

Burgess raised his shotgun to fire and managed to get off a blast, but the Cutter was too quick for him. It rolled to its right and one of the blades whipped at Burgess's suit, tearing a line across his chest. Immediately he began to bleed, but he still had enough strength to pump the shotgun and fire again. As he pulled the trigger, the Cutter yanked him from the ground. A tentacle gripped his weapon and flung it away. The beaked mouth opened and from it emerged a hollow black tube that entered Burgess's body through the hole in his clothing. The rest of the group heard him scream, even as they themselves started firing, and then Burgess's body began to swell, and a cloud of spores burst from his suit as he died.

Chunks of flesh were blown from the Cutter as Trask and the others concentrated their fire on its body, but the wounds were only superficial. They had to try to get behind it and aim for the vulnerable spot at the base of its skull. In the meantime, all they could do was attempt to keep it at bay as they manoeuvred around it, seeking their chance to strike.

The Cutter tensed its body, extended its limbs, and suddenly it was above them, clinging to the steel rafters below the garage roof. With astonishing speed, it jumped from beam to beam until it was directly above Dolan, and then dropped straight down. The four sections of its beaked mouth closed upon him, so that only his legs were visible. This time, there were no spores, and they were all forced to listen to the brief sounds of his dying. The beak locked closed and the lower half of Dolan's body fell to the floor.

Trask flung himself to the ground and opened fire with his machine pistol, but most of the bullets simply bounced off the Cutter's bony tentacles. At least one shot got through, though, for Trask saw a black eye disintegrate. It would hurt the Cutter, but it wouldn't stop it. The beast had plenty of eyes to spare.

But now Nessa, and Mackay, were moving in on it, simultaneously firing so that its attention was divided between them. Where was Lindsay? thought Trask. Had she been hurt? Then he saw her. She was standing in the shadows near Nessa and Jean, just waiting. What the hell was she doing?

Under pressure from the three shooters, the Cutter was forced to jump for the roof again, and Lindsay made her move. She threw herself to the floor beneath it, landing on her back, one of the hunting bows raised. The Cutter was above her, hanging vertically as it pulled itself to the rafters, and the hollow in its skull was briefly exposed. Lindsay released the arrow, watching with satisfaction as it hit its mark, then swiftly got out of the way as the Cutter fell like a boulder, raising dust from the floor and rattling the old paint cans on the shelves as it landed. Its limbs flailed aimlessly and yellow fluid shot from its beak before it let out a single shriek and died.

Trask went to the window. The hollow drone stood on the garage forecourt, a section of it hanging open. It looked big enough to take one Cutter, but not two, and Trask couldn't see or hear any other drones. They were done. He stepped outside, wondering what had brought the drone down on them until, even in the dimming light, he saw a trail of fresh oily footprints leading from one of the pumps to the garage door. He checked his boots, but they seemed clean. The prints were big. Probably not one of the girls, or Mackay, then: Burgess, or Dolan. God help them, because whichever one of them it was had paid for his mistake.

Back inside, Jean was standing over the Cutter with one of her big knives. That girl and her blades, thought Trask. Still, this was a rare opportunity. They'd only killed a few Cutters so far, and three of them had been too damaged in the aftermath to be of any use.

'Careful,' he said.

Jean knelt, inserted the knife just above the point at which Lindsay's arrow had entered the Cutter's skull, and began to slice. It was hard work, but the blade's serrated edge helped. With Nessa's assistance, Jean peeled back the folds of the Cutter's scalp, exposing its skull and, at its base, the hole through which the arrow had entered. It was big enough to accommodate Jean's small fist. She reached inside.

'I have it,' she said.

She yanked. There was some resistance.

'I think it's the arrow,' she said.

Mackay joined them and tugged, and the arrow came free. When Jean's hand emerged again, it was holding one of the Others. It was big, the biggest they'd yet seen. It was about the size of a kitten, a really hideous, hairless, prawn-like kitten. The arrow had pierced it through the core, killing it instantly along with the Cutter.

It confirmed what they had suspected. Like some of the Illyri, the alien Cutters acted as hosts for the Others, but the ones that the Cutters carried were more developed than any they had previously found in the skulls of the Illyri they'd managed to kill over the last year or two, or at least the handful they'd been able to get to before they destroyed themselves in a burst of spores. This one hadn't been given time to self-destruct.

Fremd believed that these Others might be of a higher order, and the Cutters enabled them to move around, to roam their new realm, for they were the rulers of Earth now. In return for hosting them, the foul Cutters got to feed on what was left of humans after the spores had emerged. Sometimes, as in the case of poor Dolan, they feasted while their victims were still alive.

'Get one of the jars,' Trask instructed. 'We'll take it back to Fremd.'

It had taken a great deal of convincing for Trask to agree with Fremd's request to examine any remains of the Others that they found. Fremd had assured him that the lab was secure and Trask had eventually, if reluctantly, recognised that to understand the Others and determine their vulnerabilities, specimens were needed. He drew the line at live ones, though, even if they'd been able to find any, and any spore sacs had to be destroyed before the remains were allowed into the bunker. Jean did that now, gently removing the sac from the underside of the Other. It was barely bigger than her thumb. She found some white spirit on the garage shelf, poured it on the sac, and set it alight, while Nessa fetched a sample jar and shoved the Other into it.

By now the sun was going down and a shaft of brilliant light burst through the dusty window. Red spores danced like dust in its beam. Damn, they'd be covered in them. The suits and vehicles would have to be decontaminated with a vengeance. He looked over at Burgess's body in its suit, and what was left of Dolan. They could bag Burgess and return him for burial. It wouldn't be pleasant for his wife and kid, but at least they'd have a chance to say goodbye, and Burgess wasn't the first who'd been buried in that kind of state. But Dolan . . .

Mackay joined him, and followed the direction of his gaze.

'God,' he said. 'What'll we do?'

'We'll tell his wife the truth,' said Trask, 'or most of it: a Cutter got him, and he died quickly, but there was nothing left of him to bury.'

'But we can't just leave his remains here.'

'We'll dig a hole. I guess someone can say a prayer. It makes no difference to him now.'

Lindsay helped Mackay to put Burgess into a body bag – they always travelled with them, but never referred to them until they were needed, a small superstition to which everyone adhered – while Nessa and Jean did the same with what was left of Dolan. Trask dug a shallow hole for him in the field at the back of the garage, but they did not mark the spot for fear of alerting still more drones to their presence. Instead, Trask's daughters scattered leaves on the grave and Lindsay said a quick prayer. Her grandfather had been a preacher of some sort and she knew all the words for the services, but Dolan got only the briefest of farewells. Something was bound to come looking to see what had happened to the occupant of the drone, and they wanted to be well on their way back to the bunker by that time.

They set out for home in the dark, driving slowly because they couldn't use headlights. True, drones might pick up the heat of the trucks and they would be visible to night-vision scanners, but there was no point in making things any easier for the invaders than they had to be. Anyway, the drones would have to be overflying the right area to spot them, and there were fewer of them to do that than before. They'd just been unlucky with the one earlier in the day.

Trask stayed with Lindsay, and his girls and Mackay followed in the truck. They had petrol, diesel, some weapons, lots of tinned food and a big sample for Fremd to examine, but it had cost them two men. At least his daughters were safe; that was something. But he didn't know for how much longer they could continue like this. Sooner or later, the Cutters would get them all, or the spores would. Their world had been turned against them. They were like cockroaches hiding in the shadows, waiting to be exterminated.

VI
THE RETURN

CHAPTER 24

The *Gradus*, the Corps cruiser assigned to monitor the mouth of the Derith wormhole, was one of the newest in the fleet. It had been named after the late Grand Consul Gradus at the request of his widow, the Archmage Syrene, who had worn her navy blue widow's robes to its inaugural voyage – a grand affair where all had feted her, and crowds had cheered. As far as the commander of the *Gradus* was concerned, Syrene and the rest of her sort could take a jump into a boiling pit of lava for all the difference it would make to him. For someone who had chosen to cloister herself in the Marque, he grumbled to himself, Syrene certainly spent a lot of time playing the grand public dame. Well, she used to, before she apparently vanished into the depths of the Marque to meditate, or play with voodoo dolls, or scratch her backside, or whatever it was the Nairenes did behind its walls.

The commander yawned. His name was Waltere, and he had been staring at the Derith wormhole for so long that he saw it in his sleep. Already the *Gradus*'s tour of duty at Derith had been extended twice, despite assurances from CentCom, the Corps' new central command, that he and his crew would soon be put to more productive use. He was growing uncomfortably familiar with that promise and it was starting to sound distinctly hollow.

CentCom had been established at the outbreak of the war, when a new structure became necessary in order to ensure that communications remained uncompromised by the Military. For Waltere, it was just another layer of officialdom and bureaucracy. The Corps seemed to be forming new subgroups and instituting additional protocols on a daily basis, all of them designed to disguise the fact – whisper it – that the war was most definitely not going according to plan. Oh, the initial attack on Melos Station had gone brilliantly, removing from the board, with one massive explosion, a good quarter of the Military hierarchy and a tenth of its ships. Unfortunately, all of the other assaults had been botched, either partially or entirely, mostly because the Corps had grown soft. That was what happened when the Military was left to handle the dirty work of conquest: its troops became battle-hardened and seasoned, while Corps forces were only good for mopping up the stragglers, or directing traffic.

The Securitats were another matter, although even they got in much of their practice from torturing civilians – Waltere had done one tour of duty on Earth, in France, and had no illusions about how the Securitats went about their business. But there weren't enough of the Securitats for them to be able to engage in full confrontations with the Military without massive Corps support, and the two organisations had their own command structures, neither of which entirely trusted the other. Meanwhile, a good chunk of the Military remained intact, although scattered or in hiding, popping out only to launch lightning guerilla raids on Corps ships and stations before retreating back to their hidden bases. But the rumours were that the Military was preparing for a massive counterattack in the hope of regaining the Illyr system and the homeworld, and forcing the Corps and its allies either to surrender or sue for peace. To be fair, those rumours had been circulating since the start of the war, when it became clear that the initial attacks designed to decapitate the Military had failed, but they'd been growing in intensity in recent times.

Sometimes, Waltere thought that he might have picked the wrong side in this fight, but it was too late to change now.

The *Gradus*, although big, had a skeleton crew of just twelve, operating in three rotations. It boasted state-of-the-art shielding and weaponry, none of which it had yet had a chance to test. Boredom had made the crew fractious and difficult. Being trapped in a tin can beside a remote wormhole tended to have that effect. Only the regular bursts of contact from CentCom through the beacon arrays confirmed that the *Gradus* had not been forgotten entirely.

Waltere blamed his ship's name. He had been present when Syrene requested – ordered, in anyone else's language, since what the Archmage wanted, she got – that the *Gradus* assume primary responsibility for monitoring the wormhole. He knew that the only reason anyone still cared about Derith was because the Archmage's stepdaughter had vanished into it, along with a handful of humans, two of whom might have been involved in Grand Consul Gradus's death. The real meat on those tenuous bones, and the only interesting thing about the mission, was that a Mech had accompanied the escapees.

Waltere had never seen one of the artificial beings. They were all supposed to have been destroyed before he was born. He didn't hold out much hope of seeing the one that had entered the Derith wormhole anytime soon. Whatever lay on the other side of that hole was bad news: a giant meteor field, a sun, a collapsing star . . . Someone had even suggested aliens. Waltere had almost laughed at that one, until he saw something flicker in the face of Syrene and some of the senior Corps officials when the possibility was mentioned. He'd said nothing, but their reaction had remained with him.

Now he sat slumped in his captain's chair, staring at that blasted wormhole, thinking of all the possibilities for glory and advancement that had passed him by while the *Gradus* floated in this backwater of the universe. It was all an illusion, of course. Waltere was not particularly bright, but he was savvy enough to know that he would never excel in the field. If he'd actually fought in the war then he'd either be dead or injured by this point; that, or given a posting far from the lines where he couldn't do any harm.

A bit like this one, he supposed.

Yallee, his second-in-command, stepped into his field of vision. Yallee wasn't very pretty, but then Waltere wasn't very handsome. With nothing else to do on board the *Gradus*, she and Waltere had begun a casual affair. It wasn't a good idea, of course, even if they were both single, because it wasn't like there was any way of getting away from each other when they fought, which was increasingly often. It was also against all regulations. They could both be court-martialled if CentCom discovered their relationship, although at least that would mean they would both be sent back to Illyr for trial. Waltere was occasionally tempted to confess, just so he could return home. If he did, he and Yallee wouldn't be going back alone. One half of the crew was permanently sleeping with the other half: they got together, they broke up, they got together with someone else. He had trouble keeping track of who was bedding down with whom. By contrast, he and Yallee had been together for so long that they counted as an old married couple by the standards of the *Gradus*.

'It's time for a drill,' said Yallee.

'Really?' said Waltere. He had a headache and the noise of the drill siren would only make it worse. 'Maybe we could just postpone.'

Nobody liked drills. It meant waking those crew members who were asleep, or disturbing those who were off duty, just to line them up before the captain's chair so Waltere could be sure that, if anything did happen, they might actually be prepared to deal with it. During the last drill, Holtus, one of the engineers, had simply refused to leave his bed, and not even the appearance of Waltere beside his bunk threatening him at gunpoint had convinced him to get out of it. Eventually, Waltere had put away his pulser and gone back to his chair. It just didn't seem worth the effort . . .

Later he'd had a talk with Holtus, who accepted that, among other things, it was bad for morale to have him disobey a direct order. Holtus agreed to appear for drills as long as they were scheduled for a time when he wasn't asleep, which wasn't ideal from Waltere's point of view but was still better than nothing. Unfortunately, when this arrangement became widely known, nobody else wanted to be woken up either, so now drills were scheduled for when shifts ended, and the time was posted a day in advance so everyone knew when to expect it. This completely defeated the purpose of drills, but nobody cared, least of all Waltere, because nothing ever happened here anyway.

Which was why, when the ship appeared from the Derith wormhole, it took him a few moments to register its presence. He could see it, but his brain, numbed by inactivity, struggled to accept the reality of it. Eventually he managed to get the words out.

'That's a ship!' he said, standing up.

Yallee turned to look. By the time she saw it, Waltere had already sounded the alert and the siren raged through the *Gradus*.

'You'd better tell them that it's not a drill,' said Yallee.

Good idea, thought Waltere. He hit his comms button.

'This is not a drill,' he announced. 'Repeat: this is not a drill. Seriously.'

Steven and Alis saw the Corps cruiser the moment they emerged from the wormhole. Steven was dizzy from the boost, so he quickly handed control of the *Nomad* to Alis.

'Rizzo?' he said. It came out sharply, like a high-pitched bark, and he cursed puberty, vowing to modulate his tones next time. Well, if there was a next time, for already the cruiser was turning towards them, its heavy cannon swivelling in their direction.

Rizzo appeared calm, however, and was quickly making adjustments to the weapons.

'Targeting,' she said.

Steven nodded at her, swallowing hard. *I'm not even sixteen*, he thought, *what the hell am I doing?*

'Three, two, one,' said Rizzo. 'Targeting complete. We have a lock.'

On the screens, the nameless vessel turned green.

Steven swallowed again. Actually, wasn't he almost eighteen? A couple of years had already passed on this side of the wormhole, if the Cayth were to be believed: technically, he was nearly old enough to drive! In another parallel universe, he'd be old enough to have a pint, legitimately, with Paul down at the Bear Arms near his Edinburgh home. Maybe his mum would have joined them: she always liked a dash of lime in her lager.

His mum . . .

'Fire,' he said.

★ ★ ★

On board the *Gradus*, the rest of the crew was still assembling when the torpedo launched. Yallee had taken the co-pilot's seat and was manoeuvring the ship to bring the new arrival under their guns. Their scanners had identified it as the same vessel that had fled into the wormhole over two years earlier.

Elvo, the duty weapons officer, was already at her post.

'Shields!' cried Waltere.

'Shields up,' confirmed Elvo. 'But it's going to hit us.'

They braced for impact, but none came. The torpedo erupted in a burst of white light while it was still some way from them. In an instant, the *Gradus* lost all power. The only illumination came from distant stars and the glow of the energy net that now surrounded them.

'All systems down,' said Yallee, but Waltere didn't need her to tell him that. He could see and hear for himself. Oxygen was their first concern. They needed to get emergency life support up and running, or they'd soon start to suffocate.

A wall of illumination appeared in the centre of the cabin. There were no Others on the *Gradus*, but it didn't matter. The torpedo's functions were automatic: arm, fire, disable.

Decontaminate.

Waltere felt heat upon his skin, and then he felt nothing else at all.

CHAPTER 25

Like all Illyri vessels, the *Gradus* was fitted with a Universal Docking Connector, allowing one ship to link with another. Alis brought the *Nomad* in under the UDC, and sent out an identifying signal to the shiny new cruiser, the electronic equivalent of a knock on the door requesting permission to enter. The crew hadn't been given time to disable the UDC before they were obliterated, and so the *Gradus*'s systems automatically unlocked the connector.

The cruiser was three or four times larger than the *Nomad*. Like most Illyri cruisers, it could be used to transport troops and equipment if required, and its bay was big enough to hold several motorised vehicles. The bay could also be adapted to provide temporary living and sleeping quarters for soldiers.

Alis remained on board the *Nomad* while Steven and Rizzo went exploring. A peculiar, ripe smell hung in the air. It took a few seconds for Steven to identify it as the faintest odour of charred meat, the aftermath of the decontamination process. No, not decontamination, Steven realised. Call it what it was: the torpedo had somehow incinerated the crew of this ship and then erased any trace that they had ever existed.

The first thing Steven did was to check the levels of food on board, fearing that the blast had destroyed everything biological. He felt a sense of relief when he opened the galley stores, for the ship had clearly been resupplied recently and the larder looked pretty full. Adjoining the galley was what looked like a greenhouse crossed with a science laboratory, where bacteria were being grown as a supplementary food source. That was all good. The Cayth had replicated more food based on their analysis of the *Nomad*'s supplies, but Steven remained slightly wary of it.

A voice spoke into his headset.

'Steven?'

It was Alis on the *Nomad*, who'd busied herself with accessing all of the information and manifests that she could from the new vessel.

'I hear you.'

'You won't believe what this cruiser is called.'

Alis knew much of the Kerr brothers' history on Earth.

'Try me.'

'You've just boarded the K-Class Diplomatic Cruiser *Gradus*.'

Steven laughed.

'You mean, as in Grand Consul Gradus?'

'The same.'

'Wow, so they named a ship after him. I'm sure he'd be happy to know that.'

He found Rizzo already seated at the weapons system, assessing its firepower and defences.

'It's much more advanced than the *Nomad*,' she told Paul. 'We could start a war with this thing.'

'It's not just the weapons,' Alis added, from her post on the *Nomad*. 'Its engines are at least a generation on from ours. It's faster and more powerful.'

'Can we keep it?' asked Rizzo. She was bouncing up and down on her seat. 'Can we? Can we?'

Steven couldn't tell if she was just pretending to be childlike, or if the possibility of so much new firepower at her fingertips had temporarily unhinged her.

'It's not a bad idea,' said Alis, 'especially given what we have to do.'

Steven felt a pang of regret. He was fond of the *Nomad*. It had been through so much and hadn't let them down, plus the Cayth had run diagnostics on it while it was in the bowels of their own ship, and the necessary repairs had been made in a fraction of the time it would have taken at an Illyri installation. But Alis and – God help us – Rizzo were right. They might be glad of the living space that the *Gradus* offered, and additional engine power and weaponry would never go amiss.

'Can we transfer the remaining Cayth torpedoes?' Steven asked.

'I did it once,' said Alis. 'I can do it again.'

He looked around the cockpit. It was gleaming, although that might not have been unconnected to the recent decontamination.

'It is a beautiful ship,' he admitted.

'Paul will understand,' said Alis.

'We can leave him a note,' said Rizzo.

Steven might not have been in command of his own ship for long, but he knew when to go along with the wishes of his crew.

'Okay,' he said. 'But I'll write the note.'

With all three of them working, it was only a matter of hours before the torpedoes were lying in the *Gradus*'s weapons bay, and all necessary equipment had been transferred from the *Nomad*. Alis then downloaded the records of all communications from the *Gradus* to the *Nomad*, which provided a potted history of the Civil War's progress. From what Steven and the others could tell, the Corps and its allies were now in control, but only within the Illyr system and a couple of outlying colonies. Beyond these, scattered Military forces were constantly harassing them. Alis was unable to find very much reference to Earth though, apart from records of craft movements to and from its solar system, and there was no reference at all to the Others. This was a Corps vessel, but information about the creatures that dwelt in the heads of the hierarchy was still apparently being kept from the rank and file. A Securitat ship might give them a better insight, if they could capture one.

Now, with the transfers to and from the *Nomad* complete, it was time to send their old ship back through the wormhole. Steven was surprised at how emotional he became as he stroked the familiar control panel in farewell, before setting it to autopilot. He stepped through the port into the waiting *Gradus*, sealing the connection behind him.

'Ready, Alis,' he said, and again his voice didn't sound right to his ears, but this time for other reasons. They all watched as the *Nomad* grew smaller and smaller, a dot sucked up by the vastness of Derith. The lump in his throat was painful, and his eyes were hot. Stupid, he thought. She was just a ship, and it wasn't like he was sending her to her grave.

But still . . .

He waited a few minutes, staring at the point where the *Nomad* had disappeared, then turned away. He patted the hull of the *Gradus*. This was his command now.

'The first thing to do is come up with a new name for her,' he told Rizzo and Alis. 'I'm not going to spend my days sitting in the belly of Gradus.'

They said nothing, probably because they were both singularly lacking in imagination, but he told himself it was because they reasoned it should be his decision, as their captain. For a moment, he considered naming it after his mother, but he wasn't sure that the *Katherine* had quite the air of threat he was seeking. Also, it immediately brought to mind images of fireworks, of wild Catherine wheels spraying circles of fire into the sky, which was definitely not what he wanted to associate with his new ship.

'The *Revenge*,' he said finally. 'What do you think?'

'*Revenge*,' said Rizzo. 'It's a good name.'

Alis nodded. It was decided.

Their course appeared on the window display. With this ship, they'd reach the first wormhole in less than fourteen hours. Steven didn't sit in the captain's chair, but instead assumed the pilot's seat beside Alis.

'You have control, sir,' she said, but unlike Syl with Paul, there was no teasing in her voice.

'No, you take her,' said Steven, and at last his voice was steady and strong. 'On my command.'

A memory from his childhood came to him: the voice of his mother reading him a story.

'Second star to the right,' he said, 'and straight on till morning.'

CHAPTER 26

Paul had only just stopped staring at the wormhole into which the *Nomad* had vanished, and was about to say something to Thula about the *Varcis*, when Derith bloomed again. Paul had momentarily forgotten about the time slip, so that hours on the other side of the wormhole were only minutes on the Cayth side. The ship grew larger, moving steadily on autopilot.

'Hey,' said Thula. 'That looks like the *Nomad*.'

A Cayth scan immediately confirmed that it was. What's more, there were no signs of life on board. Paul felt ill. Something had gone wrong. Had Steven and the others been captured, or killed? Had the Cayth somehow turned on them after all? Yet Fara and Kal appeared as perturbed as Paul was.

'We're bringing the ship in,' said Fara.

There was a tense wait while they did so. As soon as the *Nomad* docked and a final Cayth scan had declared it safe and clear, Paul, Syl and Thula entered it, with Meia hooked in over the comms link.

'Is that a *note* on the cockpit window?' asked Thula.

It was, and it was addressed to Paul. He wrenched it from the glass, unfolded it, and read it.

'Well, what does it say?' asked Syl.

Paul grinned.

'It says, "We decided to upgrade. Happy travels!"'

Meia continued to work on the *Varcis*, with Thula helping her. Paul and Syl began examining the data that Alis had uploaded to the *Nomad*, while Kal and Fara busied themselves on the other side of the cockpit, adding the stream to the combined intellect of the Cayth collective, for they too wanted to explore the new information.

'Right,' said Paul as he and Syl dug into the task at hand. It took a while to untangle the web of data, deciding what was of use and what was dispensable, but once they did, it revealed a treasure trove. Aside from including the reports on the progress of the war received by the *Gradus* – and both Paul and Syl laughed at the irony of seizing a vessel with that name – the cruiser also maintained updated records of all Corps bases and a registry of planned fleet movements for the months to come. Admittedly, the latter wouldn't be much use by the time the *Nomad* and *Varcis* were ready to go back through the wormhole, but it gave them a pretty good idea of the size and disposition of the Corps fleet, including two Corps ships, the *Satia* and the *Iria*, that were apparently in permanent stationary orbit over the earth, along with an unnamed third craft, designated only 'SD'.

'A Securitat vessel,' said Paul. At least Steven would have an idea of what he would be facing when he eventually reached their home planet. 'But it's not exactly giving us any info about what might have happened on the earth's surface.'

Syl, seated beside Paul, nudged him with her elbow.

'Try going backwards,' she said.

'Backwards?'

'Yes, see how far backwards you can get in the records. Since we've been here over two days, try two years. See what was heading to Earth two years ago.'

He looked at her, confused, and then started to smile.

'Right!' he said. 'Of course.'

Syl gave a superior sniff, then leaned close towards him.

'See,' she whispered into his ear, 'I'm not just a pretty face.'

'No,' replied Paul, but her breast was brushing against his arm – not entirely by accident, he thought – and this charged touch robbed him of any other words he wanted to add. He turned to face her, wondering, and in response she snaked her arms around him, warm and strong, pulling him into her embrace. He let himself be held for a moment before he took her golden face in his hands and kissed her, at first chastely and then fully, passionately, on the lips, and found that he couldn't stop – he didn't want to stop. It was a kiss like he couldn't remember: desperate, deep, and intense with longing. Her mouth was soft and pliant beneath his, and he could have sworn Syl swooned. Or maybe he did.

He thought he might kiss her forever, but as they pressed closer together, the white-noise murmur of the collective Cayth increased to an intrigued hum, and then a loud buzzing, like a hive of honey-drunk bees, until Paul and Syl pulled apart, reluctant but bashful, suddenly aware that they weren't alone.

'Wow,' murmured Syl, and her eyes were shining. For that moment, she looked happier than Paul had ever seen her, carefree and glowing and so very much alive. He never wanted that joyful abandon to leave her again, and he wished it could be so, and every nerve inside him seemed to be tingling too, thirsting for more.

The figures of Kal and Fara shuffled awkwardly, and then stood up together.

'We will return later,' said Fara, though she lingered for a few seconds, seeming to drink in the reality of Syl before slipping away after Kal. She shut the door firmly behind her.

Left so pointedly unattended, Syl and Paul found themselves oddly shy.

Syl spoke first. 'Well, that was a bit awkward,' she said.

'Nice of them, though,' said Paul, and he was immediately annoyed at himself for saying something so bland, so banal. Syl didn't seem to mind.

'I wondered when we were going to do that again. Or if we were,' she said.

'I wasn't exactly sure you wanted me to.'

A smile flickered at the corners of Syl's wonderful mouth.

'Then you're dumber than you look,' she said, 'because . . .'

She went silent for a moment, then seemed to make a decision.

'. . . because I love you, Paul Kerr.'

As those three words spilled out, concern furrowed the skin between her eyes, and she looked at her lap, fearful she'd gone too far.

'Ah, Syl' – Paul placed his palm on her cheek again, lifting her face, smiling at her – 'I love you too. More than I can begin to tell you. And I refuse to let you go again. Ever. I won't allow it.'

She grinned properly. 'That sounds almost like an order, sir.'

'Damn right it is, Syl Hellais. You're one of my crew now.'

'Damn right I am, Lieutenant,' she replied, 'so let's get to work,' and shoulder to shoulder they returned to the *Gradus*'s records.

As Syl had suggested, Paul ran a backwards check on ship movements to and from Earth, starting from the time they'd fled Erebos, and that was where he found what they'd been looking for: details of the evacuation of mainly Corps personnel, clear from the intense traffic of shuttles to and from the planet's surface. He scrolled further, searching the records methodically for fear he'd miss something, until Syl, who was clearly scanning faster than him, pointed at a cluster of entries. There had been a flurry of activity on a late Sunday morning, leading into early afternoon. Then the departures slowed to a jagged trickle, before petering out altogether. But the records also showed the simultaneous arrival of several large transporters through the wormhole nearest the planet, again with the designation 'SD'. They were the last ships to go in.

So the Cayth were right, and Fenuless had not been lying. They were too late: the home planet had already been sacrificed. Still unwilling to believe it, Paul frantically read what remained of the Earth entries, gnawing at his knuckles as he did so, keeping the despairing wail that ballooned in his throat in check, barely able to breathe.

Mum, he thought. Oh, Mum – I'm so sorry.

The only piece of potentially positive news was that ten of these transporters had originally been set on a course for Earth, but two had been ambushed and destroyed by the Military in the early days of the war, and they could find no sign of others being sent to replace them. Perhaps their irradiation of the breeding facilities at Archaeon had not been in vain. There was still hope. Surely there was – he couldn't countenance any other possibility. After all, if the Illyri had believed that ten tankers of spores were necessary for the destruction of life on Earth, and only eight had managed to get through, then pockets of humanity and other life might well have survived. Such slim hope.

But he had to try to put Earth out of his mind, for now – he knew that, for it was the only way he would be able to function. He had tied his future, and their ultimate salvation, to Syl, his lovely Syl.

'I'm sorry, Paul,' she said quietly beside him. 'I'm so sorry.'

He didn't know how long she'd been holding his hand, but now he turned to her and they clung together, holding on as if they were the last two lovers in the universe.

Finally they kissed again, and this time neither had the strength nor will to pull away as they became lost in each other. The Cayth's buzzing faded, turning to a background hum and then to silence as the collective turned away, and the Earth-boy and the alien-girl made their silent vows, and at last gave themselves to each other, completely, in both body and mind.

Later Paul and Syl would remember that hour as a moment of sweetest light, for they had a greater, darker mission to face: the defeat and annihilation of the Others. They could only do it together, always together.

And while they worried about the universe, Steven Kerr – a man in a child's body – could worry about Earth.

CHAPTER 27

The trip to the wormhole gave Steven time to explore more thoroughly the records kept on the *Revenge*. Even Alis, involved as she was with reprogramming the ship for the Cayth torpedoes and familiarising herself with its systems, had barely skimmed them, although 'skimming' for Alis was the human equivalent of learning by heart a couple of volumes of an encyclopedia. For every good piece of news he uncovered – a Military victory here, a Corps mishap there – he found three items of bad. One of them immediately necessitated a change of plan for the crew of the *Revenge*: Coramal, their destination, one of five Brigade bases and Military training facilities scattered throughout Illyri-controlled systems, and the planet on which Steven and Paul had been trained, was gone.

The Corps – or rather, as the report made clear, the Securitats – had decided that the Brigade bases were primary targets at the outbreak of the civil war. The Corps had always distrusted the conscripts that largely made up the Brigades, because they were human and under the control of the Military, but the Securitats seemed to indulge a hatred of humanity that bordered on the genocidal. In the Civil War, it was pretty clear on which side the Brigades would fight. Perhaps then, thought Steven, it should have come as no surprise when the *Revenge*'s records revealed that Securitat assault squads had attacked the five bases almost simultaneously and without mercy. There were, he noted, no injuries among the Brigades: all casualties were recorded as fatalities. He knew what that meant: the Securitats had killed the wounded.

The teenager closed his eyes and put his head in his hands. He remembered the staff, both Illyri and human, who had trained him on Coramal. Most had been decent, and some much more than that, among them Cairus, who had been his mentor and senior pilot trainer. Cairus had taken nothing but joy in Steven's achievements and had made him the pilot he was. Cairus was patient, intelligent, and a born teacher, but he had only taken on the role of pilot trainer after a skimmer crash severed his legs and damaged his spine so badly that even advanced Illyri medical technology could only manage to keep him alive, control the pain, and provide him with a hoverchair so he could move around. The spinal injuries meant that he no longer had full control of his limbs, and his Chip no longer properly functioned, meaning that he could not connect with a ship's systems. He created great pilots, he told Steven, so they would be able to do what he could do no longer. When they flew, so too did he.

And then there was Hague, the human master sergeant, who had been conscripted in the first months of the Illyri Conquest and had remained with the Brigades even after his period of conscription ended. On the day that he graduated from the flight academy, Steven asked Hague why he had stayed, even as he softened into middle-age. They were each drinking an illicit beer, brewed by Hague and another sergeant, Guzman, in a closet on the base. The Illyri turned a blind eye to the hidden brewery, and it allowed the sergeants to provide a small celebration for the recruits as they passed out – sometimes literally, because the ale was so strong that it made Steven's eyes water. He had only drunk one glass and was already unsteady on his feet. Even Hague, who was used to it, was looking a bit glassy-eyed. It was, Hague admitted, a particularly strong batch of ale. He thought they might have been too heavy-handed with the medicinal alcohol.

'Why did I stay?' he said, in reply to Steven's question. 'I stayed because I knew more than anyone else about keeping human beings alive in the Brigades. I'm the last of my class. All the rest were killed. Only I lived.'

He took a deep draught of beer, and swayed slightly in his chair in the aftermath.

'So, I could have gone home and let the whole damn process start all over again, or I could sign on the dotted line and try to drum into the skulls of ignorant little know-nothings like you how to survive in a universe that was hell-bent on reducing them to corpses. And that's what I did. So if you survive your period of conscription, you remember old Haguey, you hear? And when you're saying your prayers at night, you thank God for sending me to kick you in the arse when you needed it.'

Hague stretched a huge paw around Steven's shoulder and pulled him closer, breathing beer fumes all over him, but his face was deeply serious, and his eyes were those of a man who had read the names of too many dead kids.

'But most of all,' he said, 'you look after the weaker ones the way I looked after you, understand? You and your brother, you're stronger than the rest. He's starting to realise it, but it'll take you a bit longer, 'cause you're that bit younger, but you're a good 'un. I should know. I've seen 'em all – the good, the bad and the dead.'

His hand pressed against Steven so firmly that he thought his shoulder might dislocate.

'But mostly,' Hague concluded, 'I've seen the soon-to-be dead. Don't you be adding to their number.'

He released Steven, drained his glass, and stood up. He straightened his shoulders, adjusted his sleeves, and promptly collapsed unconscious. It took Steven and three of his classmates to carry him back to his bunk. They left him sleeping happily and did not see him again before they left Coramal.

Cairus and Hague: without them, Steven knew that he would certainly have been dead by now. The *Revenge*'s records indicated that the human survivors from all five bases had been taken to Krasis. Krasis was a prison world, and it housed the main contingent of the other human force within the Military: the Punishment Battalions, filled with criminals, hardened Resistance fighters, and whomever among Earth's people the Illyri had wanted to work into the grave in the official absence of the death penalty, since reintroduced. Few humans survived for long in the Battalions, and Steven and Paul had been lucky to escape being placed in them.

If Cairus and Hague were still alive, they would be on Krasis, along with the rest of the Brigades and whatever remained of the poor sods in the Battalions.

Steven opened his comms link.

'Alis?'

'Yes, Steven.'

'Course change. I'm about to send you the new coordinates.'

Alis spoke carefully.

'Steven, may I remind you that Paul's orders were to make for Coramal.'

'Coramal has been destroyed. We are going to Krasis instead.'

The pause before Alis replied went on for long enough to speak volumes.

'Krasis is a prison world,' she said.

'I know that,' said Steven. 'If it wasn't, then we wouldn't be able to organise a breakout, would we?'

'No, I suppose not.'

Another pause, even longer than the first.

'We're just one ship,' she said. 'And three crew.'

'I know,' said Steven. By then he had left the captain's cabin, walked half the length of the cruiser, and was standing behind Alis. She looked up at him in surprise.

'Which is why,' he continued, 'it's going to be the best prison break *ever*.'

CHAPTER 28

The more time they spent on the *Revenge*, and the more familiar they became with its capabilities, the more grateful Steven was that they'd ditched the *Nomad* in favour of it. Apart from its speed and weaponry, it was also equipped with advanced long-range scanners that would allow them to stay out of the way of most other vessels, with the exception of those Corps ships that were as new as their own. Nevertheless, they would remain vulnerable to discovery each time they boosted through a wormhole, as there was no telling what might be waiting on the other side. Still, that was a problem they would deal with when the time came, but to reduce the risks they decided on a roundabout route to Krasis using remote wormholes away from the main Illyri routes.

Now, sheltered by a moon in a binary system called EC3483, they watched on the scanners as a small squadron of five ships – a destroyer escorted by four cruisers – made its way past them at little more than a stone's throw in terms of the vastness of this particular galaxy. The *Revenge* identified it as a Military convoy, which probably explained why it was out here in a quiet system with no Illyri bases: the Military, like the *Revenge*, was keeping to the back roads of the universe in order to avoid unanticipated confrontations; it wanted to pick its fights. This convoy looked to be making for the Formia wormhole. Alis plotted possible courses for it, and found that two boosts would bring it within striking distance of the Corps communications station at Passienne. The Passienne base wasn't big, but it would be well defended, for it was a crucial Corps hub, responsible for the maintenance of comms beacons across five systems, as well as receiving and retransmitting the data received from them. If it could be destroyed, the Corps would effectively be blind in those systems, allowing the Military to move more freely through them.

But its destruction would be a secondary aim. Steven had learned enough from his tutors to understand how important the seizure of a communications hub might be. In war, information was the currency. With the right intelligence, a weaker force could always threaten the stronger. If the Military could capture and hold Passienne, even if only for a short time, it would be privy to all Corps communications until its enemies finally realised that the station was in hostile hands, probably when it failed to respond with the correct security protocols. At that point it would be time for the convoy to run, but not before blowing up the station.

Of course, the *Revenge* could have made its presence known to the convoy. It was out of range of the Military's weapons, and in theory they were all on the same side now. But Steven knew that if the Military captured the *Revenge*, it would never hand the ship back, and any hopes they had of reaching Krasis, let alone Earth, would be dashed. For the moment, they would have to evade their potential friends just as much as their enemies.

'First boost in two hours,' said Alis.

Steven thanked her and he and Rizzo set about preparing the *Revenge*, making sure everything was locked down while running diagnostics checks for any potential weaknesses in the hull. They found none. The time spent doing nothing much at all beside the Derith wormhole had left the ship in pristine condition. It was like a car that had only ever been taken off the showroom floor for test drives.

By the time the checks were complete, they had arrived at the mouth of the Trimium wormhole. All information indicated that it was stable, so they weren't expecting a rough boost, but even a smooth boost was mildly unpleasant. They strapped themselves in and Steven took the controls. Despite all the downsides, he still thrilled to the rush of being at the helm of a vessel while it was boosting. He had never been on a bobsleigh, or skied downhill at speed, but he imagined that the experience was mildly similar, except without the chance of complete annihilation.

Steven gave them the count.

'Preparing to boost in –'

The wormhole bloomed, but not for them. Instead the prow of a huge carrier breached space, suddenly blocking out the stars.

Steven heard someone start to scream and swear, and realised it was himself. He wrenched the controls to starboard and the *Revenge* shot across the bow of the carrier, so close that they could see faces staring at them from windows. Then they were running along the carrier's side, its bulk to their left, racing for the Trimium wormhole once more.

'They're hailing us,' said Rizzo. 'Their systems have identified us as the *Gradus*. They've sent us a security code, and are asking for the correct response.'

'Ignore them,' Steven replied.

'It's a Corps ship,' said Alis. 'Systems identify it as the *Javin*.'

'I know,' said Steven. The *Revenge* was near enough to it for him to be able to read its name on the hull, but they were closing on the wormhole. Steven didn't even bother with the count.

'Boosting,' he called, and then they were inside. It was a messy entry because of the angle at which the *Revenge* had come in and they bounced around a little at the start, but it was a short boost and when they emerged they were welcomed by empty space. But the Trimium wormhole wasn't entirely stable: it had a massive gravitational pull on this side, and Steven had to put all of the *Revenge*'s thrusters on full to avoid being pulled back into the wormhole.

The main difficulty was that they had now been spotted. Even though it was a carrier, the *Javin* was unlikely to be equipped with any craft big or strong enough to follow them through the wormhole. With luck, the *Gradus* might not yet have been missed, and their failure to respond to the *Javin*'s hail might be put down to the urgency of avoiding a collision. On the other hand, it wouldn't take long for the *Javin* to establish that the *Gradus* was not where it was supposed to be and the hunt for them would begin in earnest. Either way, the near miss at the wormhole would have to be reported, either to the station at Passienne, which was the closest Corps base, or via a small transmission drone sent back through the wormhole in the direction of the nearest beacon. If the carrier went to Passienne, it would be a problem for the Military convoy to deal with, but a drone dispatched through the wormhole would be theirs.

'We'll wait,' said Steven. 'If they send through a drone, we'll blast it and be on our way. Rizzo, prepare to target.'

Drones moved fast and were programmed to follow a non-linear course in order to avoid just the kind of destruction that Steven intended. He didn't want one to slip by, forcing them to waste time giving chase.

The scanners showed no other ships within range, but Steven still didn't like hanging around at the mouth of the wormhole. He checked the cockpit time display. It wouldn't take the *Javin* this long to prepare a drone, which meant that it must have continued on to Passienne.

He permitted himself to relax, just as the wormhole opened and the *Javin* began to emerge.

CHAPTER 29

They were saved by Steven's reactions, coupled with the buffeting of the *Javin* as it exited the wormhole. Steven hit the thrusters as the prow of the *Javin* reappeared, but he headed towards, not away from, the carrier and aimed for a spot below its keel. The *Javin*'s forward scanners had already detected the *Revenge*'s presence, but its first shots went wide as the big ship tried to recover its equilibrium. By then the *Revenge* was gliding along the underside of the carrier, where it was heavily armoured but less well equipped with weaponry.

'Shields up!' Steven ordered, but Rizzo was already ahead of him. They both knew that, at this range, the shields wouldn't be much use against a direct hit, but it was better than remaining entirely undefended.

Cannon fire ripped past their stern, but Steven was now staying so close to the *Javin* that its guns couldn't come around at the correct angle for a clean hit, and also risked self-inflicted wounds if they continued to fire. Steven's intention was clear to his crew: he was making for the wormhole again, in the hope that they could slip through and start running on the other side. By the time the *Javin* came around for another boost, the faster, lighter *Revenge* would have put a lot of space between the two ships.

But the *Javin*'s commander was no fool. A silver cloud spewed from the rear of the ship and scattered itself in the *Revenge*'s path. The *Javin* was laying mines, cutting them off from a straight route to the wormhole. Steven spun the *Revenge* and, with no time to right the ship, they returned the way they'd come, but this time upside down, with Rizzo doing her best to target the *Javin*'s weapons as they came.

'Steven.' It was Alis. 'We have to do something before they launch fighters.'

'I know, I know.'

It would take the *Javin* time to ready its fighters. They would have been locked down before the boost, because the last thing a carrier wanted was unsecured fighters rolling around in its bays, but as soon as the *Javin* was clear of the wormhole, its crew would have begun preparing craft for launch.

'We have the Cayth torpedoes,' said Steven. Unlike the weapons that had captured the *Nomad* and the *Varcis*, the *Revenge*'s torpedoes had been programmed to activate immediately upon striking a target. Now was the chance to test them.

'One of them may not be enough to disable a carrier.'

'But two of them should be. Rizzo, ready torpedoes. Target the engines. Understood?'

'Understood.'

'On my command.'

This would be the dangerous part. They'd have to put as much distance as possible between the *Revenge* and the *Javin* to ensure they weren't caught in the torpedoes' net. It would also mean running ahead of the *Javin* and then getting above it. Steven didn't want to risk another skim of its underbelly. By now its gunners would be anticipating the manoeuvre. Ahead of them was the prow of the *Javin*. Steven slipped in front of it, then turned to port and darted across the top of the carrier, almost skimming its bridge.

'Hangar bay doors opening,' Alis warned. 'Those fighters are on their way.'

Steven commenced a near vertical ascent, and the *Revenge* shuddered and bounced to the left as a shot hit its starboard side.

'Damage report,' he called.

'Minimal,' said Alis. 'No hull breach.'

But that strike was bad news. It meant that the *Javin*'s gunners now had their measure.

'The Cayth didn't give you a range on those torpedoes, by any

chance?' Rizzo asked, as the force of gravity pushed them back into
their chairs.

'I didn't think to ask,' Alis replied.

'You know, in films robots are really logical and stuff.'

'I'm *not* a robot.'

'She's joking,' shouted Steven, wrenching the *Revenge* to port. Had
he been driving a car, the move would have been accompanied by
the screeching of brakes and the smell of burning rubber, just like
back in Edinburgh when some likely lads stole a car and amused
themselves by performing doughnuts until the police came. The *Javin*
passed beneath them, and they saw the cannon fire tearing through
the darkness towards them.

'Fire!'

'Torpedoes away,' said Rizzo, and they watched the Cayth
weapons fly, leaving a blue blur in their wake.

Behind it, the first of the fighters was emerging from one of the
Javin's bays.

'Rizzo.'

'I see it.'

She targeted the fighter with their cannon, staying slightly ahead of
it so that it flew into the shots and was ripped apart. This was Rizzo in
her element. If ever anyone had been born to blow things up, it was
Rizzo. By the time the first ship had disintegrated, she had swivelled
the guns to target the second, and destroyed it just as it exited, putting
that bay out of use until the wreckage had been cleared. It still left the
fighters in the other bays – all carriers were fitted with four – but it
didn't look like the *Javin* had readied any of the others, and by then
it was too late for the carrier. It had not attempted any evasive action
when confronted with the threat of the torpedoes, probably on the
assumption that its shields would be capable of dealing with any threat
from one of its own craft, but this was Cayth technology. As before,
the torpedoes seemed to explode before they hit their target, but
instantly their nets spread, encompassing the lower half of the *Javin*.
The carrier lurched, then slowly stopped moving, but disabling a
smaller craft was a very different matter from disabling a massive ship,

especially one that had not had sufficient time to clear the gravitational pull of a wormhole. Without the forward thrust of its engines, the *Javin* found itself pulled inexorably back towards Trimium. Its forward half started to rise, so that its bow was above its stern, and then its engines struck its own field of mines. A series of explosions erupted along its hull, igniting further blasts deep in the now crippled carrier. By the time the Trimium wormhole took it, the *Javin* appeared to be almost vertical and was already on fire along most of its length. Its bow struck the lip of the wormhole and blossomed into a fireball.

And then the *Javin* was no more.

An Illyri carrier had a complement of 2,500 officers and enlisted ranks. The *Revenge* had just annihilated all of them. There was no sense of triumph though, no sense of relief for Steven, Alis, or even Rizzo. They simply stared dumbly as the wormhole closed on the destruction and loss of life they had wrought, until Steven finally spoke.

'Resume course,' he said. 'We're done here.'

CHAPTER 30

Meia and Thula returned to the *Nomad* for the final briefing before departure. The *Varcis* was at last ready, and Paul had decided that it should be Meia's ship.

'I asked her if she wanted me to go with her,' said Thula.

Paul was surprised, and just a little angry. He needed Thula to pilot his ship, for neither he nor Syl had the skills to take control of the *Nomad*, and he had also grown close to the Zulu. He relied upon him, just as he relied on Syl.

'She turned me down,' Thula added.

Paul couldn't help but let out a deep breath of relief.

'Story of your life,' he said.

'I appreciated the gesture,' said Meia.

'Shot down, and patronised too,' said Syl.

'You are not helping, lady,' said Thula.

'It is not necessary for another to join me,' said Meia. 'Also, Thula would then have knowledge of the Mech refuge. If we were captured by the Corps, I would be forced to kill him in case he gave away the location under torture.'

'Maybe it's better that you're going alone,' Thula concluded.

'Yes, maybe it is.'

The Cayth had promised to upload all that they knew of the Others onto secure servers on the *Nomad* and *Varcis*. When Fara and Kal returned – this time popping out of the wall fully formed – they confirmed that the task was complete. In addition, Fara told them, they'd inputted the location of a series of Cayth sentinels and at least forty new wormholes.

'And just in case you get taken,' said Kal, 'we have ensured that the servers on your craft cannot be accessed by other Illyri vessels, and any attempt to access them without the correct protocols will result in the destruction of the data.'

He briefed them on the necessary security formalities and then, with all preparations completed, they were all but ready to leave. They waited a final moment for Meia to run through the controls on the *Nomad* with Thula, one last time.

'Take at least a little time to master them before you attempt to enter Derith,' she said. 'Just fly around here for a while until you get the hang of it.'

'I think I'll need more than a little time,' said Thula, 'and aren't we in one hell of a rush?'

'Well, dying will not get you where you need to go any faster,' Meia replied archly. 'Let me leave before you even attempt to take off, please. I don't think I could bear to watch.'

And with that, Meia was ready to depart. They all wished her well and Syl hugged her close. Meia had saved their lives on more than one occasion. They were more vulnerable without her.

Paul didn't think Meia would appreciate a hug from him and contented himself with a handshake, but Thula had no such inhibitions and practically lifted the smaller Mech off the ground.

'Damn, girl,' he grunted. 'You're heavier than you look.'

'You need to work on your chat-up lines,' Meia replied. 'Is it any wonder that women reject you?'

And then she kissed the big Zulu on the cheek.

'Now put me down before you damage me.'

She turned back to Paul and put her hand on his shoulder.

'Remember: the Tessel system. If you have to run, that's where you head for.'

Meia departed. As they watched her go, Syl and Paul felt more lost than ever before.

'It will be harder for her now than it was previously,' said Syl, though she could have been speaking about any of them. 'She feels more than she used to: fear, loss. Loneliness.'

'I did offer to go with her,' said Thula.

'Before she mentioned that part about maybe having to kill you,' said Paul.

'Yes, before that. In future, I'll clarify these things before I make such a gesture. Anyway, we'd better get up there. I've got some practice flights to make, and I'm damned if you're all staying here while I do it. No way I'm landing this thing again to pick you up. I'm not a taxi.'

He lifted his eyes towards the skies around them and swallowed hard. Paul patted him on the back.

'I think some practice flights would be a very good idea.'

They said farewell to the Cayth and Syl heard in her mind the whisper of a billion voices, like waves breaking on a distant shore, but only Fara's voice sounded in her ear as the older woman-figure embraced the younger for the last time.

'Remember, Syl,' she said. 'Their weakness is their connectedness. They resemble a single great body: the spores are cells, but the larger ones are like limbs and vital organs. The bigger they are, the more crucial they are to the body as a whole. They are not invulnerable. They can be destroyed.'

'So I must open myself to them,' said Syl, not sure if it was a question or a statement. 'Like I did to you.'

She shuddered at the thought. Exposing herself to the Others would not be like revealing herself to the Cayth. With the Cayth, it was communication. With the Others, it would be contamination.

Fara pulled away from Syl and held her by the shoulders.

'We believe you must, yes, if you are to truly know them, if you are to find their weakness. And they have never faced an opponent like you,' she added, 'for I think the universe has never seen anything quite like you. Your mother would be proud of you, Syl Hellais. *I* am proud of you.'

Syl nodded. She tried to smile in a final farewell, but it was a twisted thing, so she merely turned away and followed Thula and Paul onto the *Nomad*, her head low and an ache beneath her breastbone. The door slid closed on the Cayth.

Thula sat down in the pilot's chair, blew air pointedly through his lips, and went to start the engines. He looked a little nervous as he did so, and he swore as the *Nomad* jumped to life.

'Jeez,' he said as he surveyed the panel before him. 'It's a relief they sent the *Nomad* back. I'm not sure that I would want to be piloting a craft I'd never even been inside. Remind me to thank that runt brother of yours when we see him again, Paul.'

'If you thank him, he'll think the Others have taken over your brain,' said Paul, who was standing near the weapons console. Rizzo had reminded Paul of the finer workings of the armaments before she left and he now intended to run through it with Syl, just in case it became necessary for her to take to the guns.

'Something certainly took over my brain when I agreed to fly this thing,' Thula replied, 'but I should remember soon enough. Steven assures me it's just like riding a bicycle.'

'A bicycle in space, with guns, and with no training wheels,' said Syl, and Thula turned to look at her, surprised that she was joining in their banter. She was folding a piece of paper tightly, but when she saw he was looking at her she grinned, and then lifted her hand and deftly skimmed a paper plane in his direction. He caught it and looked at her oddly.

'A gift,' she said.

When he unfolded it, he saw that she'd drawn a large red L on the paper.

'Your Learner plates,' she announced.

'I'd have got that without the explanation, thank you very much, Miss Chipper,' Thula said, and he chuckled as he propped it in the window.

'That's *Mizz* Chipper, I'll have you know.'

Thula sighed in mock weariness but then he became serious.

'You ready, guys?' he asked. 'Then let's do this.'

With a lurch the *Nomad* came uncoupled from the landing pad inside the Cayth ship. Paul staggered over and fell into the co-pilot's seat beside Thula, and Syl hurriedly strapped herself in at the weapons console.

'You know, Meia told me that these things basically fly themselves,' Paul said as they jolted forwards again.

'That's true,' said Thula, adjusting the thrusters. 'Until they fly themselves into something else.'

'Oh.'

The bay doors opened before them, and their future was filled with stars.

'Buckle up, kids,' said Thula. 'This is going to be a bumpy ride.'

But Syl barely heard him. The wormhole was ahead of them. They were returning to worlds that they had once known, but now changed by the years. She thought of her father and his betrayal of her. She thought of Althea. She thought of the Marque.

But most of all, she thought of Ani.

VII
THE ARCHMAGE

CHAPTER 31

The passing years had given Peris more than enough time to consider whether he'd done the right thing by fleeing the planet Earth with Danis. At the time, he'd thought that they could somehow find a way to convince Junior Consul Steyr to free them, after which they could join the fight.

But Steyr made it clear that he had risked enough by helping them to leave the doomed planet, and they should now regard themselves as prisoners of war. On the orders of the Archmage, they had been exiled to a homestead on the moon of Beros: they were captives in a gilded cage, safe but impotent, two pampered political prisoners kept at the Sisterhood's pleasure and guarded by Securitats, two ageing soldiers robbed of duty or cause, overfed, under-stimulated and left to live make-believe lives through holograms of places where they had once walked as free beings.

A quick death would have been better than this lingering one, thought Peris. Perhaps they should have remained on Earth and accepted their fate. Anything had to be better than this slow fading away. Then he thought of the Others and decided that, no, there were fates worse than this one . . .

He gazed again at the smaller moon above, satellite to a satellite, one of so many moons he'd stared at over the years. He could never look at a moon now without remembering Earth's tale of the man in the moon, inspired by the ancient blue shadows that fashioned a benevolent, craggy face, a watchful presence guiding the planet's waters into tides and eddies, quietly but unstoppably influencing the world below.

The earth had a man in its moon, but Illyr had a woman in the greatest of its moons. Influence she had beyond measure, but as for her benevolence, well, who could tell?

CHAPTER 32

In truth there were numerous females – thousands of them – on the most famous of the moons above the planet of Illyr, for the grey sphere of Avila Minor housed the Marque, the citadel of the Nairene Sisterhood, filled solely with feminine forms and girlish voices. A male Illyri had never so much as set foot on it, for to do so was against all laws and the punishment for contravening them was severe.

Right now, Ani Cienda could hear several of the Marque's females whispering loudly outside her chambers. She glanced away from the picture she held in her hands and frowned towards the door. Honestly, did they not understand that she was trying to rest, and she was most certainly not deaf?

'The Archmage has given instructions that she is not to be disturbed,' rang one voice, clear and strident.

That was Cocile, noted Ani, Syrene's former handmaiden, who was now referred to as the Archmage's 'aide'. Ani had suggested the title when she'd become Syrene's official scribe, replacing Layne, who had been killed by the Mech, Meia. Even all these years later, Ani could not help but admire the audacity of that damned Mech, for Meia had then taken on Layne's identity after disposing of her, becoming a spy disguised in a Layne-skin.

Once Meia's duplicity was revealed, Syrene was so enraged that all those who served her directly were immediately rounded up and sliced open. Random cuts were inflicted to the arms, the legs, the shoulders, the cheeks, and one unfortunate Half-Sister had even lost most of an ear by panicking and struggling. Syrene's search for imposters was more than skin-deep: she wanted to see the Sisterhood bleed; she wanted meat and pulsing arteries to convince her that no further Mech imposters hid among her Nairenes. Everybody was a suspect. No one was immune.

On hearing of Layne's demise, Ani had hurriedly offered her services as Syrene's new scribe – and she could be more than a scribe too, she reminded the Archmage, for she was the last of the treasured Gifted, the young Novices who possessed psychic powers, and whom Syrene had been moulding into her personal cohort of assassins.

What they were – and the purposes for which they had been intended – hardly mattered now though, for they were all dead, with the exception of Ani. As the only Gifted still breathing air, Ani could serve as more than a mere keeper of records, she reminded Syrene; she could be a protector, an ally. Upon hearing this suggestion, Syrene had smiled curiously at Ani, a new light in her eyes, and after several long minutes during which she probed Ani's mind – and Ani stared back at her meekly, allowing her access, up to a point – the Archmage had reached into the folds of her red robes and produced a blade.

'Give me your hand, Earth-child,' she said.

Ani held out her right hand, palm up.

'Are you right-handed?'

'Yes, your Eminence.'

'Well then, the other one, idiot.'

Turning her face away, Ani proffered her left and, without ceremony, Syrene swept the blade across the palm. Ani screamed as the skin split open, creating a deep gash of lumpy white flesh and sinew that quickly filled up with blood, spilling over and splashing to the floor.

'You look real enough to me,' said Syrene. 'Cocile, get a medic. And a mop.'

She turned to Ani again, who was kneeling at her feet, clutching her balled left hand in her unharmed right, tears leaking from her eyes. The Red Witch bent down and whispered into Ani's ear so that only she could hear.

'Now, how did you expect to be my scribe with an injured writing hand? Stupid child. Get some rest. You'll be ordained as a full Sister in the morning.'

The following day Ani was transferred from the Twelfth Realm to Syrene's private sanctum in the Fourth, with strict instructions to leave all but her most personal belongings behind, for her new role demanded fresh robes and brought with it an elevated position in the Nairene hierarchy. From that day forth, everything was kept fragrant and clean for Ani by the white-robed Service Sisters, who held their tongues and lowered their heads in her presence, such was Ani's new status and influence.

After the first week, Syrene had waved the blade at her again.

'Oh, I should cut off *both* your hands, Earthborn,' she snapped. 'Your handwriting is appalling. Is there anything else you're good for?'

Ani took a deep breath.

'Clouding, your Eminence,' she reminded her. 'I'm quite good at clouding . . .'

And as she revealed more of her powers to Syrene, she had cause to write less, and in this way she grew closer to the Archmage, and increasingly valuable to her.

The Archmage now had many aides and scribes, although much of the time she preferred that notes weren't taken at her meetings. After all, written records could incriminate, especially during a civil war that had now been raging for more than four years, and still thundered on far beyond the protective walls of the Marque.

Absently, Ani rubbed her thumb over the thick scar on her left palm, the relic of Syrene's blade. She had worried at it regularly in those early days, fretting as she tried to find her niche among Syrene's initially unwelcoming staff, so that the wound had healed lumpy and risen. She had considered getting it fixed, but it had come to represent something more to her, a constant reminder to be vigilant, and even now, as she felt it, her ears remained attuned to the noise outside. That was one thing she'd learned very quickly after her promotion: in the Sanctum, you kept your ears open, especially when it was assumed that you weren't listening. You always listened, you always watched.

'May I leave this with you then, Sister Cocile?' said the voice from outside. 'The Archmage will need it to be fitted and altered before her trip.'

Ani smiled despite her frustration with them, for that was Xela, the nimble-fingered seamstress from the Seventh Realm. Xela was the very Sister who had made Ani's gown for the Genesis Ball all those years ago, the dress that had tumbled over her shoulders like a waterfall, and had all the young Illyri officers queuing up to dance with her. It was the last truly joyful day that Ani could remember. She felt almost happy at the memory. Almost.

Lord, I was only sixteen, she thought, *just a child*. She looked again at the picture in her right hand, an old photograph printed on Kodak paper from Earth. In the image, a male and a female were gazing adoringly at the slight figure who snuggled between them: her parents, Danis and Fian, their arms around their only daughter, the child laughing at the camera, her silver hair thick as a mane, her face open and without secrets. It was a long time ago – in more ways than one – and the picture was crumpled at the edges, and worn from repeated handling.

Xela's voice carried through the door, tinged with frustration. Xela was now an aide too, a wardrobe aide, personally responsible for the stitching, laundering and general maintenance of the Archmage's vast and elegant wardrobe. When a new gown was required, Xela was entrusted with putting it together under the watchful eye of the chief Nairene designer, Sister Illan.

'The fitting will have to be done before this evening if we are to make final adjustments in time,' continued the seamstress.

'Yes, yes, only *urgent* business,' said Cocile in that imperious way of hers, and Ani knew she'd be waving her hand, wafting Xela away like a fly. Cocile was annoying in the extreme, but she was a matchless gatekeeper.

'It *is* urgent,' pressed Xela, not to be stopped.

'I said—'

Another voice interrupted Cocile now, softer and shyer, but the quietness forced others to stop and listen.

'Sister Xela, as soon as the Archmage is available, I promise I'll run down and fetch you to fit the dress. She shouldn't be long now.'

That was Lista, a Service Sister turned handmaiden – a *real* hand-maiden though, not a metaphor for a bodyguard, like Cocile. Lista helped the Archmage to dress and ran minor errands, and sometimes was even permitted to rub the Archmage's esteemed shoulders after a particularly hard day, or an unusually trying meeting, especially on those occasions when her boss was too weary to make her way to the spa for more formal treatment. Ani liked Lista: the young Sister was trusting, trustworthy, always grateful, and didn't bear grudges. Such qualities were rare among the Sisterhood. Indeed, Ani suspected that they were rare among the entire Illyri race.

Yet still, despite Lista's efforts, the squabbling outside the door continued. Other voices chimed in – Ani recognised those of Toria and Liyal – and Cocile grew more strident, and finally Ani could take no more. She sat up and quickly put away the photo, placing it into a hidden drawer in the cupboard beside her bed, making sure she locked it carefully. Then she placed her feet into the red silken slippers waiting neatly on the floor, pulled her heavily embroidered robe around her and padded to the door on silent, soft soles. She paused for a moment before she threw it open, startling the small crowd beyond into open-mouthed silence.

'What is going on out here?' she snapped. 'I'm trying to rest.'

As one they bobbed at the knee, their heads dipping reverentially.

'Your Eminence!' they cried. 'Our sincere apologies.'

And Archmage Ani nodded curtly at her assembled aides, and the eye tattooed on her cheek seemed to stare deeply into them, even as she turned away.

VIII

KRASIS

CHAPTER 33

The prison moon of Krasis lay close to the Elpia wormhole, one of the first discovered by the Illyri. Its proximity to the wormhole meant that captives could easily be transported to the worlds on which they were needed as labourers, for the Illyri had long believed that keeping inmates locked up was counterproductive.

This view might almost have seemed enlightened if it weren't for the formation of the Punishment Battalions, which were composed solely of human prisoners, the ones who had given the Illyri the greatest trouble on Earth. The automatic sentence for any human over the age of sixteen convicted of killing an Illyri – at least for those who weren't secretly tortured and murdered in reprisal by the Securitats – was exile to the Battalions for life, but it might as well have been a death penalty. Prisoners in the Battalions were often sent to mining planets where they worked until they died, or shipped in as front-line forces on hostile worlds where they helped build Illyri bases while being picked off by the local wildlife.

Repeat offenders for other crimes – Resistance fighters who had served sentences in Illyri holding facilities on Earth, only to immediately return to the fight as soon as they were released – could also find themselves on a prison transport heading for Krasis. As the Conquest grew more bloody, and the human Resistance more tenacious, the cells on Krasis had begun to fill up with those who might previously have escaped with only a two- or three-year sentence on Earth for their crimes.

Now Krasis held the last human prisoners, among the sole survivors of their kind, for with the coming of the Others, a death sentence had been passed on their entire species.

The prison population on Krasis had swollen with the arrival of those humans who had survived the attacks on the Brigade bases, including Coramal. At first, the Brigade troops had been taken to a Corps holding facility elsewhere while it was decided what to do with them, but an attempted breakout, which had almost succeeded in hijacking a Corps freighter, forced the transfer of the humans to Krasis, while the surviving Illyri Military officers were moved to standard Corps prisons.

But it was one thing for the small contingent of Securitats on Krasis to bully and torment those who had already been weakened by their time in the Battalions, and quite another to attempt the same treatment of battle-hardened fighters from the Brigades. Initially, then, the Brigade soldiers had been kept in a separate facility from the rest and were fed half-rations to break them down. They weren't forced to work, though, because the factories and labour farms had limited space, and only when workers were killed or injured could others take their place. Meanwhile, the war effort had required the seizure of all non-essential Corps vessels for use against the Military, so prisoners could no longer easily be transported to outlying mining worlds. The survivors of the Brigade massacres just sat in their cells and tried not to go crazy.

The non-commissioned officers – the corporals and sergeants – received proper rations, even though most declined the extra food to begin with, fruitlessly demanding that the same be given to their soldiers. Later they realised that this was pointless, and instead took their full rations and did their best to share them with the rest.

But conditions on Krasis remained wretched and were about to get much, much worse. An argument had broken out between a prisoner and one of the guards over a stain on bedding. All cells had to be kept in pristine condition and inmates were held responsible for any damage or dirt, which could lead to a loss of rations or a beating or, for those on punishment duty, an exhausting double shift on a factory floor, which might result in injury or death. The prisoner was a Thai Brigade soldier named Suchart. He'd told his comrades that his name meant 'born into a good life' in his own language, but whatever kind of life he'd been born into, it had ceased being good a long time before. One of the Securitats had wiped oil from his boot across Suchart's thin mattress, just for the hell of it, and now another warden was screaming at him and threatening him with a power baton for soiling his cell. Suchart, angry and almost delirious from hunger, pushed the guard and received a series of blasts from the baton for his troubles. Then, as he lay spasming on the floor, the guard had begun kicking him and shrieking in frustration. The guards were as much prisoners on Krasis as the inmates, for it was a miserable posting on a hostile moon and some, including this one, had been driven to the verge of madness by their surroundings. When the guard finally calmed down, he could not even remember why he had attacked Suchart to start with and even lifted the Thai from the floor and laid him on his bunk, before informing him that henceforth he was on indefinite lockdown and quarter rations.

Suchart had remained conscious throughout the beating and now lay on his bed and thought about one of the things that the warden had let slip in his ravings.

'*Soon you will all be dead, and then I will be free. No more prisoners! No more Krasis!*'

Using the system of Morse code taps through which the prisoners remained in contact with one another and disseminated information, Suchart passed on what he had heard to the surviving non-commissioned officers who constituted the human authority in the prison. They knew what it meant. They had feared it might be coming.

'I suspect Krasis is soon to be liquidated,' said Master Sergeant Hague. 'They're going to slaughter us all.'

CHAPTER 34

A ll was quiet on the *Revenge*. Rizzo was on monitoring duties. Once the course was set, the *Revenge* would maintain it, warning them only of ships and obstacles and, in the event that it received no response, initiating whatever evasive action the navigation computer deemed necessary.

It would take them two more boosts to reach Krasis. Not for the first time, Steven was sitting at the ship's conference table, staring at a revolving hologram of the prison: one hundred guards when fully staffed; seven different holding facilities, all separate from one another but linked to a central core by a series of covered arteries; and two primary landing pads, either one big enough to accommodate the *Revenge*, and two secondary pads for shuttles. Krasis had a carbon-dioxide-heavy atmosphere: the air was breathable, but only barely, and wouldn't permit any kind of unsupported exertion. The surface of the moon was barren. It was ugly and inhospitable; even if the cells had been equipped with windows, they wouldn't have provided much of a view.

Each holding facility had its own independent life-support system, but this would only kick in if the central core were damaged. It meant that if the *Revenge* targeted the core, which also contained the living environment for the guards, the holding facilities would keep functioning.

Huh. Steven tugged at his lower lip, a habit he'd developed as a child whenever he was faced with a problem. In this case, the technicalities of the prison break aside, it was an apparent flaw in the design of the prison. If the core did go down then the seven holding buildings would be isolated from one another since all the arteries fed to and from the core, like a bicycle wheel without a rim. That couldn't be right. They had to be connected in some way. Either the blueprints didn't include some additional walkways above ground, or they were under the moon's surface.

Steven had come up with several ideas for attacking Krasis, none of them very sophisticated, but the issue of the isolation of the holding facilities had been the main stumbling block in each. They didn't have the numbers to battle the guards on the ground, so seizing the core and opening the holding facilities from there wasn't an option. If they tried to take one of the blocks and then use its prisoners to help storm the rest, they faced the problem of having to follow an artery to get back to the core before they could move on to another block. But by then, the guards in the core would simply have sealed off the first block. Ultimately, a system of alternative underground connectors made sense. To rely on their existence was a calculated risk, but one he would probably have to take.

There! He had made his decision, and he stopped yanking at his lip. They would destroy the core first and then Rizzo's sharpshooting skills would come into play. Steven wanted to limit casualties among the prisoners, but at some point they were going to have to blast the walls of the holding facilities. He enlarged the blueprint. Each rectangular block was built to the same specifications, with tiers of cells rising along both sides of its length; catering, ablution and other prisoner facilities to the left; and guardhouses and security systems to the right. Once the central core was down, they would move in on Block 1 and blast it with targeted pulser fire, which should take out most of the guards without harming any prisoners in their cells. If they were lucky, they'd also disable the security systems, which would open the cells. If they weren't, Alis would have to go in and access them, as she was the only one of them who could. Steven would go with her, of course, leaving Rizzo to remain with the *Revenge*. Once the first block was down, they'd move on to the next, this time with whatever prisoners they'd freed as backup, moving slowly across the moon's surface on foot and using the breathing apparatus from the

Revenge, accessing each block through the theoretical underground access passages, or just being dropped from the *Revenge* once the main guard area had been destroyed. Thus, slowly, they'd take Krasis block by block.

It could work. It might work.

He had no idea if it would work.

Actually, he had a terrible feeling that it probably *wouldn't* work, but he'd never needed to attack a prison before, and it was the best plan he had. Not for the first time since they'd come through the Derith wormhole, he wished that his brother were with him.

He killed the display and left the table. To his left sat Rizzo with her feet on the main console, staring into space. To his right was Alis. She was lying on her back beside an open engineering panel. A coil of wires fed into her lower back.

The Mech's power source was not unlimited. While it had a kinetic element, much like an expensive wristwatch powered by the movement of its wearer's arm, it did require occasional charging using an induction plate. Alis's induction plate had been left on the *Dendra*, the shuttle she had originally been piloting when Steven and Paul first encountered her. There hadn't been time for her to remove it before the *Dendra* had to be abandoned, and even if there had been, she'd have been forced to reveal her identity as a Mech as a consequence. Now that her true nature was known, she used an induction coil of her own construction to charge. The process required her to put herself into a form of sleep mode until the charge was complete, although a gentle touch could rouse her from it, like someone having an afternoon doze.

Steven watched her from the doorway, her chest rising and falling slowly even though she had no lungs, no respiratory system. It was just part of her design, and allowed her to mix with the Illyri she resembled without attracting attention, like all of her generation of Mechs. He wondered what Thula would have said had he seen Alis like this, for she was usually very discreet about charging. Steven never thought that he'd miss Thula, who had always enjoyed baiting him, but he did.

Steven's feelings for Alis were complicated. He wasn't even sure that he fully understood them. He cared for her, and desired her, but he was also aware that she was not like him. Yes, Paul and Syl were not alike either, at least in the sense of being different species – and that was plenty strange enough anyway – but they were the same age, and also completely organic. And while the Illyri lived longer than humans, who knew what kind of life extension medical advances might permit by the time Paul was an old man, assuming that he and Syl stayed together for that long, or weren't killed in the immediate future, which was a very real possibility.

But Alis only looked young. She had been in existence for about twice as long as Steven, and it was her programming that caused her to behave like someone much younger. She had explained to Steven that it was adaptive, though, and could be set to age, so she could grow old at a similar pace to the Illyri. In addition, her ProGen skin could also be altered to simulate ageing, and she could choose when to die. She could even choose to die when he did, she said.

Sometimes, when he was alone, or even when he sat silently beside her, Steven tried to imagine a future with her: as he aged and she pretended to, as he grew ill and she stayed well, as his life came to an end and she elected to end hers too. They could never have children, not together, for whatever other physical attributes Alis's designers might have given her, a womb was not one of them. Oh, they could probably do something with test tubes and donated eggs, but was that what he wanted? Was it what *she* might want?

My God, thought Steven, I'm still only a teenager and already I'm mapping out my life. He felt a rush of anger and his face flushed red. His fists closed as he stood looking down at Alis, but then sadness replaced all other emotions. He was out of his depth, but he'd been out of it ever since the Illyri had captured him and his brother back on Earth, and probably even before that. He thought about waking Alis, but he was afraid of what he might say. Instead he left her where she lay, and went to join Rizzo.

He did not see Alis's eyes follow him from the room.

CHAPTER 35

Steven didn't hear Alis return. He just looked up to find her before him. He smiled at her. In preparing for the next boost and worrying about the prison problem, he had forgotten the complexities of their relationship that had been troubling him. Seeing her now made him feel both guilt for his earlier thoughts and gratitude for her presence. He believed they could work it out. After all, love could find a way, right?

'You okay?' he asked. He tried to touch her arm affectionately, but she pulled back and would not meet his eye. Steven put it down to the after-effects of the charge. The induction coil wasn't as effective as the plate and sometimes left Alis with a headache.

Alis relieved Rizzo, who returned to her weapons station, and then Steven informed them both of his plan for taking Krasis. There was silence while the others took it in.

'That's it?' said Rizzo. 'That's got to be the dumbest plan I ever heard.'

This wasn't what Steven had been anticipating. Yes, his plan had some holes, but didn't every plan? Nothing was ever perfect. He opened his mouth to say something to that effect when Alis interjected.

'There are too many unknowns,' she said. 'If there are no connectors between the prison blocks—'

'There must be,' interrupted Steven. 'It's the only possibility that makes sense.'

'But they're not on the blueprints?'

'No,' he admitted.

'Then the logical assumption is not that they may exist, but that they may not exist. Also, what will the Securitats in the other blocks be doing while we're assaulting the core and then Block One?'

'I don't—'

'What if they begin killing prisoners?'

'I—'

But Alis was implacable.

'And what will we do when they begin targeting the *Revenge*?' she continued. 'Because they will. Krasis is moderately defended from attacks from above, based on the assumption that the only parties who might ever want to free humans from it were other humans, and they didn't have the capability to do so, but that doesn't mean the guards won't have heavy weapons in reserve.'

Steven was gaping at her. He could feel himself reddening again, but this time it was as much in shame as anger. Alis was embarrassing him, belittling him. This wasn't right! She was supposed to be on his side.

'These are our lives you're playing with, Steven,' she said. She fixed him with her gaze like a scientist pinning an insect to a board. 'Ours, and those of the prisoners on Krasis. We can't go in on the basis of your plan.'

'I'm not playing!' Steven protested, and even to himself he sounded like a whining child, not helped by his voice breaking on the final syllable. 'This is the best that I can do.'

'No, it is not,' said Alis. 'Think again.'

Steven jabbed a finger in her direction.

'I can order you to follow the plan,' he shouted.

'You can,' said Alis. 'And I will ignore the order.'

'You can't do that.'

'I am a Civilian and I serve with you of my own will. You have no authority over me. Neither is this a Military mission, nor a Military craft. Come up with a better plan, Steven.'

She turned her back on him and resumed the systems check for the boost. Steven remained standing where he was, shaking with anger and humiliation.

'Why are you doing this?' he asked softly. 'Why are you behaving this way?'

Alis's fingers stopped moving. He watched her face in the glass. She was looking at him with an expression that he had never seen before, and she was no longer his Alis.

'Because I am older than you. Because my existence has encompassed too much death and suffering already. Because I am not willing to lay down my life unless the sacrifice has meaning, and has been earned.'

Her eyes shifted and her fingers began dancing over pads and keys once again. Steven turned to Rizzo, who shrugged.

'I told you it was a dumb plan,' she said.

And Steven stalked away, leaving them alone. Nothing else was said until they heard the door of the captain's cabin slam.

'That was harsh,' said Rizzo.

'It was necessary.'

'You could have been gentler.'

It was a significant reprimand coming from Rizzo, to whom concepts like gentleness seemed entirely alien, but then much about Rizzo was unknowable.

'Sometimes,' said Alis, 'I forget how young he is.'

'We're all young.'

'I'm not.'

'When my dad was dying –' Rizzo began, and Alis immediately turned her attention to the tough little Italian. As far as she knew, Rizzo had never spoken to anyone of her past.

'– he told me that he didn't feel old, not in his head,' she continued. 'He said that his body had worn out, but his mind had stayed the same as it ever was. In his head, he was still twenty, he said, but a different kind of twenty. When he was a young twenty, he said, he knew nothing and thought that he knew everything. But he suspected that he didn't know as much as he thought and was just afraid to admit it. When he was older, he knew that he didn't know everything and wasn't afraid to admit it, but he also suspected that he knew more than he thought he did.'

Rizzo put her right hand to her chest, just above her heart. It was an unconscious gesture, but said so much.

'That always stayed with me,' she said. 'I liked to think of him as being young, even at the end. For him, it wasn't about age, or how you looked. It was about what you were like inside. Being young wasn't bad. It *isn't* bad. I think it's just about being the right kind of young.'

'How did he die?' asked Alis.

'Emphysema. He smoked a lot.'

'Why do you hate the Illyri so much, Rizzo?'

Rizzo looked surprised at the question.

'I don't hate the Illyri,' she said. 'I hate the universe. But it's too big to destroy, so I just blow up the parts that I can.'

And now the old, familiar Rizzo was back, and the version whose existence had remained hidden until that moment was locked away again.

'You need to talk to him,' she told Alis. 'We're going to Krasis, one way or another, and we all need to stick together, so maybe you could try not to break his heart until we've done what we have to do.'

'And my heart?' asked Alis. She could not believe she was speaking this aloud, and to Rizzo of all people. 'What about my heart?'

'You're a Mech,' Rizzo replied. 'You don't really have a heart. And for all the pain that it brings, you don't want one anyway.'

Alis regarded Steven through the glass wall of the cabin. He was toying with a stylus, turning it over and over in his right hand. She thought that he might be talking to himself, although she could not hear what he was saying.

He looked so very young. But then, that was what he was.

As far as Alis was concerned, what Rizzo had said was interesting but not relevant. Steven was a boy who had been forced by circumstances to behave like a man before he was ready. He had done well, and his actions had contributed to their survival, but it was his skill as a pilot that had saved them. He was maturing, but he was not yet mature.

She had been engaged in a fantasy, Alis realised. She wanted to understand the nature of her own developing emotions, and to do that she had to test them. Steven had provided an opportunity to do so, to a degree: she could explore affection with him, desire, even love, or some version of it. He had become infatuated with her, and she had been content to facilitate that emotion, even to respond to it in kind. But what was love? Did it develop from other emotions, or was some seed of it present at the start? How could one know what was truly love, and what was not? Until Steven appeared, Alis had not experienced any of the feelings that this young human being inspired in her. Any affection that she felt for Tiray, the Illyri who had protected her, was unaffected by desire. It lacked that component. With Steven, desire was a crucial element. But she was coming to understand that she was not as infatuated with him as he was with her, but instead was excited by her own responses to him, by the unfamiliarity of new emotional experiences. Ultimately, this relationship could only harm them both. Lying on the cabin floor as the induction coil finished its work, and emerging from the charging daze in time to see the look on Steven's face, she knew this to be true.

And yet there were aspects of what she felt that she could not define. Emotions were slippery things.

Alis did not bother knocking on the door. They were long past that. She just opened it and stepped through.

'I am sorry,' she said.

He didn't reply. His eyes were red. If he had not been crying, the effort not to do so had left its mark.

'I'm sorry for everything,' she continued. 'What I said out there was true, but my reasons for saying it were . . . not what they seemed. I was angry. I was sad. My feelings for you are complex. I don't fully understand them – I just know that we can't go on as we are. I wanted to believe that I could be like you, but I cannot, and I think you understand this. I do love you, if love is to like, and admire, and trust. But the rest – it has no future, and will only bring us both pain. I do not want to cause you pain, Steven. I do not want you to cause me pain.'

Now he *was* crying. Alis wished that she could cry, but it was not part of her design.

'You are an extraordinary being, Steven, and you will only become greater,' she said. 'I would not have come with you otherwise. I would not have let you take me in your arms. If it is your belief that your plan for the attack on Krasis will succeed, then I will stand alongside you without objection. And if it should be that I die in the attempt, then I will do so gladly if we are together.'

She paused.

'But I really would prefer not to die.'

Even as he was crying, Steven had to laugh. It came out as a sputter, and he sprayed tears and spit and snot on the desk. He wiped his face with his hands. He was still sobbing, but she could hear that he was calming down.

'And I suppose,' he said, 'that you have a better plan?'

'I may.'

'Well, if you'll give me a minute or two, I'll come to the main cabin and you can share it with Rizzo and me.'

'I will wait for you there.'

He looked up at her.

'Thank you,' he said.

'It's no trouble to wait.'

He laughed again.

'No, *thank you*. For what you said. For all of it. For being with me.'

'I am still with you,' she said.

'Yes.'

But not as before. It hurt now, but it would be all right. They would make it so.

CHAPTER 36

Steven listened to Alis's plan. There was something familiar about it. He just couldn't remember what it was.

'You have to admit that it's better than yours,' said Rizzo.

And then it came to him.

'That's because it's from *Star Wars*!' he said.

'I have no idea what that is,' said Alis.

'My God,' said Steven, 'we're in *Star Wars*.'

'I still have no idea what that is,' said Alis.

'I don't know what he's talking about either,' said Rizzo.

'Oh, come on,' said Steven. 'You must have seen *Star Wars*. Everyone's seen *Star Wars*.'

'Alis hasn't. And of course I've heard of it, but I haven't watched it.'

'Alis isn't from Earth. She has an excuse. You don't.'

'I never liked science fiction,' said Rizzo. 'It's kind of male, and not in a good way.'

Steven gaped at her.

'You're flying a spaceship stolen from an alien race. You're actually *in* science fiction.'

'I still don't like it.'

Good grief, thought Steven. Alis tapped him on the shoulder.

'Please – what is *Star Wars*?'

And he tried to explain as the next of the wormholes loomed.

CHAPTER 37

The boosts went as well as boosts can go, and then they had their first sighting of Krasis, the prison world.

'Pure luxury,' said Rizzo, and she sniggered, for the moon ahead of them was a sad, grey thing, the most remote of seven satellites orbiting a gas giant named Tener. However, by the standards of its sister moons, and Tener itself, Krasis probably counted as a paradise.

The Krasis scanners picked up their presence as soon as they emerged from the wormhole.

'Krasis calling the *Gradus*. Respond, please.'

Alis opened the channels, both audio and visual. The head of a Securitat functionary appeared before her.

'Identify yourself,' he said.

'First Officer Yallee responding,' she replied. She'd run a check on the *Gradus*'s crew manifest and decided that Yallee was the one whom she most closely resembled.

'I am Lieutenant Reutan, duty officer at the Krasis Incarceration Complex. Your boost was not scheduled and this is a secure facility.'

'I understand, Lieutenant, but this is an emergency. We were engaged in a firefight with an unknown vessel. They attempted to board us; in the ensuing battle a dock breach occurred. Both attackers and defenders suffered serious casualties. I lost all of my crew, including the Commander, but I succeeded in capturing two of the humans who attempted to seize our ship.'

'Humans?' Reutan was interested now.

'I have identified them as Michaela Rizzo and Steven Kerr. I ran them through the standard records, and it appears termination notices have been served on both of them. I considered carrying out the order myself, but Krasis was in reach and I thought it might be more useful to hand them over to the Security Directorate. Although,' she added, 'should you decide to execute them, I would like to be involved. Their actions caused the deaths of some of my crew.'

'Stay where you are, First Officer.'

Reutan's image vanished for a time. When it reappeared, it was clear that the naming of Rizzo and Steven had set bells ringing in the Securitats' own system. Alis wasn't concerned about a message being transmitted back to Illyr, not yet. The Securitats would wait until they had confirmed the identity of the prisoners, and then a drone would have to be sent through the wormhole. If all went well, the facility would be in friendlier hands long before that came to pass.

'Can you show me the prisoners?' Reutan asked.

Alis flicked a switch and an image of Steven and Rizzo sitting dejectedly in the ship's small brig was added to a corner of the screen. Alis knew that their facial features would automatically be scanned and compared with those on record. She was just grateful that, in their excitement, Reutan and his fellow Securitats hadn't bothered to do the same with her.

'Identities confirmed,' said Reutan. 'We've activated a pad for you, Yallee. You're clear to land.'

The *Revenge* breached Krasis's atmosphere and the prison facility was revealed to her. Only three of its seven blocks appeared to be operational, for four were entirely dark. The lights of a landing pad blinked before her. A cruiser and a transporter, the latter much older and larger than the *Revenge*, waited on nearby pads, one of which had clearly been constructed recently and was little more than an area cleared of rocks. Beside it stood a couple of shuttles, but as Alis brought the *Revenge* around she saw a newer ship sitting on a raised platform beside the central core. There appeared to be some activity around it, and she noticed storage chests being loaded into it. *Interesting*, she thought.

The pad activated for the *Revenge* was one of those closest to the core. As she brought the ship in to land, a phalanx of armed Securitats, their faces obscured by breathing masks, appeared from a doorway but kept their distance until the *Revenge* had touched down and the dust had cleared. Alis killed the engines and took a moment to think. She had done all that she could. The blueprints for Krasis were downloaded to her mainframe and now she needed to gain access to the prison systems. Her finger hovered under the 'unlock' button. Once Rizzo and Steven were in the hands of the Securitats, she would not be able to protect them. As wanted criminals, they could expect some rough treatment, but it was in the nature of Securitats to seek information from valuable prisoners before killing them. Rizzo and, more particularly, Steven were both prizes in themselves and potential sources of information about the whereabouts of Syl Hellais. Back at the Derith wormhole, Fenuless had revealed that Syrene and the Nairene Sisterhood were anxious to have their lost Novice returned to them alive, if at all possible. So Steven and Rizzo were in no immediate danger of death, but at very real risk of painful interrogation and a beating along the way. Alis would have to work fast.

She said a prayer to her god, to any god, and unlocked the doors.

Alis was right: the Securitats chose not to be gentle with their prisoners. Four of them entered the brig and dragged Steven and Rizzo from it. Immediately the rest of the Securitats surrounded them where they lay on the floor. Batons rose and fell, and Alis saw booted feet kicking at the prisoners. It was all that she could do not to show concern. When she called on the Securitats to stop, it was with an air of boredom more than anything else.

One of the Securitats lifted his breathing mask and she recognised Reutan.

'You have no authority here, Yallee,' he said, and in his words she heard an uncomfortable echo of her own earlier comments to Steven. She tried not to stare at Steven now. She could see him through Reutan's legs. His scalp was bleeding profusely, and his hands were raised above his head in an effort to ward off any further kicks. Rizzo's eyes were closed. Alis suppressed her regret instinct. Her plan had been the most logical, and the one with the highest chance of success.

Both Steven and Rizzo had accepted the personal risks involved.

'That may be true, but piloting the *Gradus* alone gave me no time to interrogate them. It was only with the greatest reluctance that they gave me their names, and they would share little more. But the termination order links them to the fugitive Nairene, Syl Hellais. If you injure them excessively, and thus prevent them from providing information about her whereabouts, we may all have to answer to the Archmage.'

Even the Securitats didn't care to cross the Sisterhood. Reluctantly, Reutan ordered the prisoners to be taken to one of the core's primary holding cells. Steven managed to stay on his feet with the support of his captors, but Rizzo had to be carried.

'You kicked her too hard, Lerras,' said one guard to another as they grabbed an arm each. 'I told you not to aim for her head.'

The one named Lerras shrugged.

'She deserved it,' he said, grinning. Quietly, Alis registered his name and appearance. When the time came, she would take care of him personally, she decided.

'I can offer you the hospitality of the guardhouse, Yallee,' said Reutan as the *Revenge* emptied of Securitats. 'It's not much, but this is a prison, not a hotel.'

'I would be grateful if you could first take me to a secure communications hub,' said Alis.

Reutan looked puzzled. 'For what reason?'

'I have confidential mission information to impart to my superiors. Can you prepare a drone?'

'We'll be sending one through the wormhole imminently to inform CentCom of the apprehension of these prisoners,' said Reutan. 'But any information you have can be shared with us. We *are* on the same side.'

'I'm afraid this information is for the ears of Vice President Dyer only,' said Alis. 'It would be unwise of me to disseminate it more widely.'

'In that case . . .' said Reutan, but Alis caught the look in his eye. For the Securitats, nothing was confidential. Reutan was happy to let her use their communications system to compose a message, if she was foolish enough to believe that they wouldn't be listening to every word.

It was then that she nearly made her first error. Reutan offered her a breathing mask and she opened her mouth to refuse – she was a Mech and had no need of a respirator – until she remembered that she was supposed to be an Illyri officer.

'Thank you,' she said, pulling on the mask.

'I trust you're not armed,' said Reutan. 'No outside weapons are permitted in the facility.'

Alis spread her arms wide and turned around once to show that she was unarmed.

'I could always search you, just to be sure,' said Reutan. He thought that the young officer's uniform fitted her very well, even if it wasn't strictly regulation.

'You could always try,' said Alis, in a tone that suggested it might be the last thing Reutan ever did, at least with a full set of unbroken fingers.

Reutan decided not to search her. For now.

'After you,' he said, and he followed her across the moon's desolate surface to the looming central core.

CHAPTER 38

Krasis didn't have Chip or retina scanners or, if it did, they were not being used. It was a little bit of good luck, but Alis knew that on such small blessings did even the best of plans depend. On consideration, the absence of scanners made sense: Krasis was a prison facility for humans, and they did not carry Chips in their skulls. Also, as with Krasis's lack of significant outer defences, there was no reason why any Illyri would want to mount an attack on the prison in order to help humans escape. With war raging, even the Military had better things to occupy its time than invade Krasis to free some Brigade troops. Few figures in the Military hierarchy had any real affection for human conscripts.

All of this had made the Securitats stationed on Krasis casual in the extreme, but the prison guards were hardly the cream of the Security Directorate to begin with. Prison duty was inflicted on those who had failed in some way, while the ones who volunteered for it tended to be both lazy and brutal. For the latter, Krasis must briefly have seemed like a jolly posting, since it gave them the freedom to inflict misery and suffering on the ranks of the Punishment Battalions without any real fear of reprimand.

The prison was old. Its precast component parts had been dropped on the moon more than half a century before, since the stone of Krasis was porous and hard to mine. Inside it was all steel doors and steel bars. It smelled dry and musty, like an old tomb. The core was three storeys high and dominated by a tower at its heart, which held all of the monitoring and security systems for the prison, and was staffed at all hours. Screens around the tower displayed real-time images from the prison blocks.

Prisoners entered through a mesh tunnel that fed into a processing room, where they were shaved, stripped, put through showers, assigned to one of the blocks and given a standard uniform of a yellow jumpsuit, work gloves, boots and a coat. Since they had been condemned to the Punishment Battalions, this was the clothing they would wear until they died.

But Steven and Rizzo were not going to be processed. Instead they were placed in adjoining holding cells within sight of the main tower. Reutan took Alis's respirator and placed it in a sterilisation case with the rest. So the guards did not carry respirators as a matter of routine, she noted. That was good.

Reutan offered Alis the opportunity to shower and rest, but she declined his offer. She didn't care for the way Reutan was looking at her. He was just a step away from licking his lips and then trying to lick hers. She had no intention of stripping naked so that he and his friends could perve over her via a remote camera.

That was the other thing she had immediately noticed upon entering the core: the Securitats here were all male, just like the prisoners. Women and girls were rarely banished to the Battalions and so their numbers in the punishment ranks were few, although Alis suspected that any women sentenced to punishment duty, however strong they might have been, would not have lasted long. But there had been numerous female conscripts in the Brigades, which meant that the survivors among them must have been sent to another facility.

Alis asked to be shown to a secure terminal at which she could compose her message. Reutan took her to a screen in the base of the tower, one of five at a single hub. The rest were not being used. He had given her the one facing the door, but she deliberately walked to the other side, behind which there was only a blank wall.

'It really is confidential,' she explained.

Reutan gave a friendly shrug.

'I won't take offence,' he said. 'Perhaps you might like to join me for a drink once you're done?'

'A drink?'

'A poor imitation of cremos that we manufacture. We save the best for guests.'

They were making their own alcohol here? It just got better and better, Alis thought. Their procedures were so lax as to be nonexistent. Still, all of the guards carried pulsers, and while they may have been sloppy in their routines, they were still dangerous.

'I couldn't help but notice as we came in that most of the prison blocks appear to be dark,' she said, ignoring Reutan's invitation.

'We've moved all inmates to the first three blocks,' said Reutan.

'Why?'

'The prisoner population is too small to justify spreading it across all seven blocks, even with the addition of the Brigade intake.'

'You have Brigade troops on Krasis?'

Alis already knew this, but felt obliged to express surprise.

'It was felt that they represented a threat to Illyri stability. Their bases were closed. There was some resistance. The survivors were eventually brought here. Containing all these prisoners in three blocks is more efficient and will make them easier to handle later.'

'Later?'

Reutan waved a hand at their surroundings.

'The facility is being deactivated. We've already begun the process of transferring whatever we need to the evacuation vessels. Soon this will just be an empty shell.'

'What about the prisoners?' asked Alis. 'Where are they being moved to?'

'They're not going anywhere,' said Reutan. 'They're staying here.'

'You're just going to leave them?'

'Our instructions are to disable all support systems before departure.'

'But the prisoners will die. They'll suffocate.'

'You sound very concerned for a bunch of murderers and rebels, Yallee.'

'They're prisoners, and they include troops conscripted to fight for the Illyri.'

'To fight for the *Military*,' Reutan corrected. 'And in case it passed you by, we are at war with the Military.'

Reutan put away whatever small amount of charm he'd been attempting to use on Alis, figuring that it wasn't worth wasting his time on a bleeding-heart Illyri like this one.

'I'll leave you to get on with your communications,' he said.

Alis couldn't resist baiting him.

'What about my drink?' she asked.

'We just ran out.'

'That's a shame. Would you mind closing the door behind you?'

Reutan didn't just close it. He slammed it.

Alis rapidly inputted a series of letters and numbers into the comms recorder and set it to randomly repeat. To the Securitats who were undoubtedly watching the text appear on another screen, it would look like code, and that would make them even more anxious to decipher the message it concealed.

Then she inched up her right sleeve, revealing one of the ports in her skin. She dug for the connector and patched herself into Krasis's central computer using the comms system as a gateway. The initial rush of information was so immense that she jerked in her chair and the back of her right hand slapped hard against the console, until she started to get a handle on the flow. She looked for life support and isolated the cells in the first three blocks. That would keep their oxygen flowing.

Now for the tricky part. She found the oxygen monitors for the core, isolated them, and reprogrammed them so that all minus values became a plus below a set line. Somewhere in the prison, she guessed, was a screen showing oxygen levels, and the whole support system was linked to an alarm. She had already taken care of the alarm, but she didn't want the screen to show what she was up to. Now, if the levels fell below the new line she had set, the system would add bars to the display instead of removing them. As far as anyone monitoring the oxygen would be aware, it would appear to be more or less stable.

Finally, Alis took control of all the doors in the prison, sealing off the living quarters of the off-duty guards, and patched into the security cameras in the three active blocks. She locked the door to the communications room and settled back in her chair.

Only then did she start disabling the core's oxygen supply.

Reutan was anxious to begin interrogating the prisoners as soon as possible. He wasn't sure exactly what he wanted to ask them, but he liked interrogations. Ever since the order had come through to close the facility, life on Krasis had become even duller than usual. The workshops had ceased production, and the humans were being kept in permanent lockdown. Like every other Securitat on Krasis, Reutan wouldn't miss the place one little bit. He'd been sent there as punishment for assaulting a Junior Consul during an argument over a particularly comely aide who, it turned out, was actually the mistress of a Senior Consul, and therefore wouldn't have had anything to do with either of them anyway. But the Junior Consul had influence and Reutan had been packed off to Krasis, with orders to keep his head and his nose clean for a year or two. Once the fuss had died down, he would quietly be restored to his position in the Strategic Intelligence Section, the arm of the Security Directorate responsible for intelligence gathering through acts of blackmail, intimidation and bribery. Reutan had always been a sneak and a liar, but the Securitats had given him a way to put his worst qualities to good use.

Now he sat before a screen and watched as streams of letters and symbols appeared before him. Lerras was to his left. He had just returned from checking on the newcomers.

'How is the girl?' asked Reutan.

'Conscious,' said Lerras. 'She'll just have a headache for a while.'

'I thought she was a bit of all right,' said Reutan.

'If you like that kind of thing.'

Reutan wasn't fussy. He had been deprived of the company of the opposite sex for too long, and wasn't above spending time with a human in the absence of anything better. Especially since Yallee had turned out to be a cold one, which was a shame.

Lerras pointed to the screen.

'What does it all mean?'

'It's code of some sort. I'm running a cryptographic analysis, but so far it's come up empty.'

'It looks like random nonsense.'

Reutan gritted his teeth. The sooner he was off Krasis, the sooner he'd be able to distance himself from oafs like Lerras. He had to keep his temper, though. Lerras was one of the few Securitats on the base with whom Reutan remained on reasonably good terms. Reutan was not likeable. But then, neither was Lerras.

'That's because you're not skilled in cryptography,' Reutan replied. 'It's *supposed* to look like nonsense so that the unskilled will ignore it.'

'If you say so. I don't trust her, though.'

'I don't trust her either, which is why we're monitoring her communications.'

Lerras sat down in a corner of the guardroom, even though Reutan had not given him permission to do so.

'It's stuffy in here,' said Lerras.

'Then go somewhere else.'

But Lerras was right. It was growing uncomfortable in the guardroom, even though the door remained open.

Reutan's head started to throb. He was also beginning to experience some shortness of breath. He pulled up the oxygen monitor on an adjoining screen, but it was safely in the green zone. Something was very wrong.

Selec, one of the older prison officers, appeared at the door. He was struggling to breathe, but he still got his message out.

'First Officer Yallee has locked herself in the comms room,' he said.

And Reutan realised what was happening.

'She's hacked into the system,' he said. 'She's cut off our oxygen. Break that door down!'

Selec departed. Lerras rose and followed him, but he was staggering by the time he got to the door. Meanwhile Reutan tried to undo the damage that Yallee had done and restore their oxygen, but the system was telling him that there *was* no problem with the oxygen, and therefore was blocking his attempts to increase the supply.

The code being inputted by Yallee vanished, to be replaced by a message that Reutan could read without any difficulty at all. It said:

TOO LATE

CHAPTER 39

L erras wasn't quite the fool that Reutan took him for. He might have been a sadist, but the Security Directorate was no place for idiots, and Lerras was gifted with both cunning and a well-developed survival instinct. It was why he had remained close to Reutan, although Reutan was a nasty piece of work, even by the low standards of the Securitats. Reutan's survival instincts were almost as finely honed as Lerras's own.

Before Lerras tried to get to Yallee, he took a detour to the sterilisation units and pulled out a handful of respirators. He put one over his own face and tossed another to Selec, who was already on his knees. He scattered the rest in the direction of the guards who were still conscious, but his priority was to get through the door and beat that sweet-faced little Yallee into oblivion. There would be time for questions later, or maybe not.

Lerras told Selec to blast the door, and that was exactly what Selec did.

Alis had learned a lot during her brief time with Meia. Meia had already been near legendary among the handful of surviving Mechs, even before her experiences on Earth, and she had proven willing to share her knowledge and experience with the younger model.

She had also shared some of her upgrades.

There was a loud bang and the door was blown across the comms room, demolishing the hub of screens. Selec stood framed in the empty doorway, his pulser raised, Lerras to his right. Neither of them had made any effort to protect themselves from fire from within, because Yallee had been unarmed when she entered the facility, and had been given no opportunity to seize a weapon since then.

Thus it was a surprise to Selec when he experienced a painful blow to his chest, but the surprise only lasted for the seconds that it took him to die. Lerras heard the shot and ducked out of the doorway, but not before taking a hit to his left shoulder that spun him round and sent him sprawling to the floor. He raised his pulser to fire but the comms room was dark and he could see no signs of movement. He sent a series of random pulses into the room, causing sparks to fly from what remained of the hub, but was just a fraction too slow in reacting to the flare of light that came in response. He felt a searing pain in his right elbow, and when he looked for the source he saw a smoking stump where the rest of his arm used to be. Beyond it lay his forearm and hand, one finger still gripping the trigger of the pulser.

Lerras's agony was so great that he didn't even see the remaining guards fall under Alis's withering fire, or notice that the doors to the holding cells had opened. Neither did he see Alis toss respirators to the human prisoners, battered but upright, who then made their way back to their ship while Alis restored the oxygen supply. Alarms sounded above his head, and a voice warned that all cell doors in Blocks 1 to 3 had been disarmed, but he barely registered what he was hearing. He reached for his severed arm and with his left hand tried to work his own fingers from their grip on the pulser. He had almost freed the weapon when a shadow appeared above him, and a boot stamped painfully on his remaining fingers.

Yallee picked up his pulser and weighed it in her left hand. A hollow tube had erupted from between the second and third knuckles of her right hand. It was aimed at Lerras's head.

'You kicked my friend unconscious,' said Alis.

'Who are you?' Lerras asked, his words muffled by the mask on his face.

'It doesn't matter who I am. What matters is who you are and what you've done. I accessed your records, Lerras. You like kicking prisoners. My friend can consider herself lucky that you didn't kill her, because you've killed a lot of others in the past.'

Alis looked up at the screens on the tower. She watched the liberated prisoners battling to take control of their blocks. Some of the inmates had been hit by pulser fire from guards who, like Lerras, had had the foresight to don respirators, but the sheer weight of human numbers was already overwhelming their captors. To her right, Steven and Rizzo reappeared. They were now armed with pulse rifles. On the screens, a handful of surviving guards were falling back to the central core down two of the connecting arteries. The third, leading from Block 1, was empty, and Alis saw that the prisoners appeared to be entirely in control of it. Steven and Rizzo took up positions at the mouth of the other two tunnels and started firing at the retreating Securitats.

Alis returned her attention to Lerras, who now understood the nature of his opponent.

'You're a Mech,' he said. 'You're a damned Mech.'

'And you're nothing,' Alis replied. 'When you're gone, no one will even remember your name.'

'Do it,' said Lerras. His face was contorted in pain. 'If you're going to kill me, just get it over with.'

'I'm not going to kill you,' said Alis.

She stepped to one side so that Lerras could see the screens behind her, and the prisoners who were now streaming down the tunnels.

'They are.'

The guards in the arteries tried to hold off the prisoners while responding to the pulse fire from the core, but it was an impossible task. The tunnels were straight and empty of any cover, and Steven and Rizzo picked the Securitats off with ease. Eventually the guards tossed aside their weapons and raised their hands in surrender, but they were immediately lost beneath the swarm of escaping prisoners. Rizzo and Steven went back to rejoin Alis and protect her. She might have been a Mech, and on the side of the good guys, but she looked like an Illyri, and the Krasis prisoners didn't appear to be in the mood to make distinctions. Alis, for her part, was under fire from some guards at the top of the tower who had regained consciousness, and who were now fighting for their lives. Steven turned his pulser on them and fired a series of blasts that reduced the upper reaches of the tower to twisted metal and broken glass, and put an end to the shooting.

Alis patched Steven into the comms system, and his voice sounded throughout the facility as the first prisoners poured into the core.

'My name is Brigade Pilot Steven Kerr,' he said. 'We have seized Krasis on behalf of the Brigades and the Military. Would the officers in command please identify themselves?'

The rush of prisoners slowed, but Steven could see some of them staring suspiciously at Alis. He heard muttered threats and knew that their bloodlust was up. He didn't want to have to shoot anyone, even with only a stun blast. There were easily two hundred men before him. If they turned on their rescuers, it would be a bloodbath.

'Everybody stay where you are!'

Even without amplification the voice rang clearly around the core, honed by years of shouting at recruits on parade grounds and obstacle courses. From the crowd of prisoners emerged the leaner, yet still massive, figure of Master Sergeant Hague. He approached the tower, pausing only to glance at the wounded Lerras.

'I always knew you'd come to a bad end,' Hague told him, then continued on to where Steven and the others were waiting. He stopped before them, clicked his heels together, and smartly saluted.

'Sir!' he said, addressing Steven.

'I don't outrank you, Sergeant,' Steven said. 'I'm not an officer.'

Despite all that had happened, he was still technically a probationary pilot, with only a private's rank. If the mission on Torma had gone according to plan, he'd have received his commission as pilot officer immediately after. But of course, Torma hadn't gone to plan, which was how he'd ended up here, leading a raid on a prison moon. Maybe he should have been keeping a record of his flying hours, just in case. By now he'd have been a pilot officer ten times over.

Hague leaned forward and whispered confidentially.

'Well, I won't tell anyone if you won't,' he said.

He straightened again and stared at a fixed point somewhere over Steven's left shoulder.

'Orders, sir?'

Steven looked at Alis, who shrugged.

'It appears that you're in charge,' she said.

Steven looked around him at the sea of dirty, drawn, expectant faces, so many of them still teenagers, because the Illyri had conscripted only the young and strong. Still, he was more youthful than most of them, but Alis was right: it appeared that he was in charge.

He stretched himself to his full height, ignoring the aches where he'd so recently taken a beating, and gave his first instruction.

'Secure the rest of the facility,' he said, 'Then let's find you some decent food.'

IX
THE SISTERHOOD

CHAPTER 40

'Your Eminence, what a pleasure it is to see you again. You look absolutely ravishing!'

President Krake moved to embrace Ani, his rubbery lips sliding wetly against her ear. Briefly she was engulfed in his sumptuous robes of white and green silk, the colours of the presidency, and she smelled his heavy fragrance, mixed exclusively for him by the government's perfumers. It was rich and heady, with a hint of ripe banana, but underneath there was a note of salt and rot, for even the finest perfumes in all the conquered worlds could not hide the odour of Krake himself, seeping out from deep inside. The president was rotten to the core, a Military General who had long ago cast his lot in with the Diplomats, exchanging credibility for power, for who would ever be greater or more powerful than the leader of all Illyr, or so Krake had reasoned. The answer was nobody, of course – except the puppet-masters pulling his strings, and the quiet choreographers making him dance.

Still, appearances had to be kept up, so Ani endured his greeting for as long as was polite, and not a second more, before withdrawing. Not to be deterred, Krake put his arm around her, his jewelled fingers snaking beneath the short cape that fell from her shoulders, settling too comfortably onto her waist, pressing unhindered against the scalloped cut-out of her dress, the feature of the gown about which Xela had been most enthusiastic.

'It's discreet, but so alluring,' Xela had said, 'and, as Sister Illan says, you have the neatest figure for it, and the smoothest skin.'

Ani had lapped up the praise at the time, but she regretted her conceit now that she could feel Krake's sticky grip on that sliver of exposed flesh. She would have to have a word about that to Xela: no more cut-outs, especially when she was due to see Krake. As for herself, she would have to learn not to indulge her vanity.

'President Krake, you're too kind,' said Ani, finally putting some distance between herself and the president by reaching for the large bouquet of avatis blossoms she'd brought as a gift. She held them before her like a shield.

'These are but a little token of my esteem,' she added, 'grown in the glasshouses of the Marque. The colours are different on Avila Minor. It's to do with the quality of the ultraviolet light, I am told.'

She peered at him from between the stems, offering them to him. He looked back at her in disappointment as he took them, his grabbing hands thwarted for the time being.

'And now let me have a proper look at you, President Krake,' said Ani, her voice like sugar. 'Oh, my goodness, yes. Life is clearly treating you very well. You appear to be in the finest of health. Have you lost weight?'

'Why, thank you Archmage, indeed I have,' Krake said, preening. He was unduly proud of his breezeblock looks and his large, hulking body, which was excessively maintained and curated, if tending a little towards plumpness. If age did not wither him, it was only because he had the very best nutrition, the very best tailors and, naturally, the very best and most discreet surgeon, who tucked the president's flesh back into place whenever it started to unravel, which was often, Ani knew.

In fact, Ani knew more about Krake than he could ever have guessed. After all, he was married to the much younger Merida, a member of the Sisterhood. It was a match that had been orchestrated by Syrene a number of years before, back when the easily manipulated Krake's star was still rising, and his presidency but a dream. Merida herself was elegant and beautiful, and outwardly demure, but she was also smart and sly. This combination made her a perfect agent for the Sisterhood, and her marriage put her right at the heart of the grand seat of the government in Tannis – palatial Opula – enabling her to stroke Krake's ego while he laid bare his secrets. Merida might well be Krake's wife, and mother to his children, but she was a devoted daughter of the Nairenes first and foremost, and it was with them that her loyalties lay.

Of course, there were others who were useful to Ani, and they assumed many guises. Briefly, she caught the eye of the presidential advisor who stood behind Krake, just to his right, dressed in the gold and black of the Diplomatic Corps.

Lord Garin.

His uniform skimmed his limbs, neatly covering his firm, honeyed skin, hiding his sculpted physique from her sight, if not from her mind. Lord Garin was beautiful, both in uniform and, Ani knew, out of it. He smiled at her now – a naughty, secret smile – but she looked through him impassively, for this morning's purpose was business. With luck there would be time for pleasure later – pleasure, and the artfully leaked secrets that sometimes followed as Garin expressed his devotion to her. He gave her titbits and made her promises, and sometimes begged for her hand in marriage. Ani understood his game, for she was nothing if not practical; it was only natural that he should propose to her, because what ambitious young Lord would not dream of making the most powerful Illyri female of all into his bride, and even more so when she was so sweet-looking into the bargain? Yet she resisted his formal approaches of marriage, suspecting they might not have been offered at all if she had been just another Sister, with no power and no sway. Nevertheless, Garin was a glorious balm, and he did something to her. He did many things to her. Looking at him made her tingle inside.

'Do tell me, dear Krake,' Ani said, turning her attention back to the president, and secretly enjoying how Garin's brow furrowed unhappily at the perceived rejection, 'how is our beloved Sister Merida? I long to see her.'

'Then it shall be arranged, Archmage! She is currently in the presidential apartments in the Tree of Lights. Shall I summon her here to greet you? I'm sure she'd be thrilled to pay you her respects in person. You know, I would have invited her to join us at our little luncheon, but I'd hate her to be bored by our business talk, or confused by the more technical details of diplomacy.'

He laughed as if the thought of Merida understanding anything complicated at all, whether diplomatic details or otherwise, was an amusing one.

Ani laughed too.

'Oh no,' she said. 'Don't do that. Don't disturb her. Perhaps I can see her this afternoon. We can have a little chat, just the two of us, in your apartments. A catch-up.'

Krake was still smiling, but his eyebrows lowered suspiciously. He seemed about to find a way to insinuate himself into this meeting of the Sisterhood – Krake might have been pompous and vain, yet he was not entirely a fool – but Ani leapt in first.

'And, of course, we'd hate to bore you with our female talk, President,' she added airily. She laughed again, her right hand alighting briefly on his arm as she flirted to distract him. 'I know how devoted she is to your comfort and the care of your household. You won yourself a rare prize with her – as did she, with you – but we on Avila Minor still speak of her fondly, and often.'

We speak *with* her too, thought Ani to herself, still smiling as Krake preened some more, smoothing his clothes over his belly and puffing his chest up like a rooster. Only the week before, Merida had been spilling secrets about her husband, overflowing with information about whom he'd been meeting with, and what had been said, in one of the many informal conversations Ani regularly had with the clutch of Nairene Sisters who had been insinuated through marriage into the highest ranks of Illyri society. Syrene had certainly ensured they were placed well: a wife for a general, another for a high-powered bureaucrat; a Nairene here, another there; pretty, polite, elegant, diplomatic, and deeply duplicitous.

Merida was the most elevated of all, but she was in her thirties now and bored witless by sharing her life with the blustering figurehead president, attending functions on his arm like a shining, perfectly poised charm while expected to keep her opinions and thoughts to herself. She was but the First Lady, she regularly complained to Ani, and a lady she was expected to be at all times. Her life was lived atop a pedestal, she said, where things were put on display to be admired, but there was nowhere to go from a pedestal except down. If her husband fell from grace – and all politicians eventually make that drop – Merida had no intention of falling with him, hence her continued role as a spy for the Sisterhood, albeit under the new Archmage, Ani Cienda. Even her own offspring weren't loved and valued as dearly as her Sisters.

'Are the children well?' Ani now asked Krake.

'Very well. Little Syrene is already talking about becoming a Sister. She's only seven!'

'Well you know there's a place for her as soon as she is old enough, if you can bear to part with her. We'd be honoured to welcome her. And what of the baby, Gradus?'

Ani tried not to wince as she said the name. It was one thing naming a child after Syrene – after all, at the time of the child's birth, Syrene had been Archmage, and Krake would have been anxious to remain in her good graces – but naming his son after her first, and now deceased, husband was quite another. It said much about the limits of Krake's power that nobody of any consequence was naming children after him.

She let Krake rattle on about his young son as they slowly made their way from the anteroom into the chamber where their official meetings always took place. It was a vast space, carved out of a mountainous chunk of deep blue crystal that jutted at an angle from the ground, as if it had burst from the earth aeons before. Whether it had, or if it was but a whimsical piece of architecture, Ani could not say – the chamber was ancient, its origins unknown – but the effect was startling. Its jagged spires cut into the air, fading from deepest ocean blue through sapphire to the palest aquamarine, and then the topmost shards melted into clear glass, letting in sunlight dappled with shadows of violet. They were striking surroundings, but that was of no consequence to Krake. It was obvious to Ani why he chose these rooms, and only these rooms, for her meetings with him: they were in a direct line of sight from the Tree of Lights, the shining skyscraper that was home to five thousand of Illyr's most wealthy and powerful citizens. Those peering curiously out of their Tree of Lights windows towards the presidential palace of Opula – perhaps scanning it with their spyglasses – were more than likely to glimpse Krake in the blue room beneath the clear shards of the roof, talking to the female in telltale red. It offered visible proof that he was having yet another private audience with the public face of the mighty Sisterhood, and visible proof of his position.

As if to confirm Ani's suspicions, Krake now sat with his big face in a shaft of light, carefully angled towards the Tree, and insisted that Ani was seated with her back to it, her silver hair catching the lazy Illyr sun, the sweep of her red cape on vibrant display down the back of her chair like the tail of a bloodied peacock.

She tossed her head: let them look. Let Krake think that he mattered more than he did: such displays wouldn't cause the cleverest Illyri, the ones who really mattered, to alter their view of the puppet president. When compared to everything else Ani had to contend with, stroking Krake's ego was but a piece of grit in her shoe. She knew this and so she tolerated him. Anyway, she reasoned, she would have her reward later. She glanced surreptitiously towards Garin, and immediately looked away again to hide her secret pleasure. It was the only true inducement for keeping up this charade of consultation with Krake.

As usual, Krake had nothing of interest to share with Ani. He merely told her of developments about which she already knew, and of secrets to which she was already privy. No matter – at the very least, her presence here was a reminder of the influence of the Sisterhood. It would also serve as a useful check to Krake's deputy, Vice-President Dyer, who was the true power in the government of Illyr. Ani's regular visits to Illyr served notice to Dyer that the young Archmage of the Nairene Sisterhood was not content merely to be a passive observer, but was an active participant in Illyri life, and a figure of power in the ongoing conflict.

Dyer was a shrewd Diplomat but, more importantly, he had cargo onboard, for one of the Others lived in his head. Krake was little better than the greeter at an upmarket restaurant, but Dyer – Dyer was something else. When he and Ani met it was always by design disguised as accident, on both their parts, and they circled each other politely, giving a little here, getting a little there, holding their proverbial cards tightly to their chests, and playing their hands carefully. In public, at banquets and balls, both kept up the charade that Krake was in charge. In private, his name was rarely mentioned between them.

'And how, Archmage, is my old friend Syrene?' asked Krake as the conversation foundered. 'Do you see much of her now that she has sequestered herself in the Marque? The Archmage was so very involved in our processes and so very social. The Sisterhood must miss her terribly. I know we certainly do down here.'

'Do you now?' said Ani coolly, and Krake squirmed as she lanced him with a stare. 'I remind you, sir, that *Mage* Syrene elected to remove herself from public life in order that she might dedicate the remainder of her days to the pursuit of deeper, more profound knowledge. It was her choice, as was I as her replacement, selected by her personally. And as far as the Sisterhood is concerned, we can only benefit from the Mage's selfless immersion in learning, even amidst her personal grief.'

'Ah yes, of course. Poor Andrus. That was shocking, just shocking . . .'

And it had been, although Ani preferred not to dwell on the death of the former Governor of Great Britain, and the father of the girl who had once been her closest friend, Syl Hellais. The Other that was wrapped around Andrus's brainstem – implanted in him by Syrene, as a means of making Andrus hers – had been driven into an apparently inexplicable frenzy at about the time of Syrene's retreat from public life, with the result that Syl's father had died of a massive, explosive haemorrhage to the brain. Those at the Opera House with whom he had been sharing a bottle – or several – of cremos at the time of the incident had needed treatment for shock. One witness, the career politician Sevi, still carried a disinfectant cloth with her at all times, and obsessively wiped imaginary gore from her permanently horrified face. Needless to say, her career was not what it once had been. Few knew the true cause of Andrus's death, though. Officially, it was blamed on an undiagnosed illness caused by a bacterial infection from his time on Earth.

Ani wondered how much of the truth was known to Krake. She wasn't certain what he knew about the Others, or whether he had simply chosen not to know. Sometimes she wondered if Krake might not be cleverer than he was given credit for, although Merida assured her that this was not the case.

'But of course, Syrene did tell me personally of her intention to retire before it was made public,' boasted Krake, 'and she whispered your name as her choice of successor. She regularly confided in me, and I like to think that you and I continue this special relationship, Archmage Ani.'

'Naturally,' said Ani, who shared no confidences with Krake that she would not also have broadcast on every available Illyri channel of communication.

The president preened for a while longer, talking of nothing, as Garin watched Ani quietly over his boss's shoulder, occasionally pulling a face. She thought she might laugh so, as soon as it seemed decent, she asked to be shown to her quarters, suggesting that the president had given her rather a lot to mull over, and it would take her some time to process the ramifications of this new information.

'I need to make some notes now, to let all of this sink in,' she said solemnly. 'I'd also like to discuss what you've told me with my aides. But may I again express my deep personal gratitude for your efforts, President Krake? You are unfailingly generous with your time and expertise. And please know that I will quite understand if you don't have the time to spare for luncheon this afternoon. I realise how busy and in demand you are, and I have already monopolised you for far too long.'

Please cancel, she thought, *please just cancel.*

'Fear not, your Eminence,' he said, expansively, 'for I have allowed myself a little time later, and I am very much looking forward to dining with you, though your humility is charming.'

Oh. Oh damn.

'Wonderful,' she said, and she hoped that her face did not give the lie to the word. Just to be safe, she clouded a little as she smiled. 'I look forward to it. Now perhaps Lord Garin can show me to my rooms?'

'Certainly,' said Krake, snapping his fingers at the young Diplomat arrogantly. 'Come now! You heard the Archmage, Garin. And do ensure that you look after our esteemed guest, or you'll have me to deal with.'

'Of course,' said the young Lord. 'I guarantee that the Archmage will have no cause for complaint.'

CHAPTER 41

With a final leer at Ani, Krake left the room. Garin escorted Ani to the sweet privacy of her usual chambers and joined her inside, the door sliding quietly shut behind him. With hands like silk, he unwound the cape she held around her and slid his fingers into the cut-outs at her waist.

'I've been wanting to do that all morning,' he whispered.

Ani raised an eyebrow at him.

'Really, Lord Garin,' she teased, 'I'm not sure that's quite what President Krake meant when he said you should look after his guest.'

She reached out and unclipped the first clasp on his uniform, the one covering the golden dip below his throat. Watching him for a response, she stroked her fingers over his exposed skin.

'Well,' he replied, husky with anticipation, 'you of all Illyri should know that I believe in going above and beyond the call of duty . . .'

Some time later, Ani lay back on her pillows and listened as Garin grumbled about having to get back to work, yet made no move to leave. Ani was sated and satisfied. This time, however, Garin was not.

'Why,' Garin said as he kissed her full on the lips, yet again, 'can you not acknowledge me in public? I want to marry you, but I'm not even allowed to take hold of your hand beyond these walls. Do you not feel what we have as deeply as I, Ani? Whenever I leave you I want to shout it from the highest mountains – "I'm in love with the Archmage Ani!" – for all to hear.'

That, thought Ani, would be very bad. Already rumours were circulating about the closeness of the relationship between the Archmage and the president's senior aide. If Garin did start broadcasting the truth of it – and Ani's spies assured her that, so far, he had not discussed it even with his closest friends, but who knew how long his discretion would last? – then she might be forced to silence him. She did not want that to happen. She cared for him, but she cared more to protect her power and her position. She could see no advantage to a public union with Garin, or not yet. When, or if, the time came, it would be her decision to make. Garin, she sometimes suspected, did not fully understand where the true power lay in their relationship.

'Oh Garin,' she said, 'you say you love me, but would you be so willing to shout it if I were merely Ani Cienda, a girl who had nothing?'

'What do you mean?' He stroked her shoulder, absently using his thumb to ease a fold from the sheet that was wrapped around her, his face close to hers, his eyes not moving from her own. They were an unusual colour, she thought, even for an Illyri: as dark as evergreen leaves, as clear as water.

'What I mean is, would you be so anxious to tie your happily-ever-afters to mine if I were a creature with no power, and with no influence?'

He nuzzled his face into her hair and spoke against her ear, quiet yet insistent.

'But you're not that creature,' he purred. His lips played on her lobe and she shivered with pleasure despite herself. 'You're not, any more than I am a pauper from the alleys of Lower Tannis. Were you that nobody, and were I that pauper, then yes, I would feel the same about you. Of course I would feel the same. How could I not?'

His breath brushed delicately against the little hairs on her neck. 'But, Ani, we're not those beings. We are what we are; we both hold high stations. Why fight it?'

'But what if I didn't hold a high station?' she persisted.

'But you do!'

He pressed his mouth against her throat now, open, warm and tender, and she almost gave in, for his touch was so compelling. But then she pulled away, angry at her own weakness.

'Garin! I mean it.'

'My lovely Ani . . . Archmage Ani . . . Ani Cienda, whoever you choose to believe you are, whatever you choose to call yourself, ultimately it does not matter to me. I only dream of what we could be together.'

He brushed a strand of her hair away from her eyes, twirling it delicately between his fingers, before tucking it behind her ear as she stared down at her hands.

'Please, most precious one,' he said, tracing his fingers around the spiral of leaves tattooed on her cheek, stopping at the ever-watchful eye at its centre, 'don't let the things that we are *not* be what hold us back. Instead, let what we *are* be that which drives us forward. Marry me! Please, marry me!'

She paused, appearing to consider it, then looked at him straight on, unflinching, a challenge on her face.

'But do you actually love me, Garin,' she asked starkly, 'or am I just a good career move?'

His gaze wavered very briefly, but it was enough for Ani to doubt his answer.

'Of course I do!' he responded. 'Didn't I just tell you so?'

She shifted position, moving slightly away from him. He bent towards her to kiss her again, aware that the atmosphere between them had changed and anxious to bridge the distance.

'No,' she said, placing her hand on his chest and pushing lightly. 'Enough now. You must go. I have things to attend to. I think we're done here.'

His temple twitched as he regarded her and he appeared about to ignore her protestations – she watched him start to call up that winning smile of his, the one that always got him what he wanted – but before he could finish she, in turn, summoned her most practised glare and let it blaze cold and bright.

'I am sure your president needs you, Lord Garin,' she said, her tone tolerating no dissent. 'I fear you've attended to his guest's needs for far too long.'

At that, Garin moved away, letting go of her shoulder as if it were nothing, giving a shrug, dismissing the intimacy of their time together. His wonderful mouth turned down at the corners, displeased, and she found herself contemplating – momentarily, horribly – what it would feel like to smack him in that same beautiful mouth, to split his lip as if it were a balloon filled with blood. She wanted to hurt him, for she hated that he could hurt her.

'I'm not your plaything, *Archmage* Ani,' he said. His voice was chilly.

He had that much correct, at least: she, Ani Cienda, was the Archmage, even if Garin couldn't quite grasp what that meant in real terms. Even in the great, advanced Illyri society, there were those who believed that females were essentially a form of adornment, and even the greatest of them would sacrifice all at the altar of the right male suitor.

'Be that as it may,' she replied, 'you forget that I am not to be toyed with either. Before you propose marriage to me again, try to ensure that your motives are pure. Sometimes I fear that you underestimate my intelligence, and my position. I am no mere pawn in your game: I am a queen in all but name . . . but then I guess you've never played chess.'

'Chess?' repeated Garin. He looked annoyed. He didn't like not knowing things.

'An Earth game. The queen is the most powerful piece, not the king. Perhaps you might start considering the implications of this – in solitude – while Krake lunches with me, in private. You shall inform him that you will not be joining us, for urgent business requires you to eat later, and alone.'

Garin opened his mouth to speak, but she held up her hands and clapped them together lightly.

'Thank you, Lord Garin. That will be all. You are free to go.'

Quivering with rage, Garin stood and stared down at her, his chest heaving, before he turned and strode from the room, slamming the button that activated the exit and nearly falling over Cocile as he left, for she was crouched outside, listening, or attempting to listen, for the doors of Opula were thick and the walls impregnable. Together the two Sisters watched Garin leave, his jacket still unfastened and billowing behind him. Ani was grim, but her attendant was open-mouthed in shock.

'Sister Cocile,' snarled Ani as she rose to shut the door on her aide's appalled, blushing face, 'go find entertainment of your own, damn you. Your voyeurism is beginning to give me the creeps.'

Ani had lunch with the president in a glamorous dining room beside his office, under yet another glass roof. However, this one was held aloft by old, gnarled trees, echoing the great Palace of Erebos, and their chairs were presumptuously placed at right angles to each other, close and rather too intimate under the cosy curve of branches, hidden beneath a curtain of leaves, like lovers in a bower. How had Syrene handled him, she wondered, but then Syrene was substantially older than her young replacement, and significantly more experienced. Ani ate quickly, anxious to be gone from the presidential palace. The formal meetings with Krake were tedious enough, but the ritual of an informal lunch was nearly more than she could bear.

'Give me a kiss in parting, my dear Archmage Ani,' Krake said as she took her leave, and his lips plumped out of his shining broad face like the peeled segments of a saliva-sticky plum. 'Give me a kiss that I may pass on to your beloved Sister Merida.'

Ani's cold laughter tinkled around them, and instead she plucked the clutch of avatis blooms from where they'd been placed in a vase on the furthest corner of the table.

'Here,' she said, pressing the flowers into Krake's outstretched arms so that their heavy blossoms were crushed into his chin, their wet stems dripping onto his robes, 'give Merida these instead. I'm sure your loving wife would prefer flowers from the glasshouses of the Marque to secondhand kisses bestowed on her loyal husband by another.'

You slimeball, she added to herself as Krake regarded her drunkenly.

'Now I really must take my leave of you, President Krake,' she continued, more sweetly, as she gathered her cape around her.

'Let me call Garin to assist you,' said Krake, his features souring. He spoke Garin's name as if issuing a challenge, and Ani knew then that he had heard the rumours too. Perhaps this added to his notion that she was available to . . . *play*. Her flesh crawled at the thought, but it also reminded her of how incautious she had been with Garin. She might have been the Archmage, but her youth made her vulnerable, and she knew that powerful forces on Illyr were looking for an excuse to dismiss her as inconsequential and inexperienced – dismiss her, and worse, for there was no shortage of candidates in the Marque who might wish to replace her should any harm befall her.

'No need for assistance, my dear President,' Ani said.

She took a tiny silver bell from her pocket and rang it. Immediately several of her red-clad aides appeared to lead her away. She pressed her cheek briefly to Krake's as she left in an attempt to make amends, kissing the air near his ear. He perked up immediately and his hand reached for her as if he wished to extend the embrace, but she was already gliding away.

Ani did not see Garin again before she left. She chose not to, for if Krake suspected their relationship, then others did too, all scheming how best to use any attachment for their own purposes.

But more importantly, she knew that the absence of farewells would annoy Garin. She only wished it didn't make her feel quite so annoyed too.

CHAPTER 42

Mercifully, the Archmage Ani had little time to muse upon her bruised feelings, for she had other liaisons that afternoon and late into the night – liaisons that should prove more fruitful than her absurd dalliances with President Krake. More fruitful, and more dangerous.

With political pawns like the president, audiences were public and came with fanfare, highlighted in his official diary for all to see. Images of Ani and Krake together would appear on newsfeeds afterwards, and gossip would spread like flames in a drought, with details of what might have been said, how long they spent together, what meals were taken, what was eaten, and always what the Archmage wore, for the rise to power of the striking young Sister was an endless source of fascination for the chattering classes. Undoubtedly, the cut-outs on her misjudged dress would be copied by fashionable folk of Tannis, but she knew it would be a short-lived trend for she herself would not wear that style again. Wryly, she hoped Krake had enjoyed it while it lasted.

But there were others to whom a request to meet the Archmage was always delivered quietly and without public bells and whistles. Such invitations made the recipients feel special and valued, believing themselves to be singled out for favour. To these meetings Ani wore her red Nairene robes, and numbers were kept to an absolute minimum: the more influential the guest, the more private the audience. Ani understood full well that those whom she met under these circumstances were flattered to be the focus of the Archmage's attention. She let it be known to them that they were part of her golden circle, irreplaceable, invaluable, worth their weight in precious stones. Sometimes it was actually true. She told them secrets, she told them truths, she told them half-truths and bald lies, and in return they spilled their own secrets, believing that the Sisterhood was the great, subtle, hidden power operating in the Illyri universe.

But there were also those who convened with Ani who knew better, who knew about the Others, for they carried the ancient beings within themselves – those like Dyer. The Illyri who pulled the strings of figurehead politicians like Krake were themselves being manipulated. They might have believed themselves to have struck a deal with the parasites, convinced that they remained in control even as the Others extended their tendrils through them, but they were wrong. It was not so much the Sisterhood but the Others who were the hidden guiding force in Illyri affairs, and it was they that Ani feared most of all. They had corrupted the Illyri and pushed the entire society into a costly, brutal civil war. And it was they who could ultimately tear her beloved Sisterhood apart, because one of the most powerful of all these Others waited like a malignancy deep within the heart of the Marque. Syl Hellais had discovered it there all those years before, and it had ultimately led to her presumed destruction.

Sometimes, when Ani thought of Syl, she felt young and foolish again, transported back to the teenager she had been: impressionable, gullible and anxious to please. But she was no longer that child, she told herself, and she knew better than Syl did what the Sisterhood – indeed, what the entire Illyri race – was up against.

She corrected herself: she knew better than Syl ever *had*, for there was no doubt in Ani's mind that Syl was dead. More than four years had passed since she'd last seen her childhood playmate, four years since Syl had fled to the ends of the known universe, making her escape into the Derith wormhole from which no one ever returned.

Like Syl before her, Ani now knew of the Other that dwelt in the Marque, and she had learned something of how the creature func-tioned – how the *creatures* functioned, for they were many, implanted in the heads of numerous host Illyri, morphing and changing as required. Now they were on Earth too, infecting, spawning, always growing in number, greedy for new life, for fresh hosts, for more terrain. But the earth would not keep them satisfied forever. Eventually, they would hunger for new flesh.

By this point they must have thoroughly infested the blue planet. Of that there could be little doubt. Even though years had passed since she had left Earth, still Ani felt guilt and sadness at the thought of that lost world. It was the planet upon which her mother, Fian, had last been seen alive, and on which Fian's husband – she could no longer easily bring herself to use the word 'father' of him – had abandoned her. For that, Ani had not yet forgiven him, and saw little hope of doing so. She had been told that no life form – no human, no Illyri, no Agron and no Galatean – could possibly still survive on the planet that had once been her home. That meant Fremd was gone too, and Just Joe, and Heather and little Alice; all those in the Resistance who had saved her life had now been annihilated because the Others hungered for a new breeding ground, and the Illyri had gladly handed it to them.

Ani understood that the Others were many, but they were also psychically connected – she could find no more apt description – to one another. This did not mean that they were equal. Some were clearly more powerful than the rest, and the entity that dwelt deep in the Marque was just such a creature.

Ani thought of it as the One.

In the beginning, the One had infiltrated the Nairenes and then the Illyri like a kind of feel-good drug, drip-feeding information to the elders of the Sisterhood, for they craved knowledge like an opioid. This single, alien organism, discovered lying dormant in a meteor, had come to life in the Marque. In reaching out to it, in trying to communicate, Ezil, the greatest of the Sisterhood, had become infected: a burst of spores, an intake of breath, and it was done.

Yet at first it had seemed more like a visitation, a blessing, than an infestation. As the Other inside Ezil grew, the One communicated with this, the first of its offspring, and through it began sharing just a fraction of its great knowledge with the old Nairene. The Others were ancient, and the One had been travelling on its meteor for the time that it took stars to die, absorbing the stuff of the universe while maintaining contact with the rest of its kind, learning as they learned. For Ezil, the alien creature growing inside her became a point of connection with the secrets of existence, the arcana of creation. In turn, blinded by knowledge, she encouraged the rest of the First Five, the rulers of the Sisterhood, to allow the Others to enter them.

And all the time the One grew. It became the control tower, receiving and relaying information, sending out instructions via a form of telepathy so old and complex as to be beyond all understanding. By now, the creatures with which it communicated were wrapped around the brainstems of key Illyri – the First Five, and an unknown number of senior members of the Diplomatic Corps, for as the Sisterhood thirsted for knowledge, so too did the Diplomats desire power, and it was promised to them by the Others.

At the outset, it appeared to be a symbiotic relationship, for all the life forms involved benefited, and the hosts remained autonomous, eating, sleeping, exercising, working, and reproducing unhindered while the Others settled quietly within them, surviving while the Illyri survived, thriving when they thrived. The Others experienced the universe through the senses of the Illyri who carried them, and as the Conquests expanded, so too did the invaluable information that the Others drip-fed to their thirsty hosts.

However, as Ani wryly reminded herself, particularly as her meal with the unpalatable Krake sat like clay in her gut, there is no such thing as a free lunch. In time, the Nairenes were to find out that the Others would remain benevolent only so long as they were not crossed, and the line between the identity of the host organisms and the parasites began to blur. Doing what needed to be done to preserve the One and the Others, to extend the reach and influence of this species, became second nature to the infected Illyri, and then first nature, and then the only thing that mattered.

Yet by the time the Sisters understood the truth about their supposed benefactors it was too late, for the clock had ticked onwards on the Marque, and the time to remedy the situation had long passed, along, perhaps, with the will to do so. The First Five had tried to wriggle out of the bargain and failed. In turn, they were sacrificed to the One, connected to it permanently as sacrifices and reservoirs of knowledge, but also as a source of food and energy. The Others fed off their hosts, absorbing nutrients from them: not so much that the host organism would notice, or grow weak, but just enough to keep the Other alive. But the One was not like the rest, and its needs were greater. It required the five most powerful Sisters to feed it, and it drained them slowly and painfully as the years went by. A new deal had been made with the Others, and the Archmage Syrene had struck it. The beast was appeased and both the Sisterhood and the Others were satisfied: the Sisters had increasingly vast stores of knowledge and the power that came with it, and the Others had life.

Under the leadership of Syrene, the infection spread. More and more of the key Diplomats succumbed, either willingly or by force, for Syrene reasoned that this was the best way for the Sisterhood to keep abreast of what was going on far below on their homeworld of Illyr. Information would be relayed directly back to the One, and in turn fed by it to the Sisterhood, and so the Nairenes would always be one step ahead, always aware of what would be before it came to pass. And so, even when isolated on the Marque, they would know all.

It was thus that Syrene had learned of the death of her ally Oriel at the hand of Syl Hellais, even before the body had been found, for the powerful Other that had lived for so long within Oriel had writhed and convulsed along with the old crone as she died. Nearby, in the cavern of the Marque where the One had its domain, this vile creature had felt the pain of its offspring's passing and was filled with fury. As Oriel's dying eyes had looked into Syl's, the One within had registered Syl's face, and relayed the information back to Syrene on Erebos, where she was already orchestrating the assassination of her enemies – and by extension, those of the Others. Her wedding to Syl's widowed father had been the perfect ruse, for everyone was invited, and so everyone was vulnerable.

Into this bloodbath had arrived Syl, fleeing from the consequences of what she had done to Oriel, and into the trap that would now be sprung on her by Syrene. But then the Kerr brothers had snatched Syl away before she could be punished for her crimes.

Civil war had erupted, for the deaths on Erebos were merely the prelude to the great strike that would wipe out the Military and, theoretically, end the war almost as soon as it had begun, leaving an Illyri society ruled by the Diplomats, the Sisterhood and – through them – the Others.

That, of course, was not what happened. The Military establishment was badly wounded but not destroyed, and now the war had been dragging on for years. What Ani sometimes wondered was if all this slaughter had occurred because the Others had wanted it, and had sown the seeds of ambition in the Diplomats and their allies, or because the Diplomats and their kind were already ambitious, already desirous of the annihilation of the Military, and the Others had simply provided them with the power to do so.

Whatever the truth might be, Ani knew that all of this chaos would not have come to pass had the One not been found by Ezil all those years before. It was the original enemy, and yet she continued to feed it, for if she did not then it would devour her.

It would devour them all.

CHAPTER 43

With Cocile at her side and shadowed by her personal guards, Toria and Liyal, Ani arrived at the Tree of Lights. Illyri pedestrians stopped and gawked as the four Nairenes took the short walk between the compounds, scrabbling for devices to capture three-dimensional images of Ani and whatever fashion she was wearing that day, and the way the breeze turned her hair to waves. They nudged each other and nodded approvingly as they stared after the young, beautiful Archmage and her vibrant entourage.

Theirs was a pleasant stroll through a particularly elegant part of Upper Tannis, and Ani enjoyed the vista of sparkle and glass, the reflective spires like stalagmites growing from the white quartz streets. It was safe for one such as her to walk here, for in these rarefied confines Diplomatic rule was respected and the Sisterhood admired. Elsewhere, particularly among the poorer citizens, support still existed for the Military, and areas such as Gomor, Perl and Dannat were hotbeds of Military sympathisers, from which bombings and assassinations were ordered on a regular basis, despite vicious crackdowns by the Securitats.

But while Upper Tannis was far from such dens of unrest, still Ani formed a pleasant yet remote half-smile on her lips, and with the force of her mind she willed the wealthy citizenry to keep their distance. They did, of course they did, although they did not know the reason, and later they would wonder why they had not greeted the Archmage, or even tried to introduce themselves and perhaps make an important connection.

Within minutes, the branches of the Tree spread like a crown above the Sisters. As they waited to be granted entry, Ani understood why many who did not live here muttered privately that it had forever spoilt the iconic skyline of their beautiful, steepled city. By day it cast ungainly shadows over lesser buildings, while every waking hour a multitude of private craft buzzed about its numerous staggered landing bays like bugs around a gaudy plant, and by night its cloud of dotted lights was a random distortion amidst Tannis's spires of neat silver.

Once inside, all of that was left behind. The interior, while undeniably luxurious, was muted and discreet. Everything was cool, fragrant and hushed, from the melodious voice of the handsome concierge who welcomed them, to the pearl vases containing vast floral arrangements as white and fresh as flurries of tamed snow.

'Her Eminence, the Archmage Ani of the Nairene Sisterhood, is here to visit the First Lady Merida,' announced Cocile as she stepped forward. Ani stood back, her chin raised, a practised expression of unconcern on her face. She made it a habit not to speak to underlings in such situations, for this was all a game and she knew well enough how to play it.

'Of course,' said the concierge. He looked at Ani in something like awe. 'Archmage, it is my great pleasure to welcome you and your entourage to the Tree of Lights. We are charmed.'

Ani sighed. It was one thing her knowing how to play the game, but another to expect everyone else to understand the rules too. Being haughty was an exhausting business.

'We have been here before. Many times,' she said in a voice of cracking ice, leaving the concierge blushing and noticeably flustered as he turned from her to the screen in front of him, and tapped on it urgently.

'I'm sorry,' he mumbled, more to himself than to her. 'I'm new here.'

There was a chiming noise and a glass pod alighted softly beside his station. At once the concierge regained his professionalism.

'The First Lady awaits you, your Eminence,' he said. 'Please mind your step.'

They all got in, Ani first, perching primly on the cushioned glass benches around the curved wall of the lift.

'Very good,' said Cocile on behalf of the entourage as she brought up the rear. She smiled stiffly at the concierge and Ani noted, with hidden amusement, that Cocile was the only one to accept his offered hand to assist her in entering the pod. The concierge was certainly terribly good-looking, but then why wouldn't he be? Her people were vain, and pleasant features, like beautiful possessions, were held in high esteem. There were none who regarded themselves so highly as the residents of the Tree, and therefore their concierge would be expected to look the part.

For a moment the concierge seemed about to say something more, then changed his mind. He stepped back from the pod. The door closed and they were off, calmly being carried through the still air of the place, the crystal artery of the central trunk narrowing around them as they were borne upwards. Near the top, a neat gap opened in the clear wall of the inner crown, just as if the solid surface had liquefied, and the pod slipped through. Immediately, the glass melted shut behind them again, and they came to rest in a wide corridor tiled in sheets of mother-of-pearl. The pod door opened. Waiting for them was a female Illyri swathed in familiar red, but the fabric could never be as vibrant as the blood-coloured hair that clouded her angular skull and set off her eyes, for they were remarkable, redder yet than her hair, wide and vivid as enormous rubies pressed into the smooth golden skin of her face.

She sparkled. She was like a jewel.

'Merida,' breathed Cocile, with rare and genuine pleasure. She had been a Novice years before with the president's wife, and they were been close friends. Ultimately, Merida's looks had resulted in her departure from the Marque and her delivery like a prize to Krake. Her sharp-faced friend Cocile had been left behind, initially forlorn and, truth be told, not a little jealous, but the affection had remained between them long after the youthful bitterness had gone.

They alighted from the pod, Toria and Liyal leading, and Ani stepping out behind, though she could feel Cocile buzzing with energy and impatience at her back. Nonetheless, she moved slowly, regally, as befitted the serene leader of the Nairene Sisterhood, for Cocile needed to remember her place.

'Archmage, you are very welcome,' said Merida, bowing a little at the hips, but her eyes darted to Cocile.

'Thank you, Sister,' replied Ani, inclining her head in response. 'It is good of you to meet us in person.' Then she relented. 'As you can see, today I am accompanied by my aide, Cocile. I'm sure that you are as anxious to renew acquaintance with her as she is with you.'

She turned and nodded graciously at Cocile. Unable to contain her joy, the usually reserved handmaiden pressed forward and threw herself into Merida's outstretched arms.

'Cocile!' Merida said happily, and she laughed.

'How I've missed you,' said Cocile in response, and she kissed Merida three times, first on the left cheek, then on the right, and finally square on the lips. They both giggled. Something inside Ani felt like it was being stretched taut as she watched the little tableau play out: the touching of noses, the giggle, the foreheads pressed close together, at once so familiar yet so alien. She remembered Syl, and thought of Tanit: one friend slain by another. She looked away and swallowed down something she couldn't name, something she'd spent years trying to forget, but it was still there, circling beneath the surface, waiting to consume her if she allowed it to break through the ice and reveal itself.

'Merida,' she started to say, but it came out soft and damaged, so she cleared her throat and tried again – 'Merida, shall we go in?' – and this time her voice was strong and commanding, and they all knew it was an instruction, not a request.

Instantly, Merida disentangled herself from Cocile.

'Certainly, your Eminence.'

Once they were seated, Merida confirmed that all her staff had been dismissed for the day the moment that she learned of the Archmage's impending visit. Without another word being said, as one Toria and Liyal reached into their robes and withdrew small metal boxes from their pockets. Toria opened hers first, and out flocked a throng of tiny flying creatures in a multitude of colours, each no bigger than the tip of a pencil. Immediately they buzzed away, heading into all corners of the room, and then through the door into the presidential chambers beyond.

Liyal opened her box at the same time and tipped its contents onto the floor. A tangle of jet-black worms tumbled out and unknotted themselves before sliding off at high speed, blurring as their bodies shaped to every corner and nook that they explored.

'There's really no need,' said Merida as the electronically modified creatures, designed to sniff out signs of surveillance, searched the rooms. 'My staff are handpicked, independently vetted, and completely trustworthy. Our quarters are scanned for bugs daily and there are surveillance blockers on all our entrances. We're perfectly secure here.'

Ani ignored her. So too did Toria and Liyal as the searchers went about their business. Several silent, strained minutes passed.

'Clear,' said Toria at last, as her swarm returned to their box and were once again sealed inside. Liyal waited, her box open on the floor as worms slid back into it. She frowned as the counter inside its lid clicked to 99 then stopped, and her head cocked expectantly, waiting. They all heard it at the same time, a quiet blip, getting louder and more urgent. It was coming from the vicinity of an ornate antique chest on stubby legs, intricately carved from a boulder of fiery blue opal. Liyal walked over to the chest, bent down and retrieved a black spiral of worm from underneath it. Deftly, she uncoiled the worm, revealing a transmitter only a little bigger than a mustard seed. Without saying a word, she popped the transmitter into her mouth, ground it between her teeth and swallowed.

'Done?' said Ani.

'Done,' echoed Liyal, which was about as verbose as she ever got. She placed the worm back in the box, and closed it once more.

Ani and her guards looked at Merida expectantly. Cocile stared at her feet, as if sharing in her friend's shame.

'I'm terribly sorry, Archmage,' blustered Merida. 'Honestly, they scanned earlier. There was nothing. Are you sure that was even a bug? It was minuscule. I've never seen one that tiny. Is it even possible? I mean . . .'

Ani eyeballed her until she shut up, and then she gazed meaningfully around the opulent rooms. The only sound was a fountain in the corner as it splashed liquid silver into a bowl of hollow pearl.

'Sister Merida,' she said finally, 'we must not allow ourselves to become complacent, even when our circumstances seem crafted only for our comfort and security. There are enemies everywhere. Now, we must narrow down our list of suspects. Have you welcomed any other Nairene visitors to these rooms of late?'

'No,' said Merida.

'Are you sure? Think carefully.'

'Not lately, your Eminence. Priety dropped off her latest tome on manners, but she didn't come up. I met her in the lobby and she handed the manuscript to me there.'

Priety was the applied diplomacy lecturer to the Nairene Novices, and was unpopular and prudish, obsessed with manners, order, and hierarchy. But doubtless that came with the territory, for applied diplomacy dealt entirely with social behaviour and conduct. Off the top of her head, Priety could list every member of every family of importance in Illyri society, from their historical lineage to the ages of their children. It was a great disappointment to her that nobody ever actually *wanted* her to reel off this information and yet, despite the yawns that seemed to follow Priety wherever she went, Ani had found a place for her in the new order of the Marque. It was not a selfless act; Ani simply needed to know who was who in Illyri society, for her early years spent on Earth meant that she had come to the Sisterhood with no prior knowledge of the Illyri elite, or how they were interconnected. Priety had been indispensable in this regard.

'The manuscript was wrapped, I assume?' Ani said.

'Of course. You know Priety!'

'And you unwrapped it up here?'

Merida's hand tugged at her worried mouth.

'I did,' she said, 'right on this chair where I'm sitting. But—'

'That was a seed transmitter, Merida. They are made entirely of organic matter and contain no metals or alloys whatsoever, so are undetectable by conventional means. The transmitters are not only biological, but they are designed to roll away from light; as soon as they find themselves in darkness, they automatically adhere to the underside of whatever object is nearby. When inspected, they appear no more threatening than a piece of grit. Over time, they deteriorate like any other organic matter. They are manufactured exclusively on the Marque and have only recently gone beyond prototypes. We have chosen to keep them to ourselves, for obvious reasons, but our little searcher bugs and worms are now seed-enabled.'

She paused and Merida shuffled uncomfortably.

'If they are only to be found on the Marque,' said Merida, 'then that one—'

'Could only have come from the Marque,' Ani finished for her. 'Unless, of course, our technology has been leaked, which is not itself beyond the bounds of possibility.'

'Priety,' said Merida.

'Let's not jump to conclusions,' said Ani. 'I'd ask only that you keep this to yourself until we've had a chance to question Priety. She might be an unwitting accomplice in this: the seed transmitter could have been placed in the package without her knowledge. No need to upset yourself, Merida. I am not angry. But remember: caution always.'

'Thank you, your Eminence,' said Merida, and her face was woeful. 'You know I only wish to be of service to my Sisters.'

'Well then,' said Ani, nodding encouragingly, 'time is short, so tell me what you have learned that may be of use to our beloved Nairene Order.'

Merida poured cremos for her guests, and then shared with them her latest nuggets of Diplomatic gossip. Much of it was useful, as always, for Krake's tongue loosened when he was with his wife in the privacy of their bedroom. What interested Ani most was news of large fleet movements by the forces of the Diplomatic Corps on a scale beyond any seen so far in the war. She had heard similar rumours elsewhere and had suspicions about what they meant, but here was the confirmation she had awaited. The Diplomats were massing for a killer attack. The war had dragged on too long and an end needed to be put to it. Everyone knew that. But if the Diplomats were assembling a fleet, then they must have a target in mind. Somehow, they knew where the Military – or a significant portion of it – was massed.

Ani stood, thanked Merida, and requested the use of her pod.

'There are others upon whom I must call,' she said. 'Privately.'

'Of course!' said Merida, happy that she had been forgiven and had proven useful. 'Anything, your Eminence. Anything at all.'

'Excellent. I shall leave my aides with you. You can enjoy a catch-up with Cocile.' She turned to Cocile. 'But don't let yourselves be seen, please. Stay in here until I return. And allow no one to enter.'

Cocile – steadfast, unimaginative Cocile – did not question Ani. It was not unusual for the Archmage to order her to stay hidden while she herself left to go about secret Sisterhood business. Cocile was just grateful that today she was to remain here, in the Tree, and be permitted some time alone with Merida.

Ani moved towards the doorway and Toria and Liyal stepped in behind her.

'No,' she said. 'Thank you, Sisters, but you must stay here too.'

They both looked surprised but said nothing, which was precisely why she'd selected the mismatched pair as her personal guard: tall, rangy, feral Toria and shorter, broad-shouldered Liyal, with her unfortunate lizard-like features, were cousins in another life but now Sisters before anything else. They were loyal as hounds and they never questioned her. In her own way, Ani found that she had grown terribly fond of them.

'You can have a seat,' she said. 'You've earned a rest.'

Obedient as gundogs, they immediately sat.

CHAPTER 44

Ani didn't want to visit anyone else within the Tree of Lights – not yet, anyway. Instead, she took the pod back down to the entrance lobby, and there the same smooth young concierge greeted her, looking relieved when only one figure emerged from the capsule.

'Oh, hello again,' he said. 'I'm so glad it's you. I'm terribly sorry about earlier – I really didn't mean to offend the Archmage by speaking out of turn.' He rubbed his palms together nervously. 'Do you think she'll report me?'

Ani looked at him and felt a prickle of guilt at his distress.

'Not at all,' she replied, but the words that he heard came from Cocile's lips, and the face that looked back at him now was Cocile's: he would have sworn as much if his life had depended on it, if an axe was swinging for his neck. After all, he did not know that Ani Cienda, Archmage of the Sisterhood, could cloud minds and make others see what was not there. Few outside the Marque did, but her powers were the reason Syrene had been persuaded to keep the young Novice close once all the rest of the Gifted were dead. Ani was the last of the fledgling army of psychics, and so with a little pressing, Syrene had made it her personal business to tutor Ani, to ensure her talents were nurtured and improved as far as possible. Even Syrene had not grasped that she was being manipulated, right until the end.

There had been some initial surprise when Syrene had departed suddenly for the depths of the Marque, leaving instructions naming Ani as her successor. Wisely, few of the Sisterhood had expressed any objection and most transferred their allegiance quickly, and strategically, for they were of an Order born from an instinct for self-preservation. On the whole they understood, too, that wisdom is not the sole preserve of the old, and while Syrene might have inspired respect and fear, she was not held in any affection by the vast mass of Sisters. Meanwhile, those Nairenes who dissented openly were quickly silenced – exiled to far-off colonies – for one of Ani's first acts as Archmage was to announce plans to expand the Sisterhood's mission. They had spent too long cooped up on Avila Minor, she told her Sisters. It was time to spread the Gospel of Knowledge, and she personally handpicked those who would be entrusted with this great, noble and undoubtedly dangerous challenge. Then she named every plotter and schemer who had emerged since the death of Syrene, and within hours they found themselves bound for distant wormholes, and worlds that barely had names.

Of course, there were still those among Ani's Sisterhood who tested her trust and whispered behind their hands, but they remained careful. At least on the Marque they understood now what the young Archmage was capable of, and so were mindful of what they said or did. Still, Ani knew that notes were passed and secret drop-points were to be found in the furthest reaches of her lair. Sometimes particularly reckless accusations were traced back to their creators, and the worst of the schemers were sent to join their Sisters in barbarous lands. But mostly Ani simply read the notes and laughed at their ignorance and arrogance, then had her aides replace them with others written by herself for her own amusement; Ani had never grown out of her love of a good joke.

But here on Illyr, her clouding skills were only rumours, whispered ghosts of tales that swirled around the myth of her. They spoke of an Archmage who could shape-shift and read minds, and turn her enemies to stone or ice with her eyes; who caused creatures to devour their own young, and could summon flames to leap white-hot from within her enemies' chests, burning them to ash. But Ani knew the truth of this last myth: it had not been her but instead her beloved Tanit who burned others, and now Tanit was dead because of it.

Her pained expression caused the concierge's concern to increase.

'I did offend the Archmage, didn't I?' he said, suddenly seeing himself burned to a cinder, or turned to ice.

'No. Do not fret so,' Ani replied, in her Cocile guise. 'I can assure you that the Archmage does not feel offended or slighted.'

'Well, if you're sure. But, truly, if there's anything at all I can do . . . ?'

She looked at him as he moved his weight from one foot to the other: eager, energetic and anxious to please. And he really was terribly handsome in a fresh-faced, soft way, if you liked that sort of thing. Suddenly she had an idea, and she smiled at the thought – Cocile's rare smile – and he smiled back in relief. Slyly she stepped over to him, stretched out Cocile's hand and touched him on the elbow, allowing her fingers to linger. Cocile, Ani decided, had been alone for too long. Ultimately, she might be of more use to the Sisterhood if she had her own ties here on Illyr.

'I think there may well be something you can do,' she said, sweeter than Cocile knew how to be, 'something for me. Something . . . personal. Something nice.'

The concierge looked flustered and his face grew pink, but she held his gaze, daring him to play her game, coaxing him with fingers drumming like moth wings on his sleeve.

'I don't even know your name.'

'Cocile. And you are?'

'Rent. Rent Raydl.'

'Well, Rent Raydl, I'm glad that we have reached an understand-ing,' said Ani, and she allowed her hand to fall to her side. 'I should like to see you again, so don't let me down. Please.'

Rent bowed, going even pinker, then he seemed to make a decision. He reached out and took her hand. He held it in his own for a second while appearing to consider something and then, with a new firmness, he lifted it to his lips and kissed the tips of her fingers.

'I should like that, Cocile,' he said, gazing at her over her knuckles. She supposed it was his attempt at an alluring look.

'I'm staying at Opula tonight – come to the staff entrance and ask for me,' said Ani, 'but let's pretend we haven't had this conversation. I think that you should try to seduce me. It'll be fun.'

Unable to hold her amusement inside any longer, Ani swept out the door, and Rent stared after the receding figure of Cocile as the bright light outside lit her up, an astonished grin teasing his lips.

'Seriously, the Archmage's chief aide?' he said to nobody at all. 'Score!'

Still chuckling to herself, Ani turned left out of the building and onto the path beyond, which soon lifted into a raised walkway with a curling silver balustrade. As she climbed higher she slowed down to admire the vista that unfolded, for here was the best viewpoint of the section of the vast city that spread before her; here was Opulatum, centrepiece of Upper Tannis and the wealthiest district in all the capital. Rainbows of light bounced off every gleaming surface, and clouds tinged with blue and red whipped like paper across the shredded sky high above. She took a quiet moment to breathe in the heady air and gather her thoughts, but then a couple walked behind her, two females arm in arm in Civilian garb. They stared, and Ani nodded at them politely.

'Good day to you, Sister,' they said, and their eyes drank her up greedily: a Sister of the Nairenes, standing alone on the walkway taking in the view. What a rare sight; what a story to tell.

Ani let them pass, then embarked with a new resolve and headed along the familiar route that took her directly to the sole black skyscraper in all of diamond-white Upper Tannis. It was shiny as polished onyx as it sliced through the skyline, one central tapered column with many more rising from it, like drips on a candle that had defied gravity and melted upwards, into the air.

No words were written above its door, but none were needed. This was Securitat HQ.

And as she entered, resplendent in her red robes among so much angled, lacquered black, more eyes followed her, until the door slid closed behind her, shutting Tannis out, sealing her inside with the darkness.

Without breaking stride, Ani moved to the camera that served as a receptionist, and demanded that Vena be told of her presence.

'Oh, *just* Vena, is it?' said a female voice from the speaker, and the female guard on the screen sneered at her. 'And who the hell are you? *Just* Vena, indeed!'

Well, thought Ani, I suppose I could call her Vena the Skunk, but that probably wouldn't go down well, not here.

'I need to see your boss, sunshine,' she snapped back. 'You know the one, head of *all* the Securitats?' Although, thought Ani, I remember her when she was just another uniformed Securitat thug on Earth, and she hates me for that as much as anything else. 'How many Venas have you got in this place?'

The shock on the guard's face reminded Ani that the words she spoke were coming from Cocile's lips, not her own.

'Very well then: get me *Grand Marshal* Vena,' she conceded snippily. 'Please tell her that Cocile, chief aide to the Archmage of the Nairene Sisterhood, is here for her.'

'You have an appointment?'

'I am expected,' was all Ani said.

I'm always expected, she thought to herself; no appointment is ever necessary. The closer I am allowed to get to Vena, the easier she believes it will be to destroy me.

'I see you're still playing your childish games, Ani Cienda,' said Vena, as the Archmage was shown into her office.

It was a statement, and required no denial or confirmation. For Vena, Ani's powers weren't myths or rumours.

Ani – now once again herself, the silver-haired Archmage of the Sisterhood – merely smirked at her. She had history with Vena. Many years before, when she was but a teenager on Earth with fledgling powers, Ani had helped Syl free the Kerr brothers by clouding the minds of their Illyri guards so that they saw Vena, their boss, instead of Syl. Back then this act had made Ani's nose bleed, and her head had ached for hours afterwards, but now her clouding was sharper, clearer, and it was no longer mentally taxing either. Vena had never forgiven her, though, but then Ani figured that Vena probably wasn't the forgiving kind. She could just add it to the list, which also included a suspicion that Ani might have been involved in the death of her lover, Sedulus. Oh, Ani had no illusions about what Vena would have liked to do to her if she had not been protected by her position in the Sisterhood, and she knew that even as Archmage she was still not entirely immune from the predations of the Securitats. Vena remained the greatest threat to Ani. All of this superficial politeness — if it could even be called that — was just a veneer. Beneath it, Vena hated her and wished her dead, and Ani hated her right back.

'You've changed your hairstyle,' she said, and then laughed out loud at the absurdity of her words, because Vena didn't have any hair. As was customary, the leader of the Securitats kept her head shaved, and twin streaks were etched above her left ear. The streaks had been silver before, but now they were gold, which is actually what Ani had meant.

Vena regarded Ani sourly, her eyes hot and yellow as coals blazing from her face.

'Am I a joke to you?' she asked.

'I mean the gold,' said Ani. 'It's new. Shiny.'

For the briefest moment, there was a flicker of something almost like vulnerability in Vena's countenance. Subtly, she twisted her neck so that she could see herself in the mirror behind Ani. The glass was undoubtedly rigged with every manner of surveillance known on the planet, Ani knew that much at least. She reasoned Dyer could well be watching from his office in Opula. He often was, for Vena invited him like a spectre into these meetings, just as she was rumoured to invite him into her bedroom. Ani knew how to find out if he was eavesdropping for certain. After all, being intimate with the Gifted back when she was a Novice had taught her a few tricks, and teasing, taunting and manipulation were precisely what they excelled in. Well, *had* excelled in, past tense . . .

'Thank you,' Vena said, though the words sounded strangled, spat like pebbles from one who felt no gratitude for a compliment, as she believed praise to be her due.

Watching her and smiling encouragingly, Ani took her balled hand from her pocket and opened her fingers. Something the size of a mustard seed slipped unseen from her grasp onto the floor and immediately rolled away, searching for darkness.

Vena looked away from the mirror.

'Mind you, I didn't say I liked it,' said Ani slyly, because she couldn't resist, and preferred it when Vena was riled. But she wasn't finished yet.

'So has Vice-President Dyer seen it yet?' she continued. 'Does *he* like your new golden streaks, at least?'

'What the hell is that meant to mean?'

And there it was: Vena glanced at the glass again, now visibly flustered, with worry apparent on her face. She was clearly concerned about who might overhear Ani's comment and what they might glean from it. Ani knew only too well that Vena took her new role as head of the Securitats incredibly seriously and the implication, however vague, that she might have attained her position on any grounds except merit was bound to infuriate her. It helped to know her history, for on Earth Vena's lover had also been her boss, and there had been whispers of favouritism back then, even though she was actually very good at her job, nepotism or no nepotism. Horribly good, in fact.

Vena's concern told her what she needed to know: Dyer was almost certainly listening and watching.

'Well, if not to impress somebody, then why?' she asked innocently.

'Silver makes me think of you, and that rats' nest of yours,' said Vena, 'and I'd rather not.'

'And yet you must, for here I am.'

'Why?' asked Vena.

'Why what?'

'Why are you here? I'm busy. Some of us are fighting a war, while others are given to sitting on a private moon getting their toes pedicured. Make of that what you will.'

'Ah yes, the war – are you still battling them in the Southern Quadrant?'

'What are you talking about? We've long since cleared the Southern Quadrant.'

Ani looked baffled. 'But the Quelu wormhole . . . It's still heavily guarded.'

Vena sneered. 'A ruse. It keeps the enemy at bay while we extract the remaining metal from the mine.'

'So you do still have an operational mine at Quelu. How much is left?'

Vena opened her mouth, then stopped short.

'What are you up to?'

'What do you mean by that, Grand Marshal?' said Ani. 'Are we not all on the same side?'

'We can only assume that we are, until evidence proves differently.'

She knew that Vena's spies were trying to monitor her movements, but that was an explicit little jab by Vena's standards. If she was prepared to be so open, she must feel that she was drawing closer to assembling a case against Ani. The Archmage would have to be careful.

'Indeed we must,' she replied, 'and I hope it is true. I merely ask about the mine because my scientists are on the brink of perfecting cost-effective fuel converters for the extraction of massive amounts of latent energy, from hitherto unviable metals, on a micro level. Safely, I might add. I imagine even you can understand what that would mean for the furtherance of the Conquest, and your efforts to subdue the renegade forces that insist on thwarting us on every distant front, stalling our progress. But if you have no further need of Nairene technology, and particularly of this new, unrivalled power source, then I shall consider this conversation to be at an end.'

Ani wasn't sure what half of what she said meant, if anything, but she was pretty certain that Vena didn't either.

'You and your games,' said Vena, and her fingers curled at the air, twisting as if they were turning the neck of a rodent. 'What has this got to do with mining operations in the Southern Quadrant?'

'Radioactive elements,' said Ani. 'We need radioactive elements, specifically thorium. And that's what you're mining in the Southern Quadrant, as far as I know. I need all the remaining stock, as quickly as possible.'

'All of it?'

Excellent, thought Ani: Vena's just confirmed that there is still thorium at the Quelu mine.

'Well, yes, obviously,' she said. 'Look, if you are struggling to understand me, Vena, I shall go directly to Dyer instead, but I do feel I've made myself completely clear . . .' Ani knew she hadn't, but that was hardly the point. 'I don't doubt *he* will grasp how important this is,' she added for good measure.

Vena's eyes slipped briefly to the mirror once more. The trap snapped shut.

'I understand perfectly, Archmage. You want the materials, the thorium, so that your scientists can complete these converters. I can't offer all the Southern Quadrant stock, obviously, but I shall see what we can manage.'

'Well, as much as you can spare, and then some. At least a container load. But I need it soon. We are at a crucial stage, you understand, for the prototype is wholly unstable. I require a delivery of metals direct to the Marque, fast.'

'It'll take months.'

'I need it within a week.'

'That's not possible' – bargaining was part of the game – 'but I can get it to you by the end of the month.'

'Excellent. I shall arrange landing clearance for the delivery on the Marque as soon as I receive word from you. Remember, it must be an all-female crew. No Illyri males on Avila Minor. Don't let us down, for if you do, you will let all Illyr down.'

It sounded like a slogan to Ani. Maybe Vena could put some version of it on a recruitment poster for the Securitats, with an image of herself pointing a big finger at some unsuspecting bystander. *Don't let the Securitats down, for if you do . . .*

Vena's lips went thin and tight, and so did her face: the old loathing. It was the downside of her promotion: it forced her to deal with the one Illyri whom she most detested in the universe.

'And I in turn shall be waiting for those converters, Ani Cienda. *Archmage* Ani. They had better be as good as you say.'

They stared at each other, a challenge quivering in the air between them. Ani looked away first, but only because she thought it prudent, and Vena nodded ever so slightly in satisfaction. The meeting was clearly over. Now she stood up and ushered Ani to the entrance, steering her away from the mirror, away from Dyer's ears and eyes. At the door, she leaned forward and pressed her cheek to Ani's in customary, casual Illyri fashion. From a distance, they might almost have resembled friends.

'And you understand this,' she murmured directly into Ani's ear. 'I don't know how you got to where you are. I don't know how you manipulated Syrene into vacating her post and naming you as her successor, but I'm waiting for the day you slip up, when we all see you for what you really are. And when that day comes, I'll be ready.'

Ani glanced at the mirror and then laughed, tossing her hands in the air as if she'd just been told a tremendous joke.

'I know, and I really do hope Dyer notices your new look,' she said loudly, 'because I think it's terribly sweet how hard you're trying to impress him.'

And with a raised eyebrow and a mock-coy wave she took her leave. She had other meetings to attend, other minds to play with.

And then she had to return to the Marque, for there was the seed of treachery to crush.

X
THE END OF KRASIS

CHAPTER 45

Krasis was in the hands of its former prisoners, but their captors had not been subdued entirely. Some of the guards in the staff living quarters had managed to get to their respirators as the oxygen was cut off, and they in turn had helped to revive their unconscious colleagues and fortify the section. They were also armed. Steven had informed them that Krasis had been taken, and gave them the option of surrendering, but nobody thought this anything more than a polite formality. He, Alis, and Rizzo, along with Hague and another sergeant named Vichek, watched on a monitor as a silent argument ensued in the staff quarters – their feed provided images, but no sound – until one of the guards shot up the camera with a pulser.

'How much air do they have in those respirators?' Alis asked.

'A couple of hours,' Hague replied.

'Then we should just leave them in there until it runs out. There's no point in incurring casualties for no reason.'

'They won't wait until it runs out,' said Steven. 'We may have the advantage of numbers, but there are thirty Securitats locked in those quarters, all well trained and well armed. They'll believe themselves more than capable of regaining control of this facility.'

'The officer is right,' said Vichek. 'If I were in the guards' position, I'd blow the doors and come out firing.'

With that possibility in mind, Hague and Vichek handpicked twelve men to arm with some of the unlocked pulsers that had been transferred from the *Nomad* to the *Revenge*. Steven instructed them to take up positions of cover around the entrance to the guard quarters while the rest of prisoners moved back to the safety of the connecting arteries. A group had already been sent to the kitchens to secure food, for most of the men were weak from poor rations, and some were close to starving. Now they leaned against the walls of the connectors, devouring everything, stuffing it into their mouths with their fingers, while those with medical training tended to the wounded.

Rizzo was talking over the intercom with a Securitat named Doler, who was the senior officer in the imprisoned group. He appeared to be trying to negotiate terms of surrender, but Steven sensed that it was just a distraction. They were getting ready to counter-attack. He was sure of it.

'Do you know him?' he asked Hague.

'He's the acting governor. The old one deserted the sinking ship a few days ago.'

Alis had already informed Hague and his fellow noncommissioned officers of what she had learned from Reutan about the closure of the facility, and the Securitats' plans for disposing of the prisoners. What Hague had already suspected was now confirmed, but Steven instructed him to keep the information from the enlisted men. A few Securitats – Reutan among them – had survived the aftermath of the breakout, but they were very lucky to do so with their lives. If the prisoners knew for sure that they had been only days away from an agonising death, the remaining Securitats would have been killed within seconds.

Doler was insisting that he and his fellow guards be given a ship to take them from Krasis before they would even consider surrendering. He also wanted to speak to the officer in command.

'He'll be asking for a puppy next, and a date with an actress,' Hague continued. 'Doler is smart. He's not the worst of them, but that's not saying a lot.'

Doler announced that he was ceasing further negotiation until he could discuss terms with someone more senior than Rizzo, and cut off contact.

'That's it,' said Steven. 'They're coming.'

He raised his hand in warning and saw his men ready themselves. At that moment, the door to the guard quarters exploded outwards and heavy pulse blasts struck the central core, the impacts causing debris to rain down and a gantry to collapse. It was the equivalent of suppressive cannon fire, designed to shock and disorient as much as to kill, forcing the enemy to keep their heads down while the ground troops attacked.

The first of the Securitats emerged, some still wearing their respirators, but they were met not by the anticipated mass of prisoners who could easily be targeted, but by a small force carefully dug in around and above them – a force with teeth.

The first pulse blasts had killed two of Steven's men, but the rest were unharmed. They were all young, for the eldest was no more than twenty-five, but they had years of Brigade experience behind them, and had waited a long time for a chance to take a shot at the Illyri – better yet, at Securitats.

The fight was short, but bloody. The first Securitats were cut down as soon as they appeared, and then four pulse blasts set at full power were directed straight into the guard quarters, creating carnage in the enclosed space. A few sporadic pulse bursts followed from within, but they quickly petered out.

'Cease fire,' Steven ordered.

The core immediately went quiet. No one spoke. Even the prisoners in the arteries were silent. Somewhere deep in the guard quarters, a fire burned.

A pulse rifle was thrown into the core, then another and another. An Illyri voice said: 'We surrender. We're coming out.'

Steven's men held their positions and kept their weapons trained on the doorway, which was now a ragged round hole in the wall, surrounded by rubble.

A figure appeared from the murk, supporting another who was bleeding from the belly. Several more Securitats followed, all wounded. The rest, including Doler, were dead.

From the ranks of the former prisoners rose a ragged cheer. It was over. Krasis was truly theirs.

★ ★ ★

The remaining Securitats were placed in the same cells that had, until recently, been occupied by their captives. In total, there were only 153 humans left on Krasis, all of them former Brigade troops. The next step was to get them off the moon as quickly as possible, just in case an Illyri ship came to check on how the prison's decommissioning was progressing. Vichek was given responsibility for organising the transfer of food and other essentials to the vessels outside, and a steady stream of mechanical lifters moved back and forth between the prison and the landing pads, aided by men in respirators.

'There are only Brigade troops here. What happened to the men from the Punishment Battalions?' Steven asked. He had been expecting to see more humans than this on Krasis.

'A few days ago, the Securitats took them from their cells and loaded them into that big transporter outside,' said Hague. 'They told the prisoners they were needed for special work. When it returned, the transporter was empty.'

Steven turned to Alis and Rizzo.

'Bring Reutan to me.'

It was a much-reduced Reutan who faced Alis and the humans. His uniform was torn and a nasty cut to his scalp had left his face streaked with blood. He was trying to look as though he wasn't frightened, but he was failing. Steven gave him water and called a medic to treat his wound. Reutan relaxed a little.

'Tell me about the transporter,' said Steven, 'the one that took the Battalion prisoners away.'

And Reutan stopped relaxing.

'I don't know what you're talking about.'

'You don't know about the removal of a section of your prison population in recent days?' said Steven. 'But you were the officer on duty when we arrived. Are you telling me that a senior Securitat at a prison facility doesn't know where half of his prisoners have gone? If that's true, Reutan, then you're no good to me.'

He gestured to Rizzo.

'Put him back in his cell. Try to find one with a window, so he can watch us leave.'

It was the perfect response, and it achieved the desired reaction.

'No!' said Reutan. 'I know about the transporter, but it was nothing to do with me. Maril, the old prison governor, gave the order before he left, and Doler carried it out.'

Steven saw Hague give the slightest shake of his head. Whoever had been responsible, it was not Doler.

'What order?' said Steven.

'They were killers,' said Reutan. 'They had murdered Illyri.'

'What. Order?' Steven repeated slowly.

Reutan caved.

'That the remaining Battalion prisoners should be taken into orbit and thrown from the airlocks,' he said. 'I tried to talk my superiors out of it, but Doler wouldn't listen. He said they'd killed Illyri so they should never have been allowed to live in the first place, and that he was tired of feeding them valuable rations. He said it was time to give them a taste of real Illyri justice.'

He stared at the floor, unwilling to meet the eyes of his interrogators.

Steven struggled for a suitable reply. He could barely keep himself from attacking Reutan. He thought of the final moments of the young men on the transporter, the terror they must have felt as they realised what was about to happen.

'Alis,' he said. 'Please access the flight records for the transporter.'

Alis remained remotely linked to the prison's central operating system following her initial incursion. She had the information instantly.

'*Velder Sel*,' she said. 'Taber-class transporter. Mission: permanent prisoner transfer. Crew: six. Additional personnel, prisoner transfer: twenty. Officer commanding: Solan Reutan.'

'That's not true,' said Reutan. 'There's been a mistake!'

Alis ignored him.

'Second in command: Talder Lerras. Prisoner count on departure: one hundred thirty-two. Prisoner count on return –'

Alis paused for a moment.

'Zero.'

Reutan stepped unsteadily toward the door as if he might run away, but there was nowhere for him to go. Hague and Rizzo held him.

'There's one other detail,' said Alis.

'What is it?' asked Steven.

'The mission was voluntary.'

'My God,' said Rizzo. 'They *volunteered* to kill them?'

'Doler did it!' Reutan said. 'He changed the records to hide his involvement. You have to believe me. I wouldn't do something like that. I'm not a killer. Ask Lerras. He'll tell you. We weren't on the *Velder Sel.*'

'Lerras is dead,' said Steven. 'He died from blood loss and shock an hour ago. It looks like it's just you.'

'No, you must—'

'Take him back to his cell,' said Steven, and Reutan was hauled away by Rizzo and Alis, leaving Steven alone with Hague.

'They were our people,' said Hague. He looked older than his years, and Steven saw that there was white in the stubble on his chin.

'I know.'

'Every Securitat in this place knew what was going to happen to those prisoners. They're all responsible.'

'Indirectly, maybe,' said Steven, 'but those who gave the order and carried it out are the criminals.'

'Maybe you're right, but you can't keep this quiet. The men already suspect. They'll want justice. Someone has to answer for what was done.'

'Someone will.'

Alis returned. Steven told her to retrieve the names of all Securitats who had been on the *Velder Sel* when the prisoners were killed, and compare them with the list of survivors. When she returned, she had five names for him.

Steven wanted to be sick. His hands were trembling. He clasped them before him to hide the shaking. He felt like he was in a car that was careering out of control down a steep hill, and he could do nothing to stop it, but perhaps he was only lying to himself to make it easier.

Yet nothing could make it easier.

'I knew many of them,' said Hague. 'I knew their names. I knew the names of their families, their girlfriends. I want to do this. I'm volunteering, just like the Securitats did.'

And Steven found that he could only nod dumbly.

All work stopped as the shuttle ascended. The men watched it go, and then it was lost from view. It had six humans on board and five of the Securitats.

When it returned, the Securitats were gone.

CHAPTER 46

The final evacuation of Krasis was about to begin. Steven discussed with Hague and Vichek the nature of their mission to Earth, and Hague suggested to him that he should talk to the freed soldiers and explain what might have befallen their homeworld. Steven did so, as best he could, but he made sure that the remaining Securitats were safely under lock and key and guarded by men he could trust before he shared what he knew with the rest of them. He was afraid that the Securitats would be torn apart otherwise, even though Alis had scanned each of them – including, before their final shuttle trip, the late Reutan and his fellow volunteers – and found no trace of the Others among them.

The telling of the tale was horrible, but then how could it be otherwise? Once the commotion and shouting had died down, Steven informed the men that, of the ships captured with the prison, only the cruiser was fast enough to be able to keep pace with the *Revenge*. Between them, the two vessels could probably accommodate a force of fifty to sixty men, but that was as large a contingent as they would be able to take to Earth. For the others, the *Velder Sel* and the smaller vessels would have to suffice, but he had other plans for the remaining Brigade troops following the evacuation. He told them of the Military convoy they had seen, and advised them to make their way towards Passienne and try to link up with it. If they encountered a Corps vessel, they could either attempt to outrun it – which, in a big, slow transporter would be difficult – or seize it.

The latter would require convincing the other ship that the *Velder Sel* and its escort craft were crewed by Securitats, but Alis gave them some help in that regard by ensuring that the three ships were supplied with the most recent security protocols and all necessary codes and call signs. She also disabled the visual imaging systems on all three ships so that any curious Illyri would not be able to see the crew. Thankfully, six or seven of the men spoke Illyri well enough to be able to pull off the deception, if required, and they had five pilots among them.

'What do we do with the ship once we've seized it, sir?' asked one of the men.

'If it's better than yours, you keep it,' Steven replied. 'If it's worse, then destroy it.' He recalled a word from his childhood reading. 'Consider yourself privateers.'

'Private-what?' asked the same man, to some laughter.

'It's a polite way of saying "pirates", but with a mission to attack enemy shipping,' Steven explained. 'For better or worse, in this fight you'll have to side with the Military. Most of them may not like Brigade troops very much, but at least they won't try to kill you, and they need all the help they can get.'

The prospect of attacking more Illyri Diplomats and Securitats pleased the troops. Anything was better than Krasis, even war against superior opposition. Vichek asked for permission to lead the privateers, which Steven granted. He gave Rizzo command of the second cruiser, the *Ilfen*, which would join the *Revenge*, and which Rizzo immediately renamed the *Marauder*. She would be assisted by the last of the sergeants, an Italian named Agostino whose family, as it turned out, came from Calabria, the same region of Italy from which Rizzo's family had emigrated to the United States a generation before. It was a match made in heaven.

Alis found Steven in his cabin, immersed in the final checks and preparations.

'Are you okay?' she asked him.

He knew what she was talking about. She had seen the look on his face when the shuttle had returned following the execution of the Securitats.

'I'm trying not to think about it,' he replied.

He ceased what he was doing.

'I could have stopped it,' he said.

'Could you?'

'I could have ordered them to leave Reutan and the others alive.'

'You could have tried, but I don't believe they would have listened. They might not have inflicted the same death on them, but they would have killed them nonetheless. A blade or a noose would have worked just as well. You would have discovered them dead in their cells before we left, and every man on Krasis would have confessed ignorance of how it had happened.'

'It doesn't make me feel any better. I didn't even try.'

Alis moved closer to him. She brushed a hand through his hair, the first time she had touched him since their relationship had changed.

'I saw the same expression on your brother's face when he was forced to reduce Archaeon to a nuclear wilderness,' she said. 'I will tell you what I told him: the fact that this troubles you is what makes you a good man. Only if you felt no guilt would I be concerned for you.'

Steven wasn't sure that he agreed. Doing nothing to prevent something awful from happening didn't make you a good person, and neither did feeling bad about it afterwards. Preventing it from happening in the first place would have been the right thing to do. But he decided to say nothing more about it. It wasn't a discussion that he wanted, or needed, to have with Alis. They were on different ground with each other now, and he felt a new distance between them.

'Have you decided what to do with the remaining guards?' Alis asked.

'They can stay on Krasis. *With* life support. There's been enough killing here.'

He reached up and squeezed her hand, then released it before she could. Such small gestures were still awkward, and painful.

'Thank you, Alis. You did well,' he said. 'Without you, we would not have taken Krasis.'

'I did advise you that mine was the better plan.'

'I didn't know smugness was part of your programming,' said Steven.

Alis headed for the door.

'If it was not,' she said, 'then I believe that it should have been.'

The *Revenge* and the *Marauder* were the last vessels to leave Krasis. Steven waited until the other ships were out of sight before they finally ascended from the surface of the moon. He was well aware of the mutterings of dissent that had accompanied his decision to let the remaining Securitats remain alive, and there was nothing that he could do to stop the former prisoners from returning once he had gone and destroying the life-support systems. He just hoped that they would be relieved to have put the prison behind them, and instead concentrate on finding more worthy targets for their anger. The cell doors were on a timer and would only unlock once the last two ships were safely away from Krasis. Steven had ordered the communications array to be disabled before they left, and all drones destroyed, so the guards wouldn't be able to send a distress call. It wouldn't be too long before someone came to investigate their silence, but by then his two cruisers would be well on their way to Earth, while the rest would either have hooked up with the Military or found a base of operations from which to attack Corps shipping.

As an alternative, Alis had suggested to Vichek that one of the moons orbiting Royas, in the Evis system, might provide a reasonably secure refuge. At least two of them had water and a breathable atmosphere, and no indigenous life capable of posing a serious threat to safety. They were also within strike-and-run distance of a series of Illyri shipping routes. She guessed that it would be quite a while before the Corps began to suspect that the attacks were not the work of guerilla activity by the Military and connected them to the Brigade escapees, if they ever did.

'They won't know if we don't leave any survivors to tell,' Vichek said.

And Alis could only agree that, yes, this would probably solve the problem.

★ ★ ★

The journey back to Earth was not uneventful. As before, they did their best to steer clear of Corps and Military vessels, but on the second boost they emerged straight into the heart of a small convoy escorting a crippled Corps destroyer back to its base. It was the first test of the ability of the *Revenge* and *Marauder* to fight in unison and of Rizzo's command capabilities. The destroyer never made it back to base, and the two escorts were annihilated, but not before one discharged a drone towards the wormhole. The *Marauder* blew it up just before it entered, but it was a close-run thing.

As they drew closer to Earth, all shipping vanished from their screens. The planet had been isolated, probably because those responsible for unleashing the Others upon it did not want what they had done to become widely known. Steven wondered what excuse they had given for the evacuation and quarantine of Earth. Perhaps nobody even bothered asking, because nobody really cared.

Steven would make them care.

And if his mother was dead, he would make the Illyri wish that they had never heard his name.

XI
MEIA

CHAPTER 47

The Tessel system was largely unexplored. Planets and moons had been given only the most simple of designations: in Illyri, the equivalent of Tes-1 for the planet nearest the wormhole, Tes-1a and Tes-1b for its moons, and so on.

Right from their activation, the Mechs were used for the study of such remote parts of the universe, for it was arduous and sometimes dangerous work. A handful of Mechs could do what it took an entire crew of Illyri to achieve, for the Mechs did not need to rest or eat, and required rotas only to charge themselves occasionally.

Meia could not recall which of the Mechs had first decided to withhold information from their Illyri creators. It might even have been she who made the decision. If so, she had purged it from her memory, probably for safety. She had been duplicitous from early activation, possibly due to a fault in her programming. It was why she had made such a good spy. She had even lied to Paul and the others about her ultimate destination, and she trusted them more than anyone she had ever known, Illyri or human. But everyone broke under torture: everyone. It was only a question of how much one could endure. If they were captured, they would eventually tell their interrogators all that they knew, including the location of the Mech refuge.

So Tessel was an empty system, chosen by Meia as a decoy because of its size and the impossibility of searching it thoroughly. But compared to the neighbouring Haytalal system, Tessel was a small island. Tessel was big, but Haytalal was immense.

The journey to Haytalal had been long and Meia had experienced feelings of intense loneliness, but she had spent much of it powered down, and for the rest she had prayed and meditated, as well as engaging in more practical modifications to herself. She had despised wearing the face of the novice Layne: it had been necessary, and without the deception, Syl and the rest would never have escaped the Illyri system, but Meia felt appalled every time she looked in a mirror.

As the *Varcis* traversed the vast reaches of the universe, avoiding the main shipping lanes while occasionally bearing witness on-screen to clashes between Corps and Military ships, she had set to work on her appearance once again. She mapped an image of her old face from her memories and then began cutting and moulding, using some of the *Varcis*'s stock of ProGen skin from its medical supplies. The transformation had been less painful than before, for she had access to the correct equipment. Surgical procedures carried out with a laser blade were – not entirely to her surprise – much more precise and far less psychologically gruelling than cutting into one's face with a scalpel. But she had also come to accept the reality of pain; she might not have been programmed to experience it, but it now existed for her. The *Varcis*'s tranquillisers helped control it, but she used fewer of them than she might have done. She was glad of a little pain. It confirmed for her that she was more than a machine.

So it was something like the old Meia who approached Hayt 7, to give it its Illyri designation. It was one of the furthest planets from the dwarf star that provided its warmth – any closer, and the heat from the star would have made it uninhabitable. It lay in the upper half of a spiral galaxy that might have been considered beautiful had Meia not seen so many like it before. Hayt 7 was a desert world, but from a distance gave the impression of a planet in the process of fragmentation, surrounded as it was by multiple rings of debris chains, like the old, inaccurate diagrams of electrons orbiting a nucleus that once figured in textbooks.

Negotiating the debris fields was the most difficult aspect of accessing the planet and required Meia's full concentration. Once she was clear of them, and descending towards the surface, Hayt 7's great secret was revealed to her once more.

Hayt 7 was littered with bones.

The planet had no indigenous life forms. It was, despite its atmosphere, a long-dead world, yet scattered across it were the remains of creatures, the largest beings that Meia had ever seen. Each must have stood eighty or ninety metres in height when alive, its head shaped like a gargantuan hooked claw, its ribcage a great cathedral of bone, most of its power residing in its huge back legs while its forelimbs supported its upper body. The brief examination of its brainpan that Meia had conducted on the first sweep of the planet many years before suggested it was intelligent, a theory backed up by her other great discovery here: the wreckage from an unknown ship that had crashed on Hayt 7 in ancient times, while the Illyri were still throwing rocks at one another outside caves. The wreckage had become part of the landscape, just like the creatures and their skeletons.

Skeletons big enough to hide a ship.

And all of this she had kept from her Illyri masters – she and her co-pilots on that mission, Menos and Karel. They were not even supposed to be scouting Haytalal, and Meia was not registered on the crew manifest, but by then she had already begun hearing whispers against the Mechs, and there were also those among her own kind who were preaching that the Mechs should leave the Illyri to their godless state, and set out for the stars. At the time, Meia was concerned. As things turned out, she should have been actively frightened.

She had not seen Hayt 7 since that first visit, but she had kept it in mind, and as the extent of the Illyri treachery grew clearer – their decision to rid themselves of the Mechs and start again on AI development – Haytalal became a name shared among only a handful of the artificial life forms.

Now, as the *Varcis* descended, Meia found the ship she sought, but not with scanners or by sight. She found it because the beacon in its hull activated a response in the receiver she had planted inside herself, like a voice calling out from the desert floor and resonating inside her.

Meia brought the *Varcis* down by the torso of the largest of the dead beings, which contained within it an old Illyri transport ship named the *Morir* – the ark that had brought the remaining Mechs to safety – and waited to see what might emerge from it.

★ ★ ★

When movement came, it was not from the ship but from the nearby skull of a creature. From its mouth emerged a figure clad in layers of tattered clothing, holding a long steel rod in its right hand. The rod was topped by an intricate construction of copper wire, fused together to resemble rays emerging from a star: the image of the Divine. The figure remained standing in the shadow of the jaws, only its eyes visible through the material that concealed its face and head.

Meia left the *Varcis*. The afternoon was already growing chilly, for soon the desert night would descend. The air was thin, but Meia was untroubled by such matters. She walked across the sand until she and the waiting Mech faced each other.

From beneath the robes appeared a hand. It had sustained some damage, and Meia could see some of the bones of its endoskeleton through the holes in its skin. It pulled aside the cloth from its mouth, and Meia started. Most of the ProGen flesh was missing from its nose down, giving it the appearance of a death's head, but still she recognised the face.

'Emanis,' she said. 'I am glad to see you.'

The lie came easily to her. Emanis was a fanatic, believing himself to have been chosen by the Divine to lead the Mechs to the Promised Land. It was unfortunate that the surviving transporter should have had him on board.

'Meia,' came Emanis's reply. Then: 'You should not have come here.'

'Where are the others?'

'They sleep.'

'But you do not.'

'I watch over them. I pray in my church.'

He gestured at the skull behind him.

'Come,' he said. 'See what I have created.'

She followed him into the cranium, and marvelled despite herself at what he had wrought. He had drilled holes in the skull to admit light, incorporating them into the carvings that covered huge sections of bone so that the chinks became eyes, mouths and stars. She saw the faces of Mechs and Illyri alongside grotesque renderings of beasts both real and imagined, all incorporated into a great creation myth. Stored within Emanis himself was a history of Illyri art, and he had imitated the great artists of Illyri culture in decorating his church. Here were the spectral mourners of Machel's *The Widows of Oris*, now transformed into angels; there, the joyous lovers of Polchelti's *Transience*, but with their insides exposed to reveal biomechanical workings.

And towering over all, dominating the ceiling and upper walls, was an enormous rendering of the Creator, the Divine, containing both male and female elements, and mechanical parts alongside the organic. It was clearly a work in progress, but it bore a pronounced resemblance to –

Well, to Emanis himself.

'It is . . . striking,' said Meia, trying to conceal her unease, and failing.

'You disapprove?'

Tread carefully, thought Meia.

'No. I am merely overwhelmed. You completed all of this unaided?'

'I was happy to devote myself to honouring the Creator. Now this dead thing is a hymn of praise to the Divine.'

But Meia's eyes strayed to the ceiling, and to the incomplete depiction of that same Creator. Even its mouth was semi-skeletal, just like Emanis's own. He had hung cables from the skull and built scaffolding so that he could work on his own image.

'It will be dark soon,' she said.

'The lights are solar powered,' said Emanis. 'They retain their charge from the sun. We can remain in this church as long as you wish.'

'I would prefer to go to the *Morir*.'

'First, tell me why you are here.'

Emanis sat on a pew he had built from bones and invited her to do the same. Meia joined him, but kept her distance. The sunlight was dying rapidly, but now lamplight began to replace it. Emanis had rigged it to flicker softly, giving the impression of movement among the carvings. It was profoundly unsettling.

'The Illyri are tearing themselves apart,' she began. 'The Second Civil War is upon us.'

'Upon *them*,' Emanis corrected. 'We are not Illyri. Their wars do not concern us.'

'There is another force involved,' said Meia. 'And it does concern us.'

She told Emanis much of what had occurred on Earth and Illyr, but chose not to mention Syl, or Paul Kerr and his brother. She could not have said why, except that she felt it might complicate matters with Emanis. But she did describe the Others, and the threat that they posed to all life.

Emanis nodded at their mention.

'All things are the work of the Divine,' he said. 'Even these Others. They are a plague sent by the Creator to punish the unbelievers.'

'They destroy all creatures, whether they have the capacity to believe or not,' said Meia.

'It is the Creator's will. We cannot interfere.'

'To do nothing is to be complicit,' said Meia. 'Belief in the Divine does not absolve us of the duty to fight what is evil.'

'And who is to say that these Others are evil?' asked Emanis. 'You, Meia? If all things are the work of the Creator, and the Creator is good, then the Others are part of the Creator's plan. It is not for us to interfere. And we owe the Illyri nothing: they tried to wipe us out. They killed us in our tens of thousands.'

'That was not the work of all Illyri. Many would have objected, had they known. And some helped us. You would not be alive otherwise. None of us would.'

Emanis stood. He waved a hand, and the lamplight started to fade.

'You are wrong, Meia,' he said. 'Go back to your war. I will not wake the sleepers for this.'

'That is not for you alone to decide, Emanis.'

But Emanis was not listening to her. He stepped out into the night, and the darkness swallowed him.

CHAPTER 48

Meia followed Emanis across the sands, her infrared lenses blurring him slightly as he passed through avenues of bones. Only when they were almost at the *Morir* did he turn to face her.

'I told you to leave,' he said.

'I am not yours to command.'

'I will not let you enter. You cannot wake them.'

'They must be allowed to decide for themselves, Emanis. Now is the time for them to return to Illyr, should they wish it. Now is the time for them to show their faces and avenge the injustice that was done to them.'

'They are safe here.'

'They are not immortal. Even the power cells on the *Morir* cannot sustain them forever. What do you want, Emanis: that they should become like the bones that surround them here, relics of an extinct species?'

'Leave them in peace, Meia.'

'I cannot.'

Emanis's right hand had been concealed in his robes. Now it emerged holding a pulser.

'Then you will have to add your remains to those that already lie here,' said Emanis.

He fired, but Meia was already moving and the pulse impacted on a giant tibia behind her, shattering it. She found her own weapon and tried to draw a bead on Emanis, but he was shielded by the rib cage and she did not wish to kill him. She glimpsed a rectangle of light appear as Emanis entered the *Morir*, and then it vanished.

Meia followed Emanis's path and came to the ship. If he had tried to secure it against her, then he had failed: Meia's link to the *Morir* was deeper than any locks and codes. She spoke, and it answered, but she did not enter by the same door that Emanis had used. Instead she ran halfway along the vessel's great length until she came to a series of large hatches. She knew the layout of the *Morir*, and this was the closest entrance to the main bays at the heart of the ship, where the sleepers waited.

The nearest hatch opened at her command, but Meia did not go in immediately, wary of Emanis's pulser. But when she did risk a glance within, the corridor before her was empty.

Meia stepped inside the *Morir*.

She smelled it as the door closed behind her: a vague odour of old fires, but she could not place the source. It grew stronger as she progressed down the corridor, one of the radial arteries to the bays, which was lit by the faintest of glows from the emergency lighting that activated at her command. The corridor ended at an elevator bank, of which there were several on the exterior of the bays. Beside it was a staircase and she used this to ascend. Despite her link to the ship, she did not wish to find herself trapped in a small space should Emanis try to override its systems. She knew that he was in here somewhere, probably watching her on the security cameras. She could have attempted to form a deeper connection with the ship to disable them, but that would have meant plugging herself directly into its mainframe, which would have left her vulnerable if Emanis had installed traps to prevent any such incursion. No, she would deal with Emanis later, once the sleepers had awakened.

She had reached the first of the connecting doors to the bays when she heard Emanis's voice over the ship's speakers. The smell of burning was stronger here.

'This is your last chance, Meia. Turn back. I will not try to harm you again.'

'You have been out here alone for too long, Emanis,' she said. 'You are troubled.'

That was an understatement, to say the least: Emanis was insane. The pulser incident paled into insignificance next to that image of himself as God.

'The Creator speaks through me,' said Emanis. 'I am in the Creator, and the Creator is in me.'

Meia activated the door. Emanis began singing through the speaker. It was a hymn entitled 'I Walk Beside You Always', and as his pitch rose he multitracked his voice so that it sounded as though a choir of thousands had joined in with him.

The door opened. Meia stepped through. She was on one of the lower gangways that ran around the wall of the great circular bay. Into the walls were set alcoves, each containing a single dormant Mech. In this bay alone, Meia was surrounded by thousands of her own kind, all held in sleep mode by a small charge from the ship's power cells.

But the smell . . . It concerned her.

She approached the nearest alcove. Inside, behind a transparent protective shield, Meia could see a female Mech. She looked a little like Alis. The alcoves were not quite airtight. Meia sniffed at the seal, and wrinkled her nose at the lingering acrid stench.

She pressed a button by the shield and it slid across, revealing the Mech. A cable led from her temple into the machinery behind, designed to monitor her stasis and provide the signal to wake when the time came. The ProGen skin around the connection was charred and broken, and the monitoring systems showed no signs of life. Meia pulled away a flap of the damaged skin, exposing the burned flesh beneath. She probed deeper until she touched the Mech's skull, then worked with her fingers to manually remove the plate concealing her central processing unit – the intricate, massively complex circuit that was not only responsible for executing all instructions, but was also the source of the Mech's personality and even, for some, a physical manifestation of its soul.

Meia removed the unit, although she already knew what she would find. It had been so badly damaged that it was warped, and pieces of it crumbled away in her fingers. She looked at the name on the Mech's shirt: Olra. She searched her own memory, and found her: date of activation, specialised programming, distinctive personality traits – all were gone. Her CPU had been overloaded. Olra was dead.

Meia checked five more Mechs at random, with the same result, and all the time Emanis's singing continued.

And in that bay, Meia knew grief beyond reckoning.

Finally, she spoke.

'Did you do this, Emanis?'

The singing stopped.

'Yes.'

'Why?'

'There was little hope here.'

'So you took away all hope entirely.'

'I gave them eternal life,' said Emanis.

'And yet you spared yourself.'

'If I had not, then who would have prayed for their souls?'

His singing resumed. Meia found an input slot and connected herself to the ship. As anticipated, Emanis had installed some firewalls, but Meia breached them all. Now the ship's eyes were her eyes, and she saw Emanis. He was kneeling in the *Morir*'s makeshift chapel, bathed in the artificial light from a window carved of coloured crystal, a screen before him.

Meia secured the door of the chapel, trapping Emanis inside. She used the ship's systems to confirm that all of the Mechs on board the *Morir* were dead before slowly making her way to the little church.

And there she silenced Emanis, and sent him to be judged by God.

CHAPTER 49

The *Morir* had one more mystery to offer. All six of its shuttle bays were empty. Meia ran a trace, found signals on Hayt 13, and left behind that dead world.

Hayt 13: an ice giant, mantled by layers of water, ice, ammonia and methane, coloured cyan by the absorption of red light due to its methane clouds.

Hayt 13: uninhabitable by most forms of life.

Meia located the shuttles. They were clustered around a single spot, in the lee of a great frozen slope. She sent a signal, but received no reply. She tried again as the *Varcis* drew closer to the surface of the planet. If they were still alive, they would be in stasis. It would take them time to wake.

She prayed.

And her prayers were answered, just as she became the answer to the prayers of others.

'*Varcis*, we hear you.'

The image that appeared before her was hazy, but she recognised the face immediately.

'Menos?'

On the screen, the face of the Mech she had not seen for so many years broke into a smile of disbelief.

'Meia . . .'

Hayt 13: the Mech sanctuary.

XII

THE MERCY OF
THE ARCHMAGE

CHAPTER 50

Ani chose not to approach Sister Priety about the seed transmitter discovered in Merida's apartments straight away. Instead, Toria was assigned the task of monitoring her, and intercepting all letters and communications to and from Priety and her Department of Applied Diplomacy, but no evidence of treachery came from the surveillance. Ani had almost begun to believe that Priety might indeed have been unaware of the listening device hidden in the book of manners she had delivered, until Toria came knocking on her door just as she was about to retire for the night.

'Archmage,' said Toria. 'There has been an unauthorised communication.'

A series of seed transmitters, the tiniest yet devised, had been dispersed through every facet of Priety's life in the Marque: in her office, her chambers, even in her shoes and clothing, which was carefully removed from the rest of the Sisters' laundry and cleaned separately so that the seeds could be replaced. Now, a seed buried on the undersole of Priety's slipper had picked up a signal from somewhere in her chambers. It was coded, but Ani's analysts had deciphered it within seconds. It was a short list of Nairenes, Ani among them, with instructions for Priety to collect a batch of seed transmitters from a Sister called Beyna, who worked in the Marque's technology division, and sow them in the quarters of each of the named Sisters. The transmission was too short for its source to be traced exactly, but the analysts narrowed it down to somewhere in Upper Tannis.

On Ani's instructions, Toria was sent with three Sisters to arrest

Priety, and Liyal was dispatched with two more to seize Beyna. But Beyna heard them coming and locked herself in her cell. By the time Liyal and the others succeeded in gaining entry, Beyna had killed herself with poison.

Priety, though, was not so fortunate.

'You doubt me, Sister Priety.'

It was a statement, and the applied diplomacy lecturer seemed to wilt a little under the intensity of Ani's scrutiny. She looked to the others in the interrogation chamber, but found no pity in their eyes.

'My apologies, your Eminence, but I'm afraid I do not understand,' Priety said. Her jaw was firm and her head high and proud, but a quaver crept into her voice.

'You seem to believe that I'm a fool.'

Priety started to protest, but Ani's voice was strident, cutting across her, quieting her whimpers.

'You are a spy. You have engaged in acts of treason against the Sisterhood. A lecturer in manners, an apparent expert in protocol, yet you have shown yourself willing to sell out your Sisters to those who would destroy this order.'

'No,' cried Priety, her composure slipping. 'No, your Eminence, I would not! I would never!'

Ani held up a hand to silence her. On her palm was the tattooed eye of the Sisterhood – clear, strong-lined and unchanging. Priety recoiled from its unfaltering gaze before attempting to renew her protestations.

'Enough,' said Ani loudly. 'Do not compound your transgressions by insulting my intelligence!'

For a brief moment, Ani heard Syrene in the words that came from her own mouth, and she was grateful for her apprenticeship. There was a time when she would have been far too timid and kindly to speak to anyone in that way, particularly one who had been her own teacher only a few years before, but now the words came out smoothly, as though she had been born to this life of rule. Even Syrene would have been impressed.

'Enough with your lies!' Ani snapped, for good measure.

Priety's jowls quivered ever so slightly, and Ani thought her expression had changed, as if she might cry. Here it comes, she thought. Here comes the begging and the snivelling.

'Please,' said Priety, and her head fell forward, her eyes to the floor. 'You must understand, Archmage. I was merely concerned . . .'

At this, Ani nodded over the top of Priety's bent head, signalling to the others that this was it, this was the confession. The rest was a mere formality. In the shadows of the interrogation chamber, Kumuru, Chief Scribe of the Sisterhood, acknowledged Ani's gesture and continued annotating the record of proceedings on the screen that glowed before her. What transpired in the chamber was being recorded, but to the record Kumuru added observations about gestures, responses, tone.

There was no triumph, though, but instead a sinking in Ani's guts, for now she knew it to be true: she had been betrayed, yet again. She stared angrily at the top of Priety's skull, at the carefully whorled pattern of her closely shorn scalp, at the stupid thin plait that sprouted forlornly from her crown, twisted and fashioned to curl back on itself.

'Why, Priety?' interjected Valisus, the Marque's formidable head of security. Today she looked fiercer than ever. Beyna's death had infuriated her and she blamed Liyal for bungling the arrest. Without Beyna to interrogate, one avenue of investigation had been closed off, and they would have nothing against which to compare Priety's testimony. 'What were you concerned about?'

'I was worried about the Archmage.'

'You were worried about me?' said Ani, momentarily confused, but even as the words left her lips, she understood what the lecturer had actually meant. She was not worried about the incumbent Archmage, but the previous one.

'Am *I* not the Archmage, Sister?' continued Ani coldly. She felt little but contempt, tempered only by weariness that she'd been deceived by one whom she thought she could trust.

The older woman looked up, appalled, her ears reddening as she realised what she'd said. 'Indeed you are, your Eminence,' she said.

'Indeed I am,' repeated Ani. 'But your concern was not for me, was it, Priety? I am not *your* Archmage.'

'No. I mean yes – my concern is always for you, Archmage: you and only you. You are my esteemed Archmage.'

Priety sniffed loudly, and phlegm rattled in her throat.

'Yet you were also worried about my predecessor, about the *former* Archmage Syrene, correct?' said Ani. She spoke slowly, and never once did her chilly gaze waver. Ani could out-stare anybody.

'Only as a friend, your Eminence,' muttered Priety, 'I was only concerned as her old friend.'

'But was I not selected personally by Syrene as her replacement?'

'You were.'

'Did she not announce this herself?'

Priety nodded, her jaw tightening.

'And yet you question this?'

Suddenly Priety's pretence of weakness and begging fell away, and she looked upon Ani with undisguised hatred.

'You charlatan,' said Priety. 'You are not fit to wash the Archmage's feet. You have done something to her. She would not have surrendered her power so easily to one such as you, not after all that she had done to secure her position, and elevate the Sisterhood. Everything about you is a lie, and you will be exposed.'

'Who told you to plant those transmitters?' asked Ani.

Priety wouldn't even look at her now. 'I have nothing more to say. I demand a trial by my Sisters, as is my right. I demand—'

'Look at me,' said Ani, and her voice changed. Although her attention was fixed on Priety, every Sister in the chamber turned her eyes on the Archmage, such was the force of her will. Priety, fixed in Ani's gaze, was powerless to resist.

'Who am I?' asked Ani.

Priety stared at her.

'You are Vena, of course,' said Priety, and in her mind she was no longer in an interrogation chamber on the Marque but in the offices of Vena, a place that she had never seen but which had now been constructed for her by Ani.

'Who told you to plant the transmitters in the Marque?'

'Why, you did,' said Priety.

It had been a guess on Ani's part, but a good one.

'And who else besides Beyna did I entrust with this task?'

'Coriol. Gara. Jenis.'

Ani flicked her eyes to Valisus, but the security chief was already making for the door.

'For what purpose?'

'To establish the whereabouts of the Archmage Syrene,' said Priety, as though reciting a poem that she had learned long before. 'To find evidence that Ani Cienda is engaged in activities against the best interests of the Illyri Empire, with the aim of removing her as Archmage and facilitating her arrest, trial and execution.'

Ani had heard enough. She allowed the false surroundings to fall away from Priety and her own appearance to be restored in the older Sister's eyes. Priety blinked hard, and immediately understood what had occurred. She bolted towards the door, but was restrained by Toria.

'You have betrayed me,' said Ani.

'My devotion is not to you but to the Nairenes,' replied Priety. 'I am loyal to the Sisterhood before all else.'

'Then we will hear from your Sisters.'

The illumination in the interrogation chamber grew stronger, revealing the rest of the Council of Confidantes seated in a ring of raised seats. Aside from the now absent Valisus, there was Kumuru the scribe; Cientia, the Nairene chief of science; Saecula, the head of celestial geography; Peritia, the engineering expert; Mjek, an ageing doctor from the medical corps; Amera, Ani's former biology lecturer; Illan, the Sisterhood's chief designer; and finally, somewhat surprisingly, there was ancient Onwyn, former head of the Novice libraries, but now holder of the ceremonial post of chief librarian, for she was as knowledgeable as she was gnarled.

There were others who served on smaller advisory, technological, and exploratory councils, but these eight females, along with Valisus, made up Ani's hand-picked inner circle of nine. Toria and Liyal provided muscle, when needed. Cocile, as Ani's chief aide, was the only other Sister allowed into their meetings, and that was solely at Ani's discretion.

'Have you heard enough?' asked Ani.

The eight answered in unison: 'Yes.'

'Are you satisfied of Sister Priety's guilt.'

'Yes.'

'Are you content to leave her punishment to me.'

And for a final time, the answer came: 'Yes.'

'Then you may go. Thank you, Sisters.'

The Council departed, leaving Ani, Toria and Liyal alone with the convicted Priety. Her countenance had changed once more: she had shrunken into herself, and her eyes watered with fear.

'Please, your Eminence,' said Priety, 'don't kill me.'

'Why would I take your life?' said Ani.

Priety seemed not to hear her. 'And if you feel you must kill me,' she begged, 'let it be quick, and not the cascids. I beg of you this one mercy.'

The cascids were the ancient, hungry anthropods that patrolled the moon beyond the secure doors of the Marque. It was whispered that to be fed to them was the ancient punishment for treason.

'You're negotiating your punishment, so am I to presume that you freely admit your guilt?' Ani replied.

'Anything I did was with the best of intentions,' said Priety, and Ani could almost see the calculations she was making. 'My devotion is to the Nairenes – always to the Sisterhood before all else. This at least deserves consideration in my sentencing.'

'Sister Priety,' said Ani, 'I am not needlessly cruel. Your execution was never a possibility. I might have considered exile, once, but instead I decree that you shall spend the rest of your days here, on the Marque, where you shall be sequestered alongside your much beloved friend, Syrene. After all, you appear to want to be reunited with her more than anything.'

Priety's mouth gaped open in surprise.

'This is my *punishment*?' she said.

'Indeed it is. Henceforth, you will tread the path of the First Five. I only hope you will find the experience as illuminating as you might have wished. If you are in agreement then I shall escort you there myself.'

'I agree,' said Priety, her countenance one of awe.

'Then gather your things, Sister Priety, and say your final farewells quickly . . .'

Liyal and Toria accompanied the Archmage Ani and the disgraced Priety through the lesser-used tunnels of the Marque's inner realms. Liyal held Priety's small bag of personal items, while Toria carried a length of black cloth folded across one arm, as if she were a waiter.

'Nearly there now,' said Ani sweetly, quickening her step as they approached an apparently blank wall so that she reached it ahead of the others. She pressed the eye on her palm against one of the old rocks and immediately a great groan issued forth, and the wall started sliding to one side.

'Now, Priety,' she said, 'Toria is going to blindfold you.'

'What?'

Ani smiled soothingly.

'It is but a precaution, for the secrets of the Second Realm are known to only a few. Rest assured that they will all be revealed to you in time.'

Without further ado, Toria stepped forward and wrapped the heavy fabric across Priety's face.

They continued quickly through the tunnels, Ani activating other doors as they went, Toria and Liyal holding Priety between them, moving her along, ensuring she didn't stumble. Somewhere along the way, Liyal had disposed of Priety's bag of belongings. She wouldn't need it now.

A final door opened, and Ani told her guards to go no further.

'We're entering the Realm of the First Five,' she whispered enticingly to Priety, guiding the older Sister forward. Gradually Priety became aware of a new smell in the still air: a strange, sweet freshness. It took her a while to identify it: disinfectant. There was a low whirring noise and a fine mist settled on her exposed forehead.

'What was that?' she asked. Nobody answered, but a firm hand grasped her elbow, moving her on.

She heard the hiss of an automatic door and a mechanical voice spoke, reminding all personnel to adhere to safety procedures before entering. Another door slid softly open and she was pushed inside. A thick, heavily scented spray enveloped Priety's body, wetting her robes and making the blindfold stick to her face. She gagged.

'What's happening?' she asked, frightened, but Ani softly shushed her from close by, her voice now with a faintly mechanical tone to it, as though it were being fed through a speaking apparatus. Priety began to panic. Something was very wrong.

'I don't want to do this,' she said. 'I've changed my mind. I choose exile.'

'Hush, Priety,' whispered Ani. 'Your Sister is sleeping. Do not wake her.'

The sound of a final door opening reached the sodden lecturer, and immediately a strong odour cut through the overpowering reek of the disinfectant, a stench at once meaty and foul, tempered with decay and bodily waste. Before Priety could react, or even shout in alarm, a hand was clamped across her mouth, and she was propelled forward and pushed into a chair. Cuffs were snapped around her wrists as she struggled, and then the blindfold was unwound from her eyes. Beside her she saw Syrene, but Syrene did not see her, for Syrene was otherwise occupied.

The Red Witch sat statue-still in her chair, her body emaciated beneath her robes, her eyes the colour of curdled milk. But worse – far worse – were the tendrils and filaments of red that twisted from inside her skull, which was open like a serving dish, exposing the brain within.

But that was not all Priety saw, for it was only the beginning of the horror. A massive insectoid shape moved across the web above her as the first of its tendrils slowly snaked down towards her head.

'Now you may scream, if you wish,' whispered Ani from behind her protective mask.

And scream Priety did, over and over again, until that at which she screamed finally silenced her.

CHAPTER 51

Ani watched from behind the safety of the strengthened glass window as the One went about its work. Back on Earth, a young Illyri named Cedus had kept a tarantula as a pet, to which he would feed cockroaches. Ani felt uncomfortably like Cedus as the bulk of the One positioned itself above Priety, her skull already almost entirely concealed beneath a mass of tendrils. By now, the One was the size of a large dog, its black eyes like holes in its being, vestiges of the dark universe from which it had emerged. Still, its growth had slowed since Ani had separated it from the First Five, putting them out of their pain at last.

Only here, in this repository for the foulest of secrets, was Ani truly alone. Only she had access to this place, and the burden of what was kept here was for her to bear. It was fate that had brought her here.

Fate, and Syrene.

The Archmage Syrene used to disappear into the deep recesses of the Marque on a weekly basis – never more frequently, never less.

'She's going to meet with the First Five,' said Cocile haughtily when Ani, then still Syrene's newest aide, asked where the Archmage went on such occasions, 'though I doubt that it's any of your business.'

Cocile was a little cautious around Ani. She knew her to be Gifted, but remained unclear about her talents. She was aware that Ani had been one of the Chosen, a Blue Novice, and Cocile had feared these upstarts more than she cared to admit, for she felt that they threatened her own position as Syrene's handmaiden. Cocile liked to be in charge, or at least in charge of holding the coat of whoever was actually in charge, and she took absolute pride in her stoicism, her hard work, her discretion, and her dedication to her mistress, even to the extent of putting Syrene's needs before those of the Sisterhood itself. The Archmage would act for the Nairenes, she reasoned, and Cocile would act for the Archmage. That was how Cocile held her position. She didn't question, she didn't sulk, she took on any task, and she was wilfully blind to that which she knew she should not see. Like the Gifted, Cocile was a creation of her mistress; the only one she was more concerned about than Syrene was herself.

And then the Gifted had been wiped out – all but Ani Cienda. That blood-soaked day was one of the only times Cocile had seen her mistress cry, although her tears were not for the loss of so many young lives, but instead for the demise of her private army.

'We can start again,' said Syrene's new husband, Lord Andrus, with that strange emptiness that had become his default mode of speaking. The Other that Syrene had breathed into him so many months before, in a hot mouthful of poisonous spores, had destroyed the great Illyri he once had been, taking him over completely, although Cocile did not know that at the time. Only later would she find out about the Others . . .

'No,' Syrene had replied vaguely, talking more to herself than her spouse. 'It is too late to go back to the beginning, but they served their purpose and many of our enemies are dead. And Ani Cienda has willingly offered herself to me. She believes deeply in the nobility of the Sisterhood's cause – I know, for I have explored her mind – and that in itself is an excellent starting point. Her skills remain underdeveloped, but then she is still immature. She will only grow stronger as she grows, particularly with me as her personal mentor.'

Hearing this, Cocile had been vaguely troubled, but it soon became clear to her – and to her relief – that the young Novice was intended to fill the role of the now-dead personal scribe and second handmaiden Layne, and was no threat. As time went by, Cocile grew more at ease with Ani's presence. She saw that Syrene cared about her not so much as a Sister deserving of respect, but instead as a pretty pet being taught to fetch and sit and roll over at her mistress's bidding, and a frustrating one to train at that. She appeared to grant Ani no special affection or care, besides their daily training sessions. From these, Ani would sometimes emerge sobbing, and on more than one occasion the clear, red outline of an angry hand was imprinted on her blazing cheek.

But Ani was courteous to Cocile and went out of her way to ask her opinion, to thank her, to be considerate, just as she was considerate to so many of the Novices and older Sisters alike. She appeared to have taken the trouble to learn the name and title of every Sister she came into contact with, and endeared herself with small kindnesses, and her clear devotion to the Nairene cause.

As for Ani, she watched, and stayed quiet, for if she had learned anything from Syl it was the usefulness of observation, and she held her usually chippy tongue and practised, practised, practised. It wasn't just her clouding abilities that she honed, but also her skills as a scribe, requesting extra lessons with the bemused chief Nairene scribe Kumuru, in whose experience teenagers were all lazy and work-shy. Ani went out of her way to prove Kumuru wrong, just as she went out of her way to prove everybody who doubted her wrong, and to earn the friendship and trust of those who mattered most, including Cocile.

In very little time, the young Novice was ordained as a full Sister, and the tears of joy Ani shed on that occasion were real, for she found she had grown to love the Nairene order, and her place in it. Having a role to play, being someone who mattered, who was relied upon, who was nurtured, all of this had slowly healed the part of her that had been all but broken on that dreadful day on Erebos, when those she loved had first betrayed her and then died around her. Her workload increased, and Syrene came to rely on her, and she knew she could be happy here.

Increasingly, those who actively ran the Marque under Syrene accepted her, and more and more her attendance at official meetings went unquestioned. Her quiet figure was a shadow in the background at many a private rendezvous too, although if anyone cared to actually look properly and notice her, chances are they'd have been surprised at her presence, for it was not only on Syrene that Ani was slowly, carefully working her clouding skills.

Weeks became months, months slipped into a year, and then another, and Cocile found that she was becoming as devoted to Ani as she was to the Archmage. She confided in her, she told her things that surprised even herself as they slipped from her mouth.

And she was not alone in this.

However, Ani's path to fulfilment was marred by what Syl had told her before she fled the palace of Erebos, by what she'd said of the First Five and a creature that hid in the Marque, feeding off them; an alien entity, one of the Others, but more powerful than any they had glimpsed on Earth.

'All that is wrong with the Empire has its roots in the Marque,' Syl had contended, begging her friend to understand, and every day this statement echoed in Ani's head.

What was hidden in the Marque? Ani firmly believed that the Sisterhood had been formed with a deeply noble purpose, but if what Syl said was true, then the Nairene mission had been compromised.

As she watched Syrene, slipping away unaccompanied into the private Second Realm, week in, week out, Ani became desperate to know the truth – or perhaps the lie – of it. That was why she clouded, and why she eventually followed the unsuspecting Syrene deep into the Marque.

That was how she discovered that Syl had not lied.

What Ani saw changed her view of the Sisterhood. It was as though everything that had been in soft focus was now rendered sharp and vivid. The Sisterhood was not at fault. No, Syrene, and those like her, were the true infection.

The First Five haunted her dreams. Ezil had been the Marque's original and greatest psychic, and Ani felt sure that whatever light still flickered within the ancient, tormented Mage reached out and touched her as she slept, urging her to take action, wheedling, needling, begging, until nightmares shook Ani awake, leaving her quaking and praying for dawn.

In time she stopped sleeping and dark pools shadowed her eyes. Even Syrene noticed and asked if Ani was feeling unwell. Lista was appointed to care for her personally, and Ani wept wordlessly on the older girl's shoulder, unable to reveal the source of her grief. Finally she collapsed with exhaustion and was hospitalised. There, in the undisturbed quiet, she came to accept that she would have no peace again unless she took action. She vaguely recalled something Syl had said back on Earth, quoting a long-dead human writer: all that it took for evil to triumph was for the good to stand by and do nothing.

'I saw them, Syl,' she whispered through the window of her sickroom late that night, addressing the blackness beyond that had swallowed her old playmate. 'I saw the First Five' – she watched how the reflection of her face distorted in revulsion – 'and they were attached to that creature by tendrils, by cords of flesh and blood. They should have died long before, but that monster, the One, it keeps them alive, feeding off them. It is just as you told me.'

The memory of Syl burned brighter than ever now that Ani knew her friend had been telling the truth. She wished she could speak to her again; she wished it more than anything.

'I'm sorry I chose not to believe you,' Ani added. 'I just wanted you to be wrong. I wanted it to be a lie.'

She swallowed hard, determined not to cry, not again.

'So you know what I'm going to do, Syl?' said Ani. She waited, and perhaps the universe held its breath.

'I'm going to take control.'

CHAPTER 52

A ni clouded.

She knew herself to be one of the last truly proficient psychics in the Marque, for the Gifted training programme was no more, and none of the latest intakes of Novices showed much promise anyway. Syrene had a certain psychic ability, this was true, but Ani was so familiar to her, and such a part of her existence, that any defences Syrene might have put up against her had long since dissipated. As far as she was concerned, Ani was hers to dominate.

Only Thona, the former tutor to the Gifted, posed a significant threat, though Ani suspected she was not half as powerful as she liked to think. Meanwhile, the old clairvoyant witch Oriel was long dead, thanks to Syl, and the smattering of older Gifted Half-Sisters – now full Sisters themselves – had been dispersed throughout the Marque, their relatively minor talents left to fade through neglect, like the promise of student musicians who cease to practise regularly. Few remained who could stand against her.

So Ani began planning her coup. It took patience and discipline, and all the time she heard the voice of Ezil, real or imagined, calling to her, encouraging her, crying for her to hurry. She harnessed her power, storing it, saving it, until the night that she went to Syrene's chambers and, as the Archmage slept, put her hands to her head, flooding her consciousness, clouding her to such a degree that Syrene's own identity was lost for a time. All that was left was a shell, a mouthpiece, and from it emerged the words that Ani wished it to speak. Seclusion. Isolation.

Successor.

★ ★ ★

Then, at last, when the deed was done and the news of Ani Cienda's elevation was still being absorbed by the Sisterhood, the new Archmage led the old into the recesses of the Marque and freed the First Five from their torment: first Atis, then Loneil, then Ineh and finally Tola, all the while keeping a watch on the creature that rested in a web of tendrils above them.

To her relief, the One had not reacted, at least not at first. It did not move, but simply waited, watching from its lair. Even then, Ani thought, it knew: it had felt her inside Syrene's head and understood that this Archmage's time was passing, and another was about to take her place. A new deal was about to be struck.

Perhaps the Ore thought it a blessing, for the old females beneath it were stinking and shrivelled within the dry sacks of their own skin, and three of them had slumped into death as soon as they were disconnected from their life support, the red tendrils and fleshy cables emerging from their skulls wilting and decaying as the Sisters slipped away one by one.

Tola, however, had not gone immediately. Briefly, the old Sister's white-filmed eyes had filled with fluid – tears; it could only be tears – and the milkiness was washed away. She saw Ani then, and the faintest of smiles played on her lips. She raised her right hand as if in blessing, and then she too died, the connective cords writing from her head to lie spent and useless on the floor.

If she had ever had any doubts, at that moment Ani knew that she had done the right thing. Whatever knowledge the Others possessed had not been worth the sacrifice that the First Five had made to access it. The Sisterhood had been wise and knowledgeable in its own right once, before the Others had come. It could be so again. All that remained now was to release Ezil, the eldest. Buoyed by success, Ani reached out and pulled a fistful of life-supporting wires from Ezil's chest.

The screech that came from above her was like no sound she had ever heard before. Whatever the One had been anticipating when the connection with Ezil was broken, it was not this. Ani looked up in horror, pinwheeling her arms as she stumbled backwards over the cords and out of the way, for numerous sucking tentacles shot from the One's torso and grappled with the air, seeking new life. They wrapped desperately around Ezil again, boring into her skull and face and neck, greedy for her life force, until she was obscured from the shoulders upwards. The creature's black eyes found Ani and held her fast, glittering with ancient malevolence, demanding that the deal be done.

For a moment, Ani considered letting it die. If it perished, would the remaining Others die with it? She couldn't be sure, but she feared they would not. And how might they react to the death of their originator? She had a terrible vision of infected Illyri, overcome by the parasites they carried inside them, spewing spores into the faces of the innocent, infesting an entire society, invading Avila Minor, ripping apart the Sisterhood. She could not take that chance.

And that was when she gave Syrene to the One.

I showed her some mercy, Ani thought as she regarded the dreadful figure of the lost Syrene through the glass. She had clouded the Archmage's brain so much that Syrene barely recognised her own Marque as she was helped by Ani into its depths. It was only at the end, when Ani began suiting up, and Syrene's surroundings became familiar to her again, that she started to panic, but Ani had simply clouded her mind a little more, like an anaesthetist increasing the flow of gas, and the Red Witch grew calmer. As Ani led her forward, the One cast aside the corpse of Ezil, its suckers curling away in something like disgust before unravelling again and fixing on Syrene. Immediately, they wrapped themselves around her head, pounding at her scalp, cracking the shell around her brain.

As Syrene took Ezil's place, the Other in her head reacted to the presence of its sire and reached for it. Filaments and coils emerged from her ears and forced themselves through the bones of her skull, shattering the pan and exposing the brain.

Oh God, the blood . . .

In turn the One stretched to be reunited with its offspring, and within seconds Syrene's eyes had rolled up in her head as the three organisms – Illyri, Other, One – became a single symbiote.

It had, Ani supposed afterwards, represented a good bargain for the One. Ezil and the other four Sisters were almost entirely used up: they had little life left for the One to suck from them. Syrene might have been only one Illyri, but she was strong, and easily worth five old husks.

I gave her to that monster, Ani thought. I condemned her to a life of pain.

And Ani wondered if she and the former Archmage were so different after all.

CHAPTER 53

Ani stared mesmerised through the glass, watching the One embrace its latest prey, just as it had Syrene so many months before, a lifetime ago.

Priety finally stopped struggling. Her eyes had filmed with white and her face was crusted with blood and tears. Had there been anyone to bear witness, Ani might have found herself accused of unforgivable cruelty for what she had done to Priety; and, in truth, the Archmage did feel a certain amount of guilt, although not enough to cripple her. But there had been purpose to Ani's actions: Priety's fresh energy and life force would sate the One, at least for a time. It would gorge itself upon her vitality. Already Ani could see its body pumping, absorbing Priety's essence. She had watched the same process occur with Syrene, and the One had been sluggish to the point of dormancy for days after. It had given her time to remove the bodies of the First Five, and to incinerate each of them in the furnace used by the medical droids to burn the contaminated clothing and medical supplies of the old Nairenes.

Though it was exhausting work, all this she did alone. She had understood from Syrene that only Oriel had known the truth about the One and the First Five, and Oriel was dead, killed by Syl Hellais. It was better, thought Ani, that the One should remain a secret. Secrets had power.

But the One kept its own secrets too. Since it was in contact with all of the Others, it could theoretically have communicated to them the truth about Syrene's fate and brought the force of the Others and their Illyri hosts down on Ani. It had not. Ani could only conclude that, for now, the One was prepared to bide its time, for it had all the time that there was, and all there ever would be. The One was so ancient that its conception of the epochs was entirely different from that of the Illyri or any other race. For it, years were like seconds, and Ani had barely been Archmage for any time at all.

Ani waited. Gradually, the One's movements slowed, and it sagged in its web and curled its legs in upon itself. Only then did she re-enter the chamber.

'Syrene.'

Ani spoke the former Archmage's name, and at the same time inserted the needle into Syrene's left forearm, dosing her with an ephedrone derivative – a potent monoamine alkaloid stimulant. Instantly Syrene's back arched and her mouth opened wide. Her eyes remained white, but they moved in their sockets as Syl repeated her name.

'*Aaaaannnni,*' rasped the Archmage, '*you traitor.*'

At least, thought Ani, all this time under the control of the One hadn't changed Syrene much.

'Does it hurt a lot?' asked Ani.

'*Yesssss.*'

'I can bring it to an end.'

A pause.

'*Do it.*'

Another pause.

'*Please.*'

'First, tell me about the One.'

'*What is the One?*'

'The creature that holds you.'

'*It wants to breed.*'

'What else?'

'*To feed. And . . .*'

'Go on.'

'*It wants Syl Hellais.*'

Ani was taken aback, but of course the One would know about

Syl, for it was inside Syrene's brain; it knew everything that she did.

'Syl Hellais is dead,' said Ani.

'*It does not believe this. It has heard . . . echoes of her.*'

Oh, thought Ani, if only that were true.

'Why would it want her?' she asked.

Above Syl's head, the One stirred. She knew that she was taking a chance with the stimulant. Since Syrene was linked to the One, some of the effects of the ephedrine would rub off on the creature. She did not have long.

'*Because she is powerful, and her power would become its power.*'

The web shook. The One's legs began to uncurl. It was time to go, but Syrene had a last message for her.

'*This is not the One,*' she said. '*There is another . . . greater.*'

Ani backed away. The One was moving now. It turned to face Ani and its black eyes seemed to bore into her. Only when she was safely through the airlock did Ani realise that she had been holding her breath.

'*Kill me!*' cried Syrene, her sightless eyes searching for Ani. '*You promised! Kill me!*'

And then the tendrils tightened around her brain and she fell silent.

XIII
EARTH

CHAPTER 54

The *Revenge*, with the *Marauder* just behind it, picked up the three Illyri ships orbiting the Earth shortly after it entered the solar system. Their home was so close now, and they still had hope. All might not yet be lost for their small blue planet.

And if they were wrong?

Well, then they would wage war.

'What have we got, Alis?' asked Steven.

'The largest is a transporter, but I'm not getting any details. I would suggest that, given the secret nature of its mission to Earth, it was never registered.'

The screens gave them the dimensions of the transporter. It was much larger than any they had seen on Archaeon, which meant that the spores collected there had been taken elsewhere and then loaded onto this craft for delivery to Earth.

'And the others?'

'A destroyer, the *Satia*, and the *Iria*, a cruiser.'

At least the *Revenge*'s systems could help them with these two, and Steven soon had details of their crew, weaponry and defences. He wasn't concerned about the transporter. At best, its attack and defence capabilities would be minimal. Transporters weren't designed for a fight. In fact, because of the Illyri's presumed superiority to any other species in the universe, very few of its ships had, until recently, been battle-ready. Even destroyers, despite their name, were typically underequipped for a stand-up fight with another vessel of similar size. The Civil War had changed that, and the escort convoy they'd encountered on the way to Krasis had clearly been retrofitted for battle. But only the more advanced Corps ships, such as those used to attack Melos Station and other Military targets at the start of the war, and of which the *Revenge* and *Marauder* were examples, were really fully fledged combat vessels.

Unfortunately, the *Satia* was one of them too. Steven became worried as its specifications were revealed to him. It was worth half a dozen cruisers like his own. The *Iria* was less of a threat, but it was only a generation behind the *Satia*, and had obviously been designed by the Corps with one eye on the possibility of war with the Military, for it was a significant fighting vessel. They had one Cayth torpedo left, and after that they'd be relying on conventional weapons. The *Satia* would be the main target, but the *Iria* would have to be dealt with before they could get close to it. He wasn't sure that using Alis as the public face of their approach would work on this occasion, not with the earth reduced to a secret breeding ground for the Others.

They had some time to prepare, though. It would be days before they got to Earth and, even with the relays, it would take about two hours for any transmission from the orbiting craft to reach them. Steven handed over control of the *Revenge* to one of the newly acquired Brigade pilots and, accompanied by Alis and Hague, went to his cabin to open a secure channel with Rizzo.

The first communication reached them exactly two hours and seven minutes later. It came from the *Iria*, and was bad news from the start. To begin with, it identified both the *Revenge* and the *Marauder* by their former names, the *Gradus* and the *Ilfen*, and demanded confirmation of mission from their respective captains, Waltere and Sulus. Neither of them was likely to be answering such calls anytime soon, Waltere having been scoured from the *Gradus* by Cayth technology, and Sulus being among the dead on Krasis. But it worried Steven that the *Iria* was seeking to communicate with them personally. It was possible that the waiting Illyri had somehow been informed of a possible problem with one or both of the approaching ships, and were now on the alert.

'Delay them, Alis,' he said.

'How?'

'I don't know. Just tell them Waltere and Sulus are in a meeting.'

'I'm not your secretary!'

'Alis, this really isn't the time.'

'Fine.'

Was that a huff? It certainly looked and sounded like one to Steven.

Alis opened visual and audio channels. There was no point in trying to spin a tale of lost visuals on both the *Revenge* and the *Marauder*. That would just strain credulity from the start. At least Alis was prepared; she had found some of Yallee's voice recordings on the ship's log and could now imitate her perfectly. Also, with a flight cap pulled low on her head, she bore a passing resemblance to the dead officer.

'This is First Officer Yallee on board the *Gradus*,' she replied. 'Commander Waltere is concluding a discussion with Captain Sulus, and requests your indulgence until the meeting is over.'

This time, the delay between sending and receiving was about three hours in total: they were eating up the miles between the wormhole and the nearest relay. As soon as they passed it, communications between them and the *Iria* would be virtually instantaneous.

The image of a female officer appeared on the screen. She wore the black of the Securitats.

'This is Security Officer Pemaynell,' she said. 'Unauthorised entry to this solar system is prohibited. Under security order seven-zero-two I demand that the senior officers present themselves and explain the reason for their intrusion here.'

'What's security order seven-zero-two when it's at home?' Steven asked Alis.

'I have no idea. Must be new.'

'I hate people who go around making up new rules.'

'What do you want me to tell her?'

'Tell her nothing. Whatever answer we give will be the wrong one. Let's leave them wondering for as long as we can.'

In retrospect, perhaps they shouldn't even have answered the first message, but it was too late now. The situation was always only going to end one way: with the *Revenge* and the *Marauder* facing off against the *Iria* and the *Satia*.

'We're receiving demands for security clearance codes from both ships,' said Alis.

'Send them whatever codes we picked up on Krasis.'

It was all smoke and mirrors. Every problem they caused the Illyri, every communication that needed to be examined or decoded, brought them a step closer to home.

Two more transmissions were received from Pemaynell. The first simply repeated her request that Waltere and Sulus appear before her. The second was more interesting and set Steven's mind at rest, if only a little. Pemaynell was obviously confused – those security codes probably helped – which meant that she didn't have certain knowledge of a problem on board the two new Illyri craft, and therefore wasn't prepared to regard them as hostile without further confirmation. But she was also clear on the reception they would face if they continued on their present course.

'In the absence of a satisfactory response,' she warned, 'we are placing our fleet on full alert. If you approach within half a million miles of this world, we will respond with force.'

'Half a million miles?' Steven asked Alis.

'About twice the distance from the earth to the moon.'

'Maybe she has problems with intimacy,' interjected Hague. 'I bet she doesn't like being hugged. And someone should also tell her that she doesn't have a fleet. She's only got three ships.'

'It's one more than we have,' said Steven.

'Nobody likes a pessimist.'

Steven opened a channel to the *Marauder*.

'Rizzo, have you been listening to all that?'

'Loud and clear.'

'Let's see if they're still so bullish once we get within range.'

'Understood.'

One of their new crew spoke up. His name was Muren, and he was small, blond and sixteen. He looked less like he belonged in the Brigades than in a particularly unthreatening Scandinavian boy band.

'Sir?' said Muren. 'Won't they fire when we get in range?'

'Probably,' Steven replied.

Muren digested this.

'What'll we do then, sir?'

'We'll try not to be wherever they're aiming when it happens.'

'Okay.' It didn't appear to be the answer that Muren had been hoping for.

'Are you worried?'

'A bit, sir.'

'Do you have family back on Earth?'

'Yes, sir. My mother and father, and my two sisters. They're in Oslo. Or were.'

'I left my mother in Edinburgh,' said Steven. 'I want to find out if she's safe too. I can't do that if I let some Illyri destroyer blow us to smithereens, can I?'

'No, I don't suppose so, sir.'

'So don't go concerning yourself about what those Illyri may or may not try to do once we get closer. It's them who should be worried about us. In the meantime, I have a job for you. I want you to collect details of the immediate families of everyone on board the *Revenge* and the *Marauder*. Once we establish contact with whatever is left of the Resistance, we'll set about trying to learn what's happened to them all.'

'Yes, sir.'

Muren gave a salute and trotted off to find a stylus and a recording pad.

'Nicely done, Ste— sir,' said Hague. 'If you don't mind my saying so.'

'What about you, Sergeant? Do you have family back on Earth?'

'A sister, somewhere,' said Hague. 'We were never close.'

'Are you worried about her?'

'Not really.'

'Seriously?'

'You know how they used to say that only rats and cockroaches would survive a nuclear apocalypse?'

'Yes.'

'It's not true. My sister would survive as well. The rats and cockroaches would probably make her their queen.'

Steven thought about this.

'Well, one person fewer for us to find, then,' he said.

'Happy to have helped, sir.'

Together they stared at the images of the *Satia* and the *Iria* on the screen before them.

'That's a big destroyer,' said Hague.

'Yes, it is,' said Steven. 'I don't know what we're going to do with it once we capture it.'

Hague stared at him and then began to laugh. It was an honest laugh, huge and generous, and when Steven looked around the cockpit he saw that the sound of it had caused the rest of the crew to smile as well, even the returning Muren.

Steven smiled with them, even though he'd been quite serious in his reply.

He really wasn't sure what they were going to do with the *Satia* once it was theirs.

Day by day the tension increased as they drew closer and closer to Earth. The Illyri made no further attempt to contact them. The *Marauder* destroyed the main communications relay just beyond Jupiter's orbit around the sun. The relay was bigger than the rest, and equipped with message drones that could be sent through the wormhole. They had detected no such drones being dispatched before they reached the relay, which Steven considered a mistake on the part of Pemaynell and her colleagues. Perhaps they'd been hoping that the approaching ships would leave the relay intact, and if necessary a drone could be sent once they were safely past it. Had one been activated before the intruders reached the relay, it could have been chased down and destroyed. In this particular case, the Illyri had gambled, and lost.

They had Mars in sight when the *Satia* and the *Iria* started to come about. By the time they reached the limits of the exclusion zone, the *Revenge* and the *Marauder* were at battle stations.

'Rizzo?' said Steven. He spoke softly, and her voice came back to him over his personal earbud.

'Receiving.'

'You're clear on your orders?'

'I'm clear. Cooper will be at the helm. He is Sergeant Agostino's recommendation.'

Steven didn't need to ask where Rizzo would be. She would be at her weapons station. He, on the other hand, would be in sole charge of the *Revenge*, with Alis as backup should anything happen to him.

'Good luck, Rizzo.'

'And you. Sir.'

The moon loomed before them. The *Revenge* and the *Marauder* were running alongside each other, but now they separated, the *Revenge* moving to port, the *Marauder* to starboard, both in order to approach their assigned ships and make themselves more difficult to target in turn. For a few moments the images of the *Satia* and *Iria* were lost, and then they were no longer required, for the two Illyri vessels became clearly visible before them, the destroyer lagging behind the cruiser, but both coming on fast. The *Satia* fired first, sending two torpedoes past the *Iria* and towards the *Revenge*. Steven let them approach, a pair of blurred stars slowly increasing in size, then veered hard to starboard, skimming the surface of the moon, following the Mare Imbrium, the Sea of Showers, bringing the torpedoes with them until the Montes Appeninus mountain range appeared like a grey wall before them. It filled the cockpit windows so that even Hague swore in apprehension, and he was not alone.

Then Steven was ascending near-vertically, following the face of Mons Huygens, and the *Revenge* shook as the torpedoes struck the foot of the mountain. Steven threw her to port, drawing away from the great peak and avoiding the slew of debris from the torpedo impact.

Beside him, Alis was monitoring the progress of the *Marauder*.

'The *Marauder* has engaged the *Iria*,' she said.

Steven risked a glance at the display and saw an image of the two cruisers embroiled in a dogfight, the *Marauder* drawing the *Iria* away from the destroyer, which, even with its advanced targeting, could not risk firing upon Rizzo for fear of hitting its own sister craft.

Now the *Satia* was again visible to the *Revenge*. Steven approached it from below, limiting its use of torpedoes but exposing the *Revenge* to heavy cannon fire. Not all of it could be avoided. They took near-simultaneous hits to starboard, and alarms began to whine.

'Damage report,' shouted Steven.

'We'll live, for now,' said Hague from behind him. 'No hull breach, but another one like that and we'll be breathing stardust.'

The *Revenge* opened fire with its own cannon, raking the underside of the *Satia*. Steven watched with satisfaction as explosions bloomed along its length. Just as Agostino had made his pilot's recommendation to Rizzo, so too had Hague suggested a gunner to Steven: Biela, a Pole who Hague reckoned was only eighteen but looked ten years older than that, right down to his massive, fiery beard. Steven wasn't sure about the facial hair, but Biela could certainly shoot.

Cannon fire raged around them. The *Revenge* was hit again, but Steven did not waver from his course. He didn't think of Rizzo, or the *Marauder*, or the *Iria*. He had no mother, no brother. He no longer even had a name. There was just the great destroyer before him, and the feel of the controls in his hands. He broke his spell of concentration only once, when the stars finally disappeared and only the *Satia* remained, and that was to say: 'All weapons to me.'

Biela disengaged. The cannon ceased pounding.

'Torpedo ready,' confirmed Alis.

And Steven fired.

The *Satia* was struck amidships, its shielding no match for the Cayth missile. Whether this torpedo was somehow different from the rest, or the *Satia*'s armour caused it to react unusually, Steven did not know, but a ring of bright light surrounded the heart of the destroyer before expanding laterally, slowly immersing the ship in its glow until the totality of the *Satia* was luminescing. And as the light moved, Steven thought that he could almost see the interior of the ship, and the lives of its crew being annihilated one by one, as though the torpedo had doused it in X-rays. The *Satia*'s engines died, but the temporary energy field created by the torpedo prevented it from drifting. A small Brigade force was ready to enter the ship and claim it on command, but while Steven wanted the *Satia*, first there was the *Iria* to be dealt with.

He turned away from the stricken destroyer and prepared to join the *Marauder* in the battle.

Cooper was a good pilot, but whoever was in charge of the *Iria* was better. The *Marauder* had found itself engaged in a lethal dogfight with the technologically inferior vessel, each craft taking small hits but neither being able to deliver a knockout blow, the skill of the *Iria*'s pilot negating the superiority of the *Marauder*.

Rizzo knew her mission: if possible, Steven only wanted the *Iria* disabled and its crew forced to surrender. She had hoped to be able to oblige, but now she would be happy just to get the *Iria* under her guns for long enough to tear it apart and leave its debris floating in space. The *Iria* was currently behind them, and Cooper was doing his best to shake it off and then manoeuvre into a position that would give Rizzo a clear shot, but the damage sustained by the *Marauder* had slowed it down, and it was not responding as well as before.

'Dammit, Cooper!' shouted Rizzo in frustration, not for the first time.

'I'm trying.'

'Try harder.'

She gave the *Iria* a blast from the rear cannon, but it tricked to port and the shots went wide.

'Oh, come on!'

And then a series of blasts rocked the *Iria* as the *Revenge* arrived to help, giving Cooper the chance to pull above it and deliver Rizzo her firing opportunity. With both the *Revenge* and the *Marauder* bearing down on it, the *Iria* was lost. It tried to keep them at bay, but the *Revenge*'s hits had knocked out its rear cannon and damaged its starboard engine, causing it to list. Steven left it to Rizzo to deliver the killer shot, but as she did so, briefly turning the *Iria* into a fireball, a single round object shot from the disintegrating ship.

'It's a communications drone,' said Rizzo. 'I've got it.'

After all this, the last thing they needed was for a drone to alert the Illyri to what had happened to its ships above the earth, but a stray piece of hull from the *Iria* floated by Rizzo's sights at the crucial moment, and the drone was obscured.

'Go, Cooper!' cried Rizzo. 'Stay with it.'

Cooper reacted, shadowing the drone, but as he turned so too did it, coming back towards them instead of continuing on a trajectory out of the solar system.

'That's weird,' said Rizzo, and suddenly her earpiece barked into life and she heard Steven shouting.

'Back down, Rizzo, back down! That's not a drone, it's a—'

The mine exploded, and from it emerged a cloud of smaller magnetic minelets. Rizzo heard them strike the hull of the *Marauder*, like hail landing on a tin roof.

'Sorry, Steven,' she said.

And then the *Marauder* was gone.

CHAPTER 55

Steven watched the *Marauder* disappear. One moment it was there, the minelets like small thorns embedded in the skin of the ship, and the next it had disintegrated. The mine had been designed to take out a destroyer or a carrier, which was why the *Iria*'s commander had not used it until the *Iria* itself was doomed, for otherwise there was a grave risk of causing the destruction of two ships. The smaller *Marauder* had simply disintegrated under the force of the connected blasts. There were no bodies, no debris. It was as though it had never existed.

Not a word was spoken on the *Revenge*. Steven and Alis had lost Rizzo, but the Brigade troops all had friends, cousins, and even a brother on the *Marauder*. Now they were no more. The total, horrified quiet that filled the cabin was louder than any words.

It was left to Alis to break the silence.

'Steven,' she said.

He couldn't look at her. He remained staring blurry-eyed at the empty space once occupied by the *Marauder*, as though willing it back into existence to prove his vision wrong.

'Steven,' Alis repeated, more urgently now.

'What?' he snapped.

He was surprised to be able to speak even that one small word without hearing his voice break under the strain.

'There is another ship.'

He had forgotten the transporter. Now, on the screen, he saw it lurch into life. It was trying to escape the carnage, like some big awkward animal fleeing the hunters' guns once the rest of its herd had been destroyed.

'Take us to it,' he ordered.

The transporter was only lightly armed. It sent a few desultory shots the *Revenge*'s way, but Biela carefully targeted the weapons and they ceased firing. The unknown vessel was huge: by comparison, the *Revenge* was like a fly approaching an elephant. This was what had brought the Others to Earth. This was what had reduced his home to a breeding ground for those abominations.

This ship.

Had the *Revenge* possessed another Cayth torpedo, Steven might have chosen to cleanse the transporter. After all, he could have found some use for it. But without the torpedo, it was just a polluted ark. He wondered how many spores remained on it. The fact that it had not left Earth's orbit indicated that it might still be in use.

'They're hailing us,' said Alis.

'Open a channel,' Steven replied.

He was surprised to see the image of Pemaynell appear again. He would have expected her to be on the *Iria*, and therefore now dead. Instead here she was, alive and well on the transporter, or as well as someone could look who had just witnessed the destruction of a destroyer and a cruiser, leaving her defenceless.

'Who are you?' asked Pemaynell.

Steven let her see him. Pemaynell's face creased in shock.

'A . . . *human?*'

'My name is Steven Kerr. I'm a Brigade pilot, and also leader of this particular unit of the Resistance.'

He turned to Alis.

'Stand up, please,' he said.

Alis did so.

'This is my second in command. Her name is Alis. She's a Mech.'

Somehow Pemaynell managed to look even more shocked.

'What have you got in your head, Security Officer Pemaynell?' asked Steven.

'I don't know what you mean.'

'Is it related to those spores you're carrying on that transporter?' asked Steven. 'I figure that's why you moved to that big ship once we appeared, so that the thing in your skull could be near its own kind. Did it tell you to try to make a run for it? What's it telling you now, Pemaynell? Is it going to blow your head apart? I've seen it happen. It looks painful.'

Pemaynell gave up any effort at deception.

'It doesn't wish to destroy me,' she said. 'It wishes to destroy you.'

'Do you think that it might be willing to negotiate?' asked Steven. From the corner of his eye, he could see Alis react with surprise.

The expression on Pemaynell's face changed. She didn't speak for a good ten seconds, and Steven wondered if she was in silent congress with the Other in her head. How badly did Pemaynell want to live? How badly did the Other want to survive?

And it wasn't just about the organism in Pemaynell's head, but about all of the potential Others contained in the holds of that transporter, each capable of infecting a human host and creating many more of its kind.

'Her name was Michaela Rizzo,' said Steven, seemingly out of the blue.

'What?' said Pemaynell.

'The soldier in command of that ship your mine destroyed. Her name was Rizzo. She was my friend.'

'It is war.'

'I didn't start it. None of us did. Just you and your kind, and those things in your heads.'

'This will not help the negotiation,' said Pemaynell. 'What are you offering?'

'Nothing,' Steven replied. 'I just wanted to see if you were stupid enough to think I'd cut a deal with a murderous scumbag like you. Biela, destroy that transporter.'

'With pleasure,' said Biela.

'You're too late!' cried Pemaynell. 'Your world is gone.'

'And shut that bitch up,' Steven added.

The connection died. Seconds later, so did everything and everyone on board the transporter.

★ ★ ★

Alis watched Steven from a distance as he wept quietly for Rizzo and the men and boys lost on the *Marauder*. She felt for him, but did not want to approach. He had destroyed the crippled transporter in an act of revenge, lashing out in pain at the loss of his comrade. Again, it was the reaction of a child. Only days earlier, he had been tormenting himself for failing to protect the Securitats on Krasis. Now he was guilty of a similar crime.

Would the Illyri on board the transporter have surrendered? And what of the spores that it contained, the seeds of the Others? Perhaps, in the end, they would have been forced to kill the crew anyway, and destroy the ship in order to dispose of the spores, but now they would never know for sure.

What kind of boy would Steven have been if the Illyri had never come to Earth? Would he have been cruel? Again, Alis did not know, but she thought not. War and killing had changed him, altering his path, forcing him to draw on aspects of his nature that would have been better left buried.

And none of this would have mattered if a part of her had not once loved him, and was still filled with affection for him.

CHAPTER 56

A team, led by Hague, was assigned to explore the *Satia* and establish whether it might be possible to operate it with a skeleton crew. Despite all of Steven's assurances, the Brigade troops insisted on going in fully armed, adrenalised to the gills for a possible firefight with survivors. It was sound discipline and standard procedure, but Steven had no illusions about the capabilities of the Cayth weapon: the *Satia* had been sterilised of all life.

The *Revenge* remained docked with the destroyer until Hague gave the all-clear, and confirmed that there were two shuttles in the bay. That was good. It meant that they could move troops and supplies between the two ships without forcing the *Revenge* to dock every time.

Steven left Hague and his men to get to grips with the *Satia*, while he and Alis took the remainder of their group down to Earth on board the *Revenge*. He felt no guilt about making straight for Edinburgh. He had fought his way from Derith, and taken Krasis, all with one aim in mind: to discover the fate of his mother.

Now the *Revenge* passed over the streets and parks of his childhood and they were all empty. Human remains, almost entirely skeletal, lay scattered on pavements and outside buildings. The only signs of life came from birds, and the insects that spattered on the glass of the cockpit as the *Revenge* flew in low over Edinburgh Castle. Some of its buildings had been burned and partially destroyed. Steven spotted the wreckage of an Illyri skimmer half-buried in the remains of the Governor's House – probably shot down during the final exodus of the Illyri.

'What is that?' asked Alis.

Steven looked to where she was pointing and saw something big and grey moving across one of the courtyards, a bone in its mouth. Was it a dog, or a cat?

'My God, it's a rat!' said Muren.

He was right. The rodent was huge, probably as long as Steven's right arm. As the *Revenge* hovered, it paused and raised itself on its hind legs, showing no fear of the ship. It was joined by more of the horrors, pouring out from sewers and under piles of stones. One smaller animal tried to yank the bone from the first rat's mouth, and received a warning swipe of a paw for its troubles. When it persisted, the first rat simply dropped the bone and went for its throat, killing it within seconds. It then proceeded to feast on its kill, preferring fresh meat to old marrow, while another rat vanished with its original prize. Tentatively, more rats joined in the meal, until the dead animal was lost beneath a roiling pack.

'How did they get so big?' asked Muren.

'Human remains,' said Biela. 'They've been eating us.'

'Why haven't the spores infected them?' Steven asked Alis.

'It may be genetic, or simply practicality,' she replied.

'Practicality?'

'Like the insects, or the birds, particularly the ones that feed on carrion. The bodies get stripped down to the bone: no smell, no risk of disease. The Others might have discovered some vulnerability to infection among themselves or the remaining Illyri.'

Birds, bugs and rats, thought Steven: is this all that's left of life on Earth?

'I need to suit up,' he said. 'We're going down there.'

Steven stood before what was left of his home.

The Illyri had destroyed it, knocking in the roof and the first floor so that everything had ended up at the bottom, the living room and kitchen now just a mass of rubble and slate and broken furniture. A yellowed notice fixed to the gate informed anyone who might have taken the time to read it that the house had been rendered uninhabitable as punishment for Resistance activity, and warned against trespassing. Steven ripped it from the bars and tossed it away, then entered the little front garden. He paused for a moment, overwhelmed by memories, then started to pick his way carefully over the ruins, trying to find anything that might be salvageable, but exposure to the Scottish elements had done for most of it. It wasn't like in movies, where the hero finds a photograph of his family under a chair and slips it into his wallet. Everything was destroyed, unless he fancied trying to take the cistern of the toilet as a memento, and what hadn't been wrecked had clearly been stolen, regardless of any Illyri warnings about trespassing. He thought that he saw one of his old sweaters, filthy and damp, and the broken upper half of a statue of a dancing girl that his mother used to keep above the fireplace. He touched none of it. His mother was not here. The *Revenge* had scanned the rubble before landing and found no trace of a body beneath it. That was some consolation, at least. There was still hope.

Alis stood behind him, unrecognisable in her biohazard suit. A little further away was Biela, his back to them as he scanned the surroundings. The rest of the team remained on board the *Revenge*. They only had six biohazard suits, and the decontamination chamber could accommodate just two or three at a time.

The clouds closed in as a soft rain began to fall. Steven wondered what time it was. It felt like late morning.

'Sir?'

It was Biela.

'Yes?'

'I thought I saw something moving.'

'More rats?'

Steven couldn't keep the disgust from his voice. He'd been forced to kill one shortly after emerging from the *Revenge*. It had come straight for him, sensing food. He'd blasted it with a pulse and now bits of it were scattered across the Pattons' garden wall. The Pattons had lived next door to the Kerrs since before Steven was born. It was the only house with a painted garden wall. Mr Patton would have been really annoyed to see it splattered with a dead rat.

'I'm not sure. It looked bigger.'

Steven stepped down from the ruins.

'Muren, are you picking up anything on the scans?'

Muren's voice sounded in his earpiece.

'No, sir, but the buildings are blocking us.'

The scans could penetrate a few feet of rubble, but not a line of terraced houses.

Steven joined Alis and Biela.

'Where was it?'

Biela indicated the end of the street where Clerwood Terrace joined Greenwood Close.

'Just down there. It was fast.'

It was only then that Steven noticed that the birds had stopped singing.

'Get back on board,' he said, just as the Cutter appeared over the top of the Pattons' roof and rolled down onto the lawn, tumbling so fast that it was little more than a blur. It landed on a quartet of spindly, jointed legs, and exposed its beaklike mouth amid flailing tentacles.

'What the hell is that?' shouted Biela, but Steven was already firing, the pulser whining as he instinctively ratcheted it to full power. The Cutter exploded, showering the entire front of the Pattons' house with its insides, and putting the damage caused by the dead rat into perspective.

'Go!' said Steven, just as another of the creatures appeared from between two houses across the street, and a third emerged from an open manhole about forty feet in front of the *Revenge*. A burst of fire from the ship's front cannon sent it the way of the first, but the last Cutter was learning fast and using the garden walls for cover.

'Where is it?' asked Alis, but Steven wasn't listening, because now it seemed that every house was alive with the beasts. They were appearing at broken windows, and sliding through open doors.

Clerwood Terrace was a nest.

He and Alis laid down as much covering fire as they could while Biela entered the *Revenge* through the decontamination chamber at the rear, and then returned the favour while Steven and Alis retreated. They had barely made it inside, the door closing, when a Cutter inserted itself into the gap and lashed at them with the bladelike protrusions at the end of its tentacles. Alis fired a pulse and blew it away. The door sealed.

'Decontamination now!' ordered Steven. 'And get us off the ground.'

Thuds came from above their heads. The creatures were on the ship. They felt the *Revenge* lift off, tilting slightly beneath the awkwardly distributed weight of the Cutters. Steven, Alis and Biela remained in their suits as the decontamination chamber sent a blast of heat across them. The suits were capable of withstanding ambient temperatures of up to a thousand degrees Fahrenheit, which was more than hot enough to destroy any spores that might have adhered to them. Sweat bubbled uncomfortably from their pores. Once the process was complete, they stripped themselves of the suits and entered a chemical wash, which seemed to be set to bracingly cold, and only then were they admitted into the main body of the ship, pink-cheeked but shivering. They grabbed fresh flight suits and made for the command deck, the *Revenge* jostling as the Cutters continued to attack.

A Brigade pilot, al-Ghamdi, was at the controls when they reached the deck.

'We've managed to dislodge a few,' he said, 'but we still have two of them on us.'

Alis took the co-pilot's seat, and al-Ghamdi handed over the controls to her. An alarm sounded.

'They're starting to cut through the hull,' said Alis.

Steven ordered Biela to the cannon.

'Try and hit them,' he said. 'But be careful. Them, not us, okay?'

Biela did as he was told, manoeuvring the lighter cannon until its barrels were virtually parallel with the body of the ship.

'Tilt starboard!' he called. 'Now!'

Alis reacted instantly, and one of the Cutters was thrown off balance by the movement. It held on to the hull with half of its tentacles, but most of its body was now in front of one of Biela's guns, and then its upper half was gone in a blaze of fire, and the remaining tentacles released their grip and fell.

'One down,' he yelled.

The second Cutter appeared on the cockpit window and attempted to slice through the thick glass. Steven tried to gauge their position. It looked like they were heading back towards Princes Street Gardens.

'Aim for the trees,' he told Alis.

'We'll be very low.'

'If we don't, we'll be very dead. Brace, everyone!'

Alis descended, then pulled level only feet from the ground. Beyond the creature, Steven could see the greenery rapidly approaching. He dived for a chair and belted himself in.

The *Revenge* shot through a copse of trees, smashing them with its impact and knocking the Cutter from the glass, giving them just enough time to avoid the huge Scott Monument before they turned back to seek their quarry. The Cutter was on the ground and already running for cover. It didn't make it. Biela took care of that.

'Damage report,' said Steven.

'We have a hole in the hull,' said Alis.

Steven froze, visions of spores pouring through it and into the cabin already playing in his head.

'How deep?'

'Primary layer. We haven't been compromised, but we'll need to repair it before we leave the earth's atmosphere.'

'Are we okay until Ireland?'

'Yes.'

'Then get us there. You know the coordinates.'

Alis did. Meia had shared the location of the Irish bunker with them before they departed.

If humans had survived anywhere, it was there.

CHAPTER 57

Trask watched Fremd as he cut into the remains of the Other. Both wore protective clothing, even though they were certain that the creature's spore sac had been removed completely. Trask had supervised the operation himself in a field by an old farmhouse, surrounded by the smoking husks of three drones. His people had been fortunate: they'd come across the drones while they were on the ground and had disabled them with grenades before they could take off. Only one had contained a Cutter, though, and its response to the attack had been sluggish. They'd killed it easily.

It was the only thing about the expedition that had been easy, though. Trask was weary, weary to his bones. The previous day, he had officiated at a memorial service, for two years had passed since they'd lost Dolan and Burgess to a Cutter. It seemed to Trask that he spent a lot of time leading prayers for the dead. He sometimes found it hard to believe that it was only four years since the Others had been unleashed on Earth. The time before felt like a dream of another life lived long ago. The days dragged in the bunker, where everything – food, light, heat – was rationed, but they dragged outside as well while the humans ranged these deadly lands, scavenging for anything that might help them to survive a little longer underground.

On his darkest days Trask almost envied those who'd been taken quickly at the beginning, because for those who remained it was a slow, squalid march towards death. He marvelled that there'd ever been a time in his life when the minutes would fly into hours and hours into days, until he worried at where all the years had gone. It was one of the great mysteries of time: it sped for happiness and slowed for sorrow, until the final sorrow came to an end and it stopped entirely.

Funny, he thought – except that it wasn't, not really – how their lives had gradually drifted into something from yesteryear. The survivors were now unable to use diesel or petrol, for oil products have a shelf life, and all stocks were now stale. Trask and his people were reduced to ranging on bicycles, and transporting what they could on carts and wheeled baskets, like children and old folk used to do. The water purification and desalination plants still worked, which was something, and they had food, even if it was limited to what they could grow in the bunkers, or the occasional tinned produce they still found, but life was growing increasingly hard, and they felt more and more isolated. The bursts of radio contact with other bands of survivors were becoming rarer. Humanity was dying out.

And all because of the Others.

Frankly, even wearing a full suit and mask, Trask felt uneasy any time he was forced into close proximity to one of the parasites. He'd witnessed first-hand what they could do, watching impotently as animals and people succumbed to them, their bodies swelling agonisingly before exploding in clouds of spores. What the Illyri and the Others had done to his planet could never be sufficiently avenged.

But in his quieter, sadder moments, Trask acknowledged to himself that it would probably never be avenged at all. Who knew how many human beings were left alive?

For a time, all contact between the pockets of survivors had ceased because the Illyri had begun targeting short-wave transmissions and bombing or raiding their sources. Some transmissions had resumed since the Illyri stopped making regular sorties, but they were kept short, and most told the same story: dwindling supplies of medicines, children weakening, despair setting in. Trask and his people were luckier than most, but they were just about keeping everyone healthy through carefully rationing the last of the tinned food to add to what they were cultivating underground.

And then there was Fremd, an Illyri living alongside the humans that his own race had sacrificed to the Others. He and Trask had butted heads when they were both fighting the Illyri, mainly because each thought that he should be the one in charge of all Resistance operations in Scotland. Now, trapped in a bunker, they had been forced to work together. It wasn't easy at the start, but there was now mutual trust and respect between them, even if it hadn't quite blossomed into actual affection.

Fremd wasn't the only Illyri in the bunker either. Two others, a female named Telia and a male named Ralic, had travelled to Ireland with him. Telia was an engineer, Ralic a scientist, and both had deserted from the Military as the Illyri Conquest grew more brutal. Initially there had been anger at their presence, especially as the scale of the Illyri genocide became apparent, but both had proved invaluable to the survival of all. It was Ralic who cultivated the crops, hybridising and improving them for essential nutrients and sustenance. Telia kept the bunker functioning, combining human and alien technology to patch systems so that they continued to provide heat, light, and water and air purification. Without them, the humans would have been dead long ago. It was kind of ironic, Trask supposed, that they were being kept alive by representatives of the very species that was determined to wipe them out.

Three Illyri in the bunker with the last humans. Once there had been four, but Trask tried not to think of Althea. He'd destroyed the Cutter that killed her. He'd emptied an entire magazine into it, then gone at it with an axe. It hadn't made him feel any better, and it hadn't brought her back.

Fremd sliced into the head of the Other, revealing its brain tissue.

'It's different,' he said.

'How?' Trask asked.

Fremd used the tip of the scalpel to point at a slight swelling on the right rear lobe of the brain.

'We haven't seen this decay before.'

'I don't suppose you can remind me what that bit of it does?'

'It's something to do with the interrelationship between the host Cutter and the organism, but in this one it looks diseased.'

Fremd took a sample of the tissue and placed it under a microscope.

He adjusted the focus and an image of the tissue appeared on the screens above their heads. Trask saw what looked like particles of dust around the nerve endings, one of which also appeared to be withered.

'What is that stuff?' he asked.

'It's plaque,' said Fremd. 'Abnormal clusters of protein fragments.'

He adjusted the magnification again, zooming in on the shrunken nerve cells.

'And those are tangles,' he said. 'More proteins.'

Trask was lost.

'But proteins are good, right?'

Fremd gave Trask the kind of long-suffering look a teacher might bestow on a child who managed to add two and two, and get five. Trask hated that look.

'It depends. Some are responsible for initiating cell death, which looks like what's happening here. I see tissue loss, and atrophy.'

'Good for you. Now maybe you could explain what all that means. And without the pitying stare, please.'

'It's possible that this Other had developed, well, Alzheimer's, I guess,' said Fremd. 'Or some version of it.'

Trask knew what Alzheimer's disease was. He'd seen it take his own father, gradually robbing him of his memory, his speech, his bodily functions, until finally it robbed him of life itself. But how could an alien have Alzheimer's?

He was about to ask Fremd, but the Illyri had moved back to the dissected Other and was poking at various parts of its brain.

'Ah,' he said.

'Ah what?'

Once again Fremd moved a tissue sample to the microscope.

'Looks like it's got holes in it,' said Trask.

'More plaque,' said Fremd. 'Deformed proteins, not dissimilar to those associated with mad cow disease.'

Trask was familiar with mad cow disease as well. He recalled the carcasses of cattle being burned in great pyres to prevent its spread to humans. It was something to do with eating dodgy meat, he thought, although he couldn't be sure.

'So this thing had Alzheimer's *and* mad cow disease?' he said.

'I'm saying that whatever it had resembles both of those conditions,' said Fremd. 'But to put it simply, its neurological functions were degenerating.'

'That's putting it simply? Try again.'

'Its brain was rotting. Will that do?'

'That'll do all right. Now why was its brain rotting?'

'It could be only this single specimen, just as some humans get Alzheimer's and some don't . . .'

But Trask knew there was more.

'Or?'

'*Or* . . . the Others may have contracted something from one of the species they've infected here on Earth: humans, horses, cattle, bats. It could be any one of them – or more than one.'

'They're dying?' said Trask, and for the first time in forever, a bud of hope swelled a little in his heart.

'No,' Fremd corrected him, '*this* one was dying. I haven't seen it in any of the previous remains you've obtained, so we won't know for sure if it's widespread until you bring me more specimens.'

Fremd could see this news made Trask less than delighted, even though his face was partially concealed by his protective suit.

'The only way we can do that is by killing Cutters,' he said, 'and that's easier said than done.'

But not as hard as it used to be, Trask thought. He'd believed himself to be mistaken when he thought they were slowing, becoming less lethal, but Fremd's diagnosis of the diseased Other had given him another possible answer.

'I know,' said Fremd. 'I still need more specimens.'

'But this is hope, right?'

'Perhaps.'

'No, it's hope – and we haven't had much of that for a long time.'

'Bring me more of the Others.'

'I'll find a way.'

A red light began flashing in the corner of the laboratory, instantly joined by the noise of a klaxon. Trask moved to the nearest intercom.

'What is it?' he asked.

Maeve Buchanan, Fremd's human partner, was on monitoring duty. Her voice wavered as she spoke.

'An Illyri ship,' she told Trask. 'It looks like it's coming in to land.'

And Trask felt all hope die. He'd known this day might come. They all did. But why now, just as it seemed that the Others might not be invincible after all?

But there was no time for regrets. They had practised for an assault on the bunker. Everyone knew their positions and their tasks.

'Sound the battle alarm,' said Trask. 'We're on our way.'

A group of tense faces watched the monitor as the Illyri ship landed on a patch of high grass about forty feet from the main entrance to the bunker, which was hidden beneath a layer of earth and grass. Miniature surveillance cameras encircled the bunker at a radius of a mile, but never before had they picked up an Illyri vessel.

Beyond the bunker's main control room, the survivors had taken up their designated positions, ready to repel a frontal attack. They didn't wear masks or protective suits because there weren't enough of either to go round; and anyway, the decontamination process would kick in automatically if the bunker was breached. Further away, a small team of suited Resistance fighters, Lindsay among them, was working its way underground to come up on the other side of the craft and ambush it with grenades.

'I haven't seen one like that before,' said Trask. He had his shotgun ready, and a pistol on his belt.

'Neither have I,' said Fremd. 'It's bad news for us if they're sending fresh troops.'

'It's bad news either way.'

The ship's door opened and a figure appeared in a biohazard suit. It paused momentarily before descending the gangway to the ground. It was not armed and raised its hands in the air as it reached the grass, then stood there, waiting. It appeared to be male, judging by the contours of the suit, and it had something coloured wrapped around its neck, although the camera couldn't quite capture it.

'What's he doing?' someone asked.

'Small for an Illyri,' commented another.

Trask, who had been leaning over the desk, squinting at the screen, straightened. He tapped a button and opened a channel to Lindsay's team.

'Lindsay?'

'Receiving. We're almost at the door now.'

'Hold your position.'

'I'm sorry? Repeat, please.'

'I said, "Hold your position."'

Trask grabbed a protective suit from a locker and began pulling it on.

'What are you doing?' asked Fremd.

'I'm going outside.'

'It could be a trap. That Illyri could be bait.'

'It's not a trap, and that's no Illyri.'

'You can't know that!'

Now it was Trask's turn to give Fremd a withering look.

'When was the last time you saw an Illyri wearing a Motherwell football scarf?'

The bunker door opened and Steven watched a man slowly ascend the steps from below. He took a deep breath. It had been a huge risk to leave the *Revenge* and expose himself to possible attack, but Alis could find no way to contact the bunker, and leaving the ship seemed to be the only solution. Alis had thought him mad when he'd made her turn back to find a sports shop before continuing on to Ireland. He just had to hope that nobody in that bunker was a Hearts fan.

The man approaching him was carrying a shotgun, although it wasn't pointing at Steven, not yet. He continued walking until he was close enough to see Steven's face through his mask, and Steven could see his. Neither moved for a moment, until Steven tapped the earpiece on his suit. Trask did the same, and the receivers on the suits opened up a channel between them.

'Why are you wearing a Motherwell scarf?' asked Trask.

'I couldn't find any other one.'

'You're lucky I didn't shoot you on sight.'

And then the watchers in the bunker were treated to the strange sight of Trask dropping his shotgun and moving forward to hug the waiting Illyri.

CHAPTER 58

Alis and Hague joined Steven, leaving Biela in charge of the
Revenge. Trask assured them that they'd find more suits so
the crew could leave the ship and have solid ground under their feet,
at least for a little while. Together they headed for the decontamination
chambers. As they did so, a group of suited survivors appeared with
the intention of masking the *Revenge* with tarpaulins in order to shield
it from curious Illyri eyes.

'There's no need,' said Steven. 'They're all dead, unless there are
any here on Earth.'

Trask stared at him.

'You're serious?'

'Yes.'

Trask looked to the sky, as if expecting Illyri to materialise from
the clouds and disprove what Steven was telling him.

'Well, we'd better get under cover anyway. There are still Cutters
to worry about.'

'Cutters? Is that what you call those things with the tentacles?'

'That's right. You've seen them?'

'We killed some of them too.'

'Is there anything you haven't killed?'

Even partially shielded by his helmet, Steven suddenly looked
older than his years, and terribly tired.

'No,' he said. 'Sometimes I don't think there is. Trask, I—'

But Trask bustled him towards the bunker.

'We need to get inside. Movement attracts them. Come on.'

Then they were underground, moving into decontamination, the noise of it so deafening that Steven could not ask the question he had come all this way to have answered.

My mother. What of my mother?

They stepped from the main chamber. Fresh overalls were provided. Through the small glass window of the connecting door, Steven saw Fremd waiting for them, and Maeve. Trask moved to open it once the system had given him the all-clear.

'Trask?'

The older man turned to him.

'I went to Edinburgh, but my house was—'

Trask hit a button and the door hissed open. Standing before Maeve and Fremd was a small, middle-aged woman wearing old jeans and a patched cardigan. Steven tried to speak, but no words would come. He felt heat in his eyes, then tears. His mother held out her arms, and her son fell into them.

Later, over tea and baked beans – the former a treat usually reserved for Christmas and special birthdays in the bunker, the latter the equivalent of a Sunday roast for the survivors – Steven told them everything, from the events on Torma to the final battle with the Illyri over Earth. He kept nothing back, not even Syl's growing powers, for, if the Cayth were right, they represented the best hope of defeating the Others.

They were a small group: just Steven, his mother, Alis, Fremd, Maeve, Trask and Hague. The survivors were chatting with crew members from the *Revenge* who had been freed from duty to enter the bunker under a roster established by Hague, so that everyone would get a chance to leave the ship. Some were using the short-wave radio to try to get news of relatives and friends. Others were already asleep, exhausted by the tension and fighting of recent days and hours.

'She may not be entirely the last hope,' said Trask. He looked at Fremd. 'Tell them.'

And Fremd spoke of the deterioration in the brain of the Other, although he was hesitant, and kept reminding them that it was just one specimen.

'We need more of them to examine, though,' he said.

'We can help you get them,' said Steven, 'but it doesn't change anything.'

'What do you mean?' asked Trask.

Alis understood why Steven had spoken as he did.

'If it's caused by interaction between the Others and their terrestrial hosts, human or otherwise, then its effects will be limited to this planet,' she said.

'With respect,' said Trask, 'right now this planet is the only one I'm worried about.'

'They're not the last of these things,' said Steven. 'We destroyed one breeding world, but who knows if the Illyri established more processing plants like the one we saw? At the very least, there are Illyri out there carrying the Others inside them, and as long as they exist, they can breed.'

'But it could be the beginning of a systemic weakness,' said Fremd. 'You yourself told us that the Cayth believed the Others were connected by some form of quantum entanglement. If so, the deterioration could spread.'

'When did you get so optimistic?' asked Trask, surprised to find Fremd modifying his tone.

'When you turned out to be so pessimistic.'

'It's a Cayth theory,' said Alis. 'And we've no idea whether it produces physical effects in the Others.'

'Well,' said Steven, 'let's find some more Cutters as a first step and then at least we can establish if it's spreading.'

'Not all Cutters are hosts,' said Trask. 'You may have to kill a lot of them. Not that I'll object if you do.'

Steven started to reply, but instead he surprised even himself by yawning widely. Outside it was already night. Hague was struggling to keep his eyes open too, and Steven's body ached all over. He needed to rest. His mother's hand touched his shoulder.

'The Cutters will still be out there tomorrow,' she said to Trask.

'Let my son rest. Let them all rest for a while.'

They rose, and Steven's mother led him to a bunk. He removed his boots and lay down while his mother placed a blanket over him, brushed his hair away from his face, and kissed him softly on the forehead.

And Steven smiled. He was asleep just moments later, and slept with a peace that he had not felt in many, many months.

They spent two days hunting Cutters for analysis, while shuttles from the *Satia* brought men to the surface so they could spend some time on the planet. Contact was made with survivors in Scandinavia, France and Germany, and families briefly reunited. Information was shared, including details of what had been discovered about the brains of the Others.

The hunt was a dangerous business, because they needed to kill the Cutters without damaging them so badly that any Others they might be carrying were destroyed. The *Revenge* targeted Cutters moving in their spheres, or solitary specimens on the ground. Biela proved adept at using the light cannon to fire single shots, disabling the creatures sufficiently for the *Revenge* to be able to land and send in soldiers to finish them off. In the end, they succeeded in gathering more than a dozen dead Others. It wouldn't have been enough for a proper scientific study, but it would do for now.

While Fremd and his assistants examined them, Steven, aided by Trask in the cockpit, went looking for the nests of the creatures in the major cities in Ireland and the United Kingdom, bombing and burning as they went. They didn't get them all – that would have required teams on the ground moving house to house – but they got a lot. More to the point, they targeted clusters of spheres, limiting the Cutters' movement. In addition, as soon as they felt sure an area was safe enough, they'd search out dust-covered supermarkets and restaurants laden with tins of food, and jar after jar of sealed jam, sauce, pickles and tomatoes, and these they piled high in the *Revenge*, taking them back to the west coast of Ireland to restock the bunker's stores.

But this was just a cluster of small islands at the edge of Europe.

They couldn't do this indefinitely. Already they'd been forced to replenish the *Revenge*'s ammunition from the destroyer's reserves. They could have exhausted them entirely, and still only have secured a handful of territories from the predations of the Cutters. The Cutters were also getting clever, or the Others in their heads were. They knew they were being hunted from the air and had started hiding. By the end of five days, there was not a Cutter to be seen, but they were out there, somewhere.

After the sixth day, Steven took Trask and Fremd aside and told them that the *Revenge* would be leaving. He'd thought long and hard about the decision, and discussed it with Alis and Hague. They had agreed with him, Hague more reluctantly than Alis: the war was not here. The war was elsewhere.

The news did not come as a total surprise to Trask. He had been anticipating it, as had Steven's mother, although it did not stop her from losing her temper with her son, and scalding tears ran unchecked down her cheeks after he confirmed it to her. Devastated to be upsetting his mother, and also to be leaving her again, Steven promised to return with Paul once the Others and their Illyri allies were defeated, but they both knew it was scant consolation, and quite probably an empty promise too.

'You'd better be back,' said Katherine Kerr fiercely, 'or I swear I'll come and get you, both of you, and when I find you, you'll wish I hadn't.'

Then she found herself unable to say any more, for she was forcing down an animal howl of desolation. Her son was returning to the stars, to a war in which the possibility of victory seemed remote. If her two boys died out there on a distant world, she might never learn of it, and the rest of her life would be spent wondering.

But Steven trusted this Illyri named Syl, the one whom Paul apparently loved, the one who had saved her sons from the gallows. Syl gave him hope, he said, and his mother latched on to some of that hope, and fanned the flames of it.

And Fremd gave them more hope. Of the specimens that had been brought to him, half showed serious signs of deterioration, and three more were in the first stages of it. It seemed the original sample was not an isolated case.

On the morning of the *Revenge*'s departure, messages were received from Copenhagen and Paris. Signs of nerve degeneration had been found in the brains of more of the Others.

The creatures were dying.

The goodbyes were short, but no less sad for it. They exchanged their hugs, their handshakes and their kisses underground. Then the crew of the *Revenge* suited up and left the bunker. They waved one last time from the door of the ship before it closed and they ascended. Within days, the *Revenge* and the *Satia* had left the solar system.

For the first time in two decades, no Illyri ships flew above Earth.

XIV

THE RUINS OF EREBOS

CHAPTER 59

Ani waited in one of the towering crystal atriums of the Palace of Erebos, looking out over the Grand Hall that stood at the centre of the complex like a sparkling crystal heart, but it was a heart that had ceased to beat long ago. The little jewel of a moon now lay silent, the historic celebrations and commemorations it had hosted in its fabled heyday just the glamorous ghosts of another era. It had been this way for years now, shrouded in quiet save for the rustle of its maintenance staff of engineers and caretakers, all handpicked from within the Sisterhood. Since the brutal events that had provided the backdrop to Syrene's rushed wedding ceremony over four years previously, the Sisterhood had maintained control of Erebos, declaring itself to be custodian of the historic buildings until a time when peace might be restored to the ravaged Illyri race. Nobody had complained, for both the Military and the Diplomatic Corps were already neck-deep in bloodshed and tangled strategy; the fate of the great Palace of Erebos had been the least of their concerns. Naturally, the Sisterhood ensured that it took payment from the authorities for this custodianship, but in truth it suited Ani very well to have these private, elegant spaces to do with as she wished, unseen, and unheard.

The Palace had sustained catastrophic systemic damage during the attack by the *Nomad* when it rescued Syl from the moon. While the *Nomad* had opened fire on only a small portion of the Palace, all of its structures were interconnected, and so harm to one meant harm to all. Blood still stained the floor, and the stars left by pulse blasts were burned onto the glass like lines of Braille, ending at the exclamation mark where the *Nomad*'s cannon had ripped a new exit into a sealed tunnel, commencing the destruction of the ancient structure.

Yet again, Ani traced the story of Syl's escape with her eyes, even though she knew its details by heart. She kept the scene untouched as a memento, because everything that had happened that day felt as though it had befallen someone else, like a scene in a book or film whose title she had forgotten, with an ending that was also lost to her. All she knew was that it had broken her heart.

In a rarely visited section of Erebos, near the vast catering and service kitchens on the far side of the glimmering palace, rooms were being prepared for the arrival of the terrorist known as Aron. Ani had first encountered Aron, a member of the Military, on Earth when she was but a child. Back then, Aron had been Captain Peris's second-in-command in the Edinburgh Castle Guard, but he'd been redeployed from Earth soon after Peris left for the Brigades, and now was leader of one of the Military units fighting the Diplomats in the systems closest to Illyr. For his insurrection, Aron was a named and wanted traitor with a death sentence already passed upon him.

However, Ani remembered Aron as being smart and calculating, and he'd always been friendly, too, so when she had learned that he was believed to be central to the Military efforts, she had sent him secret word, evoking Peris's name. In time he had responded, and so she had courted him until she earned his trust, or at least until he trusted her motives enough to meet with her.

On that first meeting, he had been angry. Very angry.

'We can help each other,' she had promised him.

'Do you know that some of us are starving out there, Ani, stuck in the cesspits of outer space, dying like rats lost down a sewer, and now we're rats running out of even crap to eat? Do you understand me when I tell you how my troops suffer?'

The Diplomats deliberately targeted planets capable of sustaining life, knowing that these were most likely to be bases for Military operations. It meant that the Military struggled to grow food, and most of its outlying units were reduced to scavenging and targeting Diplomatic supply routes.

'Yes,' said Ani, 'I do understand you, and that is why I am glad you agreed to see me today, Aron. I have news for you – a symbol of my goodwill, if you will.'

She walked over to a carved cabinet and opened it.

'I have hybrid seeds,' she said, removing a small glass vial from a hidden drawer inside. She handed it to Aron and he examined the label.

'Given that these are coming from you, I'm presuming they're not just any ordinary seeds,' he said.

'Of course not! These are the latest genetic modifications, unknown even on Illyr. They're suitable for growth in the poorest soils, particularly sand or rock, for they take their nourishment from the air. The soil is just to anchor them – even broken glass would suffice. And yet they grow three times as fast, while containing many times the standard nutritional value.'

'But what about water?' he said, frowning at the vial.

'That's the clincher, for these little seeds will germinate in salt water with no trouble at all – no need for desalination. That's precisely what my labs have been working on. Of course, it doesn't have to be salt water: any alkaline solution up to a pH of 8.4 will do, and it goes without saying that they're self-propagating. It was a significant challenge, of course, but one that my scientists turned out to be more than up to.'

And it had been her scientists, not those on Illyr. They had achieved these little miracles unaided by the Others, relying instead on the Sisterhood's oldest resource: knowledge. At Ani's command and by her express wish, Avila Minor was the only part of the Illyr system in which Illyri did not carry Others inside them. The Marque had been quietly purged – or most of it had. The thing in its depths remained a threat.

'And I brought several more vials with different varietals,' Ani continued, 'so you'll even have a selection to grow. I'll have them packed on the ship when you leave. Plant them when you get back and you should be harvesting within a month.'

Ani thought there might actually have been traces of tears in Aron's eyes. Whatever he had been expecting when he came here, it was not this. He started to thank her effusively, but she held up her hand and got down to business. The seeds carried a price. In return for them, she wanted the Military-held Passienne station taken down, if only temporarily – just long enough for the Diplomats to have to reroute their communications, just long enough for her Sisters to infiltrate them and crack the code. Aron had agreed, and it was this strike force that the *Revenge* had glimpsed as it travelled to Krasis.

Ever since that first meeting, Ani and Aron had enjoyed a cautious, highly secretive arrangement: she let him know of the intended attacks that would cause the biggest losses of life, and he told her . . . well, he told her what he could and what he dared, anything that might support his quest to win the backing of the Sisterhood and its new Archmage.

Aron didn't yet understand that, even under Ani, the Sisterhood only backed itself.

But he did know about the Others. He knew that there was a strange force in Illyri affairs. The discovery by the Military leadership of the truth about the Others had come about when a Diplomatic vessel was found drifting in the Cormor system: a hull breach had left its crew dead and frozen. Two had been carrying Others, and one had been sufficiently alive to attempt to infect the Military salvage team, although their suits had saved them. The second Other had been retrieved intact, and it was this that had confirmed rumours long whispered. The information remained restricted, though: Aron had been allowed into the loop because one of his tasks was to convince, via a network of sympathisers, important Illyri with no love for the Diplomats to side with the Military. That was one of the reasons why he had accepted Ani's original request to meet, but it turned out that Ani needed no convincing about the Others.

Aron met Ani every few months, or more frequently if one of them requested it. The soldier flew in undetected on a nippy red

Sisterhood ship that picked him up on the other side of a small, somewhat unstable wormhole – unimaginatively, Ani referred to it as the Wobbly wormhole – designated solely for the use of the Sisterhood, an arrangement reached by Syrene with the Diplomatic Corps, and one that Ani had seen no reason to discontinue.

Now, as Ani received word of the incoming Nairene transport, she hurried to await Aron. The rooms in which they would meet were in an isolated, heavily shielded lodge at the eastern edge of the Palace, far from any prying eyes and ears, although Ani was certain that Erebos was now almost as secure as the Marque. Aron was escorted to the lodge straight from the little transporter, his face pale. Ani thought she detected a whiff of vomit when he entered the room too, but she said nothing, not wishing to embarrass him.

'It is good to see you again, Aron,' she said, moving to embrace him. He turned his cheek from hers angrily.

'I'm not sure I can come through that damn wormhole anymore, Ani. I swear it's getting worse. Today it was like being squeezed through a bottleneck while someone repeatedly kicked me up the backside. Someone with hooves.'

She put her hand on his arm gently, ignoring his casual use of her first name. Aron was old-school Military; despite his mission to gain support for his side, the Sisterhood retained an air of toxicity for him, and he viewed it at best as some outdated bastion of Illyri privilege and, at worst, as the enemy. He chose to have faith in Ani because he knew her from their past life on Earth, and because her information had saved many souls in these violent times; but for her Nairene title and its attendant airs and graces he had little tolerance, and for her organisation he had only disdain. It didn't matter though. What mattered was their connection.

'I'm sorry, Aron,' she said, and she meant it.

'There must be another way.'

'Well, why don't you leave it with me? I'll see what I can come up with.'

And yes, of course there were other wormholes, but she was loath to reveal their locations, not yet, for the very fact of the Wobbly wormhole's instability was its security: it would be too dangerous to bring a decent-sized ship through, and Ani didn't want to open any larger doors in the cosmos that might give Aron's troops ideas about using what would be a handy, unmonitored shortcut straight to the Illyr system, should they get the urge to ratchet their insurgency up a level.

'I would be grateful,' said Aron.

'Come,' she said, taking him by the elbow, 'let us take some refreshment. How about a drink to steady your nerves – some Meldrae, perhaps? – and then we can talk. Would you like some time to freshen up first? I can have you shown to a private room.'

Aron accepted the goblet of frosted spirits she poured for him – Meldrae was a strong, expensive, and rare liquor distilled from the leaves of the winter ferns of the snowcaps – before he allowed Lista to lead him away to an ablution facility to take a minute for himself. Ani stepped over to a window, looking out past the elaborate stonework and carvings into the gardens beyond. They were overgrown and tangled now, but she preferred Erebos this way, and had instructed that it be left to grow wild, for she felt that all the manicured and wrangled grandeur of the buildings needed a counterpoint.

'Much appreciated, Ani,' Aron said, re-entering the room and going straight to refill his cup from the decanter. 'You don't mind? That's really delicious. Beats the rotgut we have on the other side of the wormhole.'

She smiled winningly and said: 'Then I shall have to sneak a skin or two into the ship with you, when you leave.'

'I think you may just have made the trip worthwhile,' he chuckled. 'Now tell me, how is Danis? He is well, I presume? Comfortable?'

Ani did not bother to correct Aron's assumptions about her relationship with her estranged father. It would serve no purpose here.

'Oh, perfectly well. He and Peris are enjoying their retirement together as best they can, though of course he – my father – misses my mother terribly, as we all do.'

Aron scratched his chin as he considered what she said. His expression was shrewd.

'I've heard some say that they're little better than prisoners,' he said.

'If so, then it's also a little better than being dead,' said Ani. If Aron knew that Ani had brokered the agreement with the Diplomats to spare Danis and Peris more brutal imprisonment, or even a discreet execution, he did not say. In a way, Ani was her father's jailer.

'Like Andrus,' said Aron.

'Yes, just like Andrus.'

'That old turncoat got everything that was coming to him! What did he think would happen if he got into bed with the Sisterhood?'

'Careful, Aron,' said Ani. 'Remember the company you're keeping.'

Aron grunted, and took some more Meldrae.

Ani usually kept her feelings about Lord Andrus private. He had been as dear as an uncle to her, and she had been appalled at the manner of his death. Andrus had also been Syl's only living relative, and she knew how her father's death would have devastated her former best friend. With Andrus gone, all traces of Syl's genetic heritage were lost, scattered as dust to the stars, just as Ani believed Syl had been when she entered the Derith wormhole and was destroyed.

Was that true? The One had heard echoes of Syl . . .

'Andrus had one of the Others in his head,' she told Aron. 'It was put there by Syrene.'

She had shared this with no one until now. She was not even sure why she was telling Aron. Perhaps it was his use of the word 'turncoat'. Andrus had not been a traitor. Andrus had been consumed by the thing inside him.

'It makes sense,' said Aron. 'I did not know for certain, but some in the Military suspected as much after the existence of these parasites was confirmed. It doesn't excuse his betrayal though.'

'He was not himself,' said Ani. 'Hatred for him is wasted.'

Aron shook his head.

'No, my hate keeps me from giving up,' he said. 'My hate keeps me fighting, even when I'm not sure what I'm fighting for anymore.'

'Well, if it helps, I have the thorium you need for your reactors. Or I can tell you where to get it, at least.'

'Really?' Aron looked at Ani as though she were a magician, and she was gratified.

'Yes. Within the coming weeks, a delivery will be dispatched to the Marque, via the Quelu wormhole. There is still thorium mined beyond it, despite notifications that the mine had closed. Watch the wormhole and be ready to seize the shipment, for it will be full to bursting and must never get to my Marque. If it reaches Avila Minor I'll have to find a use for it, and I don't have one, despite the lies I told Vena.'

Aron looked at her in amazement.

'I'm sorry, Ani, but I don't remember you being quite this smart back on Earth. Part of me still thinks of you as younger than you are – and I feel that now, somehow, you have become older than you look. It only feels like yesterday that you and Syl Hellais were skulking about, getting into trouble, bunking off school, but I assumed she was the brains behind your little operation. You continue to astonish me.'

'Yesterday, and a million years ago, Aron. Much has changed. I have changed. I live in the largest library in the universe. I do a lot of reading.'

'Well,' said Aron, raising his glass, 'I'll drink to that, if your reading has got me more thorium. Thank you for your help.'

'Aron,' she said seriously, 'you realise that there is a price for my help. What can you offer me in return? After all, you requested this meeting.'

Aron reached into his leather satchel and produced a small transmitting device.

'I can offer you this,' he said.

An image was projected into the air before them, wavering at first and then focusing as his hand steadied and the old piece of equipment warmed up. Ani stared at the picture that appeared, little more than an electronic snapshot really, showing the face of a young human male, with long brown hair that grew over his deep-set blue eyes. Behind him was a band of older humans: rugged, square-jawed, scarred, tattooed, but Ani barely registered them. Instead she looked only at the boy. At the man. He was caught in the moment, brushing his unkempt fringe away, one eyebrow arched, his mouth slightly open, and Ani studied his features for a long while, unable to form words. It was simply not possible.

'You do know him, right?' said Aron when her silence became uncomfortable. 'Because he claims to know you. He said he was with you in the Highlands, and at Dundearg.'

Ani nodded slowly. She put out her hand to touch the picture, and it buzzed and distorted where her fingers moved.

'Steven Kerr,' she whispered. 'That's Steven Kerr.'

CHAPTER 60

Vena emerged from the washroom to find Dyer already dressed. She didn't particularly mind. While she enjoyed being with him, theirs was no great love affair and she was certain that he felt the same way. It was a relationship of convenience between two Illyri, based on many things – ambition, shared enemies, common goals, occasional physical needs – but not on any deep affection, and not on any particular trust either. They were both too experienced to really trust anyone, but they were also clever enough to realise that neither of them would ever give away anything that might endanger themselves or weaken their position. Unlike Krake and Merida, there would be no careless pillow talk. If they shared any information, they would do so deliberately, and with a purpose.

Dyer was handsome in a vague way: his features were slightly too regular to be truly interesting. He was also small for an Illyri – just a little over six feet in height – but his ascent to power had been steady and careful until he was now, to the eyes of outsiders, just one step away from the highest position in the Empire. Those outside observers were mistaken, of course: Dyer was president in all but name, and Krake knew it. Dyer let Krake have the Presidential Palace, his luxurious apartment in the Tree of Lights, his fine foods, liquors and clothing. All Krake had to do in return was whatever Dyer told him.

In essence, Dyer was the true power in the Illyri empire and the responsibility for the conduct of the war was largely his alone. It was unfortunate, therefore, that Dyer was a better politician than military tactician. He had assumed that one would equip him for the other, but he had been wrong. The attack on Melos Station, which was Dyer's idea, encouraged by Syrene, had not been matched by similar successes against the Military elsewhere, for which Dyer was to blame. His failure lay in his belief that the destruction of Melos would leave the Military powerless, that by cutting off its head, the body would simply fall dead to the ground. Instead, the Military had fragmented, scattering itself to safe havens throughout near and distant galaxies while its remaining leadership regrouped. Now Dyer and the Diplomatic forces were fighting a war on a dozen different fronts, wasting valuable resources trying to hunt down small guerilla units while Military ships struck at supply lines and vulnerable outlying bases. Despite the confident public pronouncements of President Krake – relayed through him by Dyer in the manner of a ventriloquist controlling a dummy – the reality was that the Diplomatic Corps had begun to question Dyer's abilities.

For the first time, he was in real danger of being usurped and replaced, but recent days had brought new information his way: the Military was just as weakened by the war as the Diplomats, if not more so, and was readying itself for a counterstrike directly at the home system. Its fleet was assembling, although Dyer had yet to learn the precise location of the rendezvous point. In anticipation of just such a move, Dyer was recalling his own ships and preparing to fortify the wormholes near Illyr. The problem was that there were many wormholes surrounding the Illyr system, and he could not defend them all. If he divided his forces among them, then no single Diplomatic battle group would be able to resist an incursion by the entire Military fleet. If he gambled on one or two likely wormholes and chose wrongly, the Military would enter the Illyr system unopposed. He needed to know the Military's plans.

This was why, through Vena, he had chosen to spy on the Archmage Ani, because he was convinced that she had secretly allied herself with the Military. He had felt no great fondness for her predecessor, Syrene, but at least he knew where her loyalties lay. Since her replacement by Ani, all such certainties had fallen by the wayside. Dyer did not believe that Syrene had willingly given up her position as Archmage, and his Nairene spies had described her last public appearance, in which she had announced her abdication as Archmage, and her selection of Ani Cienda to succeed her, as most odd.

But all of those spies were gone now. Sister Priety had vanished into the depths of the Marque, Beyna had committed suicide, and Coriol, Gara and Jenis had been suddenly dispatched to Morir – exiled, in other words – to found a new Nairene convent and spread the Gospel of Knowledge, although from what Dyer knew of Morir, the only thing they'd be converting on the planet were rocks and dirt. The new Archmage had deprived him of all information from inside the Marque, and she had similarly secured Erebos. She was proving far too clever and adept for Dyer's liking.

Vena appeared behind him. He did not turn, but watched her reflection in the glass. She was striking, he thought, and cold, like a dagger in Illyri form.

'What are you thinking?' she asked, and he knew that she was not expecting a lover's answer.

'I'm thinking that we have tolerated the Archmage for long enough. Either she is actively plotting against us, or she has chosen to distance herself from our cause. Whichever is true, she is not on our side, and those who are not with us—'

'Are against us,' Vena finished for him. 'What do you propose?'

'The Sisterhood has served its purpose. The Diplomatic fleet is massing, and we are preparing to strike a final killer blow against our enemies. It's time to add the Sisterhood to that list.'

'You will target the Marque?'

This was unheard of. The Marque was sacrosanct.

'Its defences are not impregnable – and it may not even be necessary to bypass them. Ships land on the Marque all the time. If we are clever, the Sisterhood will willingly admit the instruments of its downfall: a small force may be all that is required. We take the Marque, and depose the Archmage. Once she is captured – or better yet, dead – we can purge the Sisterhood and install a new Archmage to institute a rule more amenable to our own.'

Vena pressed herself against him. This was more than she could have hoped for: not just the downfall of Ani Cienda, but the end of the old Sisterhood and the birth of the new.

'And who will be the new Archmage?' she asked. Even as she spoke she knew the answer, but still she thrilled to hear it from his lips.

'You will.'

CHAPTER 61

Vena was still buttoning her service uniform as she left the Tree of Lights, her fingers trembling with excitement. Suddenly the impossible now seemed within her grasp: revenge on Ani Cienda, who, with Syl Hellais, had led her former lover Sedulus to his death on Earth; and dominion over the Sisterhood, which had rejected her in her youth, deeming her too 'unstable' to wear Nairene robes. With Dyer effectively ruling on Illyr, and Vena at the head of a new Sisterhood, they would change Illyri society – and the known universe – forever.

Yet she and Dyer remained different from each other in one crucial respect: unlike Dyer, Vena did not carry one of the Others in her skull. She had always resisted implantation, as had many of the higher Securitats. Like most of her kind, Vena was a spy at heart, and a spy knew better than to give another spy access to her secrets. The Securitats remained wary of the Others. Some of them carried the aliens in their heads, but those who did were carefully monitored and much vital information was not shared with them.

Vena found her moments of intimacy with Dyer peculiar because of her awareness of the thing that dwelt inside him. Sometimes she imagined it watching her while she was with him, experiencing these deeply physical and sensual moments at one remove, exploring her through him. In a way, it was useful for her to know that Dyer was infected: it made it easier for her to maintain her emotional distance from him.

Vena barely registered the presence of the young concierge who watched her depart, and Rent Raydl gave no sign that he had noticed her. He had decided early in his concierge career that it was always better to pretend that the Securitats, and Vena in particular, were invisible. If you paid attention to them, they might in turn pay attention to you, and that would be most unfortunate.

Regrettably, his deepening relationship with Cocile had forced him to reassess this position. It hadn't taken them long to figure out that it was the Archmage who had brought them together, but she had simply accelerated what might otherwise have been a natural, if slow, process for two innately shy, reticent Illyri. Rent and Cocile were by now very much in love, but Rent was already coming to realise that any involvement with the Sisterhood brought with it layers of intrigue. Sometimes, in his more cynical moments, he wondered if one of the reasons why the Archmage had encouraged the relationship between her handmaiden and himself was because the concierge's work at the Tree of Lights made him a potentially useful source of information, and more.

It was Rent's own fault, he supposed. It was he who had let slip to Cocile that Vena paid regular visits to Dyer at the Tree of Lights, and was widely assumed to be sleeping with the vice-president. He shouldn't have been surprised when Cocile chose to share this nugget with the Archmage – if she was not already aware of it – but he was shocked when Cocile met Rent for dinner a week later and presented him with several tiny seed transmitters. She had then encouraged him, if that was the right term for a combination of seduction and bribery, to gain entry to Dyer's apartments and scatter the seeds where he could. Most disturbing of all, Rent had agreed to do so.

Rent had no idea what Dyer and the Securitat chief talked about in Dyer's apartment, and he didn't want to know. He only hoped that, if worse came to worst, and his treachery was discovered, the Sisterhood would find a way to hide him before Vena began skinning him alive.

And deep in the Marque, listening ears took in all that had been said by Vena and her lover, and it was immediately communicated, word for word, to the Archmage.

CHAPTER 62

As Aron was preparing to leave Erebos, strapping his precious hoard of Meldrae securely into the back seat of the red craft while the Nairene pilot impatiently drummed her fingers on the control panel, there was a flurry of action on the landing pad.

'Wait, wait!' called a voice.

Aron turned to see Ani's gentle handmaiden running towards him, her red robes flapping like ragged wings. He couldn't remember her name. She was a meek and retiring creature – kindly and polite enough, but she'd never said more than a few words to him, and was not the sort to make any lasting impression.

'Yes, er – ?' he said.

'Lista. I'm Lista,' she said, before adding 'Sir!' as an afterthought.

'What can I do for you, Lista?'

'I'm coming with you,' she said, nodding emphatically.

'What? Why?' said Aron, but already Lista was clambering in through the rear door of the vessel, pushing his valuable cargo out of her way as she settled in. Clearly he had misjudged her.

'Because the Archmage said I must,' she replied, once she'd made herself at home. 'I'm to stay in the craft and you're to bring me to Steven Kerr.'

'Oh, I am, am I?' said Aron. 'Why did the Archmage not inform me of this herself?'

On receiving the revelation about Steven Kerr, Ani had seemed genuinely shaken. Their meeting had ended rather quickly after that, for she was clearly bewildered by his news, and she'd asked to be excused so that she could lie down. Of course, it had been more of an instruction than a request, but he'd obliged anyway, and watched curiously as she left the room, Lista trotting anxiously behind her. Now this same Lista was staring at him in a manner that suggested any arguments about her presence would be most unwelcome.

'The Archmage only just decided,' she said. 'She's resting at the moment. You're not going to make me fetch her, are you?'

'How do I know she sent you, though? You may mean the Kerr boy some harm. I can't go trusting every Nairene that comes running along, making demands.'

Lista sighed. Out of the corner of his eye Aron was sure he saw the pilot, Sessily, grinning, but she turned her head away when he looked directly at her, concealing her expression from him.

'The Archmage anticipated you might say as much. She said you'd know I was genuinely sent by her if I told you the following: *Nemo me impune lacessit*. It means—'

'I know what it means,' interrupted Aron. '"No one who harms me will go unpunished." I suspect the Archmage should have it printed on her business cards.'

Aron still didn't assent to Lista's presence on the flight. This was a complicated business. The usual procedure was for the Nairene ship carrying Aron to rendezvous with a Military cruiser, returning him to his own kind before heading back through the wormhole. This was done for the protection of all: Aron might have trusted Ani, but he still believed that it was better if the Archmage knew as little about the Military's operations as possible, and that included denying her and any of her Sisters access to Military vessels, for Military vessels contained Military secrets. Some of his superiors would press to have Aron thrown out of an airlock if it was found that he had allowed a Nairene access to any part of the fleet.

Aron stared at Lista. She continued to stare back at him. It struck him that she looked trustworthy, although he had no idea where he might have gotten that impression. Yes, said a voice in his head that sounded like an echo of his own, it might be a good idea to take her to see Steven Kerr after all. But just in case, maybe he could have her instruct Sessily to disable all controls once they had boosted through the wormhole, so that their ship would be entirely in the hands of the Military, and he could be certain that it was not engaged in any form of surveillance. It would make him feel better.

'All right,' said Aron. 'You can come, but you'll instruct Sessily to hand over control of this ship to my cruiser as soon as we leave the wormhole.'

'If it makes you feel better,' said Lista, which was odd, because that was just what he'd been thinking . . .

Aron was starting to feel highly confused.

'Right,' he said.

With that, Lista turned to the pilot, who had made no protest during any of this.

'Let's fly, Sessily,' she instructed.

'Yes, ma'am,' said the pilot.

Aron buckled himself in, still perplexed. He really had underestimated this Lista – she was obviously a force to be reckoned with.

But later, as Lista gagged and vomited repeatedly as they bumped and rocked their way through the nasty little wormhole, Aron couldn't help feeling a little pleasure at her discomfort.

Once they had completed the boost, a large, battered-looking cruiser came into view. All identifying marks had been removed from its matte-black bodywork, and it floated menacingly like a shark in empty dark waters. As they approached, a bay opened beneath the bow of the cruiser and their red ship was consumed by it. Perhaps it wasn't a shark so much as a whale, drinking in a cloud of red plankton.

Lista looked up from her sick bag.

'Thank heavens,' she said, and again Aron felt that odd bafflement, for he only ever heard that expression from humans, or those Illyri who'd spent time on Earth. The handmaiden must have picked it up from the Archmage.

Docking locks secured the Nairene vessel, and the all-clear sounded as the bay doors closed.

'Steven should be waiting in the control room,' Aron told Lista. She wiped her mouth, looking distinctly pale.

'You can come inside if you wish,' urged Aron, 'and freshen up.'

'Don't be ridiculous. You can hardly have me running around inside a Military cruiser, can you? Just send Steven to me and I'll let him know what Ani says,' replied Lista, then, remembering her manners, she added a reluctant 'please'.

She really was quite above herself, Aron decided as he left the craft. He glanced back just before the door closed. Lista was looking at her reflection in the shiny glass of the shuttle, smoothing her hair with her hands like a teenager awaiting the arrival of her date. For a moment, she reminded him a little of Ani.

When Aron returned with Steven Kerr, Sessily was waiting outside the shuttle, leaning against her craft like an outsized teenager spoiling for a fight. A scattering of human men gathered on the edges of the bay stared at her and she glared back, her hand hovering near a pulser strapped to her waist.

'It's okay,' said the Earth-boy in Illyri, 'they won't bother you,' but Sessily ignored him. She'd never actually spoken to a human before, and it didn't appear as if she'd missed much; this one's attempt at the Illyri tongue was rough and unpleasing to her ear. Sessily simply activated the shuttle door, barely looking at him.

As Steven disappeared inside and the door slid shut on his back, Aron could have sworn that he heard the young man whoop.

'Ani!' said Steven as his eyes began to focus in the gloom, for there it was: that unmistakable silver hair, glowing like a band of cirrus over the moon. He'd fancied he'd been in love with her once, a long time ago, but then it was easy to imagine as much of someone who'd saved your life, especially when they were beautiful, and even more so when they spoke to you as if you mattered at a time when everyone else still treated you like a child. 'I never expected you! I thought Aron said a handmaiden – '

But then he stopped. His old friend – now fully grown, and clearly significantly taller than him, even seated – was pointing a pulser at him. She watched him carefully, and the eye of the Sisterhood regarded him too from a tattoo on her cheek, peering like a face from behind a wall of ornate foliage.

'What the hell are you doing, Ani?' he asked.

Momentarily her lip seemed to quiver, or perhaps that was just a shadow thrown by the tiny lights blinking on the control panel.

'Who are you?' she said finally. '*What* are you? Steven Kerr is dead.'

'No,' said Steven, 'but if you use that pulser, then he very soon will be.'

Ani tutted.

'Tell me something only Steven Kerr and I would know,' said Ani. Her voice was rigid, her jaw firm.

'Jeez, talk about pressure,' said Steven, feeling a moustache of sweat forming on his upper lip. 'Do you have to keep pointing that thing at me?'

'Yes,' said Ani.

'Right . . .'

Steven thought quickly.

'In the van,' he started, and Ani immediately interrupted.

'What van?'

'The van we rode in together, to get away from Edinburgh. White transit van.'

'Yes?'

'Well, er, I remember you didn't pee once all the way to Inverness.'

'How could I?' snapped Ani. 'You were right there!'

'Exactly,' said Steven. 'I was right there, but I could manage quite discreetly with a bottle, if you recall.'

'Go on,' said Ani.

'I remember we were in a tiny hidden compartment, and we were thrown about all the way. And you hardly touched your juice – I'm guessing because of the toilet situation – but we ate those horrible hard scones and some squashed bananas, and then you told me about what happened to the Mechs.'

At this she remained silent, so he thought it best to continue: 'And then there was the time we played piggy-in-the-middle with a bar of soap in the lake. You were the piggy . . .'

And to Steven's surprise, the imposing female pointing a gun at his guts started to laugh. At the same time a tear slid down her cheek, so that it was almost as if her own eye and the tattooed eye were weeping together.

'I thought you were all dead,' Ani said, slipping the pulser discreetly into her pocket.

Steven shook his head.

'And I thought you'd gone to the dark side, until Aron explained how much you've helped.'

They smiled at each other. All pretence of formality and distance fell away, and Ani reached for him and hugged him tightly to her. With his face in her hair Steven felt like he was fifteen again, full of hope that all could still be made right in the universe, and he found that his cheeks were wet too. They cried together for a while, close and comfortable as brother and sister.

Ani composed herself first.

'What about Syl?' she said. 'Is it possible that she could be alive too?'

'I don't know,' Steven replied. 'I hope so. She was with my brother, but I haven't seen them for almost two years.'

'Two years?'

'Well, in fairness that would only be two days where I left them, so I'm not really worried – not yet.'

'I don't understand. What happened, Steven?'

And so he told her, as best he could, about what had happened beyond the Derith wormhole, and his trip to Krasis, and his time on Earth, and then his reconnection with the Military and their ongoing attempts to sabotage Corps operations – or as much as he dared share with her.

For this was no longer his friend from Earth.

This was the Archmage.

CHAPTER 63

The Military fleet was already massing for its assault on Illyr. It had gathered at the Myelen system, having first neutralised the two nearest Diplomatic communications outposts, along with five others chosen at random so as to confuse anyone trying to establish a pattern to the attacks. It was a motley assortment of ships, and included some carriers and destroyers that had once been earmarked for destruction as too old to be of use, alongside vessels seized from the Diplomats in raids – among them two heavy cruisers captured by the crew of the *Velder Sel*, late of the prison moon of Krasis, and the only survivor from the ships that had been sent by Steven Kerr to wreak havoc on the Diplomatic supply routes.

Also side by side on the outskirts of the fleet were three ships that had assumed near-legendary status: the *Revenge*, currently under the command of Alis while Steven was absent; the *Satia*, which now had a full Military crew, with Hague as executive officer, one step below its captain; and the *Varcis*, which was an object of particular interest since it was crewed entirely by Mechs. These three vessels formed a separate strike force led by Steven Kerr, who took his orders directly from the commander of all Military forces, Nolis.

The fleet had also gathered to it various Nomad vessels, for the wanderers had no love for the Diplomats, as well as some Civilian craft that had thrown in their lot with the Military for the same reason as the Nomads. Because of the nature of the fleet, security procedures could not be followed as tightly as Nolis might have wished. It meant that the Military was vulnerable to spies.

Now, while Steven Kerr spoke with Ani, and Nolis gathered his general staff to finalise the Military's plan to storm the Illyr system, a Nomad transporter at the rear of the fleet slipped away and made for the Krisen wormhole. It had boosted before anyone even noticed that it was gone.

XV
APOCALYPSE

CHAPTER 64

The universe was black and white; all was stars and wet-tar blackness. There was nothing else, nothing but this.

Syl's world had been reduced to sleekness and metal and monochrome. Together with Paul and Thula she lived in a floating, constricted room in space: nowhere to run, and nowhere much to walk either, unless you counted the crew quarters, the ablution facilities – smaller than those on an aeroplane – or the tiny galley; no trees, no flowers, no flowing water or bracing wind or anything much at all, besides the here and now. They had been travelling for months, but it felt like years, or maybe forever.

Once again, thought Syl, I am in a prison of sorts. First it had been Edinburgh Castle, then the Sisterhood, and now she was sealed within a battered-looking tin can kicked into the backwaters of the universe. At least this time it had been her choice.

She knew the *Nomad* backwards by this point, inside and out, for she'd studied its exterior on the countless little cameras that fed information to the mainframe. She'd counted the rivets and the chair legs in the cabin. She'd counted the panels across the ceiling, and the sachets of food that remained, and then she'd zoned out, pretending to sleep, and counted the number of days since she'd last washed properly – not just with a cloth and a bucket – and how long it was since she'd bitten into a fresh piece of fruit, or walked on land, or felt the rain, or seen another of her own kind, another Illyri, and it had stretched into weeks, then months.

She'd counted the numerous buttons and levers that Thula, and occasionally Paul, used to fly their craft. By this point she was pretty sure she knew what they were all for: that red one was starboard thrusters, that blue one was airflow, the row of yellow lights indicated minute changes in everything from temperature to air pressure to the levels of various gases outside their ship.

Sometimes she stared at the colours that blinked on the control panel, and when a light flickered on she'd play a game where she named everything she could think of that was that colour until it went off again, but she felt like she was forgetting things. Yellow wasn't her favourite colour, for while yellow was butter, daffodils, ducklings and street markings, it was also urine and bile and pus. Blue was better, for it was the sea and Earth's vivid sky. It was the burst of iridescence on a starling's wing, it was the wildness in a peacock's tail. It was sapphires. It was her father's cremos decanter. It was Paul's eyes.

Red lights flashed the most often, and red was so many things – strawberries, ladybirds, clown noses, Christmas baubles, Valentine's hearts, Aberdeen FC – but these weren't the things that came to mind. Mostly red was blood, and red was the Nairene Sisterhood.

And Syl wondered if they could feel her coming.

When they'd left the Cayth and boosted through the Derith wormhole, all had been quiet.

'I was worried there'd be a welcoming committee,' said Thula.

'Yeah, me too,' said Paul. 'Maybe they didn't manage to figure out how they lost that first ship, or just got distracted by killing one another.'

'Hey, happy birthday, chaps,' said Syl. She laughed at their perplexed faces. 'We're all three years older than we were three days ago – nearly four in fact.'

'Hey, so I'm twenty-one,' said Paul. 'Time to give up the short pants.'

'And still you don't look a day over eighteen,' said Thula. 'I guess I'm about twenty-three then. Probably should get my driving licence sometime.' He took in the crowded panel of the spaceship he was currently piloting and snorted with amusement.

'I suppose I'm legally allowed to drink,' said Syl.

She and Paul clinked their mugs of tea together.

Giddy in the moment, they all grinned at each other. It had felt like the start of a brave new adventure.

Together, as a team, they'd plotted their course as the blurred eye that was Derith disappeared behind them, and the babble of the Cayth became a memory. Paul's hand had strayed absently on to Syl's back as they spoke, and she'd liked it being there.

'Basically, we'll be travelling along two sides of a triangle to get as close to the Marque as we can,' said Paul. 'That means heading for Illyr, obviously. It may seem ridiculous, but I figure every other craft in the universe is probably hell-bent on getting from A to B as fast as possible; if we go from A to B with a detour via C, we're less likely to run into trouble.'

'I think you mean a detour via Z,' said Thula, tapping at the screen in front of him. 'We're basically going from London to Paris via, er, Moosejaw.'

'Moosejaw?'

'Yeah, Moosejaw. It's a place, okay. In Canada. Or it was a place.'

'Is that really necessary, Paul?' asked Syl. They had been gone for so long. Even though the future was frightening to her, she wanted to get back to the Marque as quickly as possible. Her destiny lay there.

'It is. I don't see any other option; the closer we get to the Illyr system, the harder it'll be to avoid detection. We need to take the back roads, and then use the back door too.'

Syl nodded. Many of the portals they were using were chosen from among those that had been revealed to them by the Cayth and added to the *Nomad*'s database. Unfortunately, all of the wormholes in the Illyr system were already widely known and heavily trafficked, except for one.

'Eradoonaliath 748,' she read as Paul enlarged the section of the star map devoted to Illyr. 'That's the Sisterhood's wormhole, near Erebos. Why is it showing up in red?'

Thula coughed and looked at Paul.

'Because it's not exactly stable,' Paul replied, 'and it's rather small.'

Thula coughed again, pointedly.

'Explain, Paul,' said Syl, glancing suspiciously at Thula. 'Please.'

If it was meant to be a request, it sounded like an order.

'Because the E748 wormhole is technically not big enough for the *Nomad*,' said Paul.

'We won't fit?'

It was Thula who answered her. 'We will fit,' he said, 'but we'll just be too close to the sides for my liking, speaking as the guy flying this rust-trap.'

They both looked at Paul, and he scratched his head with his hands, tousling his hair into a tangle. He seemed troubled.

'I can't see another way in,' he said finally. 'Every other entrance to the system will be monitored and heavily trafficked, and we'll simply be blown apart or captured the moment we show ourselves. We've no Steven to outmanoeuvre them, no Rizzo to outshoot them. It's just us.'

'Go us,' said Syl flatly. 'Go B-team.'

Thula threw her a look. Wasn't sarcasm supposed to be his job? Well then, today he'd take the high road.

'For what it's worth, folks, I brought my A-game,' he said.

What remained was the fact that by using the risky Erebos wormhole, they would inevitably attract the attention of anyone who might be on the palace moon, and the information uploaded from the *Gradus* told them that the Sisterhood now kept watch there. They had no illusions about being captured, sooner or later. As soon as they came close to Illyr, they would be taken, but it was essential that they be apprehended by the right side. Their mission was to get Syl back to the Marque. Once she was inside, she would have to find a way to confront the Other that dwelt deep within it – confront it and, if the Cayth were right, destroy it.

The question, of course, was what would happen to Thula and Paul in the meantime.

Syl looked at Paul and saw her concern for him reflected in his expression as he turned to her, a frown creasing his baby skin, and she could have cried for him and for the enormous decisions he had been forced to make, and the ones yet to be made.

'If I'm going to get squeezed to death, or popped, or whatever else might happen, there's no finer company to be squeezed or popped with,' she said.

'Nice,' said Thula, but he was smiling, just a little – and so was Paul. He squeezed Syl's shoulder in acknowledgement.

'Ditto, lady.'

'So let's get going,' said Syl. 'Let's do it, Lieutenant!'

After all, what choice did they have?

The days, weeks and months of moving through space and time, of slipping in and out of unmanned wormholes, always with one eye behind and one in front, always with a finger on a trigger – just in case – had inevitably taken their toll. Cabin fever had set in.

Paul paced relentlessly, his footfalls like a drumbeat. When he wasn't pacing, or slouched in the captain's chair, or sleeping, he read Illyri literature and history, immersing himself in the library uploaded from the *Gradus* to the *Nomad*. Thula handled the isolation by singing quietly to himself, or sometimes more loudly as if to try and fill the vastness around them with his impressive baritone. No one minded because it tamed the silence. Occasionally, when Paul knew a song, he would join in, but human music had largely bypassed Syl inside her castle, so she just listened, and wondered. Thula also wrote, which inspired Syl to begin writing too. She recorded her memories of Earth, of her father, of all that had led them to this point in their lives, leaving out only the Cayth, although in time she would add them to her account, which would come to form a crucial part of the *Chronicles*.

But more often than not she zoned out and got lost inside her own head, reaching beyond the windows and airlocks of the *Nomad*, searching the universe for signs of intelligence, trailing tendrils from her mind towards the distant planets that occasionally bobbed like fruit floating in water below them, or above them, or alongside them. There had to be more, she reasoned, for hadn't they met the Cayth? And yet they'd seen no other life at all, and she had felt nothing but gnawing loneliness as she stretched her psyche into space. Rocks orbiting distant suns were barren, or molten, or hidden under swirling fumes of brightly hued poison. There was nothing there. Sometimes she clung to Paul, desolate and filled with despair, and sometimes she pushed him away, for she wanted to be alone, to think, to plan.

Slowly, steadily, they moved closer to the Illyr system.

CHAPTER 65

The *Nomad* arrived in the system that hid the entrance to the wormhole E748 without incident, save for the odd scattering of asteroids, and the occasional mindless, heedless drone speeding blind to who knew where, and most recently a quick duck away from a distant, dark craft that looked like a transporter, although they could see no markings upon it.

'Military,' said Thula.

Paul nodded. It made sense. Only a Military craft would have reason to hide its identity, although he wondered what this one was doing so close to Illyr. That was dangerous. They'd managed to monitor enough distant signals and communications to know that the war still raged. Paul had a brief, foolish notion to go after the transporter and seek its help. Maybe it could take them to someone in the Military who would have a better idea about how they might gain access to the Illyr system without being crushed or spotted, and thence to the Marque.

He pushed the thought away. He knew that he was frightened and looking for a way out. He felt sure that he would die near Illyr.

Syl said nothing. She was wondering what she would find. She was thinking about her father.

And Ani.

CHAPTER 66

The shuttle carrying Ani back to Erebos barely made it through the wormhole intact, and was forced to make an emergency landing on the outskirts of the palace grounds. Ani was profoundly, painfully sick as soon as they emerged. She had cut her forehead deeply and it would require stitches, while Sessily had fractured her right arm.

'The wormhole is losing its integrity,' said Jolia, one of the Illyri technicians who came to the aid of the Archmage. 'It's unsafe for further boosts.'

'Secure it with a warning beacon,' said Ani.

She was sorry to be losing the Sisterhood's private wormhole, but grateful that she would never have to use it again. They had been away for two days in total. The delay had been necessary for Ani to receive her new guests.

From the rear of the shuttle, five figures emerged. They were dressed in what looked like Nairene robes, but Jolia recognised none of them. As far as she was aware, only Sessily and Lista had been on board the shuttle when it left with Aron. Jolia had already been mildly surprised to find the Archmage on the damaged shuttle instead of Lista – the Sisterhood had been informed that the Archmage was 'meditating' in her chambers – but she knew enough of Ani's powers of deception not to be too shocked. An additional five Sisters, all new to her, was another matter entirely.

As they drew closer, the five strange Sisters drew veils over their heads and faces, but not before Jolia caught a glimpse of damaged skin on the neck of one. Visible in the wound was not flesh or blood, but cables and circuits.

Ani took Jolia's chin in her right hand, turning the technician's face towards her.

'What do you know of organic circuitry?' she asked.

'A little,' said Jolia. 'Actually, more than a little.'

'Good,' said Ani, 'because I have a special job for you . . .'

CHAPTER 67

The shifting red mass of E748 bloomed before the *Nomad*, its edges rippling as they faced it head-on. It was like looking into the open end of a ghostly trumpet, but it wavered and shimmered, and bulges randomly appeared in its surface as if clumsy fingers were prodding against its interior. Something in its left side began to swell like a massive bubble under a layer of skin, tight and angry and seeming ready to pop. Beyond was the suggestion of distant nebulae, but nothing more.

The three passengers on the *Nomad* stared into the mouth of the wormhole and tried to hide their fear. For once, none of them seemed to have anything to say.

Paul made the first move, and his voice and manner were efficient. He was back in charge.

'Right, crew,' he said, 'this is the big one, the last boost. Status, Thula?'

Thula didn't even need to look at his system readings.

'More unstable than previously thought,' he said, 'as I'm sure you've noticed.'

'Is it safe, Sergeant?' There was an edge to Paul's voice.

'No, Lieutenant, it is not safe.'

'But is it safe *enough*?'

'I couldn't say. All I can tell you is that the *Nomad*'s readings caution against entering, or even approaching it for that matter.'

'As does my stomach,' whispered Syl from her seat – Rizzo's old seat – beside the guns.

'So we can't use it?' said Paul. He might have been angry, but equally he might have been relieved – it was hard to say.

'With respect, sir, you have not let the *Nomad*'s readings stop us before. Or my advice, for that matter.'

Paul almost smiled.

'I guess I haven't. Okay, so what do we think? Syl?'

'Is there another way?'

'No, not without retracing our steps and entering through a major wormhole, which would leave us open to being captured by a Corps ship and imprisoned.'

'Or worse,' said Thula.

'I didn't want to say it, but yes, probably worse.'

'It's just semantics anyway,' said Thula. 'It's not like we have much choice.'

'Well,' said Paul, 'it's not going to get any more stable with us just stalling here, looking at it. Let's do it. Secure the ship for boosting. Syl, when you're done, you keep the weapons seat. I'll co-pilot. Strap yourselves in tightly. And let's put on helmets this time, to be safe. Oh, and make sure you have a working oxygen supply too, just in case. We'll worry about everything else when we make it to the other side.'

'If we make it to the other side,' muttered Thula, but if Paul heard, he chose to ignore him.

'One more thing,' said Paul, and he marched over to Syl, took her face in his hands and kissed her on the lips. It was meant to be a firm, quick peck, but Syl clearly had different ideas, and Paul was happy to go along with it.

'Oh, come on,' said Thula as the kiss went on and on, and if he could he would have revved the engine in annoyance.

Paul pulled away, and his face was pink.

'Sorry,' he said.

'I'm not,' said Syl, and she was smiling as she buckled herself into her seat. 'That was lovely. Ready when you are, Thula.'

Thula tried to hold a steady course, but the pressure inside E748 was tight and constricting, and Syl felt the squeeze worse than ever before, the sensation of being stretched like an elastic band twanged to breaking point. Light split and warped beyond the window as it was distorted against the inner walls of the wormhole, separating into a spectrum, and then another spectrum, and then, as a massive thud smacked the *Nomad* from the side, an entirely new array of colours seemed to burst like fireworks beside her, sparking images she'd never seen before, and would probably never see again.

The vibration grew in intensity until they were being shaken wildly. Syl's head was tossed about on her shoulders, her body straining and bruising as it was thrown against its supports. The *Nomad* let out a deep moan, and she thought fleetingly of whale song as, almost in slow motion, metal buckled towards her. For an instant it seemed like a trick of the mind, but she knew that it was very real as a panel collapsed painfully on top of her leg, a great weight that held her in place and would not be lifted.

And still they were buffeted, a mere paper ship on a sea of madness. A rivet popped from the floor below Syl and shot upwards, embedding itself in the roof panel. Another followed, fast and direct as a well-aimed dart. She heard herself shout a warning as more rivets turned into projectiles, and she looked towards Paul and saw that he was twisted in his seat, turned towards her desperately, as powerless as she was. He was wearing his oxygen mask, and she grabbed hers while Paul tried to secure Thula's as the Zulu battled to control the ship, the muscles in his neck thick with effort, the veins in his temples popping. He shouted something incomprehensible as lights sparkled and played on the cockpit windows before collapsing and floating away in swirls of broken hues. There was an ear-splitting screech, and every indicator on the dashboard burst into life at once before forming columns of illumination that stretched like iridescent worms.

And as Syl watched, the hull of the *Nomad* crumpled in upon itself, and Paul was struck by a thick lump of metal. They were sent spinning through space as Thula lost all remaining control of the ship. Paul – ominously silent, and limp as a rag doll – was ripped from his seat, his buckle compromised, his straps flapping uselessly, and his body slammed helplessly into Thula. The controls snapped in Thula's hands as he was thrown away from the panel, his seat wrenched from its moorings, big, strong Thula rendered as fragile as driftwood on a storm of chaos, spinning until he crashed into the far wall, still strapped tightly into his broken seat. A starburst of red exploded onto the shining chrome as his leg made contact, and splintered glass rained down on his head.

But that wasn't the worst of it, for the *Nomad* itself seemed to be breaking up around them, howling and roaring like an animal in great pain. Syl could see the sky where it shouldn't be seen. She felt cold, so very cold . . .

They had finally run out of luck.

The last thing Syl saw was Paul's sweet, sweet face, his eyes already closed. The last thing she heard was her own anguished scream.

And still the faraway stars shone calmly at the end of E748, glimpsed as if through the wrong end of a telescope, eyes blinking but not seeing.

Chapter 68

. . . perhaps she was dead. There was a very bright light, just like in the movies, but surely, surely death couldn't hurt this much . . .

. . . perhaps she was in heaven. Everything was white, and there was music, but surely, surely heaven would not hold such pain . . .

. . . perhaps she was in hell. There was red, so much red, and she felt so very hot, as if she were burning up, but she was completely numb too, and surely, without a doubt, hell would be riddled with pain . . .

. . . perhaps she was alive. There were voices, and her head throbbed, and a cool cloth covered her aching eyes. But she found she could remember, too − bits, at least, as she recalled Paul in the blood-splattered *Nomad*, his eyes closed, his body flopping like a doll's, lifeless and broken, and now she wished more than anything that she was dead.

Syl started to scream.

CHAPTER 69

When Syl woke up, she wasn't in heaven and she wasn't in hell. She didn't know where she was. She was lying on her back in a small, white space with curved walls, a closed door, and a circular window in the ceiling opening up into a star-filled black sky. She winced against the whiteness around her, forcing her pupils to close, and then she focused more slowly, taking in her environment. Tubes ran in and out of her body. Her head itched, but when she tried to lift her hand to scratch it, she found her arms were strapped to the bed beneath her, loosely enough to move a little, but tightly enough that she couldn't reach anything.

'Hey!' she cried as she pulled against the bonds, but her voice was hoarse and weak. 'Untie me!'

She heard a babble of muffled voices growing nearer, and she yelled again, louder now, just as the door flew open, and in swept two females, both wearing the distinctive red robes of the Nairene Sisterhood.

'What is it?' said one, looking around as if expecting an invasion. She was tall and well rounded, and her plump, pale face was tattooed with shapes that might well have spelled words in an unknown alphabet, although without the translation they looked like random doodles. 'Why are you shouting?'

'Where am I?' said Syl, still struggling against her stays. 'Am I a prisoner?'

'Well, you're not exactly going anywhere, if that's what you mean,' said the other female. She was somewhat older, but not nearly as old as her snow-white hair might have suggested. She kept it short, so it sprouted from her head like the bristles on a broom, and she wore an expression of restrained amusement.

'Where am I?' said Syl.

'The Palace of Erebos, in our medical suites.'

'But you're Nairenes.'

'Obviously. We control this facility.'

'How did I get here?' – and then Syl remembered, and she nearly choked on the next words as they spluttered, panicked, from her mouth – 'Where's Paul?'

'Paul?' said the white-haired Sister.

'She means one of the humans, I think, Velarit,' said the other.

'Yes, the human men! What happened to them?'

'They're alive, which is about the best that can be said for them,' said the Sister called Velarit. 'And please stop shouting. We thought there was a problem.'

'Of course there's a problem!' cried Syl. 'I'm tied to a bed and I don't know what the hell is going on. I need some answers.'

Velarit ignored this.

'Syl Hellais,' she said, 'I shall inform the Archmage that you have awoken. She is anxious to see you.'

'The Archmage?' The horror echoed loudly in Syl's voice.

'Naturally,' said Velarit. 'Who else? She has taken a deep personal interest in your progress. As soon as she knows you're awake I imagine she'll be here promptly.'

'No!' shouted Syl.

'And please,' said the second Sister, 'be more polite to her Eminence than you are being to us. It is because of her that your life has been saved.'

'Only so she can watch me die again, more slowly,' said Syl, and she was furious to find that tears of fear and self-pity had filled her eyes and were flowing down her cheeks. Her nose started running too, but there was nothing she could do to stop it, and no way to wipe it. She sniffed loudly. 'Please, please just untie me.'

But the Nairenes departed without another word. Syl sank back against her bed. What had she expected? How could she have been so foolish? She was on Erebos, far from the Marque, and back in the hands of the Archmage.

Minutes later the door opened again and through it glided a figure in deep red flowing robes, veiled in familiar fine lace, straight and poised, moving with the elegance of a creature fully at ease in its skin. She was alone and pointedly shut the door before turning back to face the bed, slipping the veil onto her shoulders as she did so.

'Ani?' said Syl. She'd have recognised that silver hair any-where, but this Ani was markedly taller, distinctly older, fully grown and fully beautiful. But that wasn't all that was different about her: her cheeks were now adorned with intricate tattoos of spiralling tiny-leafed vines, and from them watched the tattooed eyes of the Nairene Sisterhood.

'Syl!' cried Ani, and she flung herself down beside her beloved friend, burying her face in Syl's neck and crying fat, wet tears into her hair.

'Oh Syl,' she said. 'Four years gone. Nearly five years, even, and I thought that you were dead!'

Syl couldn't move with the weight of Ani on her chest, and the ties at her wrists meant that she couldn't return the embrace either, but she wasn't sure she wanted to. Four years, said Ani, but for Syl it was a matter of mere months. The things that had been said on their last parting still rang in her ears, and then there was the small matter of Ani's red robes, and the mark of the Sisterhood indelibly staining her skin.

Ani pulled away, looking confused.

'Ah,' she said, 'you're still restrained.' She laughed as she stood up − a dry, forced, adult laugh so unlike the teenage giggle Syl remembered − and moved to undo the stays. 'It was just to stop you damaging yourself. You were unconscious, but still you kept trying to scratch the wound on your head.'

Ani stopped what she was doing and stared into Syl's face, studying her.

'Look at you, though,' she continued. 'You've hardly changed at all. You still look so young—'

'I don't understand,' interrupted Syl. 'What are you doing here, Ani? Where's Syrene? Why are you wearing those robes?'

Ani looked surprised, and then she bit her lip as if to control a grin, and for an instant there was a glimpse of her mischievous younger self. But immediately it was gone again, and she was an adult once more.

'Of course – you don't know yet! Well, how could you?'

She twirled, smiling as Syl watched, perplexed, and red silk shimmied and fell around Ani in slow, lazy waves.

'Lady Syl Hellais,' she said, 'you are looking at none other than the new leader of the Nairene Sisterhood. I am the Archmage Ani.'

In response, Syl said a very rude word.

Ani glowered at her, her face turning red, and Syl looked back, filled with dismay and disbelief. As they sized each other up, like two dogs before a fight, Syl did what came naturally: she opened her mind, searched for Ani, and found her. Syl felt Ani's thoughts bubbling hot, churning around her as though she'd immersed herself in a pot of boiling oil, and she experienced the flashes of anger, hurt, pride, arrogance, and power, and with them the truth of what Ani had said, followed briefly by something else, something like love – before Ani's thoughts were closed to her with the force of a trap snapping shut.

'No!' snarled Ani. 'You stop that!'

Syl withdrew, and the old friends continued to regard each other suspiciously – one clearly older than the other, fully grown, and self-assured like she'd never been before, the other younger, but angrier. So much angrier.

'How?' said Syl finally. 'How *could* you?'

'From where I'm standing, I'd say you're hardly in a position to criticise me,' said Ani.

'But the leadership of the Sisterhood, Ani? Have you lost your mind? I knew of your loyalty to it because you remained on Erebos, but to become its Archmage . . .'

She looked away from her old friend, finding herself repulsed by the tattoos so reminiscent of those she'd last seen on Syrene's cheeks, by that cold, dead eye that nonetheless seemed to be watching from a place beyond here, where there was no life, and no hope.

'I stayed because I wanted to fix things,' said Ani. 'I told you that – and it's exactly what I'm doing.'

'By becoming what we hated?'

'What *you* hated, Syl, not we. Not I. You were always determined to believe the Sisterhood was completely bad, but you were wrong. We were a noble order before Syrene corrupted us, and I am reclaiming that nobility for all my Sisters. Syl, I've done so much already, but with you beside me I could achieve so much more. I would like you to join us. Put on your robes again, and help me to cure this society of its ills.'

'And if I won't?'

'Then you're free to go.'

'Really? But I'm tied to a bed.'

Ani sighed, as if frustrated by a particularly irksome child, and resumed loosening Syl's bands.

'There,' she said when she'd done. 'I repeat, you're free to go.'

Syl sat up and swung her legs around, but immediately she felt dizzy, nearly toppling off the bed in the process, and Ani leaped to steady her, holding her tight. Syl leaned against her, her head swimming, her heart beating so hard she could see it pulsing in her eyes, and she found that Ani was strong and steady, and the touch and smell of her were achingly familiar. They stayed like that for a long time, neither saying anything, neither knowing what to say. Almost shyly, Ani's stroked Syl's back and Syl let her. Now that she was sitting, she wished that she had stayed lying down. Her head throbbed, and her body felt so weak that, had Ani not been supporting her, she would have fallen to the ground. Her eyes closed. She had dreamed that Ani was the Archmage. She had dreamed of wormholes.

'Ani,' she murmured finally. 'How did I get here? What happened?'

'We found you. We were monitoring the wormhole because it was due to collapse – just like you're about to do, I think.'

Ani eased Syl back onto her sickbed.

'Paul,' said Syl. 'Where's Paul?'

Ani pulled away, but she left a steadying hand on Syl's shoulder.

'He's not . . . great.'

'But alive?'

'Yes, he is that. He's in a medically induced coma. When we found him we didn't think he'd make it, but the medics resuscitated him – several times, I believe – and they say he'll recover in time. Perhaps less handsome than before, but only a little. His friend Thula claims that a broken nose adds character to a man's face.'

'Thula! What of Thula?'

'Ah, Thula. Actually, I was delighted to meet him. Steven mentioned him repeatedly, and favourably.'

As Ani casually dropped Steven's name into the conversation, she could barely conceal her pleasure at Syl's surprise. Steven, too, was alive!

'You saw Steven?'

'Only the other week. He's with the Military, but that's a conversation for another time. Goodness, we really do have a lot to catch up on, don't we? Perhaps now that you seem to have stopped being quite so angry, and if you feel up to it, we can start to talk. Properly. Like adults.'

Ani summoned a nursing Sister, and Syl was given a syrupy liquid to drink, and an injection that cleared away some of her nausea and sharpened her thinking a little. Feeling slightly more in control of herself, Syl arranged her thoughts.

'Okay,' she said. 'Start with Paul, please.'

'You and he are still an item then, I gather?'

'Yes,' said Syl, defensive now. 'We are, very much so. More than ever.'

Ani nodded, her features bland.

'I don't expect you to understand,' said Syl.

'I understand perfectly well, Syl. I'm not made of stone. But I do think you're making life very difficult for yourself.'

'It hasn't exactly been easy of late, you know, Ani – and it was Paul who made things bearable; it was Paul who pulled me through, who lifted me up every time. It was Paul who believed in me, even when I'd stopped believing in myself. It was Paul . . . it was always Paul.'

As she said it, she realised just how true it was, and she thought her heart would break at the idea of losing him. Her words dried up, and she felt as though there were pebbles in her throat. Ani watched her, and her eyes were kind.

'Well,' she said briskly, after a few beats, 'he took a really nasty bump on the head, but he's got that thick Scottish skull, you know,' – she smiled encouragingly – 'and I guess that saved his life. Everything else that was broken or injured can be fixed. We're fixing him now. But it will take time, Syl, lots of time, so we need to keep him asleep. He's peaceful, he's well cared for, and he's having the best medical treatment available.'

'When—'

'Tomorrow. You can see him tomorrow.'

Syl seemed about to argue, but then nodded.

'That would be good. Thank you. Tell me about Thula, please.'

'Thula's fine. We're rebuilding his foot – it was crushed during the boost – and he's completely deaf in one ear so he's shouting rather a lot because of it, but Lista is taking extra special care of him. He seems to have realised we're not going to kill any of you, so he's finally stopped threatening my staff. Or perhaps Lista has distracted him.'

Lista: the name was familiar to Syl.

'Lista? Do I know her?'

'You certainly should. You took her white robes that last day on Erebos and gave her your dress to wear. That's how I met her. I saw your dress in the crowd during the evacuation. She was trying to hide, the poor thing – I felt so sorry for her. If Syrene had found out, she'd have had her exiled, or maybe even killed. Anyway, I hid Lista until I could get her some new service robes. She works for me now, and she's intensely loyal. But she thought you were called Tanit, because that was what you told her.'

A cloud passed across Ani's features as she spoke Tanit's name, and the distance between Ani and Syl, which they were trying carefully to bridge, revealed itself once again. Syl knew that Ani had loved Tanit, had even been *in love* with her, and yet Syl had killed Tanit in front of her.

'I'm sorry, Ani,' she said, because she was sorry: sorry for the pain she'd caused her friend, though she felt little actual remorse for Tanit's death. What she'd done had been necessary – kill, or be killed. 'I'm truly sorry for what happened that day. I wish there could have been another way.'

She wanted to explain, to lay it all out body by body, corpse by corpse, detailing the killing spree that Tanit and the other Gifted had started, and had been hell-bent on finishing, beginning with Elda and ending, almost, with Paul Kerr. However, she knew an apology followed by an explanation would seem like no apology at all, so she left the words unsaid. Automatically, she reached for Elda's amulet around her neck, the one with 'Archaeon' scratched on its surface, but found that it wasn't there. It must have been lost in the accident.

'Are you looking for this?' said Ani. She slipped her fingers under the neckline of her own gown and pulled out the familiar necklace, its ugly brown locket flopping against her chest, all wrong against the sumptuousness of her robes. 'I've been keeping it safe for you since they scanned you for internal injuries – no metal is allowed in the scanners.'

She turned the locket over and over in her hand as she spoke, and it pivoted on its clasp.

'I remember what you said about Elda, Syl, and I'm sorry that I didn't believe you. I know all about Archaeon, all about Syrene's plans and schemes, for how could I not? I hold her position now and have access to everything that was once hers. I even sleep in her bed, but before that I was her scribe. I was her trusted aide, the last of her beloved Gifted, and she kept me close. I know how she warped the Gifted to suit her own purposes, but I also believe that Tanit was not to blame for what she was made to do. She was a child, Syl. We were all children, manipulated by adults for their own ends. And yes, I loved Tanit. I loved her deeply.'

Syl stayed quiet while Ani spoke on, her voice flat and low, as if this was a story she'd repeated to herself many times.

'I think that Tanit loved me back, Syl, in her way, but I know she worshipped Syrene above all others. I recognise now what kind of creature Syrene was trying to turn her into, and would have turned me into as well if she could. I have thought it through more often than you could know in the years since you killed— well, since Tanit died. I believe you did what you felt you had to do to stop Tanit. I wish it had not been so extreme, so final, but for the life of me I can't imagine what the alternative might have been. In the end, perhaps Tanit's death was a mercy. After the crimes that she and the other Gifted had committed – the murders, the burnings – they could not have been saved. Maybe they were corrupted beyond salvation, but they were corrupted by those who were older than them, and who should have protected them.'

There were tears in Ani's eyes, but they remained unshed as she talked, and she looked past Syl, twirling the amulet, her eyes focused on nothing at all.

'I have had four years to mull it all over, to come up with other endings to their tale, and I have, countless times, yet still I've never been able to completely convince myself of the possibility of any of them. But you – you had minutes, if not seconds to make a decision. And your life was threatened too. For what it's worth, Syl, I understand what happened. I don't like it one bit, but that's neither here nor there. And I'm no longer the child I was. I have moved on, and I too have done things I'm not proud of in the interim. Many things. I now know the universe isn't black and white. Sometimes it's just grey. But then, sometimes it's filled with colours so beautiful you can't even begin to imagine.'

Ani stopped and seemed to notice that she still held Elda's locket between her fingers. Absently, she brought it to her lips, then slipped it back under her robes. Syl did not protest. Perhaps Ani now needed that reminder of the past more than she did. Instead she reached for Ani's hand.

'I've missed you, Ani Cienda,' was all she said.

'It's good to have you back, Syl Hellais,' said Ani, and they both smiled a little, and for that moment it was enough. Ani turned to leave, declaring that she did not wish to tire the patient out, and as she made for the door Syl asked one last question, the one that she had been most afraid to have answered.

'Ani, what of my father?'

But Ani was gone.

CHAPTER 70

Syl remained on Erebos, confined to the medical suites over the days that followed. Her injuries were still healing, most visibly an immensely itchy but relatively superficial cut on her forehead. In addition her thighs were bruised black from the force of the collapsed panel that had kept her in place for the worst of the turbulence. However, for this she was vaguely grateful, because the chief medic, Velarit, said it was probably the anchoring weight of that panel which had saved her life. She found she was breathless too, as her lungs had been compromised, which left her more tired than she could recall ever being, seemingly able to hold a conversation for more than half an hour at most before she needed to lie down to sleep.

It didn't matter, because there was no one much to talk to anyway beyond the polite yet crisp staff in Nairene red, who were under strict orders from the Archmage to keep secret the fact that the fugitive Syl Hellais, and two wanted humans, were now recuperating under the care of the Sisterhood.

Paul remained comatose and Syl had to remind herself continually that it was drug-induced, and for his own good. Naturally, she drifted in to see him, sometimes twice a day, sitting alone by his bedside, but he was oblivious to her presence, his eyelids closed, their skin blue-tinted and fragile but unmarked – unlike the rest of his face, which was cross-hatched with welts and cuts. His nose was obviously smashed, as was the socket bone above his left eye, and his hair was shaved away, revealing a long, angry gash on the side of his head, but the rest of him was hidden beneath temperature-controlling sheeting. On her first visit, Syl had carefully pushed back a corner of the covers and found Paul's hand, but even that bore the scar of the burns that had been inflicted on him the last time he was on Erebos, and she swallowed hard as she stroked it, appalled at what had happened to him because of his contact with her people.

Tenderly, carefully, she felt for him with her mind, but he was so heavily medicated, that she found nothing but cool, blue light.

Thula was technically off-limits too. For he remained in the rehabilitation wing of the facility and Syl was not allowed to visit him without protective clothing because the delicate rebuilding of his foot could be compromised by cross-contamination. Syl went to speak with him once or twice, but mostly she was content to wave at him through the thick window separating his room from the units, and chat with him over the intercom system. She tried not to wince when she saw the mangled stump of his leg, neatly crisscrossed with a cage of synthetic bone, and tubes pumping blood, but Thula appeared untroubled by it, and found the whole process fascinating. Lista was often with him, which Syl found . . . interesting. Lista always looked delighted to see Syl, greeting her enthusiastically, and Syl felt more than a little ashamed, for she had abused Lista's trust and good nature twice. At least Lista didn't hold grudges.

But it was Ani to whom Syl wished to speak more than any other. However, her old friend had left after their first conversation, promising she'd be back when Syl was stronger, but she had not returned.

'The Archmage has been called away on important business,' Velarit said briskly when Syl questioned her, but Syl wasn't entirely sure this was true. She had so many questions to ask, questions that Ani would doubtless be uncomfortable answering, and perhaps this was why she stayed away. It was more than frustrating: Syl wanted to know how her father was. She wanted to know about Earth, about Steven, about the war.

About the Others.

As her body grew stronger, she grew more fearful that her enemies would discover her presence on Erebos. She was entirely reliant on Ani's goodwill, and the discipline of the Sisters attending her, to prevent her from being taken by the Corps or the Securitats. She needed to get to the Marque, and she recalled Ani's invitation to return to the Sisterhood.

And then what? The Cayth believed that she had the power to destroy the Others, but they hadn't exactly been clear on how she might go about doing that. And if Ani was Archmage, then she must surely know about the Other in the bowels of the Marque, the creature Syl needed to get to. How, wondered Syl, could the Ani she used to know smile so peacefully and speak so calmly when that abomination was buried deep in Avila Minor, infecting the very heart of everything over which Ani reigned and about which she professed to care so much? Was she in league with it? Had she, like Syrene, struck a bargain with the Others?

Or was Ani herself perhaps infected by one of the parasites, a parting gift from Syrene before she so mysteriously retired? Syl had not sensed one of the creatures inside Ani, but Ani had registered her probing before she had time to get beyond superficial emotional responses. The very idea of her friend's possible contamination caused her to jerk awake, stomach churning and heart pounding, in the deepest hours of the long, dark nights. Syl desperately wished to know why Ani had replaced Syrene, and how - *how*? Once that became clear, so too might the steps she had to take.

As the days stretched on and Syl's body healed, her capacity for concentration grew and she began to play games with her mind, burrowing into the heads of the unwitting medical staff, collecting misshapen segments of the truth, like jigsaw puzzle pieces that she attempted to fit together into a picture that made sense. She gently asked questions too, seemingly innocuous or innocent, but the answers she received surprised her:

Syrene had declared to her Council of Confidantes her intention to relinquish the position of Archmage in favour of Ani Cienda. The news had been met with consternation, but Syrene would not be swayed and confirmed that she intended to join the First Five in a life of isolation and contemplation. In the immediate aftermath, Ani had purged the Council of Syrene's supporters, demoting some, sending others into exile, replacing them with Sisters whose loyalty to the new Archmage was not in question. Ani had also retained Syrene's handmaiden Cocile as an aide, along with loyal Lista, and she had two personal guards who were near her at all times, close and connected as shadows.

Yet none of it made sense: how had a young upstart like Ani risen to the top so quickly?

The answer, of course, must be because she could cloud minds, although when Syl had fled the Marque four years earlier, Ani's powers were still in the process of development. As one of Syrene's precious Gifted, she had been rigorously tutored and encouraged to practise, and so it was probable that this training had continued – indeed, intensified – once the other Novices who possessed similar psychic abilities were all dead. Syrene must have invested all of her hopes in Ani, and all of her efforts. Perhaps Ani had ultimately become strong enough to manipulate the Archmage herself. In a piece of poetic justice, could Syrene have created the instrument of her own destruction?

The more Syl thought about it, the more she became convinced that she'd stumbled across something that looked like a seam of truth: it was insane, but somehow Ani had clouded her way into Nairene history.

That afternoon, Syl awoke from a nap to find Ani standing at the end of her bed, as though the Archmage had somehow become aware of the direction of Syl's thoughts. As Ani looked down on her friend with a concern that was almost motherly, Syl put her hypothesis to Ani, and asked if she had become Archmage through the use of her psychic gifts.

'You mean like this?' said Ani.

Syl felt a pang in her head, followed by a quiet, electrical buzzing, and Ani's image blurred before her. As Syl's vision refocused, the young Archmage shimmered out of view and in her place stood Syrene, scarlet-robed, proud and terrifying, her overripe lips swollen to bursting point, her hairline shaved even further back than before, the curlicued tattoos on her face squirming into her hair as if trying to escape the sharp gleam in her enormous eyes. Those orbs bored into Syl and, as she watched, they enlarged and extended, turning black as if filling up with oil, and they grew deeper too, like caves burrowing into a mountain. The tattooed coils became a writhing infestation of thin, red snakes, and they turned and slithered out of the hair and back towards the hollow eyes, more and more of them, until the sockets became a tangled nest of vipers.

'No!' shouted Syl, and immediately Syrene was gone. Only Ani stood before her, looking slightly put out.

'Spoilsport,' she said. 'I was just getting started.'

'You've grown stronger,' said Syl, hoping her voice sounded steadier than she felt. 'So much stronger.'

'As have you, it seems,' replied Ani. 'I sensed that you never once believed Syrene to be present. You knew what I was doing. Nobody else has been able to see through the illusions.'

They regarded each other carefully.

'Why did you come back here, Syl?' said Ani.

'I will tell you, if you first tell me what happened to Syrene. I want to know everything.'

Ani considered this, her head cocked to the side like a bird's, a gesture Syl had grown familiar with over many years, and then Ani sighed and sat herself down on the edge of the bed.

'I know I can trust you, Syl, if only because you hate the Sisterhood, and you hate Syrene, and they are the only ones who would benefit if you revealed the truth I'm about to share with you. Anyway, who would believe you?'

And so she told Syl all.

The light had changed by the time Ani's story was done, and Syl looked upon her friend with fresh eyes – a child before the adult that was the Archmage. What Ani had done, what she had achieved, was both extraordinary and somehow terrible. In her way, Ani was the most formidable Archmage yet. Trapped in the Marque with the One, Syrene and Priety must have understood that better than anyone.

'I wanted her to suffer as the First Five had suffered,' said Ani, speaking of Syrene, 'but I also needed a channel of communication to remain open. The One is different. It's more powerful than the rest. The Others are embedded in Illyri society. By keeping the One alive, and linking it to Syrene, I thought that I could learn more about them.'

'And did you?'

'In a way. Syrene told me what the One wants.'

The room felt too small to Syl, too warm. She sensed the answer coming. Perhaps she had sensed it from the time of her first sighting of the One, and had heard it confirmed in the Cayth's prophecy, but had chosen to remain deaf to it.

'She says it wants you, Syl.'

There was silence for a time. It was Syl who broke it.

'What will you do?' she asked.

'What do you mean?'

'About the One. And about me.'

'Hide your presence from it, of course, just as I've kept you hidden from the Corps and the Securitats. We've been lucky: their attentions lie elsewhere. A great battle is imminent, Syl, perhaps the last battle. The Military – or what's left of it – is preparing for an assault on Illyr. The Corps knows that it is coming, but not when, or where: its forces are marshalled but it can't strike until it knows the location of the Military fleet, and so far that has been kept secret. Dyer is in charge, not Krake. Dyer is the real power behind the presidential throne. He has help too, because Vena is by his side. She's now head of the Securitats, and she whispers in Dyer's ear from the other side of his bed.'

Syl blanched at the mention of her old enemy's name. Vena, who blamed Syl for the death of her former lover, Sedulus, had tried to have her killed on the Marque. Syl had presumed that Vena was still back on Earth. Actually, she'd been hoping that Vena might have died, preferably painfully.

'Together, Vena and Dyer have proved to be a considerable threat,'

Ani continued, 'and even my spies have struggled to infiltrate their lair, although some progress has recently been made. Whatever, the future of our society may well be decided in a matter of days.'

Ani put her head in her hands, as if carrying the weight of all she'd just said had been a heavy burden, and when she spoke again her voice was muffled.

'I can't predict the outcome, but I do know that it will be horrific. Countless lives will be lost, and at the end our true enemy will remain undefeated. The Others will prevail and continue to contaminate whichever side triumphs.'

'And which of those sides are you on in all this?'

'I am on the side of the Sisterhood.'

'That's no answer, Ani.'

'Then I am on the side of the Sisterhood above all others, and after that I will ally myself with the just. The Corps and its allies have shown themselves unfit to rule. They have infected our race with an alien parasite, which, if it is allowed, will eventually consume us entirely, just as it has consumed life on Earth, and who knows how many other worlds. And – '

She paused.

'Go on,' said Syl. Tentatively, she made forays into Ani's thoughts, and saw a red wall of rage fractured by a fissure of fear.

'The Securitats are planning a move against the Sisterhood. It seems that I have goaded Vena for too long, and she has always had her eyes on the Marque. To seize control of the Marque, she will have to kill me. But I will not permit it to fall to one such as her. The Sisterhood will defend the Marque, and give what aid we can to the Military.'

Ani sat back in her chair.

'So,' she said, 'here we are. I have bared my soul to you, but you have not bared yours to me.'

'You haven't told me everything yet,' said Syl. 'You haven't mentioned my father.'

It was as though she had punched Ani, and the girl behind the tattooed mask of the Archmage was revealed once more.

'No. Syl, it's—'

'Just tell me.'

Ani couldn't meet Syl's eyes.

'I made a mistake,' she said.

'What mistake?'

'I underestimated Syrene. When I gave her to the One, I assumed that it would simply take her as it had taken Ezil and the rest of the First Five. But there was a link between the Other in her head and the parasite that had taken over your father. Maybe it was because he had become infected through Syrene, and the entity that had infected him was a product of its spores. It was her revenge, Syl. She couldn't harm me, and she couldn't get to you, but she could hurt him. She could hurt him so badly.'

Syl began to weep.

'She killed him, Syl. She instructed the Other in his head to destroy him along with itself, and it did. I'm so sorry.'

Syl turned her back on her friend, faced the wall, and let her grief overcome her.

CHAPTER 71

The spies – the traitors – brought the news to Dyer at the Tree of Lights. The Military fleet was assembling at Myelen.

Dyer did not react instantly. He took time to think, then gave his orders: a pincer movement, with a Diplomatic task force descending on Myelen on separate fronts, using the two wormholes in the system – Myelen 1 and Myelen 2 - to launch a devastating surprise attack. Dyer presented the plan to his commanders, but most of them were career Diplomats who had found themselves elevated to command status. Only a handful of Dyer's commanders had any battle experience, and their objections to the splitting of the Diplomatic fleet were overruled in the rush to capitalise on the new intelligence received. This was their chance to strike at the Military while its forces were packed into a single system, with nowhere to run. It was how wars were won.

Later, the *Chronicles* would record that President Krake himself tried to change Dyer's mind – his plan for surprising the Military required him not only to divide the task force, but also to deplete by half the fleet defending the Illyr system – but by then the die was cast. The first component of the Diplomatic force would move in on Myelen 1 from Obruscar, the main Corps base just one wormhole boost away from Illyr, and only two boosts from Myelen. The second, though, would require many more boosts in order to reach the second Myelen wormhole, and the safest route would take it close to the Derith wormhole.

Dyer had been advised of the disappearance of the *Gradus* at that same wormhole, but his Nomad spies informed him that the *Gradus* had been captured by Military forces and now formed part of its battle fleet. Satisfied that there was no reason to be concerned about Derith, despite the waves of unease coming off the Other in his head, Dyer gave the order for half of his task force to pass within sight of it on its way to Myelen.

CHAPTER 72

When Ani returned the next morning, concerned for her friend and troubled afresh by the part she had played in the death of Andrus, she found Syl sitting upright on the edge of her bed. She was scrubbed clean, though her face was pale and her eyes were red from crying. She had changed out of her white hospital gown and was wearing the red robes of the Sisterhood.

'What on earth are you doing, Syl?' said Ani.

'I'm giving myself to the Sisterhood,' Syl replied bleakly. 'Again.'

Ani was all but dumbstruck. 'But why would you do that?' she asked.

Impatiently, Syl brushed a runaway tear from her cheek.

'I can't hide forever, Ani. I must face the One. I don't have a hope in hell of winning if I don't even turn up for the battle, do I?'

'But . . . but you could die. You will – you'll die, I know it!'

'Someone has to do something, Ani. What if I'm the only one who can?'

Ani was shaking her head – no, no, no – and her features crumpled in devastation as she battled the potential horror of losing her friend all over again.

'Please no, Syl,' she said. 'I can't. I couldn't bear it.'

'You said that the One wants me,' Syl said, and she found a new firmness both in voice and in purpose as she spoke. 'Well, I want it too, Ani, and you're going to give us both exactly what we desire.'

★ ★ ★

The Diplomatic task force moved through space: five carriers and eight destroyers, supported by twelve heavy cruisers. To starboard, the Derith wormhole rippled.

Rippled, then bloomed.

The Cayth fleet emerged so suddenly that even the lightest of the task force vessels did not have time to come about before the first of the torpedoes were unleashed upon them. Had any of the Diplomatic crews survived long enough, they might have glimpsed a single female figure standing on the otherwise empty bridge of the Cayth command ship, a goddess of war made flesh. Fara watched as the Illyri were utterly destroyed, and their vessels – now cleansed entirely of tens of thousands of crew – left to drift like ghost ships through the blackness.

The Cayth retreated back into the Derith wormhole, and it was as if they had never been.

CHAPTER 73

The Diplomats' communications arrays were down, so even if the Derith component of the task force had made its rendezvous point, there would have been no means of communicating that fact to the other half at the Corps base at Obruscar. The commander at Obruscar, Deyla, unable to raise her opposite number, Ilar, sought clarification of her orders from Dyer. Despite the urgings of Krake and others to recall Deyla, Dyer decided to gamble.

The order was given to attack the Military fleet.

On Illyr, a pair of assault cruisers stood ready on the massive landing pad at the heart of the Securitat headquarters in Upper Tannis. Inside each craft was a strike team composed entirely of female Securitats, heavily armed and clear on their orders: to secure the main control facility on the Marque, subdue all opposition, and apprehend and execute the Archmage Ani. The Securitats involved had all been warned of the possibility of psychic manipulation, so would shoot her on sight.

Vena waited in the control room by the landing pad. She was in contact with Dyer's senior aide, Neian. As soon as the Military fleet was engaged, and a Diplomatic victory assured, Neian would instruct her to seize the Marque.

Vena was calm. She had waited a long time for this. A few more hours would make no difference. She sat quietly, a whetstone before her, sharpening the knife that would cut the throat of the Archmage.

CHAPTER 74

The Battle of Myelen – the greatest confrontation between the rival Illyri factions since the First Civil War – was a disaster on many fronts. The loss of life dwarfed even the attack on Melos Station, which had marked the start of the conflict, and no Illyri family was left untouched by it. The *Chronicles* attest that Illyri society never recovered from Myelen and its aftermath.

Most of all, it was a catastrophe for the Diplomats. The Military fleet was taken by surprise as the Diplomatic task force emerged from Myelen 1, and five ships, including the great carrier *Tesos*, were lost in a matter of minutes, but years of guerilla warfare had taught the Military tactics that were beyond the capacity of Deyla and her captains to deal with. Had the Derith force survived, it is possible that the attack might have succeeded, but as soon as the first shock of their appearance had faded, the Diplomats found themselves facing not a bunched fleet of vessels, but ships diverging in multiple directions before they converged again as small, disciplined squadrons, each with a specific target. Already they were inflicting damage on the Diplomats and distracting them from the larger hunt.

Meanwhile, the Military vessels, including the six surviving carriers and more than a dozen destroyers, began boosting out of Myelen, to make straight for Illyr. The Military had already been poised for its own assault on the Illyr system within hours, and all plans were in place. When the order to attack was given, its commanders made their move, aware now that at least a section of the Diplomatic fleet was tied up at Myelen. The Military fleet emerged through the Melos wormhole, the place where so many of their fellow soldiers had died.

Anticipating some possible level of sentimentality and desire for revenge on the part of the Military, Dyer had fortified Melos, but with one quarter of his fleet now engaged in a battle that it was destined to lose, and another quarter floating lifeless near Derith, his forces were hopelessly divided. The Military had expected to encounter some opposition at Melos and had prepared for a hard battle, but Dyer's combination of one carrier, two destroyers and a number of heavy cruisers was not sufficient to hold back the Military. The Military destroyer *Entia*, the first vessel to emerge at Melos, was torn apart by the minefield laid on Dyer's instructions, but in doing so it carved a path for the ships that followed, as well as alerting their commanders to the presence of the mines and causing them to take action to destroy them.

Hopelessly outgunned, the Diplomatic ships turned tail and ran.

News of the Military incursion reached Vena on the landing pad just seconds before sirens began to wail in Securitat headquarters, echoed by similar warnings from Corps facilities nearby. The order came through from Neian: Vena and her Securitats were to stand down and await further instructions from the vice-president. There was to be no assault on the Marque.

Vena tore the communicator from her ear.

'Marshal?' asked one of the control room staff, who had listened to the exchange with Neian. 'What are your instructions?'

'Tell the pilots to prepare for lift-off,' she said.

'But the orders were—'

'I give the orders here,' said Vena. 'So clear me a flight path. *Now.*'

At Melos, two craft curled away from the main fleet. They were the *Varcis* and the *Revenge*, and together they set course for the Marque.

CHAPTER 75

The Marque's defences were on high alert. The Archmage had ordered that no ship was to be permitted to land unless first cleared by her. All vessels approaching the Marque were to be tracked by its weapons systems and automatically targeted. If they did not break off their approach, they were to be destroyed.

The Marque was huge, and thousands of Sisters lived within its walls. Ani had exiled or isolated all of Syrene's loyalists, and taken care of the spies that Dyer had cultivated, but even she could not purge the Sisterhood of every possible source of opposition and dissent. There were those who resented her for her youth and her arrogance, and others who hated her simply for being Earth-born. Some were ambitious and dreamed of being Archmage, and some knew that any such hopes for themselves were futile, but were angry and bitter enough to destroy that which they could never aspire to be.

Vena had found one such Sister, just one, and had carefully groomed her during the years of Ani's rule, keeping her identity a secret, holding her in reserve for such a day as this one. Her name was Soler, and she and Ani had one thing in common beyond the robes that they wore: Soler, like Ani, had loved the Gifted called Tanit.

Now, as the two approaching Securitat ships were ordered not to approach, and the guns of the Marque locked on them, Soler – clever, hurt, bitter, and a genius, in her way – activated the virus that had been lurking in the Marque's defences for almost a year. Guns were rendered impotent, landing pads left undefended, and doors remained unlocked. By the time Toria tracked her down and killed her, the first cruiser had touched down, and the Marque's hallways were already echoing with the sounds of screaming and dying.

The second Securitat cruiser was some minutes behind the first, having been delayed by congestion in the routes off Illyr as Diplomatic and Civilian crafts reacted in panic to the Military assault. The cruiser was now unable to find a safe landing pad: as soon as the breach in the Marque's defences had become apparent to the Sisterhood, the Nairenes had rushed to manually secure as much of their stronghold as they could, barricading doors and parking lifters and loaders on the landing pads, making it impossible for a ship to use them without incurring damage. With no other option, Keyra, the pilot of the cruiser, had ordered her gunner to aim for a light loader that was currently lying on its side on a pad adjoining one of the Marque's huge greenhouses. This meant bringing the cruiser down until it was almost level with the loader: Keyra didn't want to leave a crater on the pad that might endanger her cruiser. The gunner, Corae, hit the loader side-on with a heavy pulse blast, reducing it to scattered pieces of metal and clearing the way.

Sisters emerged from a doorway beside the pad and began firing handheld pulse weapons at the cruiser. Corae turned the cannon on them, reducing them to their constituent parts just as she had done with the loader.

'Prepare for landing,' said Keyra. They were the last words that she ever spoke. The *Revenge*'s first torpedo struck before the cruiser had even touched the pad, and the second turned it into only a memory. While it burned, the *Varcis* came in beside it and the Mechs emerged to join the fight.

The explosion from the cruiser's destruction shook the Marque, sending dust down upon Vena and her surviving Securitats. The Sisters had been sturdier in their defence than Vena had anticipated – in fact, had she not known better, she might have said that it was almost as though they had been anticipating just such an assault, and only Soler's sabotage had facilitated Vena's entry into the Marque. In the aftermath of the blast she tried to raise Keyra on her communicator, but to no avail, and she understood that no reinforcements would be coming to join her. Pulse blasts came from in front and behind, and a Securitat fell to the ground beside her. Vena returned fire, killing the pair of security Sisters before her. She instructed the four remaining Securitats to dig in and hold back the Sisters, for Vena was almost at her destination. All was not lost. If she could capture the Archmage, the Sisters would be forced to stand down while Vena negotiated their surrender.

But, in truth, Vena knew that she would not allow Ani to live, just as she knew that she herself would never escape the Marque alive, not now. And what did it matter, after all? If the Military had managed to get through the Melos wormhole, then the war was over, and a reckoning was coming for Vena and those like her. There would be no mercy for her, just as she would show no mercy to Ani Cienda. The Archmage would not outlive her.

Vena arrived at Ani's chambers, marked on the map that Soler had smuggled out to her. If Ani was not here, then Vena would just make her final stand in this place, but she was certain that this was where Ani would have sought refuge. Soler had told her that the Archmage's chambers functioned as a secondary control room if the main one was seized. From there, the Archmage could direct and coordinate the defence of the Marque.

Vena hit the door release. A Sister turned to face her, and Vena recognised Liyal, one of Ani's devoted bodyguards. Liyal fired a pulse, but it was off target, while Vena's was not. Her shot took Liyal in the chest, killing her instantly.

Vena moved quickly into the chambers. To her right knelt a Sister in red robes, apparently meditating before a wall of ancient books. Vena stepped towards her, and the Sister started to rise. Her veil fell away, and Vena saw the face of Ani Cienda watching her calmly. Screaming, years of barely controlled rage pouring out of her, Vena threw the Archmage to the floor, then holstered her pulser and pulled the knife from its scabbard. She grabbed Ani by the hair, not even stopping to wonder at the lack of fight in her. Vena raised Ani again to her knees, exposing her neck, then drew the blade across her throat. There was a gush of blood and Ani's body shook.

Vena released her hold and stepped back, watching the body fall, waiting for Ani to die at last. The Securitat was breathless, panting, but she was smiling too. Finally, it was done.

The Archmage's body grew still. The blood stopped flowing, to be replaced by a stream of milky fluid that slowly became a trickle. The Archmage slowly stood, and now Vena saw for the first time the scarring behind her ear and around her hairline, and noticed that this figure was slightly shorter than Ani Cienda.

Vena backed away from the Mech, shaking her head in disbelief, and as she did so, a terrible pain shot through her body, beginning in her back and working its way through the core of her being until it seemed that it must surely erupt from her chest. There was a coldness to it, and then the chill was gone and there was only the warmth of her own blood flowing from the wound. She turned slowly. Meia stood behind her, and in her hand was a blade not dissimilar to Vena's own: a little thinner, perhaps, but just as sharp. Somewhere in the distance all firing ceased, and there was only silence.

'Any last words?' asked Meia.

'Bitch,' said Vena as Meia's knife finished its work.

CHAPTER 76

Syl and Ani stood before the glass and stared at the One. It seemed to register their presence, for it moved on its web the better to face them, and Syrene and Priety both jolted in their seats, as though reacting to a sudden electric shock.

The tiny communicator in Ani's ear vibrated.

'Speak,' she said.

Meia's voice was in her head.

'The Marque is secure. Three Securitats were taken alive. The rest are dead.'

'And Vena?'

'Deceased. She cut Alegna's throat. Alegna is most unhappy about it.'

It had been Meia's idea to substitute the Mech named Alegna for Ani. The ProGen skin job to alter her appearance had been rushed and crude, but it had worked.

'Good,' said Ani. 'Please give my thanks to Alegna, and apologise on my behalf for any discomfort she may have suffered.'

'I will. Ani?'

'Yes.'

'I can join you, if you'll let me.'

It was with Meia alone that they had shared their plan to allow Syl access to the One, in those few short days before the anticipated assault on the Marque. It had been a crazy, intense time, filled with fear, planning and small, seized moments of joy at their reunion. Meia had not objected to the scheme – for the pair who stood before her were so clearly no longer children asking her permission, but adults, united and decided – yet she was well aware of the risks involved. She wanted to be with them to help if she could, but Syl and Ani both knew that this was beyond even Meia's capabilities. They just hoped what was to come was not beyond Syl's.

'You'll be of more use elsewhere,' said Ani. She adjusted the communicator so that Syl could hear Meia's voice. 'You can talk to both of us before you leave. Syl can hear you now.'

'Syl?'

'Yes, Meia.'

'Don't die.'

'I'll do my damnedest, Meia, I promise. Thanks.'

Ani cut the signal as the One regarded them with its dark, alien eyes.

Meia returned to the *Varcis* and joined the remaining Mechs. Only a dozen had survived: twelve, out of tens of thousands. The thought brought rage to Meia.

Alegna came on board last, a scar across her neck where the ProGen skin had been sealed. She took a seat behind Menos, the pilot, and he turned briefly to pat her affectionately on the hand. The *Revenge* hovered off their port bow.

'Steven?' said Meia.

'We hear you,' came Steven Kerr's voice from the *Revenge*.

'The Archmage has instructed us to leave the Marque.'

'Is she okay?'

'She has her own work to do, as has Syl, and as do we.'

'The fleet has passed Cryos Station,' said Steven. 'We have Diplomatic ships massing at Illyr. It doesn't look like they're about to go down without a fight.'

'Then,' said Meia, 'I suggest we give it to them.'

The door to the inner chamber hissed open, and Ani and Syl stepped through. Both wore protective suits and hard plastic masks over their faces, but they were unarmed.

The One had changed since the last time Syl had been in its

presence. It was still largely transparent, and its system of hearts could be seen beating in unison, along with the pinkish-yellow cloud of brain behind its eyes, but the gripping tentacles on its body that allowed it to move on its web had withered away to be replaced by harder, chitinous limbs, and the same substance seemed to be creeping across its belly and lower back. As Syl watched, a section of the One's skin hardened and changed colour. It was growing armour, she realised: it was aware of the recent change in the Diplomats' fortunes from the Others implanted in the Corps hierarchy. The One was preparing to defend itself.

She noticed that, underneath it, Priety was on the verge of death. Her old teacher had been drained almost entirely of life: the One had clearly been drawing on her life force to power its transformation. Beside Priety, Syrene looked much older than Syl remembered. Her skin was wrinkled, the filigree tattoos on her face sagging like snagged threads, and her hands and arms were mottled with liver spots.

Priety's mouth opened wide and a death rattle sounded in her throat. Her body sagged as the last of the life left it, and immediately the One began withdrawing the tendrils that connected it to the corpse, pulling away from it as a thing unclean. The fleshy coils and tubes curled towards Syl and Ani, and Ani took a step back in alarm, but Syl remained where she was and kept the One at bay with the force of her will.

She had not discussed with Ani the details of what she was going to do, in part because she was not even sure herself. She would not know until she was facing the enemy, but now that she was in its presence she still remained uncertain. She only understood that she had to offer herself to it, or at least allow herself to be taken, and without resistance, because only then could she enter it, become one with it, and – she hoped, she prayed – manipulate it. It wanted her, which gave her the advantage. Syl had entered a seller's market.

Almost to her own surprise, she found that she was not frightened. Even as she drew closer to the One and stared up at it in its web, she felt only a nervous anticipation of the unknown. And awe; she felt awe.

She recalled Derith and the Cayth. She remembered what Fara had said from lips that matched her own mother's: she was a being unlike any other, and she recognised the truth of it, for she contained universes within her. She had crossed boundaries in time and space that no Illyri before her ever had. Outwardly, she remained unaltered, but inside she had felt the change, the shift in the cosmos, as her psychic powers – a gift of her conception, carefully nurtured – morphed and grew beyond all proportion. Ani had powers, but Syl *was* power.

It was now or never and, should everything go awry, the death of a young Illyri would go all but unnoticed, and the universe would roll on regardless.

Syl Hellais might, ultimately, prove to be nothing, but she sensed that she could be everything.

She reached up and pushed her mask away. She heard Ani scream a warning, and then the One was upon her.

The Military fleet was in sight of Illyr when the first of the Diplomatic ships came into view. The Diplomats had regrouped quickly; even with the loss of half of their ships at Derith and Myelen, what presented itself to Nolis and the other Military commanders was still an armada of impressive power, and one equipped with vessels considerably more advanced than most of the Military fleet. It was also obvious that Dyer had not been entirely foolish, holding in reserve much of his firepower in case the Military breached the Illyr system.

The first of the Diplomatic ships surged forward. The final battle for the soul of the Illyri was about to begin.

Red. Syl saw red.

She understood that the One had consumed her head, smothering her it with tendrils. She could feel them probing at her nose, her mouth, her ears. She did not resist. She let them come. There was pain, tiny explosions of it, but it hurt less than she had expected.

As she allowed the One to enter her, so too did it reveal itself to her. Once again she found herself in contact with a consciousness that was old, and vile, and eternally hungry, all teeth and mouths, containing within itself billions upon billions of lives lived and lives lost. She roved with it through time and space, watching stars collapse and great galaxies being sucked into black holes. She saw worlds fall to it, entire species succumb until they were reduced to dust, and the memory of each creature that had become its prey was shared with her, for it retained what it absorbed, creating a repository of all the universe's dead.

Deeper she delved, ever deeper, as, back on the Marque, the One dug at her skull, and the tips of the first tendrils licked at her brain stem. Instantly Syrene's consciousness was nearby, a trapped creature reduced to madness, screaming over and over, but Syl ignored it. Time ceased to have meaning for her, because time had no meaning for the Others, and she was becoming one with them. Planets formed and fissures gaped in the fabric of the universe. All was colour, then no colour at all. She followed the life paths of billions of Others simultaneously as they were born, bred, and died, moving back, sire upon sire, and always there was hunger, so much hunger. They were ceaselessly, endlessly ravenous, consumed by a craving that knew no end, and no limit.

Syl's mouth was filled with flesh. Her nostrils were blocked. She was unable to breathe, so the One breathed for her. Somewhere, a distant, younger version of herself was lifted from the floor of the chamber in the Marque and spun in the air like a marionette dancing for its master. She experienced a tightening at the base of her neck, and a sensation like a bone needle penetrating her spine.

Now she was the One, and the One was her, and she felt it searching through her consciousness, seeking the source of her gifts, a vampire gnawing for the vein. Ani still screamed her warnings, a voice like an echo through just one of Syl's senses, though Syl hardly heard it for now she had thousands more. But Ani was wrong. Ani was—

The pain stopped. Syl opened her eyes. She was no longer in the Marque, but in the hollow heart of a distant world, and before her squatted an entity awesome in its immensity, barely younger than the oldest star, a creature that contained within it the first dust of the universe. It resembled the chitinous beast that the One might yet become, given aeons, its hide hard, pitted and marked by ancient injuries, its legs like broken trees in some great forest beyond imagining, fissured, cleaved columns no longer capable of supporting the mass above them. Its mouth was a yawning maw, caves within caves. Its dark eyes were filled with the memory of stars, and from its back emerged hollow spears of bone that had forced their way through the rocks above ages before, stretching into space. This was the Beast, the source of the One and of all the Others, the first and oldest of its kind, and as its body jerked it pushed clouds of spores through the spines and into the void, dispersed in the hope of claiming new worlds in its name. Syl was but a mote of dust before it, a germ, encased in the One.

She was an infection.

The Beast recognised the One, accepting it because the One was its own, and Syl's poison began to spread within it.

Above Illyr, Steven and Meia were fighting for their lives, the *Revenge* shadowing the *Varcis*, each staying close to the other: firing, warning, protecting. To starboard, they saw explosions burst from the carrier *Demion* as a Diplomatic destroyer poured fire into her. Voices cried losses in their ears: the *Xomon*, the *Folia*, the *Vare* . . .

They were losing. They had come all this way and made it back to Illyr to join the fight, and they were losing.

The Beast was not as it once had been.

It was in every one of the Others; it saw through them, lived through them, experienced the universe through them. When one of its offspring ceased to exist, the Beast felt its pain. Now the Others on Earth had begun to wither and die, and the Beast did not understand why. A weakness of some kind, perhaps: an infection. To protect itself, the Beast had closed itself off against them, isolating the source of potential contamination.

But it had done so too late. There were now dark patches in its memory and cracks in its ancient defences. It was through one of these cracks that Syl Hellais entered it.

Syl sensed the Beast's realisation of its error. It had absorbed her through the One, and in doing so had unleashed her upon itself. As Syl moved through its consciousness – pricking, bursting, destroying it from the inside, cell by cell – the Beast tried to force her away, breaking the connection through the One, but Syl would not permit it to be severed. So the Beast tried to kill her, constricting her with the One's tendrils, depriving her of oxygen, but still she fought it. The Beast began to panic, and in panicking revealed more of itself to her, like an impaled man struggling to free himself from the spike who, in his torment, impales himself still further. Syl was at its very core, and so at the core of all Others, infecting them as they had infected untold species. The Beast's thoughts were hers, and so was its rage. In its fury, it showed her what it was about to do. She saw Illyr and the ships fighting above it. She was in the Others curled around the brainstems of the Diplomat crews, and the gunners who poured fire upon the Military fleet, but she was also in the parasites that walked with their hosts on Illyr and on Earth, and the hundred other worlds colonised by the Illyri. She watched as Illyri mouths opened, as their bodies swelled, and then spores poured forth, infecting her entire race as the Illyri were sacrificed to the Beast. She heard herself scream, and for the first time she felt real fear.

And the Beast exploited her fear, and turned it upon her.

Ani stared in horror as Syl exposed herself to the One, and was powerless to prevent her from being yanked from the floor of the Marque so that she now hung suspended above it, dangling from the end of a mass of tendrils that covered her head to the shoulders. Ani didn't know how to react. Was this what Syl had intended? Did she know what she was doing?

Suddenly Syl's body began to jerk and thrash, and her arms flailed uselessly at the air. This was wrong. Syl was in trouble, and if Syl was in trouble then they all were, but Syl was also her friend. Syl had always been her friend.

Ani took a deep breath and removed her own mask. She stepped forward and touched her hand to the nearest tendril. It curled almost delicately around her arm and was quickly joined by others that wrapped themselves around her young, fresh body, her head, her face. She closed her eyes as her lips were forced apart, and then all was redness.

Syl was dying. She was drowning in blood, suffocating in spores. She tried to concentrate, but the Beast was tormenting her through the One, using it to inflict pain upon her, distracting her while it tried to sever the link with her. The Beast now knew that it had been mistaken. It could not take Syl Hellais's powers and absorb them into its own. She was too strong for it – for them – yet not so strong that she could not be killed. The Beast would destroy her and then wipe out her species. There would be others, and the Beast was old enough to have learned patience. It felt the psychic connection with the girl slowly disintegrating, tendril by tendril. Soon it would be gone entirely, and then –

There was a new consciousness. It intruded upon the Beast, drawing its attention away from Syl before it could finally purge itself of her. It was another girl, linked to Syl, but not like her, not as powerful or as strong, but with such force of will: Ani, the Archmage, the one who had sacrificed the younger for the five ancients. As she appeared, so too did the previous Archmage, the being named Syrene, and the Beast felt her presence twisting inside its thoughts like a thorn. It sensed hatred from her – for Ani, for Syl, for all things, but most of all for the Beast – and in her dying Syrene also unleashed herself upon it, ripping at it in her death throes just as Ani clouded its vision with mist, but not so much that it could not find her, could not lash out, could not—

Kill her.

Syl felt the moment of Ani's death. She experienced it as a rush of fire through her being that scorched her raw, and a darkness that consumed her as her friend's light was extinguished. She heard Ani cry out, an exclamation of surprise as much as pain, as something deep inside her body, some vital part of her, was punctured by the One. Syl sensed Ani's consciousness searching for her, reaching like a hand stretched out by one who is drowning.

On his moon of exile, Lord Danis woke to the sound of his daughter calling for her father and he shouted her name in turn, over and over, as a great wave of love and regret washed over him, leaving him broken by its passing.

And then she was gone.

The *Revenge* was crippled. It had taken a shot to port that had disabled its engines, and its weapons systems were fried. The *Varcis* had stayed with it, a bird trying to keep the predators from its stricken mate, and had fended off two attacks, but now the hunters were converging. Steven counted two Corps cruisers approaching, and most of a squadron of fighters from one of the carriers. Beside him, Alis had accessed the *Revenge*'s workings and was trying to bring the weapons back on line at the very least, so that it might be able to defend itself, but Steven saw now that it was too late.

'Meia,' he said.

This time she appeared before him as a hologram, just as his face was before hers on the *Varcis*.

'I see them,' she said.

'You have to leave us.'

'I won't.'

'Meia, I'm ordering you to go. You won't survive against them.'

'I don't take orders from you, Steven.'

'Please.'

Meia stared back at him.

'What would have been the point of all we have gone through if I were to desert you now?' she said, and he had no answer for her.

Meia smiled. 'I will see you again, Steven. There is another world beyond this one.'

And their enemies descended upon them.

★ ★ ★

Syl was no longer herself. She had no name, and she had many names. She was a being created by the universe, forged from the light of a strange star, for this moment, and for this purpose: to undo the error of creation that had spawned the Others. She was within the Beast, and of the Beast, and so she tore it apart first, taking its consciousness to pieces, psychic agony becoming physical pain. Its primeval hide fractured and burst, its hearts exploded one by one, and the spines from which it spewed forth its spores forced themselves back into its body, piercing it straight through and impaling it in the dust and stone of the dead star that would serve as its mausoleum.

And as the Beast trembled in the moment of its dying, Syl Hellais – Syl the Destroyer – turned all her rage and grief at the loss of Ani Cienda on the offspring of the Beast, and on all those who would have used them to further their own ends. She saw the Diplomatic armada above Illyr, and one by one she crushed every ship – every carrier, every cruiser, every destroyer – until only fragments of them remained, and the dead floated before what was left of the Military fleet. Then she turned her anguish on those on Illyr and its dominions who carried the Others inside them, and even as the parasites inside them began to perish along with their sire, she snuffed out their lives, so that thousands upon thousands fell in an instant. It was Armageddon. It was apocalypse. It was a new plague of her making.

On its distant world, the Beast shuddered and died, and in the Marque, the One curled in upon itself and ceased to move. Its tendrils withered, and its web collapsed beneath it. Freed from her bonds, Syl fell to the floor, and the chamber echoed to her screams of rage, for she wanted to keep killing and never stop.

But in time she grew still and silent. She turned and stared into the lifeless eyes of Ani Cienda, whose remains lay crumpled and broken beside her. She reached for her friend and drew her to her breast, and only then did she weep for all that she had lost.

XVI
HOPE

CHAPTER 77

When Paul Kerr finally awoke, it was from a dream in which he was dying in a wormhole, although that had simply been the conclusion of a longer dream of aliens, and parasites, and war, and a girl with golden eyes and bronze hair whom he had loved like no other.

Now he opened his own eyes, slowly, carefully. He was in a white room, dimly lit. There was some pain, but it was tolerable. He stayed very still as the memory of the dream faded. In time he heard a door open and he looked in the direction of the sound. A woman in white robes entered and began fussing with his pillow, followed by the girl with the golden eyes, and then a boy like himself, but younger. Others were behind them, and he searched for their names and found them: Steven, Thula, Meia and Alis.

'Syl.'

He spoke her name. She took his hand.

'Did we win?' he asked.

'We did,' she said. 'But we lost so much . . .'

They laid Ani to rest in the Marque. A line of Sisters stretched from her chambers to her tomb, and each one took her turn to help bear the Archmage on her last journey. Syl and Meia, along with Cocile and Toria, carried her bier for the last steps. They placed her shrouded form in the glass tomb below a great dome that looked out upon the universe, so that her resting place would always be filled with light, as befitted a child of the stars.

CHAPTER 78

The calls for Syl Hellais to be made president began almost as soon as she set foot on her homeworld of Illyr for only the second time in her life. Krake was under arrest and the Military authorities were anxious to restore the normal functioning of Illyri society as soon as possible. The Diplomat voices that might have dissented against such an elevation for Syl Hellais had almost all been silenced, for few had survived her wrath, and those infested by the Others were now all dead, annihilated along with the parasites inside their own heads.

Yet there were some, even among the Military, who feared her too, and whispered quietly of the threat posed by one so young and powerful, even as more devious minds wondered how her abilities might be harnessed and used to serve a new Illyri Conquest. What, Syl thought, might they have said had they known that it was she who had been responsible for the deaths of so many? It was assumed that those Illyri who had been carrying Others in their heads had died because the Others inside them had died, a consequence of Syl's annihilation of the Beast, but that was not the case. They had died because Syl had willed it. The Military knew that she had destroyed Corps ships and their crews along with them, but that could be glossed over as a necessary act to bring a brutal conflict to an end. But if they learned that she had, in her rage and grief, targeted all those who had colluded with the Others and ultimately contributed to the death of Ani Cienda, they might not be so understanding. Syl did not fear those who were already plotting. She was more extraordinary than any of them could ever guess, and could snuff out any threat before it was even spoken aloud.

She was just tired of death.

But Syl did not wish to be president, and the more they pressed her, the more she resisted. She found herself repeatedly drawn back to the Marque, where she would spend hours sitting by Ani's tomb, speaking with the ghost of her friend. Sometimes Meia would come to her, or Alis, for some of the Mechs remained concealed in the Marque in the guise of Sisters, while the rest had gone into hiding. The Illyri had turned on the Mechs once before, and Meia was unconvinced that they would not do so again. Cocile was being spoken of as Archmage, which surprised Cocile almost as much as it might have surprised Ani – and left the lovelorn Rent Raydl concerned at what this might mean for him – but others, hearing that Syl had rejected the presidency, had begun to wonder aloud if she might not consent to become Archmage instead.

Syl wanted none of it. She had no place here. She told Ani so, as she whispered to her beneath the stars.

Paul was waiting to meet Syl when the shuttle from the Marque landed in Upper Tannis after yet another of her sad-eyed trips to Avila Minor. They were living together in a lovely apartment in one of the older sections of the city, and Paul was enjoying exploring Illyr while his medical treatment continued. Thula was staying nearby and he and Paul saw each other nearly every day, either by choice or at the medical centre.

Steven had returned to help rebuild Earth at the first possible opportunity after the war. He'd taken all the other humans with him as well as a team of Illyri volunteers – mainly scientists – who wanted to help right the wrongs that had been done in their name. Danis and Peris had gone with them. Ani's death had dimmed the light of Illyr for both of the old soldiers.

'I'll see you back down there, big bro,' Steven had told Paul on parting. 'I'll give Mum your love. Oh, and I'm taking the top bunk.'

They'd laughed and bumped fists, then hugged, but many weeks had passed and Paul missed his younger brother. He missed his mother too, and now Thula had begun to talk about going back to Earth.

As for Paul, he tried not to think about the future. He needed to give Syl time, just as he needed his own health back so that he might be of use to her again, and not a burden. Because of his injuries, he walked with the aid of a crutch, but the doctors had assured him that the need for it would become less and less over time. He was still in some discomfort. He tried to hide it from Syl, but nothing could ever truly be hidden from her. He watched her now as she approached, and something in his chest tightened painfully. How he wished that he could help her, or heal her, but he did not even know how to begin. All he felt equipped to do was love her, and hope that this might be enough.

'Let's go home, Lady Syl Hellais,' he said, and he reached for Syl's hand, but to his surprise she did not take it.

'Syl?'

Paul stopped and turned to face her. She met his eyes, fierce and wilful, and there was a challenge written large across her troubled and, oh, so very lovely face.

'But where is home, Paul?' she said. 'Where is home for the likes of us?'

How different she is now, he thought – a million miles away from the contrary sixteen-year-old he'd met playing dress-up on the streets of Edinburgh, a million-billion-trillion miles in every which way – and yet somehow still the same, because the essence of the Illyri girl with whom he'd first fallen in love remained. They had come so far together, they'd crossed galaxies, and he knew he couldn't bear to be without her.

'Home?' he said, without thinking it through. 'My home is wherever you are, Syl.'

And as the words left his mouth, romantic and foolish and rash, even to his own ears, he recognised that they were also true. Yet still trouble stirred him, roiling like storm clouds on an internal horizon, for there was within Paul a desperate craving for the only home he'd ever known, the place where he'd been created, the world for which he'd fought before he'd met Syl, before she'd opened his universe,